Rhys Bowen is the *New York Times* Royal Spyness Series, Molly Murphy Mysteries, and Constable Evans. She is a recipient of the Agatha Best Novel Award and an Edgar Best Novel nominee.

Praise for Rhys Bowen

'The latest addition to Molly's case files offers a charming combination of history, mystery, and romance.' *Kirkus Reviews* on *Hush Now, Don't You Cry*

'Engaging . . . Molly's compassion and pluck should attract more readers to this consistently solid historical series.' *Publishers Weekly* on *Bless the Bride*

'Winning . . . The gutsy Molly, who's no prim Edwardian miss, will appeal to fans of contemporary female detectives.' *Publishers Weekly* on *The Last Illusion*

'This historical mystery delivers a top-notch, detail-rich story full of intriguing characters. Fans of the 1920s private detective Maisie Dobbs should give this series a try.' *Booklist* on *The Last Illusion*

'Details of Molly's new cases are knit together with the accoutrements of 1918 New York City life . . . Don't miss this great period puzzler reminiscent of Dame Agatha's mysteries and Gillian Linscott's Nell Bray series.' *Booklist* on *In a Gilded Cage*

'Delightful . . . As ever, Bowen does a splendid job of capturing the flavor of early twentieth-century New York and bringing to life its warm and human inhabitants.' *Publishers Weekly* on *In a Gilded Cage*

'Winning . . . It's all in a day's work for this delightfully spunky heroine.' *Publishers Weekly* on *Tell Me, Pretty Maiden*

TELL ME PRETTY MAIDEN

~ A Molly Murphy Mystery ~

RHYS BOWEN

Constable • London

CONSTABLE

First published in the USA in 2008 by Minotaur Books,
an imprint of St Martin's Press, New York

This edition published in the UK in 2016 by Constable

13 5 7 9 10 8 6 4 2

Copyright © Rhys Bowen, 2008

The moral right of the author has been asserted.

A CIP catalogue record for this book
is available from the British Library.

ISBN 978-1-47211-848-6 (paperback)

Typeset in Times New Roman by TW Type, Cornwall
Printed and bound in Great Britain by CPI Group (UK) Ltd, Croydon CR0 4YY
Papers used by Constable are from well-managed forests and other responsible sources

 MIX
Paper from
responsible sources
FSC   FSC® C104740
www.fsc.org

Constable
An imprint of
Little, Brown Book Group
Carmelite House
50 Victoria Embankment
London EC4Y 0DY

An Hachette UK Company
www.hachette.co.uk

www.littlebrown.co.uk

To my son, Dominic, who is making his way in the hard world of musical theater, in the hopes that his mother will one day see him a Broadway star
And with thanks, as always, to John, Clare, and Jane for their editing insights

'Tell me, pretty maiden, are there any more at home like you?'
'Oh yes, kind sir, there are a few. Kind sir, there are a few.'

'Tell Me, Pretty Maiden,' Florodora,
1901 Broadway musical

One

New York City, December 1902

My feet were freezing. We Irish have been known to embroider the truth, but on this occasion I was being literal. The boots leaked badly, letting in snow and slush, and I could no longer feel my toes. If I had been sensible, I would have gone home immediately, but I have never been known for being sensible. Besides, I was on a case. A good detective wouldn't leave her post just because of a little frostbite.

Winter had arrived in New York with sudden fury on the day after Thanksgiving, blanketing the city with snow and bringing traffic to a virtual standstill. Since then the roads and sidewalks had been shoveled and swept to make passage possible, but great mounds of snow and ice were piled in the gutters, and the wind that swept in off the Hudson cut through the warmest of winter coats. And this evening I wasn't even wearing a coat. I was wearing a threadbare jacket, knee britches, and hobnail boots. My hair was piled under a cap and my face was dirty. I was, in fact, posing as a street urchin.

It had seemed like a good idea at the time, when I put on the clothes in the warmth of my little house on Patchin Place. My

1

assignment was to follow a certain Mr Leon Roth and I had already learned the hard way that women who loiter alone on the city streets at night are likely to be arrested for prostitution. Street urchins, on the other hand, are plentiful and invisible. For good measure I took a broom with me and made half-hearted attempts at being a crossing sweeper while I watched and waited.

I had actually picked up all of twenty cents for my pains. But I hadn't expected Mr Roth to take so long. And I was rapidly coming to the conclusion that no job was worth risking pneumonia.

This had promised to be a straightforward assignment. A wealthy Jewish couple, the Mendelbaums, had hired me to check the credentials of the young man they wanted their daughter to marry. He had been produced by a matchmaker, which seemed to be normal for their tradition, and he seemed to possess all the qualities that would make an ideal husband. These qualities included a Yale education and a considerable private income. But New York was not the shtetl of their forebears, where everyone knew the habits of everyone else. These parents cared about their daughter and wanted to make sure that her intended harbored no secret vices – and was as rich as he claimed.

I had taken on the job with enthusiasm. It was one I thought I could handle without danger, one not involving the sordid peeking and sneaking of a divorce case. Besides, the fee was generous and if I carried out my duties to my clients' satisfaction, then they might well recommend me to their friends. It had been easy enough to check on his place of employment at a major shipping and importing company and to learn that he was expected to go far. I hadn't yet managed to obtain the details of his bank accounts, not having had much opportunity myself to know the inner workings of banks.

And now I was checking into his moral character, which was proving more interesting. I had stationed myself outside Mr Roth's address and watched and waited. He lived not too far from me, in an apartment hotel on Fifth Avenue. This was not the swank part of Fifth Avenue, up among the Vanderbilts and Astors on Central Park, but the lower part of that street, south of Union Square. It had once been the most fashionable address in the city, but not any longer. The big brownstone houses were mostly divided into apartments. Gone were the carriages and liveried footmen. It was still respectable but definitely not glamorous.

The first few days of my task convinced me that Mr Roth was also respectable but not glamorous. I had managed to follow him to the Knickerbocker Grill, where he met with other young men and drank nothing stronger than water, to the Manhattan Theater where he saw a production of *A Doll's House*, by a Swedish playwright called Mr Ibsen – by all accounts a rather gloomy sort of play if one could judge by the sober pictures outside the theater. I even followed him to Macy's new department store where he bought a silk ascot.

I was almost ready to report to the Mendelbaums that their daughter could marry Mr Roth with confidence when he came out of his house in a great hurry one evening and hopped on the Broadway trolley. I lifted my skirts in unladylike manner and sprinted, managing to haul myself aboard the trolley at the last moment, and then alighted after him at Forty-second Street.

As soon as his feet touched the cobbles, he took off at such a great pace that he had been swallowed up into the crowd by the time I managed to disembark – skirts and petticoats making it impossible to leap down from a vehicle the way he had done. It was a little late for theaters, but the street was still chock-a-block with diners emerging from restaurants, touts advertising new plays, newsboys shouting the latest headlines, hawkers, flower sellers, beggars, crossing sweepers. Since the sidewalks were still piled with snow and ice, the crowd was walking in the street, bringing carriages and cabs to a halt.

Mr Roth was heading west. I fought my way past the Victoria Theater and the Republic, with the electric glow from their marquees lighting up the street scene and making it seem quite merry. Then, on the other side of Seventh Avenue, I thought I caught another glimpse of his homburg, far ahead of me now and still moving toward the Hudson. It was then that my suspicions were roused. Of course I could have given him the benefit of the doubt and believed that he was running a little late for a theater performance, but I couldn't see any more theater marquees beyond this point. In fact the crowd had now thinned out and the street ahead looked decidedly darker and less savory.

I walked more cautiously. It was rumored that Forty-second Street was rapidly becoming a den of vice. The better class of prostitutes was now moving away from the Lower East Side and brothels were now to be found side by side with theaters and restaurants, especially on the west side of Broadway. I wandered up and down for a while, hoping he might re-emerge from some building, or that I might spot him in some restaurant, until I realized that I was also being observed. The constable patrolling his beat was eyeing me with suspicion as he passed me the first time. When he returned some half an hour later and I was still there he crossed and came over to me.

'Waiting for someone, miss?' he asked, his hand idly fingering his nightstick.

'Uh, yes. My cousin,' I said.

'This is no place for a young girl at night,' he said. 'If I were you I'd beat it while you're safe. You look respectable enough, but my opinion of you might change if I find you here next time I come around.'

I took the hint and went home. I had been arrested for prostitution once before while observing a house in a more respectable part of the city than this. A woman out unescorted after dark was always suspect in the eyes of the law, and I had no wish to spend another night in jail. I didn't even have Daniel to bail me out these days, since he was still suspended from his duties with the New York police force, pending a trial, and was currently out of the city.

On the way home a young boy swept the slush and muck for me to cross the street and then said, 'Spare a nickel, miss.'

That gave me an idea. I had been in the middle of packing up a box of clothes to send to my former lodger Shamus O'Conner and his two children, Shamey and Bridie. They were now living in the country where Shamus was employed by a farmer and young Shamey was already helping him with the farm chores. It was an ideal situation for them, healthier and safer than life in the city, but I still missed them terribly. I had become used to young Shamey clattering down the stairs, yelling, 'Molly, I'm fair starving again. Could I have some bread and jam?' And to Bridie snuggling close to me and taking my hand.

Among the clothes I had been given, outgrown by a friend's son, were britches and a jacket that were too big for Shamey. It occurred to me that I should put them to good use while he waited to grow into them. So the next day I acquired a newsboy's cap and a pair of old boots from a pushcart on Hester Street, and the transformation was complete. When I went to observe Mr Roth that evening, I was no longer a respectably dressed young lady called Molly Murphy, but one of a thousand street urchins, hoping to make a penny by sweeping the crossings clear of muck.

It was too bad my assignment had coincided with the early snowstorm. It only took me a few minutes to feel profoundly sorry for the children who really had to face this weather in such rags. I felt profoundly sorry for myself, too, to tell you the truth. I would have gone home on the spot, but I was definitely on to something interesting.

For the second night in a row, Mr Roth had hurried to West Forty-second Street. What's more I hadn't lost him this time. I had kept pace with him all the way to the block between Eighth and Ninth avenues, where he had disappeared into a faceless building. An hour later he still hadn't come out again. Forty-second wasn't like Elizabeth Street, where girls sprawled on the stoops in provocative poses or called out ribald comments to passing men. These uptown houses of ill repute had discreet name plates: Fifi, or Madame Bettina. They could have been any normal apartment or office buildings. This particular one had no plate or card beside the door, just a dark, narrow staircase leading up to God knows what. I hadn't liked to follow him up there. I had an aversion to brothels since I was almost press-ganged into one. Besides, dressed as I was I would be tossed out again on my ear.

I had just come to the conclusion that this was a foolish endeavor and that the numbness in my feet was a sign that frostbite was taking over when he came running down the stairs again. What's more, he was carrying a large brown paper parcel this time. He walked briskly to the corner of Eighth Avenue and hailed a cab. I was now truly intrigued. I hadn't heard of brothels making presents to their customers. I simply couldn't guess what might be in the parcel and I had to know. Ignoring the warnings in my head, I went back to that doorway and made my way up those stairs.

The staircase was poorly lit and there was peeling oilcloth on the stairs. I stumbled my way upward until I saw a line of light spilling from under a door. I drew level and listened. No sound of girlish laughter. No sound of female voices. Silence, in fact. Then I almost fell back down the stairs as I heard a noise I hadn't expected. A loud mechanical clatter. Cautiously I pushed the door open to see an old man working away at a treadle sewing machine. On a table beside him were pattern pieces laid out on cloth. A dummy held a suit pinned to it. That was when I realized that Mr Roth had just paid a visit to his tailor.

I was trying to close the door silently again when the tailor looked up and saw me. 'Get out of here, you no-good kid,' he shouted and made as if to throw his iron at the door.

I fled. As I made my way back to the Sixth Avenue El I felt red-faced and foolish. Only I could have suspected drama in a simple visit to a tailor. It's part of my Irish temperament, I'm afraid. We enjoy making great drama out of the most mundane events. My one relief was that I had told no one of my plans and so nobody knew about my silliness except me.

I had been pretty much on my own for the past week or so. Daniel had spent Thanksgiving with his parents in Westchester County and had not yet returned, and my neighbors and good friends Elena Goldfarb and Augusta Mary Walcott, usually known by their irreverent nicknames Sid and Gus, respectively, had been invited to Vassar for a reunion with other girls of their graduating class. I had therefore welcomed this assignment. I wasn't good at doing nothing and being alone. Sid and Gus had returned the night before but I gathered they had brought friends to stay and I hadn't liked to interrupt. I had no idea when Daniel would come back. Maybe not for a while. If he had finally told his parents about his current unfortunate predicament, then maybe they had pressed him to stay out of town with them until the whole matter could be settled. It occurred to me that he could at least have written to let me know his plans. Men are always so bad at that kind of thing.

I was just approaching the corner of Sixth when I saw a scuffle going on. A couple of my fellow street urchins were facing one another. One of them was a tall, skinny chap, about my own height, and he was facing a little runt half his size. But it was the runt who was obviously the attacker.

'Go on, beat it. This is my spot,' he was shouting in his high, childish voice, 'and if ya ain't careful, I'll fight ya for it.' He raised his hands in true prizefighting stance.

I stopped to watch, not giving much for the little one's chances. Instead the older boy shrugged. 'Keep it. Ain't no good anyway,' he said, then shouldered his broom and strolled away. There was something about the way he walked that made me follow him. It took me a good half-block before I realized what it was that had made me suspicious. He walked like a girl. Boys saunter. They plant down their feet carelessly. They kick at things. This one was treading carefully, taking small steps. I smiled knowingly to myself. It was no street urchin but another girl in disguise, like me.

Two

Intrigued now, I fought my way through the crowd to catch up with her. Why another woman should want to dress up as a street urchin, I had no idea. The only other female detective I had met in New York City was Mrs Goodwin, but she was employed by the police and wore a uniform. I was determined to keep this woman in sight until I could find a suitable opportunity to confront her. At least I didn't have to worry about her fighting temperament.

Then I heard the rumble of an approaching El train over our heads. The young woman suddenly dashed up the steps to a station platform. I went to follow her, but I didn't have a ticket. She pushed through the barrier and onto the train while I was left fuming and waiting in line at the ticket booth. For the second time in one evening I was furious with myself. If she truly had been another woman detective, then maybe we could have worked together and helped each other on occasion. God knows how hard it is to survive as a woman in a man's world and how lonely such a profession can be.

My small back alley of a street called Patchin Place was in wintry darkness as I approached it, picking my way along the narrow trough that had been cleared through the snow. As I fished in my pocket for my front door key I realized I dreaded the prospect of an empty house on a cold, dismal evening. I'm really not a creature designed for the solitary life at the best of times, and at this moment I longed for nothing more than a roaring fire, hot drink, and good company. I knew where I could find all of the above, but I hesitated to burst in on my neighbors so late in the evening, especially when they were entertaining friends whom I had not yet been invited to meet.

For a long moment propriety battled with longing. Being of a Celtic disposition, of course longing won out. I picked my way across the street and knocked on their door. It was opened by Sid wearing her customary gentleman's velvet smoking jacket, her Turkish cigarette in its long ebony holder resting gracefully between her fingers. She was the picture of bohemian elegance but she was eyeing me with horrified suspicion.

'What do you want?' she demanded. 'Go on. Clear off.'

'Sid, it's me. Molly,' I said.

A surprised smile spread across her face. 'Bless my soul, so it is. What on earth are you doing out this late, dressed in that extraordinary manner? No, don't tell me. Gus will want to hear it too, and I know our guest will be thunderstruck to meet you.' She was already chuckling as she ushered me into the house and then threw open the drawing room door with a dramatic gesture.

'Prepare to be astonished, Gus,' she said. 'And as for you, Elizabeth, here is a street urchin hot on your tail.'

I stepped into the delightful warmth of their drawing room. A big fire was blazing in the hearth. The heavy burgundy velvet drapes shut out the chilly night. A low table held a brandy decanter and steaming mugs as well as a copper bowl of figs, dates, and nuts. My friend Gus was sitting in the high-backed Queen Anne chair on one side of the fire, a beaded black shawl around her slender shoulders, while the person on the other side of the fire was my fellow urchin, whom I had lost on the train station. Her cap was now removed to reveal a fine head of dark hair. She had half risen from her seat and was eyeing me with fear.

Gus recognized me immediately and came toward me, arms open. 'Molly, my dearest, pray tell what is going on. Is this some festival we are missing? The night of the street urchins? Surely not the Holy Innocents?' She dragged me toward the fire. 'Goodness, your hands are freezing. Sid has just made some toddy for Elizabeth. Sit here while I fetch you some.'

I was firmly pushed into Gus's seat by the fire and felt my hands and feet tingling back to life. My fellow urchin was eyeing me with interest as Gus returned with a steaming mug and thrust it into my hands. 'Take a sip of that and then tell all,' she said.

I sipped and felt a delicious glow spreading down through my body. 'Holy mother, that feels good,' I said. 'I thought I was about to lose my hands and feet to frostbite. What a ridiculous idea to dress up as a street urchin on a night like this.'

'I came to that same conclusion myself,' the visitor they had addressed as Elizabeth said in a rich, cultured voice. 'You must have had a very good reason for doing so.'

'I was following a man into an unsavory area,' I said. 'Women who loiter on the sidewalk are liable to be arrested for prostitution. Urchins are invisible and plentiful, especially since every crossing currently has a sweeper or two in attendance, as you've just found out.' I smiled at the woman who threw back her head and laughed.

'You saw me, did you? Dismissed by a pint-sized bully. What a humiliation. But he looked a tough little devil and I had no wish to take him on and come home with a split lip for my pains.'

'So you were following a man, Molly,' Sid prompted.

'Yes. I've been asked to check on the character and potential vices of a young man. I'm supposed to see if he'll make a suitable husband.'

'And he was venturing into a disreputable part of the city? Tut, tut.' Sid chuckled.

'Only to visit his tailor as it turned out,' I admitted. 'So far his behavior has been exemplary.'

Their guest was looking at me with interest. 'Do I take it that you are some kind of detective?'

'I am,' I said.

'A very good one too,' Gus added proudly. 'I haven't introduced you properly, have I? Molly Murphy, this is Elizabeth Cochran Seaman. Molly has solved all sorts of dangerous cases. You'll find her a fellow adventuress with stories to tell almost as good as your own.'

'Fascinating,' the woman said. 'A woman detective. I don't think I ever met one before.'

'Are you not a detective yourself?' I asked. 'What other reason could there be for skulking around dressed as a boy on such a cold, unpleasant night?'

'I'm doing a little investigation of my own,' the woman said, smiling enigmatically. 'Into the plight of newsboys.'

Sid came over to perch on the arm of the woman's chair. 'This, my dear Molly, is none other than the famous Nelly Bly.'

'But I thought you just introduced her as Elizabeth,' I said, and flushed at their laughter.

'My sweet, Nelly Bly is her pseudonym,' Sid said. 'Surely you must have heard of her. She is very famous.'

'Infamous, rather, wouldn't you say?' Nelly, or was it Elizabeth, chuckled.

'I'm sorry. The name is familiar but I really don't know . . .' I mumbled.

'You have to remember that Molly has been in America less

than two years,' Gus said, coming to put a comforting hand on my shoulder. 'Your most infamous exploits were all over by then, and perhaps news of them didn't travel to Ireland.'

'It may have reached Dublin,' I said, laughing too now, 'but not the backwater where I lived. We got the news of Queen Victoria's death two days late.'

'Well, let me fill you in,' Sid said. 'Elizabeth is a newspaper reporter. She specializes in exposing corruption, injustice, that dark underbelly of society that we should know about. She is worse than you at putting herself in harm's way to achieve it, too.'

'She got herself arrested so that she could report on conditions in a women's prison,' Gus said, 'and she went undercover in an insane asylum.'

'From which they almost wouldn't let me out,' Elizabeth added.

'And didn't you cause a ruckus in Mexico?'

Elizabeth laughed out loud again. Truly she had a most infectious laugh. 'I did indeed. I reported on the corruption surrounding their elections. I was lucky to have got out of that one alive.'

'So what adventures have you undertaken recently?' I asked. 'I've read the newspapers diligently since I came here and I don't think I've noticed your name.'

'My dear, I have been playing at being a staid married woman,' she said. 'Only just recently it has begun to pall. And when I heard that the city newsboys were talking of forming a union, I thought what a good story it would make and resolved to look at their plight for myself. Hence the disguise.'

Gus looked across at Sid. 'Aren't you pleased that all our friends have so much spunk?'

'They wouldn't stay our friends for long if they didn't,' Sid said. 'Life is too short to have boring friends. I must say it was delightful to discover that not all of our Vassar classmates had succumbed to matrimony and domestic drudgery.'

'What about that girl who had gone up the Amazon?' Gus exclaimed. 'Her description of anacondas made me long to see for myself. Should we take a trip to the Amazon, do you think, Sid dearest?'

The fire and the hot toddy had brought back life to my hands and feet and I was feeling comfortable and drowsy. It occurred to me that conversations like this did not take place in many drawing rooms. Young women were supposed to swoon at the thought of a giant snake, not wish to rush up the Amazon to see one. I gazed at them fondly. Gus's eye caught mine.

'Molly, where are our manners? You look quite worn out. Have you been overdoing things while we've been away? Have you eaten tonight?'

'Yes, thank you,' I said, not wanting to impose.

'And has Daniel the Deceiver been treating you well during our absence?' Sid asked.

'Daniel is still away, as far as I know,' I said. 'I've not heard a peep from him since before Thanksgiving.'

'Just like a man.' Elizabeth chuckled. 'It never crosses their minds to think that we women might be worried and want to hear from them. But why would you want to hear from a deceiver, may I ask?'

'That is all in the past,' I said, feeling my cheeks turning red at the thought of explaining this. 'He is a reformed character. But Sid and Gus still insist on using the epithet.'

'Because he still doesn't treat Molly how she deserves to be treated,' Sid said. 'Too self-centered by half.'

'Aren't all men?' Elizabeth said. 'My husband is better than most but if he has a pet project then all else is shut from his mind. I once waited over an hour for him to pick me up from the station, because he was rearranging his stamp collection and had forgotten the time.'

I decided that I should probably go home and let these old friends enjoy one another's company. I rose to my feet. 'If you ladies will excuse me,' I said. 'It's been a long day and I should get out of this ridiculous outfit.'

Gus took my arm. 'Molly, do stay and have a late supper with us,' she said. 'Sid has found some lovely ripe cheeses and we've a bottle of claret we're dying to try.'

'It does sound tempting,' I said, 'but I think I should go home and let old friends reminisce.'

Nelly Bly also got up. 'And I should also go and change before there is any talk of supper. I've been an urchin long enough today.' She held out her hand. 'It was my plea sure to make your acquaintance, Miss Murphy.'

'Molly, please,' I said.

'And I am Elizabeth. I prefer not to use my infamous nom de plume when I am not working.'

Her handshake was firm, almost like a man's.

Gus held open the door for me. 'Tomorrow you must come to dinner, or will you be out sleuthing again?'

'I suppose I must, if I'm to do this job thoroughly,' I said, 'although I rather think that the young man will turn out to be just as represented.'

'Lunch then,' Sid said. 'We won't take no for an answer.'

'Thank you.' I smiled at them. 'Then I definitely accept.'

'Unless Daniel the Deceiver puts in an appearance,' Sid said dryly, 'then we'll be cast aside again, you mark my words.'

'Absolutely not,' I said. 'I am not a puppet on a string. I don't jump to Daniel's commands. And if he can't be bothered to send me one note in over a week, then he can wait until I'm ready to see him.'

'Well said, Molly,' Elizabeth applauded. 'Spoken like a

Vassar graduate. I take it you didn't go to that esteemed institution?'

'I went to no institution at all,' I said. 'I was educated, to a certain extent, with the daughters of the local landowner, but then my mother died and I had to stay home to raise three young brothers. I'd have dearly loved to further my education, but it just wasn't possible.'

'There is always time,' Elizabeth said. 'These two women possess an impressive library and a wealth of interesting and informed friends.'

'I know,' I said. 'I have taken full advantage of both. Now if you'll excuse me, I look forward to continuing this conversation tomorrow. Now I hear soap and a washcloth calling to remove this grime from my face.'

I left them laughing merrily and closed the front door feeling in much better humor. I crossed Patchin Place and was about to put my key in the front door when I was grabbed violently from behind. My arm was wrenched behind my back as an elbow came around my throat.

'Got you,' a voice hissed in my ear. 'Don't try to struggle or it will be the worse for you. I could snap your neck in a second it I wanted to.'

Three

For a moment I was too terrified to move, and when I tried to struggle I found that my attacker had me in an impossible stranglehold; an arm crushed my windpipe so that I couldn't even cry out.

'Right. Let's take a look at you,' the voice continued in low, threatening tones, and I was dragged backward to the lone street lamp. 'Okay, who sent you? Who put you up to it, huh? Have the Hudson Dusters now got boys breaking into homes for them?'

The iron grip on my neck was released just a fraction. My heart had started beating again and I recognized the voice.

'Daniel,' I croaked, trying to turn my head toward him. 'Daniel, let go of me. It's me. Molly.'

The hands let go of me as if I was burning.

'Molly? Are you all right?'

'I will be when I can talk again,' I whispered.

'I'm so sorry. I had no idea,' he said, then glared at me. 'What in God's name do you think you are doing? I thought I'd arrived just in time to nab a burglar.'

'I've been out on a case,' I said. 'The situation necessitated a disguise.'

He turned me toward him, his big hands resting on my

shoulders. 'My dear girl, when will you give up this absurd notion and start living a safe and normal life?'

'I have to earn a living,' I said evenly, although the closeness of his presence was unnerving.

'I have enough to worry about at the moment on my own behalf, without having to worry about you. You have to stop taking these absurd risks, do you hear?'

'As to that, I was taking no risk at all,' I said calmly. 'I merely wished to be invisible on a city street. Besides, I earned twenty cents for my pains, sweeping a crossing.'

I reached into my pocket and produced the coins. He looked at them and suddenly burst out laughing. 'Molly Murphy, what am I going to do with you?'

'Right now you could tell me why you didn't write all the time you were away,' I said, 'and then I suppose you could kiss me.'

'Didn't write? You knew where I was.'

'Daniel, you said you'd be away for a couple of days over the holiday,' I said angrily. 'It turned into a couple of weeks. I was concerned. Besides, I thought you might possibly be missing me.' I pulled away from him. 'But since you obviously weren't, I see little point in standing out here in the snow discussing it. I'm freezing to death in these clothes. I need to get inside.'

I stomped ahead of him to my front door. Daniel followed. I opened the door, then turned to face him. 'And another thing, what were you doing at my doorstep at this hour of the night?'

'It's only ten,' he said, 'and I wanted to make sure you were all right as soon as I returned to the city.'

'Well thank you kindly, sir. As you can see, I'm hale and hearty.' I went to shut the door. He put out his hand to block me.

'Are you not going to invite me in, Molly? When I've come all this way in the snow?'

'What, and risk compromising my reputation?' I said. 'A young woman who lives alone and admits a man to her house late at night risks terrible censure from society.'

At this he laughed again. 'Now you sound exactly like Arabella. Since when did you ever care a fig what society thought of you?'

'I might have turned over a new leaf, while you've been away,' I said. 'I may have need of a respectable suitor someday.'

'Molly, don't torment me like this,' Daniel said suddenly and pushed his way into the front hall beside me. 'You know what I've been going through recently.'

'Too busy to write to me what ever it was,' I said. 'What happened – did you get invited to such brilliantly fashionable parties with Arabella's set that you couldn't turn them down?'

'I'm sorry.' He sighed. 'It's been a worrying time. My father caught a nasty grippe that we feared would turn into pneumonia. For a while it was touch and go, so I couldn't leave in such circumstances. I was at his bedside day and night. You know how frail his heart has become.'

At this news of course I felt rather silly and shallow. 'Is your father now recovered?' I asked.

'Mercifully yes, thank God. And then the snowstorm stranded me for a few extra days, and my mother was trying to persuade me to stay even longer.'

'Ah, you did finally tell them the truth about your predicament?'

'I told my mother something of it – that I was having a spot of bother with the current commissioner of police.'

'Daniel, you promised you were going to level with them. How can you let your own family go on believing that you're still flourishing as a captain of police when you're in such deep trouble?'

His eyes flashed dangerously. 'What did you expect me to

say to a man with a weak heart – to an ex-policeman who retired with full honors? That his son had been kicked out of the force in disgrace, accused of being in the pay of a gang?'

'No, I suppose in the circumstances . . .' I said weakly.

'And as you pointed out yourself, John Partridge is only police commissioner until January. I have to be patient for another month and then who knows. Maybe someone more sympathetic to my cause might be chosen for the job.'

'I'm sure your fortunes will change, Daniel,' I said. 'John Partridge is only being stubborn. He already knows you were set up. It would be most unfair to keep you on suspension any longer. You're one of their best men. They'd be fools if they didn't reinstate you, with an apology.'

'Let's hope they are not fools then,' Daniel said. He stood there staring at me.

'What?' I asked.

'You look damned alluring in that ridiculous outfit, with that smudge on your nose and those wisps of red hair escaping from that cap.' He ran his finger experimentally down my nose and over my lips.

My resolve had never been strong where Daniel Sullivan was concerned and I could feel it melting. 'I think you should probably go, Daniel,' I said. 'Before we both act imprudently.'

'You're right. We wouldn't want to act imprudently,' he said, his eyes challenging mine. 'But as I recall you yourself invited me to kiss you not a few moments ago.'

'As long as it just stops with a kiss,' I said. 'Our kisses have a habit of progressing to something more, and in our present situation . . .'

'I understand,' Daniel said. 'If only things were different. If I had prospects . . .' He let the end of the sentence trail off into silence.

I took his hands. 'Daniel, don't worry too much. I'm sure it will all be all right in the end.'

'I'm trying to share your optimism,' he said, 'but if you'd been through what I've just experienced . . .'

I thought it wiser not to mention my own recent experiences. Men like to believe that they have the harder lot. I reached up and stroked his cheek, then recoiled. 'You haven't shaved, Captain Sullivan. Shame on you coming to visit a young woman without attending to your toilet first.'

At this he laughed, grabbed my wrists, and drew me close to him. 'I recall another occasion when you were not so particular about the state of my whiskers,' he said.

I recalled that occasion all too well. 'And it is not to be repeated until your situation is resolved,' I said, putting my hands on his jacket front and exerting firm pressure to keep him at bay.

He nodded. 'Very well then. One kiss and I'll go. But tomorrow let us have fun for once. The snow up in Westchester County was amazing. I'd love to show you what it looks like – not gray city slush, but untouched sparkling whiteness. I'm sure you've never seen such snow in Ireland.'

'You want us to go up to Westchester? I'm afraid that's not possible. I have a case I'm working on.'

'Then not as far as Westchester. Surely you can spare some time for Central Park. They have an ice-skating rink and children will be tobogganing. We could take a sleigh ride. You can spare an hour or two for that, can't you, Molly?'

I was truly weakening this time. 'I'm sure I can,' I said. 'The man I am following is safely at work in his office during the day with no time for getting into trouble.'

Daniel beamed as if I'd just given him a gift. 'Then I'll call for you at eleven. How long has it been since we had a day's outing together?'

21

'Too long,' I agreed.

'Until tomorrow then.' He took me in his arms and kissed me gently on the lips. Our lips were still cold from the frigid night air, but they quickly warmed up, as did Daniel. The kiss turned from chaste to demanding and before I allowed myself to respond, I stopped him. 'Daniel, no.' I held him away, my hands on his cheeks. 'Not wise. Go home.'

'If you insist,' he said with a sigh, and went.

Four

Of course the moment I had shut my front door I regretted sending him away, and the very next moment I remembered something else. I had promised to have luncheon with Sid, Gus, and their friend, the intriguing Nelly Bly. Now what was I going to do? I dearly wanted to do both. I debated the matter and in the end Daniel won out. I reasoned that Sid and Gus had their guest to entertain them, whereas Daniel had been through such hard times that he needed me more than they did.

So early next morning I went across Patchin Place to explain, and to beg to postpone our luncheon by one day. My friends naturally found this amusing.

'You see, Gus. What did I tell you? I knew she'd cast us aside the moment that man walked back into the picture. He snaps his fingers and she drops everything to attend to him,' Sid said with a wink.

'I do not, in normal circumstances,' I replied hotly. 'It's just that it's been so long since Daniel and I had a chance to behave like a normal couple and go out to enjoy ourselves. I assure you that I do not come running every time Daniel Sullivan snaps his fingers.'

'Do you think we should let her off just this once, Gus?' Sid asked.

'She obviously enjoys this man's company, although I can't think why,' Gus replied.

'I suppose he is what might be described as handsome, in a roguish way.'

'And he may be trying to make amends for his past behavior.'

They were both watching me with amusement as they carried on this conversation.

'If you must know,' I said, interrupting, 'I really want to see the ice-skating and tobogganing in Central Park. I've never experienced such things in my life. It doesn't really snow in my part of Ireland.'

'Of course.' They nodded sagely together. 'That would be the only reason.'

'You two are quite exasperating sometimes,' I exclaimed. 'But I do beg your forgiveness for my rudeness. Please apologize to your friend Elizabeth and tell her I look forward to taking lunch with her tomorrow.'

As I went to leave, Gus called after me, 'And what do you plan to wear for this outing in Central Park?'

'Certainly not my waif's britches,' I said. 'I do have that big woolen cape. That should keep me warm.'

'Quite wrong,' Gus said, looking at Sid, who nodded.

'Well, I don't possess one of those delightful outfits trimmed with white fur that one sees in the women's magazines,' I said. 'The woolen cape is the only warm outer garment I own.'

'You have the very thing, don't you, Gus?' Sid said.

'I do, indeed.' Gus rushed up the stairs and soon reappeared holding a mid-length red velvet cape, lined with fur.

'Holy Mother of God,' I exclaimed as Gus thrust it at me. 'I couldn't possibly wear this.'

'You don't think the color goes well with your red hair?'

'Not at all. But it's much too fine. I couldn't borrow such a garment from you without worrying that I'd spoil it.'

24

'Nonsense.' Gus laughed. 'I hardly ever wear it. Better you give it an outing than to let the moths have their way with it. Go on. Take it. Dazzle Daniel and everyone else in Central Park with your appearance.'

She insisted on trying it on me and I left their house feeling like a queen.

Daniel's eyes widened when I appeared at the front door in all my finery. 'You look – absolutely stunning,' he said. 'New clothes? Your detective agency must be doing well.'

'Only borrowed for the occasion,' I said, 'but my agency is doing remarkably well. I've had one assignment after another since I got back from Ireland. I rather think that Mr Tommy Burke was pleased enough with me to refer me to his friends.'

'It's nice to know that the trip to Ireland turned out to be successful after all,' Daniel said. He slipped my arm through his and escorted me down Patchin Place. Turned out successful after all, I thought grimly. One brother killed, one banished, and I could never go home again. Hardly a resounding success. But at least I had put Tommy Burke in touch with his lost sister. Maybe his money would help the freedom movement and somehow help make up for its lost leader.

'Watch your step!' Daniel snatched me back as I was about to walk out into the path of a carriage charging down Greenwich Avenue at a ridiculous pace.

'Right,' he said. 'Let's see where we can best hail a cab.'

'Daniel, you can't afford this anymore,' I said without thinking. I saw from the set of his jaw that this was the wrong thing to say. I had just been telling him how my business was flourishing, and now I reminded him that he was on suspension with no pay until he knew of the outcome of his case.

A cab drew up beside us and I got in without saying another word.

'So what case are you working on that involves dressing up as a ragged boy?' he asked.

'Very simple, really. A Jewish couple wants to make sure that the young man the matchmaker has found for their daughter is all that she says he is.'

'And is he?'

'So far his behavior has been beyond reproach. I followed him to Forty-second Street—'

'Aha,' Daniel said.

'—where he was collecting a suit from his tailor,' I finished.

'If your case involves the Jewish community, you should ask your friend Mr Singer to do some snooping on your behalf,' Daniel said. 'Do you ever see Mr Singer these days?'

I knew the comment was meant as a barb. There had been a time I had considered marrying Jacob Singer, when Daniel had still been engaged to Arabella Norton and I had believed we had no hope for a future together.

'I haven't seen him in a while,' I said. 'Besides, he wouldn't move in the same circles as this Mr Roth. Jacob is active among the poor and downtrodden. This young man is a recent Yale graduate who is employed in the family shipping business and dines out at the best restaurants.'

'He sounds highly suitable,' Daniel said. 'Why are these people employing you?'

'To find out if he has any hidden vices,' I said, giving Daniel a wicked smile.

'And has he?'

'Not that I've yet discovered, but most men do, you know.'

Daniel looked at me, then sighed. 'And so you are fully occupied while I sit twiddling my thumbs. It's all wrong, isn't it? Men are supposed to be out earning the daily crust while young ladies are supposed to sit home idly playing the piano or doing their embroidery, waiting for their lord and master to return.'

'Not this young lady,' I exclaimed. 'I've never had an idle day in my life and if I did I should die of boredom, as, I suspect, most women in such situations do. And we are only speaking of the privileged few. For most women their life is drudgery from sun up to sun down.'

'True enough,' Daniel agreed, 'although I hope there will come a future time when you are content to learn to play the role of housewife and mother.'

'We'll have to see about that, won't we,' I said.

He went to say something but I stopped him. 'Let's not talk about it anymore,' I said, patting his hand as one would calm a child. 'As you said yourself, today is for having fun. We're nearly there. Look how the snow sparkles in the sun.'

The cab pulled up beside the wrought-iron gates leading into Central Park. The cabbie jumped down and helped me from the cab as if I were a fine lady. Daniel paid and then offered me his arm. I felt like a fine lady as we swept together into Central Park. Just as we were about to enter, a surprised voice called, 'Why, Captain Sullivan, sir!' And the constable on guard saluted Daniel.

'Hello, Jones,' Daniel said. 'How are you?'

'Fair to middling, sir,' the constable said. 'Can't complain and this duty is pleasant enough. A few pickpockets, lost children, lost keys, and that's about it. Except that today we've been told to be on the lookout for a burglar from New Haven, Connecticut.'

'A burglar from Connecticut? Must be a special kind of burglar to have them alert the New York police.'

'Ah well, as to that I couldn't say. But he may be behind a string of robberies and he's killed those who tried to stop him.'

'What makes them think he's coming to the city?'

'His getaway vehicle was found, having run into a tree on the highway in the Bronx. He's currently a student at Yale, which would explain the New Haven burglaries, but his family lives here in New York and the police suspect that he may have been trying to get home. Halsted is the name. Society man, too, if you can imagine.'

'That name rings a bell,' Daniel said. 'Halsted. Now, where have I met him?'

'If you meet him again, be sure to arrest him,' the constable said with a chuckle. 'That would put you back in their good books, wouldn't it? I tell you straight, Captain Sullivan, we need you back on the job with all that's going on at the moment.'

'Oh, really? What *is* going on?' Daniel asked.

'Well, there's this new Italian gang, for one thing. Straight from Sicily, so I gather, and meaner than anything we've seen so far. They make the Eastmans look like pussycats.'

'Do they, indeed. What do they call themselves,' Daniel asked, 'and where are they operating?'

'They've no defined territory as far as I know, but they're behind all kinds of criminal activities – protection rackets mostly, but robbery, violence, extortion, murder – you name it and they've a hand in it.'

'Like the Black Hand boys?'

'Like them, but worse. The Black Hand thugs keep to their neighborhoods. These guys seem to be operating all over. And they'd kill a man as soon as look at him. They call themselves the Cosa Nostra. No idea what that might mean. It's Italian, sure enough.'

'Just what we needed, another gang,' Daniel said with a bitter laugh. 'Let's hope we can nip this one in the bud and stop them before they take hold. There are plenty of Italians to recruit into gangs in New York.'

'You're telling me, Captain. Plenty of trouble, too. And you try getting one of them to squeal. They've got this code of silence and we just won't break it. Now if they put you on the job, sir, you'd know what to do. When do you think you're coming back?'

'I wish I knew, Jones,' Daniel said. 'I'm being kept in limbo – on purpose, I'm sure. But if we get a new police commissioner in January, he may show more sense than this current fool.'

'I do hope so, sir.' He looked around. 'I should be getting back to work and I should let you enjoy your stroll with your young lady.' He saluted again as Daniel and I walked on.

'One of the best,' Daniel said. 'One of the few that didn't turn against me.'

'I'm sure none of them is against you, now that the truth is out.'

'But is the truth out, that's the question? There has been no trial as yet. That rat Quigley has yet to confess.'

'It will all come right, I'm sure,' I said, and gave him an encouraging smile.

East Drive had been cleared of snow, which now lay piled in great mounds that urchins were sliding down on sheets of cardboard, giving out hollers of delight. Better-dressed children passed us, dragging proper sleds or carrying ice skates, and accompanied by nannies.

At that moment there came a delightful tinkle of bells and a horse-drawn sleigh passed along East Drive, its occupants looking as if they had stepped straight from a Currier and Ives Christmas scene with their fur-trimmed bonnets and muffs. They were laughing merrily as if they hadn't a care in the world. I found myself thinking of Arabella Norton. Daniel might have been riding in such a sleigh had he not broken his engagement to her.

'So did you see anything of Arabella when you were home?' I couldn't resist asking.

'I was not about to make my presence known or to go out

into society given my current circumstances,' Daniel said dryly, 'even if I had wanted to do so – which I didn't.'

He started to walk faster, almost dragging me along beside him.

'Whoa, hold your horses,' I said, tugging at his arm. 'I can't stride out like a man, you know, much as I would like to.'

He looked down at me and smiled. 'Forgive me,' he said. 'As you know, I have much on my mind. Let us go and see the skaters and forget all our cares. If you'd like to, we could try it ourselves.'

'In which case I rather fear I should be sitting on my backside on the ice more than anything,' I said, 'since I've never been on skates before.'

'You'd have my arm firmly around you,' Daniel said, 'and I have skated on the pond behind our house since childhood.'

'We'll see when we get there,' I said. 'At this moment I'm just enjoying being in the snow. It hardly ever snows in my part of Ireland, and if it does it's only a light dusting that soon melts in the rain that follows it. My, how it dazzles. Come on, let's walk where nobody has trodden before.'

I started to run across what had been a meadow and was now an expanse of pristine whiteness. The snow crunched deliciously under my feet and I looked back at the trail my footprints had left.

'If I were a criminal, you'd have no trouble following me, would you?' I called out. 'Come on, Daniel. What are you waiting for?'

'Molly, a little decorum, please, and besides, you don't know how deep the snow might be.'

'Nonsense,' I said. 'It doesn't come over the tops of my boots. Don't be such a ninny. See?'

I took two more steps and suddenly found myself sinking into snow up to my knees. I hadn't realized until this moment how very cold the snow could be. It almost took my breath away.

'Daniel, help me out,' I gasped. I glared at him as he started laughing.

'Don't say I didn't warn you,' he chuckled.

Feeling foolish and angry, I bent down, scooped up a snowball, and threw it at him. It hit him square in the chest.

'Good shot, Molly,' I yelled with delight.

For a second he looked startled, then he brushed himself off. 'Right,' he called. 'You asked for it!' and he bent to make his own snowball.

I struggled free of the snow and started to run. A snowball hit me in the back. I paused, scooped, and threw back one of my own, then picked up my skirts, raising them to a level that bordered on impropriety and ran on again, squealing in delight like a ten-year-old. At the edge of a meadow the ground rose in a series of tree-covered hillocks. I headed in that direction as another snowball whizzed past me.

'Missed me,' I shouted, but I could hear him gaining on me. The hills and trees were ahead. We could turn this into a game of hide-and-seek. The snow was deeper here again, however, and I clambered and slithered up the nearest slope. Daniel still hadn't caught up with me. I started to run down the other side, then almost stumbled over something beside the tree. It was white and I didn't realize what it was until almost too late. I grabbed onto a bare tree branch and pulled up, recoiling in horror. It was a woman's body.

Five

She was young and beautiful, with a delicate little elfin face surrounded by rich chestnut hair, and she was clad only in a flimsy white dress and white stockings with dainty little black evening shoes. Her porcelain flesh was as white as the snow and she looked like a large white china doll lying there.

'I've got you now. You're at my mercy,' Daniel shouted as he came blundering over the rise. Then he saw my face. 'What is it?'

Silently I pointed to the ground at my feet.

'God Almighty,' Daniel exclaimed, although he was usually most careful about swearing in my presence. 'Don't touch her and stand back. I want to get a good look at the scene of the crime. There will be footprints.'

'Scene of the crime?' I asked nervously.

'Young ladies don't usually wander out into the snow with no warm outer garments and certainly not in those shoes. She was probably killed and brought here.'

He came forward cautiously and examined the ground around the dead girl.

'Strange,' he muttered. 'I see no prints but those the girl herself made. How can that be?'

He squatted beside the girl, lifted her wrist, then dropped

it again as if it burned him. 'I felt a pulse. She's still alive. Quickly, help me off with my jacket. We must warm her up.'

'My cape is warmer,' I said, untying the neck before he could object. I helped Daniel raise the girl from the snow and we wrapped the fur-lined cape around her.

'We must get help fast,' Daniel said. 'And a warm drink. You stay with her. Here, put my jacket around you. I'll go and alert the constable at the gate. I'll be as fast as I can.'

He ran off while I knelt in the snow, cradling the unconscious girl in my arms. Her flesh felt so cold to my touch that it was hard to believe she could be still alive. But as I looked down at her face I saw her eyes flutter open and look around in wonder. They were an incredible blue and her wide-eyed stare only added to her doll-like quality.

'Don't worry. You're safe now,' I said in a soothing voice. 'Help is on the way. You're going to be all right.'

The eyes fluttered shut again and I held her to me like a large child. I looked around me at the desolate winter landscape. It was hard to believe that I was in the middle of a city and that just over that hill there were crowds of people. Daniel was as good as his word. Just as I was beginning to feel the cold badly without the benefit of my cape, he came back, wading through the deep snow with a cup of cocoa in one hand, and the constable from the park gate, red-faced and panting, following at his heels.

'Well, I never did,' the constable exclaimed.

'She hasn't regained consciousness, then.' Daniel dropped to his knees beside us.

'She opened her eyes for a moment,' I said.

'Wake up, my dear,' Daniel said gently. 'We've got a nice hot drink for you. Try and take a sip.'

He put the cup to her mouth. She recoiled in fear as the warm liquid touched her, but then ran her tongue experimentally around her lips. Daniel tried again and this time she managed a sip or two. After a few minutes of patient ministration, he was able to get the whole cup down her. Her eyes opened again and she stared at us in complete bewilderment.

'We should get you home,' Daniel said. 'Where do you live, miss?'

She continued to stare without responding.

'You're in Central Park. Do you know how you got here?'

No reaction.

'You're safe with us,' Daniel said gently. 'We are police officers. We're going to take good care of you. Now, what is your name?'

She looked up at me with the same bewildered look on her face.

'Tell us your name and address and we can take you home,' I said, smiling at her.

No response.

'Maybe she has some identification on her,' the constable suggested.

'I think that's unlikely,' I said. 'She's wearing the flimsiest of gowns and no kind of overcoat.'

'No pocketbook?'

I shook my head. 'No pocketbook.'

'Maybe that's it then,' Constable Jones said. 'Maybe she was out for a morning walk and she was robbed in a desolate part of the park and the thief stole her outer garments and pocketbook.'

'It's possible,' Daniel said. 'Were you attacked? Let me see if you were hit on the head.'

He went to touch her hair but she recoiled in alarm again.

'Let me,' I said. 'She'll feel more comfortable with a woman.' I smiled at her. 'I just want to see if you got a nasty bump on the head. I won't hurt you.'

I tried to feel her scalp but she was starting like a nervous colt. 'She may have a bit of a bump just over her right temple,' I said, 'but I don't see any blood. Besides, we saw her footprints, and no others. If someone had hit her over the head to knock her out, would she have got up and started walking again? And look at those impossible little shoes. She'd never have intentionally gone for a walk in those.'

'But she did walk this far under her own steam and then she must have collapsed with cold.' Daniel was still frowning.

'No other footprints, you say?' The constable stared at the snowy ground, which clearly displayed the dainty trail coming from the northeast. 'And no sign of foul play, as far as we can tell? Her dress was not disturbed or in disarray?'

From the way a glance passed between him and Daniel, I could tell what he was hinting at.

Daniel coughed discreetly. 'If she walked here alone, we can hardly find out any more until she's been examined by a doctor, or can tell us herself.'

'Her dress was in no kind of disarray when I found her,' I said. 'She was lying as if asleep,'

'What ever happened we must get her into a warm environment as soon as possible,' Daniel said. 'In the absence of a name and address we'd better take her to the closest hospital.'

'That would be the German hospital, Lenox Hill, on East Seventy-seventh,' the constable suggested.

'Not far at all, then,' Daniel said. 'If we could carry her to the nearest park gate, we could hail a cab. That would be quicker than summoning an ambulance. Do you think we could manage it?'

'No trouble at all,' the constable said. 'I'll wager she weighs no more than a feather. Look at her, she's all skin and bones. She doesn't look as if she's had a decent meal in months.'

He was right in a way. There was no spare flesh on her. I could easily span the tiny wrist I was holding between my thumb and first finger, and yet she didn't look gaunt or starving, and from what I could see, her dress and shoes were of good quality.

'Are you sure you can't tell us your name?' I asked her again. 'It would be so much nicer to go home than to be taken to a hospital, wouldn't it?'

The girl only stared at me with large, hopeless eyes.

'Maybe she doesn't understand us,' Daniel said. 'Maybe she is a new immigrant who speaks a different language.'

I tried my schoolgirl French on her and Daniel tried some German, but we got no response. As Daniel and the constable lifted her gently between them, she attempted no kind of struggle, but lay passively, her head lolling like a rag doll's. We soon found a path cutting across from the East Drive and were walking on a swept surface again. The wet snow had soddened my skirts and stockings by now and my teeth were starting to chatter even though I had Daniel's jacket around my shoulders.

We soon emerged onto Fifth Avenue and Daniel hailed a cab that whisked us a few short blocks to Seventy-seventh. As Daniel carried the girl through the austere entrance of the hospital, and then down that echoing white-tiled hallway, she showed alarm and attempted to struggle, but she was so weak that he held her easily imprisoned in his arms. Soon she was lying in a hospital bed, wrapped in warm blankets and being attended to by nurses. I retrieved my borrowed cloak just as an imposing, bearded doctor arrived on the scene and we repeated our story for him.

'Out in the snow, dressed like this?' he demanded. 'Such folly.' He had a strong German accent.

'We were thinking that maybe she wasn't out in the park willingly. That maybe she had escaped from an abductor or assailant,' Daniel said.

'Ach so. I will take a look at her. Move away, please.' A

screen was placed around her bed while the doctor examined her. He came out almost immediately, wiping his forehead.

'She is clearly severely traumatized,' he said. 'She won't let me touch her.'

'Then it's possible she was assaulted in the park?'

'From what I could see, I'd say the answer is no,' the doctor replied. 'Her undergarments are tied with an old-fashioned drawstring and don't appear to have been touched in any way. I should have thought that any potential attacker would have snapped the string in his lust, or at very least not bothered to tie it up again.'

'And as to other kinds of assault?' Daniel asked. 'She didn't appear to have been struck on the head and knocked unconscious, did she?'

'Again, not from what I could see. She became so alarmed every time I moved near her that I thought it best to let her recover before we examine her further. So you have no idea who she might be?'

'She wouldn't answer any questions or communicate with us in any way,' I said. 'Captain Sullivan thought she might not understand English.'

'Captain Sullivan? You're in the military, *mein Herr*?'

'New York police,' Daniel replied curtly.

'*Das ist gut.* Then we don't have to file a police report.'

'No, that's been taken care of,' Daniel said. 'So we can leave her in your care for the time being, can we?'

'Of course.'

'I'll give you my card.' Daniel fished in his pocket. 'And we'll come to visit her tomorrow.'

'Hopefully by the next time you come she'll have fully recovered and we'll have contacted her family.' The doctor gave a jovial smile.

* * *

I glanced back at her bed as we left. The screens had been wheeled away and she was lying there not moving, eyes closed, looking as if she was carved from white marble.

Six

'I'm not sure that I'm in the mood for ice-skating after that escapade,' Daniel said as we stepped into brilliant winter sunshine. 'How about you?'

'I'm feeling thoroughly wet and sodden,' I said, 'in need of a change of clothes and some hot tea.'

'I'll call us a cab and take you home.'

'You'll do no such thing,' I retorted. 'All this extravagance with cabs.'

'Then I'll let you pay for it,' Daniel teased, 'since you made a fortune over in Ireland and are currently working on another lucrative case.'

'It wasn't exactly a fortune,' I said, 'and in my business I need to put money by for the dry times when no client shows up at my door. Besides, I was brought up to be frugal. I've a good pair of legs and they can take us to the nearest El station.'

'I'll agree with that,' Daniel said, eyeing me appraisingly. 'You've certainly got a good pair of legs.'

'Captain Sullivan!' I exclaimed in mock horror.

'Well, you showed them to half the world as you danced across that snowy meadow,' Daniel said, smiling.

We walked in silence for a while. 'You're very subdued,' Daniel said. 'Still thinking about that girl?'

'I can't stop thinking about her,' I said. 'Poor thing. What an awful ordeal. She could so easily have died if I hadn't run away from you and looked for somewhere to hide.'

He nodded. 'A rum business, wasn't it? I'll be most interested to hear an explanation of what really happened.'

'It seemed to me that the girl had had a bad fright of some kind,' I said. 'The way she flinched away when anyone tried to touch her. And yet there appeared nothing wrong with her except for extreme cold.'

'I wonder if she isn't perhaps a mental patient, wandered away from her caretakers,' Daniel said. 'She could be delusional.'

I thought of those blank blue eyes. 'You may be right. If she is a mental patient, her family will have reported her missing by now.'

By the time the El reached Eighth Street, my petticoats and stockings had dried and I found myself regretting that I had not tried the ice-skating.

'Maybe we could go skating tomorrow,' I said. 'Knowing Sid and Gus they will undoubtedly have proper skating outfits. I have already agreed to have lunch with them and with their friend Nelly Bly.'

'Nelly Bly?' Daniel exclaimed. 'The newspaper reporter? She is an acquaintance of your friends?'

'Sid and Gus know everybody worth knowing in the city,' I said with a smile. 'And she seems such an interesting woman.'

'A dashed plucky one, from what one reads,' Daniel aside. 'She has put herself in harm's way on numerous occasions, including traveling around the world in seventy-eight days. I'd dearly like to meet her.'

'Then I'll ask Sid and Gus if you may be included,' I said. 'We can visit the hospital in the morning, lunch with Nelly Bly, and then have time to fit in an afternoon of skating before I have to shadow Mr Roth to his evening pursuits.'

'Couldn't you take an evening off and let us extend our skating into dinner somewhere?' Daniel asked.

'And what if that's the one night that he goes on the town, or meets with undesirable people?' I said. 'I have been hired to do a job, Daniel. I don't recall you taking evenings off when you were on a case.'

'That's true enough. But in my case, I was on the trail of criminals and it was important that they were caught.'

'Oh, I see,' I said haughtily. 'You still think that my occupation is not serious, is that it? I've been in dangerous situations myself, you know.'

'Which is why I would be heartily glad if you forsook it for a safer profession,' Daniel said. 'But I admire your loyalty to your clients and your determination to see the job through. I'll be content to wait for a dinner engagement until the assignment is over. When will that be?'

'I'm planning to observe Mr Roth for at least two weeks,' I said. 'If I have no hint of any deviant behavior in that time, I shall report to my clients that their daughter may safely marry him.'

'So any young man only needs to behave himself for two weeks to make an ideal husband?' Daniel asked.

'I didn't say that. But two weeks should be enough to form an impression of him, and two weeks is about the amount of time the client is paying for.'

Daniel laughed.

'I'm starving,' I said. 'It's past lunchtime and we haven't had a bite to eat.'

'We could go to the restaurant at the Hotel Lafayette,' Daniel said. 'They do a good lunch plate.'

'We're supposed to be economizing,' I said. 'I'll make you lunch at home. I've a good soup and some cheese.'

'Very well, I accept,' Daniel said.

Finally, we reached Patchin Place.

When I unlocked my front door, I found a letter lying on the mat. It was in a woman's flowery hand, one that looked strangely familiar. I picked it up.

'Now who would have written to me?' I said out loud.

'Maybe it's another assignment?'

'No. Letters to the agency are held at the post office,' I said. 'I don't want my clients knowing my home address.'

Never having been known for my patience, I ripped the envelope open. The stationery smelled of perfume. I glanced at the letter.

My Dear Miss Murphy:

I can only hope you are safely returned to New York by now. I have just received a long letter from Grania Hyde-Borne in Dublin, apprising me of the amazing events that took place. My dear Molly, I had no idea that I would involve you in such danger. I never intended to place you in harm's way and I beg your forgiveness.

Please come to visit me at your earliest convenience. I would dearly love to apologize to you in person, and also to hear the truth about my poor Rose and about Cullen. And there is the little matter of extra money that I owe you, although now I fear I can never pay you enough for what you went through.

Oona Sheehan

I stood there with the letter in my hand.

'Who is it from?' Daniel asked.

'It's from Oona Sheehan,' I said angrily.

'The actress?'

'The very same. The one who put my life in jeopardy on the trip to Ireland with her dirty schemes.'

'So what does she want now?'

'She's writing to apologize in person, so she says. But I think the truth is that she wants to hear about what happened to Cullen Quinlan. She was in love with him, you know.' I didn't add that I had fallen in love with him just a little myself.

'Cullen Quinlan?'

I felt myself turning red. 'The leader of the republican brotherhood. A very great man.'

'Ah,' he said. 'So are you going to go and pay her a call?'

'I don't see why I should. It will only open up old wounds, talking about it again.'

Daniel peered over my shoulder. 'She says she wants to pay you the money she owes you,' he said. 'At least you should collect that. You earned it.'

'I definitely did that,' I retorted bitterly. 'Very well, I shall pay her that visit, if only to let her know how thoughtless and cruel her actions were.'

'I don't envy Miss Sheehan,' Daniel commented with a dry laugh. 'Why did you not go to collect your fee as soon as you got home?'

'I just wanted to forget the whole business,' I said. 'Too many painful memories.' But even as I was speaking I was toying with Daniel's words. He had said 'home.' I could never go back to Ireland and it gave me a thrill of delight to realize that New York really was my home now.

'I'll go to her rooms right away, and get it over with,' I said.

'Not right away, I hope. Were we not going to eat first?'

'Trust a man to think of his stomach in times of stress,' I said. 'Very well, let me put the soup pot on the stove and you shall have your meal.'

After the meal had been cleared away, I changed into my business costume and attempted to put up my hair into a neat bun.

As I was doing this I remembered that I still had the striped black-and-white two-piece that Miss Sheehan had lent me to wear. I found it in my closet, looking in definite need of cleaning and pressing. For a second I wondered if she'd be angry at the state I was returning it in. Then I reminded myself that she owed me far more than she could ever repay.

I shoved the garment into a carpet bag, said farewell to Daniel, and off I went.

Miss Sheehan's address was Hoffman House on West Twenty-fifth Street. I was expecting some kind of apartment building and was surprised to find instead that not only was it on Madison Square, but that it was an elegant hotel. Madison Square is a leafy oasis in the summer, but the sky had clouded over and trees stretched gaunt black branches over gray and dirty snow, making the scene feel quite forbidding. The wind had whipped up again, too, and I was glad to step into the warmth of the hotel foyer. As the doorman closed the gilt-and-glass door behind me, I stood with my feet sinking into thick carpeting while I stared up in half admiration, half fascination at the large oil painting that dominated the back wall. It depicted nymphs and satyrs, all revealingly nude and lusty-looking. One might expect such things in a museum of art, but in a hotel it was shocking, even for one like myself who has sampled the bohemian life.

Obviously it possessed fascination for other New York visitors, too, as an elderly couple poked their heads in through the front door behind me.

'See, Mary, what did I tell you?' the man said.

'Terrible. Wicked and terrible. Don't you dare look, Joseph.'

I smiled at their names as well as their reaction, then went over to the reception desk.

'I'm here to see Miss Sheehan,' I said. 'My name is Murphy. She is expecting me.'

'Let me see if Miss Sheehan is in residence,' the clerk said and disappeared, leaving me unable to take my eyes off the painting. He soon came back with an almost gracious smile on his face.

'Miss Sheehan will be happy to receive you, Miss Murphy. Please take the elevator to the tenth floor. Room number 1006.'

The elevator operator saluted smartly and whisked me upward. As the door opened on ten, a rather striking older woman was standing there. She was swathed in some sort of ginger fur – lynx maybe – and it went well with her wiry mane of hair, giving the impression of a lioness on the prowl. She nodded to me solemnly and said, *'Bonjour,'* in a deep, mannish voice. I was sure I had seen her before somewhere but it was not until the elevator man said, 'Going down, Madame Bernhardt,' that I recalled Miss Sheehan telling me that the Divine Sarah also kept a suite of rooms at the Hoffman.

Talk about mingling with the mighty, I thought to myself. If only the folks in Ballykillin could see me now, hobnobbing with the rich and famous. The thought flashed through my mind before I had time to remember that there was nobody in Ballykillin any longer. No family. No friends. All gone. And I was going to have to relive some of my most painful moments for the woman I was about to see. I hesitated in the mirror-lined hallway and almost turned back. But I put on a brave face and rapped smartly on her door.

She was looking as stunning as ever, wearing a silk robe of dark, rich green that accented the copper hair. For once this wasn't piled on her head but spilled over her shoulders. Her face bore no trace of makeup but in truth it needed no help. It was simply the epitome of beauty. One looked at her and gasped. I could well understand why so many young men became besotted with her. I had been resolved to be cold, efficient, and distant with her, but when she stood at the door and opened her

45

arms wide, saying 'Molly, my sweet child. Thank you so much for coming,' I found myself accepting her embrace and even murmuring some kind of thanks of my own.

She drew me into a drawing room overlooking the park, elegantly furnished with brocade chairs and sofas. A huge bowl of out-of-season fruit was on a side table, along with the sort of floral tributes that seemed to accompany Miss Sheehan wherever she went.

'Take off your coat, do,' she said, 'and do sit down. I'll have Yvette bring us some tea.' She motioned to a dainty little brocade armchair beside the window. She rang a small silver bell and a slim dark person in a black-and-white uniform appeared, bobbing a curtsey. 'You rang, madame?'

'Yes. Tea for two please, Yvette.'

The maid jerked a halfhearted attempt at a curtsey and went.

Quite a change from Rose, I thought to myself. Her last maid had been a broad country girl from Ireland and she had been brutally murdered.

'Life must go on,' Miss Sheehan said sadly, as if reading my thoughts. 'I chose a new maid as different as possible from Rose so that I was not reminded of her. Madame Bernhardt's own maid suggested her. They come from the same town in France, so one understands.' She paused, looking at me critically. 'So how are you, Molly? From what Grania writes, you had a most harrowing time.'

'Yes, it wasn't too pleasant,' I said. 'No thanks to you.'

She reached out and touched my hand. 'I felt so awful when I realized what I had let you in for.'

'You knew from the very start what you were doing,' I said angrily. 'You used me.'

'Yes, but I never thought . . .' she said. 'Molly, I would never have exposed you to such danger, had I known. I thought it was a simple assignment. Can you ever forgive me?'

She took my hand and smiled her most enchanting dimpled smile. Against my better judgment, I felt myself soften and managed a weak smile of my own.

'And could you possibly bear to tell me all about it? I only have Grania's account and she has left out a lot of details I would dearly like to know.'

'All right,' I said, and started to recount the events. I tried to be as brief as possible and to stick to the main facts, but it was hard to tell the story without dwelling on my brothers and on Cullen. As she listened, she put a lace handkerchief up to her mouth. 'Our brave Irish boys,' she muttered. 'Such a waste.'

'As you say, such a waste.'

We sat there looking at each other.

'He was a fine man, wasn't he, Molly?'

'One of the best,' I agreed.

'And did he speak often of me?' she asked.

I didn't like to say that he had long forgotten her. 'All the time,' I lied.

'If only I could have been there,' she said. 'But I have a duty to my public. They count on me, Molly. I brighten their little lives.'

For a while I had been feeling pity for her. Now that vanished as easily as a pricked bubble. 'I can't stay long, Miss Sheehan,' I said. 'I have brought the clothes that I had to wear when I left the ship, because my own were not available to me. I'm afraid you'll need to have your maid give the outfit a good cleaning.'

I had started to open the bag, but she waved me away. 'Keep them, please. You should have helped yourself to any of my clothes that you wanted. Couturiers are always giving me things to wear. I have far too many. Come and see – is there anything else you'd like?'

She took my hand and tried to drag me toward her bedroom. She was trying to be friendly, and I have to admit I was sorely tempted. Who wouldn't want to help themselves to a Worth gown or two? But I remained steadfast. 'You are most kind, but no, thank you.' There was the little matter of the money she still owed me. I hated asking for money but I had completed the assignment for her, hadn't I? And almost been killed in the process. She did owe it to me. I took a deep breath. 'If you want to repay a debt,' I said, 'there is the money you promised me.'

'Promised you?' She looked up with dramatic surprise.

'When you asked me to deliver your luggage, remember? An extra hundred dollars?'

She flushed prettily. 'Oh, that. Of course. How silly of me. I'd completely forgotten.'

Obviously, a hundred dollars was a mere trifle to her. She fished around in her purse, then gave me an embarrassed smile. 'I appear to be out of checks,' she said.

'You can mail it to me,' I said. 'You have my address.'

'Of course,' she said with relief, then looked around with impatience. 'Yvette? What has happened to tea?'

'Coming, madame,' came a voice from far away. 'They are sending it up in the service elevator at this moment.'

'You see. Tea is on the way.' Oona patted the seat beside her again. 'And while we wait, I have to confess that there was another reason I brought you here. I have another little assignment for you.'

I might have known, I thought.

'Oh, no thank you,' I said, jerking my hand away from her. 'What is the phrase? Once bitten, twice shy.'

'But it's not for me, this time,' she said hastily. 'It's for my dear, dear friend Blanche Lovejoy.'

'Blanche Lovejoy?' I asked. The name somehow rang a bell.

'You must know Blanche,' Oona said. 'Everybody knows Blanche. Her name is a household word.'

'I haven't been in New York long,' I said, feeling stupid. 'Although I know I've heard the name.'

'She is only one of New York's best-known and best-loved entertainers. She was in *A Country Maid*, and *Springtime Follies*. Both of them huge hits.'

Neither meant a thing to me, but then I hadn't exactly had the money to go to the theater much.

'She hasn't had a show on Broadway for a year or so,' Oona went on, 'but she has a new show opening this week at the Casino. Best location in town. She has high hopes for it, because frankly the leading roles don't come so easily when an actress turns thirty-five.'

'Sarah Bernhardt seems to have no problem,' I said. 'I bumped into her going into the elevator. She must be over forty.'

Oona laughed merrily. 'Close to sixty, my dear. But then the divine Sarah is an institution. For the rest of us mere mortals our careers are over when we lose our looks. I have five more years, at best.' She gave a wonderfully dramatic sigh and put a hand to her breast.

'And what will you do then?' I couldn't resist asking. 'I presume you're accumulating a nice little nest egg.'

'My dear, I shall marry well,' she said. 'Before I'm too old I shall let some very rich man snap me up and spend the rest of my life in pampered luxury.'

'Artie Fortwrangler, for example?' I asked, referring to a young man I had met on the ship.

'Oh merciful heavens. So you bumped into Artie, did you? I don't intend to be that desperate.' She laughed. 'I was thinking more of a European. A duke maybe, or an Italian prince.'

Yvette burst upon this scene of self-adoration with a curt 'Your tea, madame,' putting the tray down so firmly that the teacups rattled. 'Do you wish me to pour?'

'No, thank you, Yvette. That will be all,' Oona said, waving her away.

As she retreated, Oona muttered, 'I suppose French maids have a certain flair, but they always make one feel that they are doing one a favor and are being ill-used. Rose was so amiable.'

I wasn't going to allow her to slip back into reminiscences about Rose. 'So to return to Blanche Lovejoy,' I said. 'You told me she has a new play opening this week. Why do you think she needs my services?'

Oona leaned closer to me, as if she didn't want to be overheard. 'Because, my dear, she thinks that the theater may be haunted.'

'Haunted?' I couldn't help smiling. 'What does she think I could do about it? She needs a spiritualist if she wants communication with the dead.'

'She believes the ghost is trying to kill her. She wants someone from the outside to prove to her that she is not imagining things, that she is not going off her head. You can do that for her, can't you?'

Seven

I came out of Hoffman House and paused to turn up my collar against the bitter chill of the wind that blew down Twenty-fifth. I was annoyed that I had come away empty-handed – I didn't think that she'd post that check without more prompting, and I wasn't sure what to do next. I had half-promised Miss Sheehan that I would visit Blanche Lovejoy, and I had to admit that I found the assignment intriguing. Ghost hunting was something I hadn't tackled before. But I already had a case I was working on for at least another week, which would be too late for Miss Lovejoy. That's not to imply that she would have been killed by then. She had apparently invested a considerable amount of her own money in the venture and was threatening to close the show before it opened if she didn't feel safe in the theater.

Then there was the girl we had found in the park that morning. I knew she was no longer my business, but I couldn't get her out of my mind. I had to make sure she was all right and safely home among her loved ones. And I was dying to know exactly what had happened to her. My mother had always warned me that my curiosity would be the death of me – if one of my other sins didn't put an end to me first.

So how could I possibly juggle two assignments at once? I couldn't be in two places at once, that was sure. Miss Lovejoy would presumably be at the theater primarily in the evenings, which was exactly when I should be following Mr Roth. What I needed was an employee. Then suddenly it came to me. I had the perfect person to work with me. Instead of mounting the steps to the Twenty-third Street El station, I kept walking on Twenty-third until I came to the brownstone where Daniel had rooms. His landlady, Mrs O'Shea, was delighted to see me.

'Why, Miss Murphy. You're a sight for sore eyes, and that's a fact. You'll no doubt cheer the poor man up,' she said. 'Grumpy and gloomy doesn't describe it these days, does it?'

'He's going through a bad time,' I said. 'Is he home?'

'Just got in some ten minutes ago,' she said. 'I was just about to ask him if he'd like to join us for supper. I don't like to think of him brooding alone up there.'

'I'll go on up then,' I said.

'You're most welcome to stay for supper, too,' she said. 'I've made enough Irish stew to feed half of New York.'

'Thank you, but I have to be somewhere else this evening. But I'll pass on the invitation to Daniel then, shall I?'

'Most kind of you.' She beamed as I went to climb the stairs. 'I bet you'll be glad when this is all over and you and the captain can get on with your lives again,' she muttered confidentially. 'He's of an age when he needs to settle down with a family of his own.'

'I will be glad when his current problems are over,' I agreed, and went up the stairs before she could ask any questions I couldn't answer.

Daniel looked startled as he opened his front door and saw me standing there.

'Molly, what on earth are you doing here?'

'Well, that's a fine way to greet the woman who is supposed to be the love of your life,' I said.

'But we parted only two hours ago,' he said. 'Even the most

ardent lovers wouldn't miss each other in such a short space of time. Unless, of course, you regretted sending me out into the snow last night with only one chaste kiss and have come to make amends?'

'I've come to do no such thing,' I said. 'It's a business proposition I have for you.'

I didn't wait any longer to be invited but pushed past him into his rooms. It's funny how you can always tell a man's residence from a woman's. That lingering herby smell of pipe tobacco, the austere polished wood, rows of serious-looking books, leather armchairs with no fluffy cushions, nothing frivolous or unnecessary. I swear, if Victorian men had been responsible for decorating their houses, there would never have been a solitary stuffed bird or aspidistra in sight.

I seated myself into one of the leather armchairs on either side of his fireplace without being asked.

'You saw Miss Sheehan?' Daniel asked. 'Did you get the money she owed you?'

'She was conveniently out of checks,' I said. 'She promised to mail it to me. I'll believe it when I see it, but she did offer me another job.'

'After what she put you through the first time? I hope you turned her down.'

'It's not for her but for a friend. And I have to admit that it sounds intriguing. Another actress. Blanche Lovejoy.'

'Blanche Lovejoy?'

'You know her then?'

'Know her? She's a big star, or rather she was a big star a few years ago. There was a time when a Blanche Lovejoy musical comedy was always playing on Broadway. And before that she made her name in vaudeville. I remember seeing her when I was a college student. Some of her songs were very risqué. So what does Blanche Lovejoy want you to do for her?'

'I'm not quite sure yet, but I'd like to pay her a visit at the theater this evening. However, this is where I run into a problem. I already have an assignment. I should be shadowing Mr Roth in the evenings.'

'You certainly can't do two jobs at once,' Daniel said.

'No, I can't. Unless—' I paused for dramatic effect. '—unless I take on someone to help me. A business associate.'

'Really? Can you afford to do that? And would they do a good enough job?'

'I hope so,' I said. 'It was you I was thinking of, Daniel.'

'Me? You're asking me to come and work for you?'

'You have the right qualifications for the job,' I said, trying not to smile, because I was actually enjoying this moment. 'And you told me yourself that you're sitting home twiddling your thumbs while I have more work than I can handle. I'm offering you a chance to keep your hand in at your detective skills. I'll give you seventy-five percent of the fee.'

'Only seventy-five?' He was smiling too now.

'Administrative costs, you know. I have an agency to run. Now what do you say? Have I found myself a new associate?'

Daniel frowned. 'If it ever got out that I'd been working for a woman, I'd be a laughingstock when I returned to the force,' he said.

'Not working for a woman, Daniel. Working with a woman. You know that you and I could make a great team. You'd be the biggest asset my little agency ever had. I know I can't pay you what you're worth but at least you'd have some money coming in – enough to pay for cab fares to take your lady friend to Central Park.'

I saw him frown again, and swallow hard, his Adam's apple dancing above the starched collar.

'If you don't want the job, I'm sure I can find someone else who would do it for me. I believe that Ryan O'Hare is unemployed with no current play on Broadway. He'd definitely find it a huge lark to play the detective.'

That did it, of course. I knew that Daniel despised my friend, the flamboyant playwright Ryan O'Hare.

'You'd surely never dream of working with such a creature,' he said. 'Think of the reputation of your business. No prosperous Jewish family would ever consider letting such a man work for them!'

'Then take the assignment yourself, Daniel. It's absolutely up your street. Following a man around unsavory neighborhoods – who better to do it than you?'

'You're right,' he said. 'Nobody could do it better than I. Except that I am well known among the criminal element.'

'I don't think that Mr Roth will be mixing with the criminal element,' I said. 'At least I sincerely hope he won't.'

'I suppose I could try this one assignment and see how we get along,' Daniel said at last.

'If we can't work together for a few days, then I see little hope in planning any kind of future together,' I said. 'It's about time you learned that I will never be the demure miss who waits at home for her lord and master, doing her embroidery and playing croquet.'

He looked a little startled at this outburst, then he had to nod. 'No, I can't see you being anyone's lapdog, Molly. It is one of the things I admire about you. And maybe I can teach you a thing or two about detective methods.'

'Maybe I can teach you a thing or two about mine,' I said. 'Shall we shake on it?'

I reached out my hand. Daniel took it, then pulled me toward him. 'Sealed with a kiss,' he said and planted his lips firmly on mine. This time I let him kiss me, returning the kiss with full fervor.

Mrs O'Shea's tap on the door was the only thing that prevented the encounter from going on a little too long.

'Did Miss Murphy tell you that you're invited to supper, Captain Sullivan?' she called through the closed door.

'I'm afraid I won't be home for supper, Mrs O'Shea,' Daniel called back. 'I've a detective assignment.'

I grinned. 'And I have a date with a ghost,' I said.

Eight

The Casino Theater on Broadway at West Thirty-ninth was where Blanche Lovejoy's new play was about to open. I wasn't at all sure what I could do for Blanche Lovejoy. How did one prove that a theater was or wasn't haunted? If I made actual communication with a spirit, she'd stop production and that would presumably put a lot of people out of work, unless she could find another theater at the last minute. And to be quite honest, I wasn't at all sure that I wanted a face-to-face encounter with a ghost, especially a malevolent one that was trying to kill Miss Lovejoy.

As soon as I spotted the Casino Theater, I could tell that Miss Lovejoy wouldn't want to move to another theater unless it was absolutely necessary. It was a magnificent-looking building – more sultan's palace than theater, with carved stonework, archways, vaulted windows. Lit only by the electric lights from the buildings around it, the stonework seemed to glow. On one corner a round tower seemed to reach up into the heavens and I could just glimpse the metallic dome on top. There was a sign on the marquee, although it wasn't yet illuminated.

OPENING NEXT WEEK,
Miss Blanche Lovejoy makes her triumphant return in
Ooh La La.

The engraved glass front doors were firmly locked but I finally located the stage door down an alleyway. I went in and found myself in a dimly hit hallway.

'Where do you think you're going?' a voice from the darkness demanded.

I must have jumped a mile. I hadn't seen the little kiosk built into the wall and the man's face in the window floated like a disembodied head. 'We're not open to the public,' he said. 'So I must ask you to leave right away.'

'I have a message for Miss Lovejoy,' I said. 'From Miss Oona Sheehan. It's urgent.'

'From Miss Sheehan, huh?' I could now see that he was an older man with a round face and not much hair, and most of him was hidden behind the booth in which he sat, making me feel that I might be talking with the man in the moon. 'What a lovely gracious lady she is. So you know Miss Sheehan, do you? She worked here a couple of years ago.'

'I know Miss Lovejoy will want to see me as soon as she has a minute,' I said.

'From Miss Sheehan, you said?' He repeated the words.

'Yes.'

'They're in run-through. We open next week.'

'I won't disturb her until she has a minute free,' I said, 'but Miss Sheehan was most insistent that the message be passed along tonight.'

He squinted at me, sizing me up. 'Well, you can't be trying to get a job,' he said. 'We've all the chorus girls we need.'

'Do I look like a chorus girl?' I asked.

'You'd be surprised. It takes all types, my dear. When they first come in here, all fresh-faced and no lipstick or rouge, you'd think they were somebody's granddaughter, straight from the farm. Soon they start dressing themselves up and painting their faces and then they look like everyone else in this ridiculous profession. Some of them aren't changed by it, but for some of them it goes to their heads. Well, it would, wouldn't it? Stage-door Johnnies with more money than sense, flowers, champagne out of slippers. Nonsense all of it and it makes some of the girls go off the rails. I try and keep an eye on them. Sort of grandfather figure . . . I'm Old Henry. That's what they call me. Old Henry.'

I could tell he liked to talk and that we'd be there all night if I wasn't careful. From far off I could hear the *thump-thump* of music and then female voices raised in song. Then squeals. Then a deep man's voice shouting, 'Wait, don't go!'

'Coming to the end of act one,' Old Henry said. 'That will be the bathing number. You can tell by the shrieks. If you go through now, you'll have a chance to see Miss Lovejoy in her dressing room between acts.'

'Thank you.' I gave him my brightest smile.

'And what did you say your name was, young lady? You have to sign in before I let you go any farther.'

'It's Kitty Kelly,' I said, coming up with the first Irish name that popped into my head. I scribbled it on a sign-in sheet. 'And how do I find Miss Lovejoy's dressing room?'

'Follow this passage to the end. Go left. Up some stairs. Round the corner and then down the hall. You'll see her name on the door with the star on it. But don't go anywhere near the stage or you'll get me in trouble. Miss Lovejoy don't like outsiders watching until it's all just so. Thinks it brings bad luck. Very superstitious theater folk are, you know.'

I was about to leave when something struck me. 'Henry,' I asked, 'does this theater have a reputation for being haunted?'

His expression changed instantly. 'Hold on. You better not be tricking me, young lady. If you're one of them lady newspaper reporters . . .'

'No, why would I be?' I said.

'Then why did you ask that about the place being haunted?'

'Because I'm sensitive to these things. You know that we Irish have the second sight – and I got a definite feeling of a hostile presence.'

He leaned out of his booth. 'For pete's sake, don't go saying that to Miss Lovejoy. She's in a bad enough state as it is.'

'Why? What happened?'

'Silly little accidents, really, but she thinks there's more to it. A scenery flat falling over when she was singing, and a breeze almost starting a fire when it knocked over one of the candles onstage. Theaters are big drafty places. Accidents do happen. But she's scared it's something more. There, I've said more than I should. You can ask her yourself, if you want to hear more.'

'I will,' I said. 'You can be sure I will.'

I set off down a narrow passageway that became darker and darker until, by the time I reached the steep iron stairs, I had to almost feel my way upward. The stone wall felt cold to my touch and unseen breezes wafted around me. I could hear more jolly music coming from what sounded like far below me now, but up here it was chill and quite deserted. I told myself firmly that I didn't believe in ghosts, but my heart was beating rather faster. When I saw a billowing white shape out of the corner of my eye, I almost tumbled back down the stairs until I realized it was a curtain, hiding some kind of doorway.

Then I was angry with myself for being so stupid. I who had taken on my brothers in a dare to sit in the churchyard all night after old Dan O'Haggerty had been buried. I came out to an iron platform from which a spiral staircase dropped straight down into a cavernous backstage area. A backdrop and pieces of scenery blocked the brightly lit stage from my view, but I could hear the echo of voices, although I couldn't make out the words. Then, just as I left the platform to take the passage to Miss Lovejoy's dressing room, a horrible scream filled the theater. I told myself that it was only part of the play, but it made my blood run cold.

Almost immediately afterward there came the pounding of running feet and the iron stairway vibrated as a bevy of chorus girls came running up.

'Did you see it?' one of them was whispering.

'I didn't see anything, myself, but Clara swears she felt it moving behind her. She said it made her go all cold and shivery all over.'

'Poor Blanche. This will be the end of her if it goes on.'

They were coming toward me. I hadn't yet found Blanche Lovejoy's dressing room and there was nowhere to hide, so I flattened myself against the wall for them to run by me. This turned out to be a mistake. The first girls saw me moving in the darkness and started in fear. One of them gave a little scream.

'It's up here. I can see it now,' another one whimpered.

'It's all right, ladies, I'm quite human, I can assure you,' I said loudly.

'What are you doing up here? You'll get in awful trouble.' A tall blonde pushed past the others. 'Miss Lovejoy don't allow no public before opening night.'

'She sent for me,' I said. 'She knows I'm coming. I was told to wait in her dressing room.'

'She won't be in no state to talk to anybody,' the lanky girl said. 'She'll need a sedative after what happened.'

'What did happen?' I asked. 'I heard the scream.'

'She saw a face at the window,' one of the girls whimpered.

'Window?'

'In the scene she was doing, she is supposed to open the window and look out,' the tall blonde said. 'She went to the window and saw a face outside, staring at her.'

'Did any of you see it?'

'We weren't onstage,' another girl said. 'But Clara said she was waiting in the wings and she felt something brush past her – something cold and clammy, she said.'

'Trust Clara,' the blonde said with a sniff. 'She's a bundle of nerves all the time.' She glanced back down the stairs. 'We'd better beat it. We'll be in big trouble if we're not in our dressing room when Blanche comes up.'

As one they ran on together like a gaggle of slim white geese, all jockeying for position. I found Blanche Lovejoy's dressing room. It had her name and a star on the door. I wasn't sure what to do next – wait in the dark hallway and risk scaring Blanche to death or go ahead into her dressing room and risk scaring her equally when she entered. But she wouldn't want me down in the theater either. I decided to go into the room. At least I'd look less threatening in brightly lit surroundings.

Just to make sure, I tapped on the door. When it opened slowly and I saw a hideous form on the other side, it was all I could do not to scream and run. But I stood my ground and found myself staring at an old woman, bent over and with a nose like a witch's. I almost believed she was the ghost until she cocked that head, like an old bird, and said, 'I don't know you. Go away. I'll not have you upsetting Miss Lovejoy.'

'I don't intend to upset her,' I said. 'I've come to help her. Oona Sheehan sent me – to help deal with the ghost.'

'Well I never.' The old woman was still looking at me with birdlike eyes. 'You'd better come in then.' She ushered me into a small, cluttered room. I had expected a star's dressing room to be spacious and glamorous, like Oona Sheehan's rooms at the Hoffman House, but you could hardly swing a cat in here. Straight in front of me there was the dressing table with its mirror surrounded by electric lightbulbs and sticks of grease paint strewn higgledypiggledy all over the table. On one side there was a screen, blocking off part of the room and hung with several costumes. In the other corner there was an armchair and a table beside it with a bottle of Irish whiskey on it.

'You heard the scream, did you?' the old woman asked. 'Something else must have happened then.'

'She saw a face at the window when she went to open it.'

'Oh dear. She'll be in a proper state then. I'd better find her calming mixture.'

'Calming mixture?'

'Her doctor makes it up special. I'm not quite sure what's in it but Miss Lovejoy says it's like laudanum, only better. Opium, I suppose. Or morphine. Or both. Wait – that's her coming now. You go and sit over there so you don't startle her.'

She motioned to the armchair. I obeyed just as the door burst open and two people came in. I suppose I had been expecting Blanche Lovejoy to be another Oona Sheehan – a delicate beauty. But the woman who came in was more carthorse than race horse. She was big-boned, with an almost mannish face and a great mound of brassy blonde hair that made the face seem even bigger. She had a booming deep voice. What's more, she was swearing like a trooper.

'Jesus, Robert, don't you damned well dare try to patronize me as if I was a goddamned idiot child. I know what I saw and I am not going out of my head and you blasted well better do something about it, or this show is not going to open. You hear me?'

'Blanche, please, be reasonable.' The second person had come halfway into the room. He was a small, round, bald-headed man, with sagging jowls and a mournful expression like a blood hound's, and he reached out to touch her. 'Blanche, baby, sit down and have a drink. You'll feel better. Come to think of it, I could do with one, too.'

'I am not your baby. I'm nobody's baby. Get out and leave

me alone,' she shouted. 'And drink your own whiskey. You can go to hell, all of you.'

'But what about act two?'

'I'll come down for act two when I'm good and ready.' She said. 'If I'm good and ready.' She literally shoved him out of the door and slammed it shut. 'Martha, I need my calming mixture.'

'Of course you do, my darling precious one,' Martha said. 'Why don't you lie down and Martha will bring it for you.'

'And a drink,' Blanche added, sounding like a petulant child now. 'A big drink.'

Her eyes turned toward the bottles on the table and she saw me.

'What's she doing here? Who let her in? What did you let her in for?' she demanded.

Before Martha could answer, I got to my feet. 'Miss Lovejoy, I'm here because Oona Sheehan sent me,' she said. 'I'm Molly Murphy. She said you needed my services.'

'Molly Murphy?'

'Private investigator,' I said. 'I gather you've been having a spot of trouble in the theater.'

I saw light dawning on her face, a face that must have been made for the theater. All her expressions were larger than life – her anger, her despair, and now her radiant smile.

'Miss Murphy – you came. Thank God,' she said.

Soon I was sitting beside Blanche Lovejoy while she reclined behind her screen and worked her way through a large tumbler of neat whiskey.

'I was so excited about this play, Miss Murphy,' she said. 'I had such high hopes for it. After all this time, a chance to star again on Broadway. I even invested my own money in the production and that wonderful songwriter George M. Cohan wrote a new song just for me. It's called "That's the Way the French Do It!' Rather naughty, you know, but that's what my public has come to expect. I made my name singing naughty songs in vaudeville, after all, didn't I?'

I nodded as if I was aware of this.

'And the part is just right for me. All the leading roles in musical comedy recently have been for silly little girls. As if I could sit on a swing in *Florodora* like that awful little Nesbitt girl. I'd break most swings unless they had iron chains. The public doesn't want real women anymore. It wants girlish fantasy. Sixteen-year-olds who flutter their eyes and exude innocence coupled with budding ripeness. And look at me – among all that budding ripeness, I'm just an old overripe tomato.'

I thought the drink and the calming mixture might be making her maudlin, so I interrupted. 'So why don't you tell me what's been happening at the theater?'

'This theater, my dear Miss Murphy, is haunted.' She delivered the line as if she was playing to the top balcony. Then she raised herself from her reclining position. 'Ever since we started rehearsals here little things kept going wrong. Unimportant things to begin with – a table falling over and spilling water over the stage. My dress getting caught on a nail and ripping.'

'They could happen in any theater, I should imagine.'

'Of course. That's why I didn't think twice until I realized that all the accidents were directed at me.' She took another generous gulp of whiskey and coughed. 'That dress that got ripped on a nail. I went back and examined the wall, and there was no nail! It was perfectly smooth. And then the accidents became more serious: the scenery flat that crashed to the ground just inches from where I was standing, and that candle that fell over and started a small fire. If it had fallen in the other direction it would have landed on my skirt and I should have burned to death.'

'But what makes you think it's a ghost, Miss Sheehan?' I asked.

'Because I have seen it,' she hissed. 'It is all dressed in black with a white face and dark eyes full of hatred. It was staring at me today when I went to open the window. After I screamed people ran behind the set but there was nobody there. So who else could it be but a ghost? And you can feel the presence, too. At least I can feel it. The horrible chill as if someone is drowning me in cold water.' She reached out and grabbed my hand. 'You're Irish. You must have contact with the spirit world.'

'Not personally,' I said, 'but I do believe that we Celtic people have second sight. And if you listen to my mother, half the people in my village have seen a ghost at one time or another.'

'There, you see. I knew you'd be·the right person when Oona suggested you.'

'But what exactly do you want me to do?' I asked.

'Watch out for me. Follow me around. I want to know if you can see the ghost, too, because if you can't there is only one other option.'

'And what is that?'

'That someone is deliberately trying to kill me.'

Nine

'First call for act two,' came a boyish voice from the hallway. Then there was a rap on Blanche's door. 'Act two, Miss Lovejoy.'

'Somebody is trying to kill you?' I asked. 'Do you have any idea who that could be?'

'None at all. Everyone here adores me. That's why I have to believe that it's a ghostly presence.'

'Have you spoken about this to the police?'

'I thought of doing so, but they would only laugh at me. That's why I need you, Miss Murphy. Molly, dearest. You'll be able to get to the truth about what's happening to me. You will do it, won't you?'

'I can try,' I said uneasily, because in truth I was wondering if the ghostly presence might not be induced by too much alcohol and calming mixture.

Blanche looked at me imploringly. 'Come down to the theater now and watch. You can slip into a stage box, but don't let anyone know you are there. If the ghost has appeared once tonight, he might well appear again.'

'Very well,' I said.

Blanche stood up while Martha fussed around her, putting a large number of hairpins into that great mound of hair.

'We'll have to find some way to explain your presence,' Blanche went on, as she examined herself in her mirror. 'There is no point if you can't be right beside me all the time. Can you dance?'

'Not at all,' I said. 'I might manage a poor attempt at a waltz, but that's about it.'

'Not good enough for the chorus then,' she said. 'They have several ballet numbers on their toes. Can you sing?'

'Well enough for singsongs and church, but that's about it.' I gave an uneasy laugh.

'Then how are we going to explain your presence backstage?'

'I could help with the props,' I suggested.

'Then you wouldn't be allowed to follow me upstairs and you'd be too busy fetching and carrying to keep watching me.'

'Then how about your dresser?'

I heard a disgusted gasp from Martha.

'But everyone knows I've had Martha for years.'

'You could say that Martha is getting—' I was about to say 'too old' but stopped myself under her eagle gaze. 'That you're training me to take over from Martha some time in the future,' I finished.

But Blanche shook her head again. 'If you are my dresser you wait in my dressing room. You'd have no reason to be hanging around backstage.'

'Act two beginners onstage, Miss Lovejoy.' There was another firm rap on the door.

'I have to go,' she said. She rose unsteadily, then a big shudder ran through her body. 'I don't want to go down there. What if the face is there again? How can I perform if it's there, watching me?'

'There, there, my little love,' old Martha cackled. 'It will be all right. Nothing will harm you with all those people around you.'

'I'm sure it will be fine,' I added. 'Just as I'm sure there is a logical explanation for all this.'

'But the face at the window. I saw it. I swear that I saw it.'

'Maybe one of the stagehands peered through the window for a lark and now is too scared to admit it,' I suggested.

'I wish I could believe you,' she said and suddenly reached out and gripped my hands fervently. 'Come down with me. Stay close to me.'

'But you hadn't thought of a good reason for my being there.'

'You can watch over me from one of the stage boxes,' she said. 'That's close enough to see everything. And when I have time I'll try to think how I can have you beside me all the time.'

Images of me dressed up as a cat or pretending to be a potted plant flashed through my mind, and not for the last time I wondered what I was doing here, and thought how much simpler it would have been if I'd been shadowing Mr Roth to his favorite restaurant.

'Don't forget your wrap, darling girl.' Martha placed a woolen wrap firmly around Blanche's shoulders. 'We don't want you catching cold, do we?'

'Martha has presumably been with you for a long time,' I muttered as we went down the hallway side by side.

'She was my nurse, when I was a child,' Blanche said.

You could have knocked me down with a feather. I'd have taken Blanche for a product of a city slum with her foul mouth and her mannish ways.

'I wasn't always like this,' she said. 'I ran away from home with a man who turned out to be no good when I was sixteen. He left me with a child. I could never go back. It was either the theater or prostitution. Luckily, I had a good voice and could make people laugh, or I'd be dead by now.'

'And the child?'

'Was given up for adoption by some do-gooding church ladies' society. I've never seen her since.'

We reached the end of the hallway and Blanche went ahead of me down the stairs.

'Straight ahead to the pass door,' she whispered as we reached the wings. 'Don't let anyone see you.' Then she handed her wrap to a stagehand and was suddenly a different person. She swept toward the stage with her head held high, making her entrance like arriving royalty.

It was easy to slink past unnoticed in the dark chaos backstage. Scenery flats, pillars, ropes, spotlights, props were everywhere – whole rooms waiting to be assembled in seconds. The chorus girls were lined up beside the stage, some of them doing stretches or jumping around to keep warm. The overture for the second act had begun and the light jaunty music that filled the area was in strange contrast to the darkness and chaos of the wings. I climbed over a rope hanging from somewhere above and reached the door. Then I pushed it open just a crack and squeezed through.

Instantly I was in another world. In the half-light from the stage, this looked like the interior of a sultan's palace. Every inch of wall and ceiling that I could see was carved in a Moorish style with arches and niches and geometric designs. On either side of the stalls rose two tiers of ornate boxes, looking like pictures I had seen of Indian palaces, and were hung with rich fabric curtains and drapes. If a maharaja or an elephant had walked past, I shouldn't have been too surprised. Behind the boxes a carved balcony ran around the rest of the theater and from this balcony pillars fanned out to support the ceiling like exotic blooms. The thought crossed my mind that one could sit here and gaze in wonder without having to watch a play as well. No expense had been spared in the design of this theater. No wonder Miss Sheehan had said it was the plum. No wonder Miss Lovejoy was reluctant to move somewhere else.

I was about to find a way into the stage box when I noticed two figures sitting in the third row of the stalls. One of them was the round little man that Blanche had addressed as Robert. The other was a striking dark-haired man with classic features.

The overture finished. The dark-haired man shouted, 'Blanche, where are you? You're late. The curtain would have gone up by now.'

'Go to hell, Dessie.' Blanche swept onto the stage. 'When we have a curtain working, I'll work with it.' She suddenly switched on a radiant smile and became someone quite different.

'Claudette, is zat Monsieur Wexler's motor car I 'ear?'

While their attention was focused on the stage, I slipped past the men in the stalls and found an entrance to the stage box. Then I sat concealed behind the drapes in the darkness and watched.

I have to say it was a very silly play, but then I suppose most musical comedies don't rely on their plot. From what I could gather, Blanche played an impoverished French countess who opened her château as a seminary for young ladies. A motor car with several American artists has broken down near the château, and Blanche has convinced them to stay and paint in the area, since the owner of the car is reputed to be a millionaire. But she is falling for the most handsome (and considerably younger) Monsieur Teddy Wexler, even though she knows he is impoverished.

There were the requisite love songs. 'Let's bill and coo like the birdies do,' and 'My sweet Monique, you're quite unique. I can't wait to dance cheek to cheek.'

And then there were the naughtier songs that apparently had made Blanche famous, including that one about 'the way we do it in France,' in which all the lyrics were supposed to be part of a cooking demonstration but were laden with double entendres. 'For dessert we like a good ripe pear, or a nice little tart will do.'

Grudgingly, I had to admit that I could see why Blanche had become a star. Her presence dominated the stage. Her big, booming voice echoed through the theater. Her winks and innuendoes in the naughty songs would make half the women in the audience blush and reach for their fans and handker-chiefs while all the men roared with laughter.

The play ended with no more ghostly appearances and I made my way back to Blanche's dressing room.

'So what did you think?' she asked.

'Delightful, just delightful,' I said. 'I'm sure it will be a big hit.'

'And you saw nothing – strange?'

I shook my head.

'Thank God for that. Maybe the evil presence will know that you are watching out for him and retreat.'

I thought secretly that any self-respecting ghost would not have been put off by the likes of me, but I merely nodded encouragingly. 'So when do you need me again?'

'We have our first dress rehearsal tomorrow at seven,' she said. 'Company meeting at five. If you and I plan to arrive early – say by four, we can have time to talk while Martha dresses me.'

'Have you decided how I can infiltrate your company without arousing suspicion?' I asked.

'I am always quite exhausted after a performance, aren't I, Martha?' Blanche said, raising a languid hand to her face. 'No energy left to think. But by tomorrow I'll have thought of something. I know I will.'

'Then what should I tell the stage door keeper when I arrive?'

She frowned, which instantly made her look older. 'You are a detective. What do you think?'

'I already signed in with a false name,' I said. 'Kitty Kelly.'

'How very clever, isn't she, Martha?'

'So I'll just tell him that I'm to report straight to you on an urgent matter. It's your show. Nobody will dare question me.'

'That's right. The very thing.' She turned her dazzling smile on me. 'Molly, I am glad that you came. You are going to save my show, my career, and my sanity. I know it.'

'I'll do my best,' I said uncertainly, then remembered that we hadn't discussed money. 'Would you be paying me by the hour or shall we settle on a flat fee?'

I could see that she hadn't thought much about the financial aspect of this either. 'Oh,' she said. 'Yes, of course. Your fee. Would fifty dollars cover it, do you think?'

I hesitated. If I found out the truth in the next few days, then fifty dollars would be just fine. If I was expected to show up at the theater night after night, then I'd be out of pocket. I decided that fifty dollars in the hand might be worth more than a hundred in the bush. 'That would be fine to start with,' I said. 'If this looks as if it's going to require more than a week or so, we'll discuss it again.'

'More than a week or so? God forbid,' she said. 'I can't perform in a haunted theater for a week or so. You have to find out the truth for me quickly, Molly. I'm counting on you.'

'As I said, I'll do my best.' I turned to the door. 'Until tomorrow then, Miss Lovejoy. Goodbye, Martha.'

'Oh, and Molly,' Blanche called after me, 'if there are any newspaper reporters hanging around outside, don't breathe a word about the theater being haunted. I'm absolutely terrified that if news of this leaks out, we'll scare the public away from opening night.'

'Of course not,' I said.

As I came out of Blanche's room and made my way back through the narrow passageway, I was conscious of eyes on me. I spun around. A man was standing in the shadows at the far end of the hall. Just as I was wondering if I was looking at the ghost, he retreated and I heard the sound of a door closing. Not a ghost then. They didn't bother with doors. Besides, I had recognized him. He was the lean, dark-haired man who had watched the performance from the third row of the stalls.

Just why was he watching Blanche's dressing room? I wondered. Was he watching out for her, concerned for her welfare, or was it something more sinister? This was no time to go back and confront him but tomorrow I'd find out who he was. The fact that he was safely seated in the stalls and no ghost had appeared in the second half of the performance seemed significant to me.

I made my way down the dark stair and reached the stage door.

'You saw Miss Lovejoy then, did you?' Old Henry asked. 'Gave her the message all right?'

'I did, and I'm going to be coming back tomorrow to help her out with something, so I'll see you then.' I gave him my most friendly smile. He could prove to be a useful ally.

'Button up your coat,' he said. 'Awful fierce wind out there tonight. Cut right through ya.'

'Thanks, Henry,' I said, and stepped out into the night.

I had only taken a couple of steps down the alleyway when I noticed a dark shape looming in the shadows. It was large, featureless and grotesque. I gasped and was about to flee back to Henry when it spoke in a normal man's voice.

'Pardon me, miss, but are you part of the play?'

I saw then that the strange appearance was due to an enormous shawl the man wore over his head and shoulders against the cold, so that just his eyes were showing.

'I didn't mean to scare you,' he said, noting my reaction. 'It's just that it's so damned cold tonight. Are you one of the chorus girls?'

'Not exactly,' I said, 'but I will be working with the play.'

'So you'll know then if it's true that the ghost appeared again tonight?'

'Ghost?' I feigned innocence.

'You must have heard about the ghost. They're saying the theater's haunted. They're saying the ghost is trying to kill Blanche Lovejoy.'

'Who is saying?' I demanded. 'What is this – third-hand gossip?'

'Oh no, miss. I work for the *Herald*. My sources are quite reliable.'

'If you work for the *Herald* I suggest you go and find some real news and not a fairy story,' I said and walked away before he could stop me.

It seemed that the story of the ghost was common knowledge already, whether Miss Lovejoy wanted it to be or not.

Ten

I had a dream about the girl in the snowdrift that night. It was strange and nebulous, the way dreams are, but it was permeated with fear and I awoke feeling that I needed to visit the hospital to see if there was any news. I had expected Daniel would report on last night's assignment, but there was no sign of him before it was time to get ready for lunch with my friends and with Elizabeth, aka Nelly Bly. I also remembered he had expressed interest in meeting Nelly Bly, so I waited for him as long as I dared before I went across Patchin Place and knocked on their door with Gus's fur-lined cape over my arm.

'Molly, come in, we're dying to know all,' Gus said, sweeping me through to the kitchen at the back of the house. 'How did the skating go? Was the cape all right? Did it keep you warm?'

'It was perfect, thank you, and I hope I've returned it in good condition,' I said, 'because it was put to a use I hadn't expected.'

'Really?' The occupants of the kitchen looked up with interest. Sid was stirring pots on their big kitchen stove while Elizabeth, or was it Nelly, sat at the table with a glass of sherry in her hand. 'Dare one ask what kind of use? I hope you were sensible, Molly dear.'

'More than sensible. I helped save a life. We found a girl in a snowdrift in Central Park. She was scarcely alive so we wrapped her in the cloak and whisked her to the nearest hospital.'

Elizabeth leaned forward in her seat, her face alight. 'My dear, how very interesting. Who was she and what was she doing in a snowdrift?'

'We don't yet know,' I said. 'She regained consciousness but didn't say a word. It was almost as if she didn't understand us. We thought that maybe she spoke another language.'

'I wonder what she was doing alone in Central Park then,' Sid said. 'Young ladies who speak no English don't usually wander around alone, especially in the swank uptown area. They stay in their neighborhoods, don't they?'

This was a valid comment. 'It's all very intriguing,' I said, 'because she was not dressed for an outing in the snow. She wore no coat, and only a flimsy white silk dress.'

'Maybe she had been robbed and her coat had been taken. The criminal element in this city would kill for less than a winter coat in weather like this.'

'I would agree,' I said, 'except that she only had dainty little evening slippers on her feet and they were soaked through. She wouldn't have intentionally gone out at all in those.'

'What a fascinating mystery,' Sid said. 'So will you find out more?'

'She can't walk away from something so delicious,' Elizabeth said. 'It's an investigator's dream. If she doesn't pursue it, I shall do so myself.'

'I'm going back to the hospital today,' I said. 'I hope to hear good news. That she has recovered her faculties and her family has been contacted.'

'Do keep us informed, won't you, Molly,' Gus said. 'You know how we love a good puzzle.'

'And you can drop me a note and keep me informed as well,' Elizabeth said. 'I'll give you my card. I'm moving into the Fifth Avenue Hotel while I carry out my research.'

She took out a calling card and wrote the Fifth Avenue address on it.

'You plan to come in and out of the Fifth Avenue Hotel in your newsboy's rags?' I asked. 'Won't that attract attention, to say the least?'

'I think I've given up wearing a disguise,' Elizabeth said, 'especially such a chilly one. I'll do my research in future by interviewing boys at those awful hovels where they live like little rats. And then I'll feel guilty when I come back to the warmth and civilized comfort of the hotel.'

'You know you don't have to leave us, Elizabeth,' Gus said. 'You know you are welcome to stay on here as long as you like.'

'You are very kind, but you more than anybody should know that I like my independence and don't wish to be beholden to anybody. You should rejoice that one woman in the universe beside yourselves is her own woman, comes and goes as she pleases and is not slave to the dictation of a male, or of a male-dominated society.'

'Add me to that list,' I said.

'So how was your little outing yesterday morning, apart from finding the girl in the snowdrift?' Sid asked with a sweet smile. 'Did you get your skating in first?'

'Unfortunately not,' I said. 'I was running away from Daniel when I stumbled over the girl.'

'Running away? My dear, had he tried anything improper?' Elizabeth asked.

I started to laugh. 'On the contrary, I had just aimed a snow-ball rather accurately and he was seeking revenge.'

Amid our laughter Gus asked, 'Sid, dearest, how is lunch

coming along? I'm sure our guests are getting hungry. Maybe we should move our conversation to the dining table.'

Sid lifted the lid of a large cast-iron pot and poked at something inside. Then she sniffed appreciatively. 'Almost ready, I think.'

'Daniel had expressed interest in joining us,' I said, 'but I haven't heard from him this morning, so I don't know where he can be.'

'So he has finally come to realize that we are intelligent company?' Gus asked.

'It has more to do with Nellie Bly being present, I fear,' I said, laughing.

'Anyway, since lunch is now ready, it's too bad for him. What are we eating, Sid?'

One never knew what was coming next when Sid was cooking. It could be anything from Mongolian stew to Moroccan couscous, depending on my friends' whim and which part of the world was currently capturing their interest. Before I could ask, Sid put the lid back down and announced, 'Coq au vin. We decided to opt for simplicity and winter comfort today.'

Elizabeth nodded. 'One can't go wrong with French food, can one?'

It was at times like this that I had to stop myself from grinning. I, who had grown up in a peasant's cottage, who had lived on potatoes and turnips and the occasional bit of mutton in a stew when we were lucky, was now living among people who thought that coq au vin constituted a simple meal. I wondered if there would ever be a day when I took this life for granted.

'The table's laid, so why don't you go through and I'll serve,' Sid said. 'If you'd be good enough to carry the wine, Molly. It has been near the stove so I'm sure we must have chambreed it sufficiently.'

I carried the wine bottle and soon we were eating the most

delicious chicken, which was cooked so tenderly that it absolutely fell from the bone. There was crusty bread from the French bakery around the corner on Greenwich Avenue to accompany it and afterward that big bowl of figs, dates, and nuts, with a dessert wine.

Sated and a little tipsy, I made my way home, having promised to keep them all apprised of the fortunes of the girl we rescued from the snow. I desperately wanted to know how she was faring and was annoyed that Daniel hadn't appeared all day. I wondered if he had had second thoughts about working for me, or was angry with me for forcing him into a situation not of his choosing. Then I told myself I was being too sensitive. I had offered him a job. He could have turned it down if it wasn't to his liking. Maybe something important had come up this morning. Maybe he had been summoned to police headquarters or even to the commissioner's office. Whatever the cause, I was determined to visit that hospital with or without him before I went to the theater at four.

I hurried to dress in my business suit and was just on my way out when I bumped into Daniel, trudging through the deep snow up Patchin Place.

'Well, here you are at last,' I said. 'I've been waiting for you all day. I was about to dismiss you as an unreliable employee.'

'Don't joke, Molly,' he said.

'Why, what's wrong?'

'I think I might have caught pneumonia,' he said, holding a thick woolen scarf over his mouth.

'Oh no. You're sick, are you? Come into the house and I'll make you a cup of tea or something. Then we'll get you home to bed.'

'That's the best invitation I've had in a long while,' said the voice from inside the scarf.

'Not that sick then,' I replied dryly, and shoved him into the house. 'Here, let me feel your forehead.' I put my hand up to touch it. It was freezing cold. I tried his cheeks. Equally cold. 'No fever,' I said. 'So it's not pneumonia.'

'It could well turn into pneumonia,' he said peevishly and slumped at the kitchen table. 'I got thoroughly chilled to the marrow working on your damned case last night. Do you know that that Roth fellow stayed out until 2 a.m?'

'Jesus, Mary, and Joseph – then he's not the paragon we thought he was after all.'

'I didn't say he was doing anything sinful all that time,' Daniel said, unwrapping the scarf as he spoke. 'He was at Delmonico's, with friends. All young men like himself. But they talked and talked and they were the last to leave. The waiters practically had to throw them out in the end.'

'He was drunk, then?'

'Not in the least. They only had a couple of bottles of wine all evening.'

'So nothing detrimental to report?'

'Yes. That I was frozen to the marrow and this morning my throat was distinctly scratchy. So I stayed in bed all morning as a precaution and got Mrs O'Shea to make me hot chamomile tea and broth.'

'Oh, you poor dear man.' I laid on the sarcasm so thickly that he got the message.

'Better to be safe than sorry,' he said. 'You're going to have to treat your employees better than this if you want them to stay, Miss Murphy.'

'I spent one evening following Mr Roth dressed only in rags, remember?'

'Yes, but you were home before ten. I was out until two,' Daniel said.

'Surely you've had similar duties in the police department?' I said. 'Your men patrol the streets all night, every night.'

'That's why I became a captain,' he replied with a reluctant grin. 'I did my share as a young officer and then I left it to my juniors.'

'Exactly what I'm doing. Leaving it to my juniors.'

Daniel glared at me as I laughed. 'Oh, come on, Daniel. You'll know to wear something warmer tonight. Buy some hot chestnuts or a hot potato and put it in your pocket. That'll help you keep warm. And take along a flask of brandy.'

'You expect me to go out there again?'

'Somebody has to,' I said. 'I'm due at the theater at four and my evenings are going to be occupied by watching over Blanche Lovejoy.'

'What does she want you to do for her?'

'Protect her from a ghost,' I said. 'No, don't laugh. She is mortally afraid, Daniel. She thinks her theater is haunted.'

'And just how do you plan to protect her from a ghost? I don't see you wearing a large crucifix around your neck – and where is your holy water?'

'The aim is to prove to her that there is no ghost and that she's imagining things. Either that, or . . .' I broke off.

'Or what?'

'Or someone in the cast is trying to scare Blanche Lovejoy and make sure the production is shut down.'

Daniel reached out his hand and grabbed mine. 'Molly, be careful. If someone is resorting to such desperate measures, they may resent your trying to stand in their way. I should think that backstage in a theater is a great place for nasty accidents. Make sure one doesn't happen to you.'

'Don't worry,' I said. 'Nobody knows why I am there except Blanche, and she's going to arrange it so that I have a good reason for being near her at all times. I'm to meet her at four, which doesn't give us much time to visit the hospital.'

'Oh, about the hospital,' Daniel said. 'Would you really mind going on your own today? I don't think I should risk being around so many sick people, not in my present condition.'

'Daniel, you've got the beginnings of an ordinary little cold. But I don't mind going alone, if you'd like to stay here and rest before this evening's assignment with Mr Roth.'

'You're a heartless slave driver, Molly Murphy,' he said, but in a good-natured way.

Eleven

I arrived at the German hospital just as the clock on a nearby church was striking three. That gave me one hour to see my mystery girl and then get back to the theater. I inquired which ward she had been taken to and found her lying, as still and white as the first time I had seen her, in a bed at the far end. For a moment I wondered if she had died, but as I stood beside her those clear blues eyes opened and focused on me. I thought I saw some recognition there.

'Hello.' I gave her my warmest smile. 'Do you remember me from yesterday? I was the one who found you in Central Park. How are you feeling today? Recovered from your ordeal?'

She continued to stare at me, but didn't say a word. Nor did her expression change.

'Have they managed to contact your relatives yet?' I asked.

Again, not a glimmer of anything in her eyes.

I saw a nurse coming down the ward with some medicine on a tray. 'Has this young lady spoken at all yet?' I asked.

'Not a word,' the nurse said.

'Do you think she doesn't understand English?'

'We've tried several languages but she just stares blankly.'

'So you obviously haven't managed to contact her family.'

'Not as far as I know. How are you connected with her?'

'I was the one who found her in a snowbank yesterday.'

'Mercy me. The poor child. Well, maybe she'll come around soon with loving care and nourishing food.'

She continued on her way. I went to seek out the doctor we had seen yesterday and found him coming out of a ward down the hall. He recognized me right away.

'The young lady. You have seen for yourself, no? She does not respond to anything. Maybe the blow to her head?'

'She did receive a blow to the head then?'

'We had to sedate her before we could examine her properly, and yes, there was a bump on one side of her head, and some bruises and scratches on the same side of her body. But nothing that seemed severe enough to cause such deep amnesia.'

'If she was hit on the head in the park, and presumably knocked out, then how did she manage to walk to the spot where I found her on her own?' I said, speaking more to myself than the doctor. 'And why bruises and scratches just on one side of her body?'

'A tricky puzzle,' the doctor said. 'I wish I knew the answers.'

'And that was the extent of her injuries?' I asked. 'No signs of other – uh – kinds of assault?'

'No sign at all.'

'Well, that's one piece of good news, isn't it?' I said. 'So, is something being done to locate her next of kin?'

'We have informed the police about her. We can't do any more,' he said. 'Physically she'll be strong enough to leave us any day.'

'And if they don't manage to locate her family?'

'If her mental condition doesn't improve, then she'll have to be placed in an institution. We need our beds here for the sick.'

'You're sure this isn't just a language problem?'

'My dear young lady, we have tried,' he said. 'If you don't understand a language, there is always some way of communicating, isn't there? Gestures and smiles and words that languages have in common, like *mama, papa.*'

'Yes, I suppose you are right,' I agreed. 'Oh dear. I had hoped for better news today. I'll come back tomorrow and bring her some good broth – something nourishing. Maybe you'll have better news by then.'

'Let us hope so,' he said. 'Goodbye, fraulein.' He nodded gravely and moved on.

I was in deep gloom as I walked down the long tiled hallway. Nurses drifted past in crisply starched pairs. Loud moans came from a ward on my right. I hate hospitals, I decided. Maybe it was that smell of disinfectant that doesn't really mask the sweeter odors of sickness and death. Then I noticed a figure I thought I recognized coming toward me. The meticulous outfit, the neat blond beard, the homburg, the silver-tipped cane – I couldn't be mistaken. It was the young German alienist I had encountered on several occasions previously.

'Dr Birnbaum,' I called and waved, making the nurses turn toward me and frown.

His face lit up as he saw me and he clicked his heels smartly. 'Miss Murphy. What an unexpected pleasure. What brings you here?'

'Visiting a patient,' I said. 'And you?'

'I'm here to consult with an old friend from my student days in Vienna,' he said.

'Of course, how silly of me. This is called the German hospital, isn't it? You'd feel right at home here.'

'Although I am Austrian, not German. There is a difference, you know.' He smiled. 'And I treat the mind and here they only treat the body.'

A magnificent idea was forming in my head. 'You're an absolute godsend, do you know that?'

'Am I? In what way?'

86

'There is a patient here, a young girl, who doesn't seem to be able to speak or understand anyone. I found her yesterday unconscious in a snowdrift in Central Park. We brought her here and she has recovered, but still won't speak.'

'Has it occurred to anyone that she might be deaf?' he asked.

I felt really stupid. 'What an obvious thing to have over-looked,' I said. 'But would you take a look at her yourself? I'd feel much happier if I knew that everything was being done to communicate with her. And if she really were suffering from a disease of the mind, then you'd be the very person, wouldn't you?'

'I can't examine a patient here uninvited,' he said, 'but I can ask my friend to make an introduction to her attending physician.'

He always was one for correctness, I remembered.

'Thank you, Dr Birnbaum. That's a load off my mind. And if you could possibly let me know what you find, I'd be most grateful.'

I thought he might say that divulging such information would also be unethical, but he nodded and said, 'I'll pop a note through your front door when I return home this evening. It's good of you to take such an interest in a stranger.'

'Oh, you know me.' I laughed. 'I never could keep my nose out of other people's business.'

I came out of the hospital and stood breathing deeply, filling my lungs with the cold, smoky, familiar New York air to rid my nostrils of the cloying hospital smell. Then I walked back along Central Park, making my way to the Fifty-eighth Street El station. As I walked, I found that my brain was buzzing. Daniel and I should have taken more trouble to examine the site where we had found the girl yesterday. We should have retraced her footsteps and seen if we could have located her coat, or the place where she was attacked. We might have seen the footprints of her attacker. We may even have been able to see where she entered the park and where she encountered him, or them.

I decided I probably had a little time to spare. When my business began to show a healthy profit, I'd buy myself a watch. A good detective needed to know the exact time. I was dying to take another look at the spot where she had lain. If I hurried I'd be able to see if we had overlooked any clues. I entered the park through the same gate through which we had carried her out yesterday, retraced our steps along the path, over the East Drive and into the central wilderness area, and there it was. I could still see exactly how she had lain in the snow and where I had knelt beside her. I stood looking down at her imprint in the snow, trying to picture how she had fallen, and how long she had lain there. I found that I was shivering in the cold as the sun had dipped behind the horizon. If I couldn't stand here for long, dressed warmly in stout boots and a woolen cloak, then how could she have survived at all, if she had lain there for any length of time?

I examined the site closely for any telltale clues – a locket or a handkerchief with her initials on it would have done nicely, but alas, there was nothing. Our footsteps had disturbed the snow around her, but on the other side of the dell her neat little trail of footprints was still clear. With mounting excitement I followed them, around a little hill, across a stretch of flat lawn, until they joined a path and were lost among countless other footprints. I followed the path for a while, hoping to see if a footprint might be recognizable, but after a while I had to give up. Still, I had learned one thing: she had not been attacked anywhere near the spot where we found her. She had not been carried to the spot. She had walked there under her own steam and had come from the north. Not, therefore, from any of the polyglot ghettoes of lower Manhattan.

The same clock chiming the three-quarter hour reminded me that I had a job to do and I'd be late if I didn't hurry. I slithered and skidded my way through the park until I reached Columbus Circle and the end station of the Sixth Avenue El. It was four o'clock on the dot when I stepped into the hallway at the Casino Theater. I was red-cheeked and gasping for breath because I had run all the way from the train, and had to stand in front of a very surprised Henry while I caught my breath.

'Well, fancy seeing you again,' he said. 'Anything wrong, miss?'

'Nothing. I just thought I was going to be late and that would never do on my first day,' I said.

'First day?' He looked suspicious.

'I'm going to be joining the company,' I said.

'As what?'

'I can't say yet, until I've met with Miss Lovejoy. Is she in her dressing room?'

'No, miss, she went front of house, meeting with Mr Barker and Mr Haynes. And that young songwriter guy, whatever his name is.'

'So who are Mr Barker and Mr Haynes?' I asked.

'They're the men that count,' Henry said. 'Mr Barker is the director. He's got money in the show as well. And Mr Haynes – he's the choreographer. He's the one with the creative talent, at least according to himself, of course.'

I laughed, but I didn't rightly know what a choreographer was and didn't like to show my ignorance by asking. I also didn't think it would be wise to barge into a meeting and maybe put Blanche Lovejoy in a spot, especially if she hadn't yet managed to come up with a good reason for explaining my presence in the theater.

'I think I'll go up to her dressing room and wait for her there,' I said. 'Will you tell her that I'm here if you see her?'

'I will indeed, miss,' he said. 'So you're really an actress! That baloney about bringing a message from Oona Sheehan was just a ruse to meet Miss Lovejoy, wasn't it? Come on, now. You can't fool Old Henry. I can't tell you how many times I've seen that trick played before.'

'No, I really was bringing a message from Oona Sheehan. Honestly.'

He touched the side of his nose with a knowing grin. 'And that message was that Miss Lovejoy should give you a job in her production?'

'Something like that,' I said, trying to look sheepish.

'I'm surprised she fell for it at this stage,' he said. 'I know Miss Lovejoy. She likes order. She likes everything to be perfect. Changing things at the last minute just isn't like her. You must be mighty talented, or a really big draw.'

'Neither, I promise you. I'm sure I'm going to play the most minor of parts and disturb things the least possible.'

'Chorus, you mean?' Henry looked puzzled now.

'I'm really not sure, yet,' I said. 'Wait until I've spoken to Miss Lovejoy.'

'Let's hope the other girls don't resent you,' Henry said, going back to his newspaper. 'Most girls would kill to get a part in a production like this one.'

I left him with those words echoing through my head. Had somebody not been awarded the role she felt she deserved? Was somebody maybe trying to get even with Miss Lovejoy? But then surely it wasn't one of her cast members. If Blanche got so spooked that she decided to close the show, then they'd all be out of work.

Twelve

Martha admitted me to Blanche's dressing room.

'She's expecting you,' she cackled in that scratchy witch voice of hers, staring at me with those strange, hooded, birdlike eyes. 'Give me your cloak. I'll hang it up for you.' I complied although I could have easily hung the garment on the hook myself.

'I gather she's downstairs meeting with the producer and some other men,' I said. 'I thought it wiser to come up here.'

'Definitely. She doesn't like to be caught out. Not Miss Lovejoy. Even as a little child she hated to be caught out and then find herself at a disadvantage. Always did like to be holding the reins and in the driver's seat. A headstrong child, that's sure enough.'

'And you were her nurse, so she tells me,' I said.

'I was. I raised her from infancy onward. And I cherished her, too. It broke my heart when she ran away from home like that. I worried about her more than they did, I think. And it was the happiest day of my life when she came to find me again.' When she smiled, she looked just old and kind. But the smile quickly faded. 'Of course I didn't approve of what she had become. Taking her clothes off in front of men – and those songs. I couldn't blame her family for disowning her. But I stuck by her, and now, as you see, she's as respectable as a lady can be in her profession.'

'How long have you been with her then?'

'Well, it must be at least twenty years since she found me in Massachusetts and brought me down to New York to be her dresser.'

Which made Miss Lovejoy close to forty. This show must have been a last attempt to play the romantic lead and obviously it was vitally important to her that she succeed in it.

'So tell me, Martha,' I began cautiously, 'do you have any thoughts yourself about this ghost? You don't believe in ghosts, do you?'

'I wouldn't say yes or no to that,' she said, again nodding in birdlike fashion. 'I've not come face-to-face with a ghost personally in my life, but I've met some people who would swear that they have. And all I can tell you is that Miss Lovejoy is very nervous. It's got her good and rattled, I can tell you – and she's come through a lot, my darling Blanchie has. It takes a lot to get her rattled.'

As she was finishing this speech I heard the sound of footsteps coming toward us along the passage and suddenly the door burst open. Blanche Lovejoy came in, looking as out of breath as I had been a few minutes earlier.

'Any sign of her yet, Martha?' she demanded, then saw me. 'Oh, there you are, Miss Murphy. I was wondering if you'd changed your mind and weren't going to show up.'

'Not at all,' I said.

'I was expecting you to come through to the stalls so that I could introduce you to Robert and Desmond.'

'Henry said you were having a meeting, but I didn't know whether you'd welcome my presence,' I said. 'I thought you might find me awkward to explain, so I came up here to wait.'

'Ah, well, can't be helped,' she said. 'I'll just have to make a general introduction at the cast meeting. But I've warned the boys that you'll be joining us.'

'You've decided how to explain my sudden appearance then?'

'Brilliant, my dear.' She gave me her most dazzling smile. 'I had the most brilliant idea. I'm slipping you into the cast because I owe Oona Sheehan a favor and you are her cousin, just arrived from Ireland and seeking a theatrical career. Isn't that perfect?'

'Yes, I suppose so,' I said.

'Of course, I'll drop Oona a note, just in case anyone asks her,' she went on, pacing the room like a caged tiger and waving her arms as she spoke, 'and I've even found a good way to have you onstage most of the time – and get us an extra laugh as well. Guess what, Molly – I'm going to make you a bluestocking. We'll find you an ugly wig with pigtails and give you glasses, and you'll be the pupil who never joins in the fun. In every scene where the girls are onstage, you'll stand in a corner with your nose in a book. You can even wander across the stage with your nose in a book during scenes in which the girls aren't present. And I'm going to add lines. When I dismiss all the girls, you'll stay where you are until I say, 'Come along, Josephine,' and you'll look up with exaggerated surprise and follow the rest of them. After the first time that should get us an extra laugh, don't you think?'

I smiled and nodded, although the reality of being onstage, in the spotlight in front of hundreds of people, was just dawning on me and making my stomach clench into knots. I could never admit to being shy, but I've never appeared in public either. I had no idea what it might feel like to be expected to perform.

'But isn't it to die for?' she continued, still pacing. 'Sometimes I surprise myself with my own brilliance, don't I, Martha?'

'You do indeed, my angel,' Martha replied, although I couldn't tell whether sarcasm was involved. It was impossible to know what she was thinking or feeling.

'It's a perfect little setup,' Blanche went on, undaunted. 'You'll be onstage with nothing to do but pretend to read, and you'll have all the time in the world to observe. If there's a scene in which your presence on stage would be quite wrong – the love scenes between me and Arthur, for example – then you can wait in the wings, with your nose still in the book. They'll all know that you are my new protégée so they won't dare to move you.'

She paused and looked at me, her eyes sparkling triumphantly. 'So what do you say, Molly? We'll show them I'm not going out of my head, won't we? We'll catch that ghost.'

'I'll give it my best shot, Miss Lovejoy,' I said with what I hoped was enthusiasm.

'Right. Let's get to work.' Blanche pulled out a script. 'We've just got time to go through it once together. You'll have to muddle through as best you can at tonight's dress rehearsal, but take it home and study it so you've got your moves down pat before tomorrow. I've written you into the scenes and I've marked your position on the stage. Remember, in a play nothing is random. Every move is in the master script and the spot you stand in never varies by an inch. Since you are supposed to have your nose in a book all the time, I suggest that the book is this one. That way you'll know what comes next.'

She opened the first page and started going through it at a great rate. 'So the first scene in the garden, the girls will be playing tennis and you'll be standing against the back wall. For heaven's sake, don't lean on it or it will fall down. You'll be here, next to the rosebush. Then when the girls rush off to tell me the news, you'll look up from your book, realize they have gone, and hurry after them, exiting stage left.'

She continued to bark out instructions until I was hopelessly confused. I was feeling inadequate and worried that I'd make a mess of things until I realized that I was the one doing a favor here. If she wanted me to be onstage to protect her, then she'd have to forgive a few errors. Another thought struck me.

'It's a dress rehearsal. What am I supposed to wear?'

Blanche glanced at Martha. 'You'll need a costume,' she said as if this might not have occurred to her before. 'I don't know if we've anything suitable in wardrobe so we may have to improvise for tonight's dress rehearsal and probably tomorrow night's, too. It's supposed to be summertime in the play. Do you have anything like that garment you are wearing, equally dowdy, but lighter weight?'

I realized then that Blanche wasn't all sweetness and light, but I ignored the insult. I suppose my business suit could be described as dowdy.

'I have a plain muslin,' I said, but she shook her head.

'No, these are good class girls. I don't think muslin would do, do you, Martha?'

'I'm sure Madame Eva will be able to make something for her in a hurry if you asked nicely,' Martha said. 'She's supposed to be a schoolgirl, isn't she? So what she needs is a schoolgirl outfit. Checked gingham or black with a white bow or white with a black bow at her neck. Something plain but wholesome.'

'Right, as always.' Blanche nodded with satisfaction. 'Come on then. If we hurry we can make it to wardrobe before the meeting.'

I was whisked along the hall, up yet another flight of steps, and into a room that was positively cluttered with racks of costumes, bolts of fabric, boxes of wigs – and half buried under all this a table containing a sewing machine, and sitting at the table a hunched old woman dressed head to toe in black. She looked even more witchlike than Martha. She had similar sharp features and her skin looked horribly sallow in the dim light. I don't know how she managed to sew in there and how she didn't go blind doing it. She glanced up, frowning, as we came in.

'It's all right, you don't have to make a fuss,' she said in heavily accented English. 'I said they'd all be ready by five and they are all ready. See – the last of the tennis outfits, all hanging and ready for the girls to pick up.'

'You're a miracle worker, Eva,' Blanche said, and produced her beaming smile. 'And I'm glad you're done because I have one teeny little extra job for you to do.'

Eva's scowl turned to me. 'Who's she? I haven't seen this one before.'

'She's new. She's going to be joining us. We felt the chorus needed comic relief so she's going to be the studious girl who never joins in. Could you whip up something plain and unflattering for her?'

'Could I whip up?' Eva demanded, waving her arms dramatically. 'What you think I have, a magic wand here? Where is this plain and unflattering fabric, huh?'

'Not for tonight, silly. Of course not for tonight. But before opening night. That's all I ask. Four more days. And she'll need a wig. That red hair is so un-French. I thought black, plain, two pigtails.'

'And how should this ugly dress look?' Eva demanded.

'What do you think? Plain black with a white bow?'

'She'll look like she's going to a funeral,' Eva muttered.

'All right. Plain white with a black bow. Schoolgirlish. Young.'

'I'll take her measurements and see what I can do,' Eva said.

'Oh, and spectacles,' Blanche added. 'And black boots.'

'Anything more?' Eva asked. 'You want me to make her a

ball gown, in case you change your mind and this girl turns into a princess in the middle of the play?'

Blanche leaned over and planted a kiss on her cheek. 'I'll be forever in your debt, Eva dearest. Stay with her, Molly, and let her take your measurements, then come down to the stage when you hear the bell.'

I nodded, noticing that she had called me Molly. I had thought we had decided on an alias, but I suppose nobody was likely to recognize me, especially under the black wig, glasses, and ugly dress. But I couldn't say anything in front of Madame Eva.

'So what do you want me to wear tonight?' I asked before Blanche could disappear.

Blanche glanced at Eva. 'You couldn't find her a plain skirt and shirtwaist?'

Eva shook her head. 'I'm not running a department store here. I don't keep clothing on spec.'

'Then it will have to be your own clothes, Molly. I must dash.' And she was gone. Eva took my measurements, tut-tutting in horror that I wasn't wearing a corset and had such a large waist.

'What man you think you get with a waist like that?' she demanded. 'You should see Miss Lovejoy's waist. A man can encircle her waist with his hands, even at her age.'

A distant bell summoned us to the stage. I heard the sound of feet tramping from all over the theater and joined the grow-ing crowd as we hurried down the stairs. I got more than one inquisitive stare as we made our way to the stage. Most of the cast took up positions sitting cross-legged on the floor while Blanche and the men I had seen in the stalls the day before sat on the sofa and chairs that were part of the set. I slid to the floor at the back of the crowd.

The director, Mr Barker, the one she had called Robert,

gave a speech about all their hard work coming to fruition. The choreographer, Desmond Haynes, the slim dark-haired man who had been watching Blanche's dressing room when I came out, gave his own speech, mainly directed to the dancers, about the importance of the straight line and the pattern. A distinguished-looking white-haired man, who turned out to be the conductor, talked about tempo and signals and watching him and not rushing the cancan number. There were more instructions, some questions, and then Blanche gave a pretty speech about how she was counting on every single one of us not to let her down.

As they spoke I studied them in turn: round little Robert Barker with his worried frown, supercilious Desmond Haynes, the various actors and actresses and chorus girls. And there was the backstage crew, lurking in the wings. Did one of them have a secret grudge against Blanche Lovejoy? How was I ever going to find out?

Blanche got to her feet. 'All right, everybody. Overture and beginners down here at six forty-five. Oh, and before you go, I have one small addition to our happy family. Molly dear, would you stand up?' I stood, feeling all those eyes upon me. 'This young lady is the cousin of none other than Oona Sheehan, so of course I had to find her a small part in our play.'

'I hope you're not thinking of making her an extra maid and taking away more of my lines,' the older actress who played the maid said peevishly.

'Of course not, darling. Wouldn't dream of it,' Blanche said. 'Molly will be an extra pupil in my school.'

'But we've got all the chorus numbers worked out perfectly,' one of the girls complained. 'We don't have time to relearn anything now.'

'Molly will not be part of the chorus. She will be the studious girl who never joins in. Onstage but not part of the action.

Now this is all new to her so you must help her. Right, off you go.'

The stage cleared in seconds. I ran to catch up with Blanche. 'Where should I go?' I asked.

She considered this. 'Probably best if you change with the girls in their dressing room. It would create resentment if I had you get dressed with me. Up the staircase and to the end of the hall.'

She ran ahead of me. I was following, picking my way past props and scenery, when my arm was grabbed roughly. Desmond Haynes was glaring down at me. 'You listen to me, girl,' he said. 'This is a stupid idea of Blanche's. She always was too softhearted. The theater is no place for amateurs and I take it you are a rank amateur?'

I could only nod.

'I have worked these girls until their routines are perfect,' he said. 'Do anything to spoil what I have created and I'll have you out of here so fast your feet won't touch the ground. Do I make myself clear?'

'Absolutely,' I said.

As I climbed the stairs to the dressing room, my heart was hammering. I couldn't help wondering if Mr Haynes was looking for an excuse to get rid of me as quickly as possible. I also wondered whether this was only because of artistic sensibilities or because he sensed my presence as a threat.

Thirteen

I tapped on the door to the girls' dressing room, but they must have been making quite a racket in there because nobody answered. So I turned the knob and went in. This room wasn't at all cozy like Blanche's dressing room. It was long and narrow, with a mirror and wooden ledge down one wall, hooks for clothing on the other, and a few stools. And it was crammed with half-dressed females. I must say I felt a little like Daniel of the Bible story entering the lion's den. Twelve pairs of cold eyes stared at me.

'Hello,' I said. 'I was told to come in here and get ready.'

'Move over, Connie,' a voice said. 'Better give up your space to Miss Important here. Mustn't upset the boss's new favorite.'

'Look,' I said hastily, 'this wasn't my idea. I didn't beg for this chance or anything. Oona and Blanche cooked it up between them. I feel very awkward about the whole thing.'

'So you should,' the tall girl I had met the day before said. 'Do you know how many actresses are out of work in this city? Actresses and dancers who have studied hard, worked hard, and are dying to get just one chance at success? Now along you come with no audition, nothing. And I'll bet no experience either, right?'

'Not much,' I said. 'I was in a couple of plays in Ireland.'

I could say this without lying because I had been an angel in the nativity play at church and once we'd put on a production of *Dick Whittington and His Cat* when I took lessons with the girls at the manor house. I was the cat, naturally.

'Okay. Put your stuff down wherever you can find a space,' the tall girl said. 'I'm Lily, by the way.'

'Molly. Pleased to meet you,' I said.

'You'd better get a move on. Where's your costume?'

'I don't have one yet. I have to wear my street clothes tonight.'

I saw the looks and giggles and nudges. I was obviously going to be an object of entertainment for them.

'Then you'd better get on with your hair and makeup,' Lily said. 'Or are you planning to leave them the way they are?'

'Oh no. There's a wig coming for me tomorrow, but I suppose tonight I should put my hair into pigtails, because that's what Blanche wants.'

'It's Blanche, notice, girls.' Lily jabbed the next girl in the side. 'On first-name terms with the star. Well, let me give you a word of warning, kid. Miss Lovejoy is a stickler for correctness. You'd better not call her Blanche in public or you'll be sorry.'

'Thanks for the warning,' I said. I took a brush out of my purse and started to attack my tangle of curls. My hair is a disaster at the best of times and today I had run against a fierce wind. It took awhile to comb out the knots and force my hair into two pigtails. Then, of course, I had no ribbons to secure them. By asking around I managed to scrounge two unmatching scraps of ribbon.

By now the girls were all in white tennis outfits, which were daringly sleeveless, with skirts above the ankle. I watched in fascination as they sat on stools, tying their ballet slippers and applying their makeup. They had boxes full of sticks of various colors and they were applying these to their faces in grotesque amounts. The girl next to me must have caught me staring.

'Where's your makeup?' she asked.

'I don't have any,' I said.

'You'll need your own makeup. The girls don't like to share,' she said. 'But I suppose I can help you out just this once. Help yourself.'

I looked at the long array of the greasy sticks.

'I'm afraid I've never put on my own makeup,' I whispered. 'Can you give me a little hint?'

'You're supposed to be a bluestocking, didn't she say? Then you'd look pale. Not like us. We have to look healthy. So you'll get by with a base of number five. A touch of rouge on the cheeks and of course carmine two on the lips. When you're done, I'll show you how to do the eyes.'

I did as I had observed and soon my face stared back at me, quite brown and countrified.

'I thought I was supposed to be pale,' I said.

'The lights are terrible at making us look washed out,' she said. 'That's why we need extra color to start with. Now do your lips and here.' She reached across with some rouge on her finger and gave me a generous red circle on both cheeks. Then she insisted on painting a black line along my eyelids and out at the sides of my eyes. By the time she was done I looked like a doll. But then so did everybody else.

'So what's this I've been hearing about a ghost?' I whispered as the girl dabbed a final coating of powder onto my face. 'Is it true that the theater is haunted?'

She laughed nervously. 'Well, none of us has actually seen the ghost, but we did see that table tip over and the candle almost catch Miss Lovejoy's skirt on fire. And we were backstage, waiting in the wings to go on, when that scenery fell. And I can tell you there was nobody near it when I looked. So it's definitely odd. And it's always Miss Lovejoy.'

'You don't think anybody could be trying to frighten her, do you?' I asked.

She looked surprised. 'As a joke, you mean?'

'More serious than a joke. To make her leave the play, maybe?'

'Who would want to do that? Miss Lovejoy doesn't allow outsiders during rehearsals and all of us just jumped at the chance to be in a play at the Casino.'

'Has Miss Lovejoy any enemies that you know of?'

The girl laughed. 'Plenty, I expect. When you've been as famous as she has, I expect she's trodden on toes and offended heaps of people. But everyone here wants this play to be a hit, especially Miss Lovejoy. She hasn't had a hit in years and she's turning forty soon. So if she decides to call it quits, we're all in trouble.'

At that very second there was a loud rap on the door that made me jump. Then the callboy's voice, 'Overture and beginners in fifteen minutes.'

The girl got up from her stool. 'That's us,' she said. 'Come along. I'm Elise, by the way, and I know you're Molly.'

I smiled. 'Thanks for your help, Elise.'

The girls were crowding toward the door, pausing for one last glance in the mirror, patting at their hair and smoothing their dresses. I could feel the tension had mounted, as if this was a real performance and not just a dress rehearsal. And suddenly I picked up that tension. I was about to go onstage, with only the faintest idea of what I should be doing. My stomach twisted itself into knots. Why did I get myself into these crazy situations, I wondered. Why couldn't I find a nice normal job, in a bookstore or a ladies' tea room – even as a governess. Anywhere safe and ordinary and away from danger.

I didn't have time for any more thoughts because I was swept downstairs with the tide of people, as the leading actors mingled with us schoolgirls. There was complete silence and our feet on the iron treads echoed through that lofty backstage area like the sound of an invading army. I followed the girls around to the far side of the stage and stood at the back of the line as they waited to go on. It was chilly back there, and drafty, too, with wafts of cold air swirling around my legs. I could see why so many of the actors wore woolen wraps. As we waited I had time to examine my surroundings. The backstage area was cavernous. I couldn't even see the ceiling, but looking up I could pick out various walkways and ropes and pulleys disappearing into the blackness, looking like parts of a monstrous spider's web. All sorts of opportunities for someone who had managed to sneak into the theater with mischief on his mind.

'Beginners onstage,' came the call and the girls marched out to take up positions. I had my book open and went to my designated spot against the wall. I also remembered not to lean on that wall as it was only made of painted wood and canvas. It was bright as day onstage and quite warm, too. Beyond the curtain the orchestra struck up the overture. I found it hard to breathe. Thank heaven I didn't have to say any lines or I would have opened my mouth and nothing would have come out. After what seemed an eternity the curtains opened. Spotlights glared down on us. The girls came to life.

'We're learning how to make a smash, how to win the game of love,' they sang. The song was all in tennis vocabulary, but cleverly angled to reflect the game of life. I kept my head down and my eyes on my book, as instructed, but I found that I could see quite well around me. The song concluded in a dance number, then the maid appeared, clapping her hands briskly.

'Madame the Countess is waiting for you for your deportment class, you naughty girls,' she announced. 'Off with you.'

The girls ran off. I waited for a fraction of a second then followed the last in line, not looking up from my book. I thought I heard a chuckle from the orchestra pit. I had survived my first scene.

The rest of the first act was a blur. On stage, then off again. Stand against the wall. Sit on the stool in the corner. Follow the girls. Wait for Miss Lovejoy to call for me. It all became a jumble of confusion. I was exhausted by the end of the act and glad to go up to the dressing room. The other girls were making more quick changes and it made me glad that I'd be wearing one outfit for the entire play.

Then we were summoned for act two. Not so many scenes this time, as the real action, the love story between the countess and the penniless painter, had really taken over. I wandered on-stage once at the wrong moment, because I thought the scene was over, but they were still in the middle of an embrace. I looked horrified and hurried off again, getting a laugh. Then we were all onstage for the big ballroom scene. The countess has discovered that one of her paintings is worth a fortune. She will be rich again and gives a ball to celebrate. I had to sit at a table to one side, my head, as usual, in my book, completely ignoring the jolly scene going on around me.

In the middle of a silly song about what every girl should know, suddenly the lights flickered and a cold wind crept around my shoulders. I shivered and looked up from my book. Others on the stage had noticed it, too. I could hear the tension in their voices as they spoke their lines. Then suddenly a violent burst of wind blew across the stage, sending candelabras and potted plants crashing down, blowing off hats, tablecloths, anything that wasn't firmly anchored. A candle fell onto a chorus girl's skirt and the flimsy fabric went up like a torch. Two of the actors dived onto the girl, rolling her on the ground to put the flames out. Girls were screaming. I dashed to the side of the stage, fighting the strength of the wind coming at me full in the face. Nobody was there.

Suddenly there was a great shout from the auditorium. 'Everybody stay where you are. Nobody move.'

And Robert Barker came storming in through the pass door.

'This has gone on long enough,' he bellowed, making a lot of noise for such a small man. 'I aim to get to the bottom of this right now.'

He stomped across the stage and saw me standing in the wings.

'It's coming from this machine,' I said. 'Do you know how to turn it off?'

'Simple,' he said, and disconnected the electricity. The wind died immediately. 'A wind machine,' he said angrily. 'Some damned fool's idea of a practical joke.'

'I came out immediately after it started,' I said. 'There was nobody here. Besides, the whole cast is onstage for this scene.'

'So what were you doing out here?' He was glaring at me.

'I told you, I ran out to see if I could catch whoever was doing this. Miss Lovejoy told me about the ghost. I thought I'd keep an eye out for it.'

He went on staring as if he was trying to read my mind, then he pushed past me onto the stage. 'Stop that blubbering,' he snapped to some of the chorus who were clutching each other in fear. 'It's all explained. It was the wind machine. Some fool connected it to the electricity by mistake. Nothing to get upset about.'

'But who connected it?' Blanche asked in a trembling voice. 'You know the whole cast is onstage for the final scene. Who could have done it?'

'Wally!' Robert Barker bawled. The stage manager appeared. 'Were any of your crew on this side of the stage just now?'

'No, sir,' Wally replied. 'We were all working on that tree

that you said didn't have enough leaves. All back in the props room, except for Tommy, who had to work the final curtain.' Tommy stuck his head out from the other side of the stage to acknowledge his presence.

Barker checked the boys who manned the spotlights. They were all in their places.

'You see,' Blanche said, her voice taut with fear, 'it isn't human. It's a spirit, a malevolent spirit, and it's determined to wreck my play. How can we possibly open when this kind of thing could happen at any moment. It wasn't just aimed at me this time. That poor girl could have been burned to death if those dear boys hadn't acted so rapidly and bravely. As it is, her costume is destroyed. Look at it.'

The girl in question was now sitting on one of the chairs, sobbing quietly, while the young men still attended to her. One side of her skirt was a charred brown mess.

Blanche smoothed down her own ballgown. 'The show must go on,' she said in a firmer voice. 'We will not let it daunt us.' She turned to the girl with the burned skirt. 'You, child, are you hurt?'

'I don't think so, Miss Lovejoy,' the girl answered with a trembling voice.

'Then we will pick up where we left off. Maestro, if you please, we'll take it from the top of the song. Henry, have those props stood up again. Places, everyone.'

I had to admire her courage. She was obviously really shaken. We all were. Some of the chorus girls really looked as if they really had seen a ghost. They moved around like mechanical toys, some of them holding hands for support. Even the men in the cast glanced at each other warily. I went back to my seat in the corner.

The show ended with no more interruptions. We lined up to take our bows. I was embarrassed to find that I'd get a featured player's bow with the gardener, the cook, the messenger boy, and the dressmaker. I'd have much rather not taken a bow at all, but Blanche insisted. I don't suppose for a moment it was to reward my talents. She wanted me near her onstage until the very end.

We were a subdued bunch as we trudged wearily up the stairs to the dressing room. Once we were safely inside everyone made a fuss of Irene, the girl whose skirt had caught on fire. They helped her undress and found that she did have burns on her hands and the hair had been scorched off her arms.

'Go home and put butter on them,' Lily instructed. 'You were lucky, Irene. I thought you were a goner.'

'Abe and Joe were so quick. They put the flames out right away,' Irene said, with admiration in her eyes. 'They were wonderful. I don't know how I'll ever thank them.'

'Oh, I expect you'll find a way,' someone said, getting a general laugh and making me realize that chorus girls weren't all little angels.

I watched how the other girls removed their makeup and followed suit. Somehow I'd have to buy the necessaries of stage makeup before the next dress rehearsal. I wondered if I could ask Blanche for expenses over and above my fee. This little jaunt could turn out to be an expensive business.

Beside me Elise had taken off her ballet shoes and was attending to her feet. She was unwinding bandages and pulling pieces of cotton wool out from between her toes. One of the pieces of cotton had blood on it.

'Oh no. Did you hurt your foot?' I asked.

She looked up at me, amused. 'We're on our toes a lot in this show. It's hell on the feet. Look.' And she showed me a dainty foot with bruised, blistered, and bloody toes. 'All part of the job,' she said. 'Some dancers have worse feet than mine.'

'I'm glad I'm not expected to dance then,' I said. Those girls had looked so dainty and ethereal as they glided over the stage on their toes. I had no idea that they paid such a price for that delicate motion.

As we came out of the stage door, we were met by a crowd of young men. At first I thought they might be suitors but one of them came up to us as we emerged, his notebook at the ready. 'So what happened tonight, girls? Did the phantom strike again?'

'We're not allowed to talk about it,' one girl said and walked primly past him.

'So something did happen!' the reporter said, eyeing the rest of us for the one most likely to spill the beans. 'There might be something in it for the girl who gives me a hint.'

Lily slipped her arm through his. 'Take me out to supper, ply me with wine, and I might very well let down my guard,' she said.

Elise leaned close to me. 'Miss Lovejoy will kill her if this gets out,' she said. 'If she asks you, don't rat on Lily, okay? Act innocent. Pretend we know nothing.'

'All right.' I nodded.

'And just wait until it's a real performance,' Elise went on. 'You won't believe the crowd you'll find out here. You have to positively fight your way past the admirers. And you never have to buy your own supper, you know. There is always some stage-door Johnnie waiting to take out a chorus girl. It's nice, really. Of course some of them want payment for the supper, if you know what I mean. I never let it go farther than a kiss or two, but some of the girls are rather free with their affections. Every season one or two of them wind up in trouble. Just make sure you're not one of them.'

'Oh, don't worry,' I said. 'I have a very jealous beau of my own. He doesn't like the idea of my being on the stage to start with. If he hears about the stage-door Johnnies, he'll be standing by that door waiting for me every single night.'

'You're lucky to have someone like that,' she said wistfully. 'I keep hoping one of those rich young bucks will take a shine to me. But I'm too wholesome-looking. They go more for the flamboyant types, like Lily. And Miss Lovejoy herself, of course. She has her pick. Or she used to have her pick when she was a little younger.'

I went home deep in thought. Whether Miss Lovejoy liked it or not, news of what happened in the theater tonight was going to leak out. And another thing struck me. The one person we hadn't seen tonight was Desmond Haynes. Mr Barker had been watching from the stalls, so it was possible that Desmond was also out there, but I hadn't seen him, and he hadn't come through to the stage after the calamity.

Fourteen

By the time I got home it had started to rain, a miserable sort of freezing sleet that soaked me through between the El station and Patchin Place. So I was tired and dispirited as I trudged through the slush to my front door. I had an absurdly irrational hope that Daniel might be standing there, waiting for me, but of course there was no sign of him.

'Drat the man. Why can't he ever appear when he's needed,' I muttered and realized instantly how ridiculous I was being. When he was there I told him to go away and when he wasn't there, I wanted him. I suppose this was because our relationship had to be put on hold until the charges hanging over him were finally settled and, frankly, I didn't trust myself when we were alone together.

Tonight, however, I didn't care about being cautious. I needed to be hugged and held and to feel safe. The incident with the wind machine had shaken me up more than I cared to admit. I told myself that it could only have been started by ordinary human hands, but I still remembered the chill draft around my legs before that great blast of wind. The theater had definitely gone cold. Maybe I was starting to believe that a malevolent spirit might just be responsible.

It was too late to barge in on Sid and Gus, so I let myself into my little house and went around lighting all the gas brackets. I looked for a note from Dr Birnbaum, but there was none, which was also vexing. He had promised to deliver a report on his way home. I hoped that his strong code of ethics hadn't gotten the better of him and he wasn't going to divulge his diagnosis to me. I went over to the stove and made myself a cup of tea. I remembered then that I'd promised to bring some nourishing food to the girl at the hospital. I had no time to make a soup now. I'd have to buy something on my way to visit her tomorrow.

My dreams that night were troubled. Somehow the mute girl in the snowdrift mingled with the ghost in the theater. 'You see, I have robbed her of her voice,' he said. 'She will never speak again.' And he laughed a horrible laugh that echoed through the theater and through my head. I woke with my heart racing and found it hard to get back to sleep with the consequence that I dropped off just before dawn and woke late. I was still pottering around my kitchen in my robe and slippers when there was a knock on my front door. I fully expected it to be Sid or Gus, on their way back from the French bakery with croissants, coming to invite me for breakfast, and was horrified when the caller turned out to be none other than Dr Birnbaum. He was immaculately turned out as always in a great coat with an astrakhan collar, his gold-tipped cane tucked under one arm.

'Holy Mother of God,' I muttered. 'I'm sorry, Doctor. I wasn't expecting a gentleman caller this early. I thought you'd be my friends from across the street. Please forgive the attire.'

He smiled. 'My dear Miss Murphy, I assure you that I have seen more shocking things than your dressing gown during my years as a doctor.'

'In that case, come on in,' I said. 'I've just made a cup of tea. Can I pour you one?'

'Thank you, but no. I have just had coffee at my hotel. I

came to explain why I did not leave a note for you as promised. I saw the girl, and what I saw disturbed me greatly.'

'Can she speak yet?' I asked. 'Did she say anything?'

'Nothing. Not a word. She stared at me blankly as if she didn't understand or hear me.'

'But she is not deaf?'

'No. I tested her hearing and she reacted normally to sounds out of her range of vision. She hears. She also has the power of speech, I believe. The sisters tell me that she moans in her sleep and she has no abnormalities that I could detect. I can only conclude that some great trauma has robbed her of her wits.'

'Poor girl. How terrible,' I said.

'It is indeed. I remember that my mentor, Dr Freud, in Vienna had such a girl as a patient. She also appeared to be mute until Dr Freud was able to cure her through hypnosis. I should dearly like to work with this young woman and see if I can help her regain her senses and her voice.'

'Oh, do you think you can help her? That would be wonderful.'

'If I am given the chance,' he said. 'Nobody has come forward to identify her. If she is not claimed soon, I rather fear that she will be shipped off to the insane asylum.'

I gasped. 'Oh no. They can't do that.'

'What else is to be done with her? When her body is healed she can no longer take up space in a hospital bed. And when she's in the asylum she will be beyond my reach. That institution has its own doctors and its own methods, which I hear are primitive beyond belief.'

'We can't let that happen, Doctor,' I said. 'I'm not going to let it happen.'

'How can you stop it?'

'Let me think,' I said, pacing around the room. 'We can put an advertisement in the New York newspapers, and I have a friend on the New York police force – a female officer called Mrs Goodwin. I'll ask her to look into any reports of missing girls. Somebody somewhere must be worried that this girl hasn't come home.'

'There are lost girls aplenty in New York – girls who have run away for one reason or another.'

I shook my head. 'Not this girl. She was nicely dressed. She was wearing delicate little evening shoes.'

'Then let us hope that your friend can assist us,' he said. 'And as to the advertisement in the newspapers, I will be happy to take that chore upon myself. I find her case most interesting, and most challenging.'

I saw then that scientists and ordinary folk like myself saw things very differently. I was worried about the girl. Dr Birnbaum saw her as a challenge.

He gave a little bow. 'I bid you good day, Miss Murphy. Let us stay in touch, *ja?*'

As I opened the front door I saw a figure standing outside, arm raised and about to knock. I gave a little gasp of horror, then recognized Daniel, swathed in the scarf again.

'You nearly scared the living daylights out of me,' I said, laughing.

'Sorry, I suppose I do look a little intimidating,' Daniel said and was about to come into my house when he saw Dr Birnbaum standing in the hallway. 'What's this, Molly?' he asked.

'You mean who is this, surely,' I said.

'I mean a gentleman caller at this hour with you still in your night attire,' he said in a cold voice.

I laughed again. 'Oh, Daniel, don't be so silly. This is my friend, Dr Birnbaum, from Vienna. He is an alienist, Daniel. He agreed to look at the poor girl in hospital and came around specially to report on his findings.'

'I see.' Daniel's voice was still expressionless.

'Dr Birnbaum. May I present Captain Sullivan,' I said formally. 'Captain Sullivan, Dr Birnbaum.'

Daniel extended a hand but Birnbaum clicked his heels and bowed, making for a rather embarrassing moment.

'I will take my leave then, Miss Murphy,' Dr Birnbaum said, putting his homburg back on his head. 'You will let me know if your friend has any news.'

'I will. And thank you.' I escorted him to the door and closed it behind him to find Daniel still glaring at me.

'Molly, have you no sense of propriety?' he demanded. 'You let strangers into the house dressed like that?'

'As to that, Daniel Sullivan, this robe reveals no more of my body than any dress would and the man is a doctor. He has presumably examined plenty of females clad in considerably less than I am wearing. And for your information, I only opened the door because I thought it was Sid and Gus coming back from the bakery with rolls. Now are you satisfied?'

'I suppose so,' he said grudgingly. 'So what news did your German friend have about the girl?'

'That she is as capable of speech as you or I, and that some great trauma has robbed her of her wits. He believes he can restore her to sanity through hypnosis.'

'Really? Well, that's good news, isn't it?'

'It would be but they may not keep her in the hospital much longer. If her next of kin is not found, she'll be shipped off to the insane asylum.'

'Dear God.'

'As you say. I'm going to do all I can to prevent that from happening.'

'And what can you do, pray?'

'Dr Birnbaum is placing advertisements in the papers and I'm going to see your colleague Mrs Goodwin. She can find out if any reports of missing girls fit her description.'

'Good thinking,' he said. 'Oh wonderful. You've just made tea.'

I poured him a cup and he sat, cradling it in his hands.

'So I see your pneumonia is already on the mend,' I said sweetly.

'Don't mock. Yesterday I felt terrible. Now I will admit that it has turned into no more than the usual grippe.'

'Did you have to stand out in the elements until the early hours again?'

'Fortunately, no. Mr Roth had an early night. His lights went out at ten. Mercifully, I went home to bed. I think we can probably conclude this case, don't you, Molly? You can report that the young man is wholesome enough to marry anyone's daughter.'

'There's one more aspect of the case that I haven't yet managed to investigate properly,' I said. 'His business and financial transactions. No bank or businessman will discuss such things with a woman.'

'Of course not.' Daniel nodded. Before I could respond to this typically male insult he went on, 'And you're right. That is something I can do easily. And during the daylight hours without getting chilled to the marrow. So what about your new assignment – did you encounter the ghost?' He looked up, smiling.

'As a matter of fact we did,' I said. 'At least somebody or something caused a horrible disruption during the play last night. The wind machine was turned on and blew over scenery. One poor girl's dress was set on fire. There was absolute panic.'

'And what makes you think that this was caused by a ghost? It sounds more like a human prank to me. Surely ghosts don't have to resort to wind machines. Their mere presence, wafting across the stage, would cause the same kind of panic.'

'You're right,' I said. 'But there's only one person in the theater I couldn't account for when the incident happened.'

'And does he or she have a motive for causing havoc?'

'I don't know yet,' I said. 'My next task will be to find out.'

'So you're going to continue with the case?'

'Yes, I am. I've been given a part in the play. Come to opening night and you'll witness your Molly onstage.'

'Really? As what?' He looked amused.

'A harem dancer,' I said glibly, then laughed at his reaction. 'No, I won't give away the part I play. You'll have to come and see for yourself.'

'And how long do you think this farce will go on?'

'It's not a farce, it's a musical comedy.'

'You know what I mean. The farce of ghost hunting.'

'Until I get to the truth.'

'I hope she's paying you well.'

'I hope so, too,' I said. 'But who knows, maybe this job will turn out to have extra benefits. Maybe I'll make a name for myself and become a big star. And you can wait at the stage door and drink champagne from my slipper. That's what they do, you know, the stage-door Johnnies. I gather the chorus girls are constantly whisked off to dine with rich men.'

'Who then expect more than supper, I suppose,' Daniel said. He put his hands on my shoulders again, looking down at me with a worried expression. 'Oh, Molly. I can't wait until this nightmare is over. I want to get back to my normal life again. I want to be able to support you so that you can stop taking these ridiculous risks.'

'And take up embroidery?' I demanded.

He laughed. 'No, I don't suppose you'll ever take up embroidery. But I worry about you, you know.' And he hugged me to him. This time I let him, feeling the roughness of his jacket against my cheek. But my thoughts were racing. Did I look forward to giving up such a precarious way of life someday? It was true that I did worry about money when no cases came in for a month or so, and I had faced danger from time to time. But why did women have to make an absolute choice between their accepted role and men's world of commerce? Nelly Bly seemed to have bridged the gap, I decided. Maybe she could tell me how it was done.

Fifteen

'I can't stand here all day.' I broke away from Daniel's arms. 'I have so much to do, I don't know if I'm coming or going. Talk about it never rains but it pours.'

I had just finished that prophetic phrase when a letter came flying in through my mail slot. This was a surprise in itself as letters were a rarity. My correspondence for the detective agency was held for me at the post office and I had no circle of friends outside of New York. So I picked it up with anticipation. The handwriting was perfect copper plate on good velum stationery. I opened it, scanned to the signature, and said in surprise, 'Oh, it's from Miss Van Woekem.'

'Good God,' Daniel said. I noticed he'd been doing a lot of swearing around me recently. 'What can she want?'

'If you hold your horses a minute I'll tell you,' I said. I read the note out loud. 'Dear Miss Murphy. I must speak to you immediately on a matter of great urgency. Please call on me at your earliest convenience.' These last two words were underlined boldly.

'Well, I'll be . . .' Daniel said, without finishing the sentence. 'What on earth can she want so urgently with you?'

Miss Van Woekem, I should perhaps explain, was an elderly lady of impeccable pedigree, not prone to flights of fancy or to exaggeration. She also happened to be godmother to a certain Miss Arabella Norton, Daniel's erstwhile betrothed.

'Maybe Arabella has displeased her and she wishes to make me her goddaughter instead,' I joked, but Daniel continued to frown. 'This would happen now, when I've no time,' I said, 'but I suppose I'll have to go. I'm rather fond of the old thing and she does sound upset.'

'Perhaps I should go with you,' Daniel suggested. 'I might be able to help.'

'I'm not sure, Daniel,' I said. 'It may be something she wants to keep private from her usual circle and she counts you among them.'

'Counted,' Daniel said. 'No longer.'

'All the same, I think I had better go alone. I don't know if this is a personal matter or a professional one. I'll report back to you if I'm not required to keep confidentiality.'

'As you wish,' Daniel said, feigning indifference.

I patted his cheek. 'You are a silly thing. You know very well that you wouldn't take me with you if you were summoned on police business.'

'Of course not. It would be more than my job is worth.'

'There you are then. I'm a professional detective, just like you. And I'm not trying to get rid of you, but I have to get dressed and out of here or I'll never get my work done today.'

After he had gone I felt guilty, of course. He was obviously struggling with his current situation and probably needed companionship and reassurance. But then one of us had to earn some money and right now that person seemed to be me. I rushed upstairs to wash and dress, all the while trying to decide in which order I should tackle the many things I had to accomplish today before tonight's dress rehearsal.

Probably my first task should be to find out if anyone held a grudge against Blanche Lovejoy or would want her show closed for any reason. I wasn't quite sure how to do this until I realized that I knew people who were connected to the theater. Obviously, the first person on that list would be Oona Sheehan. It was she who had sent me to Blanche, after all. And then there was Ryan O'Hare, the flamboyant and completely outrageous Irish playwright. If anyone knew juicy gossip, it would be Ryan.

I wrote down both names in my little notebook.

Then I scribbled 'buy greasepaint etc.' Oona would know where to do that.

But there was also my other worry – the mute girl in the hospital who could be transferred to an insane asylum any moment. What chance would she ever have of regaining her speech and her senses in that terrible place? Dr Birnbaum was going to place advertisements in the New York newspapers and I had promised to speak to New York police matron Sabella Goodwin. In truth Mrs Goodwin's official title was matron, but the police had recently begun to use her as a detective in undercover assignments, in cases where a woman's presence would raise less suspicion than a man's.

I decided to go to her home, rather than to police headquarters, where my presence would be awkward, to say the least. I took out my pen, ink, and writing paper and wrote her a note, in case she wasn't at home. It was hard to tell with her strange schedule. Sometimes she would be out on the streets all night and might just have returned. Then I washed and dressed and set off at a lively trot.

Mrs Goodwin lived within walking distance from Patchin Place, on East Seventh Street, but over on the East Side near Tompkins Square. The neighborhood had a more refined air than Greenwich Village, with well-scrubbed front steps and well-dressed children playing in what remained of the snow in the park. Her home was a solid brownstone, with pots containing bay trees on either side of her front door. I knocked and was delighted to hear approaching footsteps. My bright smile waned, however, when a cross voice demanded, 'Who is it?'

'It's Molly, Mrs Goodwin. Molly Murphy.'

The door opened to reveal Mrs Goodwin, clad pretty much as I had been an hour previously: her dark hair, now tinged with gray, lying loose over her shoulders, her body wrapped in a large red flannel robe and slippers.

'Molly dear,' she said. 'You've caught me at a bad time. I just got home after a night's duty on the streets. I was literally halfway up the stairs to bed.'

'I'm sorry,' I said. 'I'll go away and come back another time then. When it's more convenient.'

'Was this just a social call, or something important?' she said.

'I had come to ask for your help,' I said, 'but I can leave you the note I brought in case you weren't home.'

She sighed. 'Since you're here, you'd better come in. I don't suppose it will kill me to wait another half an hour before I go to bed.'

'If you're sure,' I began but she frowned and dragged me inside.

'Now then, what is today's great drama?' she said as soon as she had seated me in an armchair beside a well-banked fire. 'You are well, I hope?'

Her look said volumes.

'Quite well, thank you,' I said hastily. 'I've come to you about a baffling case.' And I recounted the whole story of the girl in the snowdrift.

'I know she is nothing to do with me,' I said, 'but I want to see her safely home.'

Mrs Goodwin was still frowning. 'I'll do what I can,' she said, 'although it might not be as easy as you think to trace her next of kin. Girls run away from home all the time because they are in trouble, because they quarrel with their parents, or because they dream of the bright lights and the big city. Or they run away with a young man who subsequently betrays them and abandons them. As often as not, they fall in with bad company and wind up on the streets.'

'This girl didn't look like a prostitute,' I said. 'Her style of dress was demure.'

'Not all girls in that trade look as if they are,' Mrs Goodwin said. 'If she was in a brothel that catered to a high class of clientele, she would dress appropriately. And there is a certain type of man who is attracted to the virginal and vulnerable. Do we know the state of her virginity?'

'No, I haven't asked that question. I was told that she hadn't been assaulted in that way.'

'Then I would suggest that finding out would be a next step. It would mean we were dealing with a girl who had recently run away and not fallen into the hands of a pimp or a madam.'

'But what about the terrible trauma?' I asked. 'The one that has robbed her of her speech?'

'Until she regains her speech and tells us, we have no way of knowing. From what you tell me, I suggest that someone was deliberately trying to get rid of her. You say she suffered a blow to the head. Perhaps someone intended to knock her out and leave her to freeze in the park. By the time her body was found he could be far away with an alibi.'

'How terrible.' I shuddered, reliving the cold of that snow against my own bare skin.

'People do terrible things every day,' she said. 'Some of the sights I have witnessed seem beyond belief. Mothers who kill their innocent little children, men who beat their wives, men who kill for a bottle of liquor or a new coat. Life, I am afraid, is very cheap in New York City.'

'But you will do what you can, won't you?' I asked. 'You'll

go through the reports of missing girls. You'll ask around at headquarters. I've given you the description.'

'Yes, I'll do what I can,' she said with a weary smile. 'But you have to realize that you can only do so much. She is not your sister. You have no obligation here. You can't solve all the troubles of the world.'

'I'd like to give it a darned good try,' I replied, making her smile.

After I left her, I decided that my next visit should be to Ryan O'Hare. He had rooms at the Hotel Lafayette, near Washington Square, and at this relatively early hour was likely to still be at home. I was told at the front desk that Mr O'Hare was indeed in residence and tapped cautiously on his door. I say cautiously because one was never quite sure whom one might find in Ryan's rooms. He had, shall we say, an extensive and diverse circle of friends. But this time my knock was answered by a very sleepy 'Come in.'

I opened his door and found the room still in darkness, the heavy drapes drawn.

'If that's you, Jacques, be an angel and put the coffee on the table,' a voice muttered from the gloom.

'Ryan, it's Molly,' I said. "I'm sorry to disturb you but it is after eleven.'

'Molly?' The voice sounded instantly wide awake. 'What a lovely surprise. Open the curtains, my angel, so that I may feast upon your beauty.'

'Enough of your blarney, O'Hare.' I laughed as I went over to the window and pulled back the drapes. Ryan was now sitting up in a very regal-looking four-poster. His long dark hair was tousled, he was wearing a frilled night shirt, and he looked remarkably attractive. He patted the red silk eiderdown beside him. 'Come and sit and talk to me. I have been positively starved of your company of late.'

'Yes, I know,' I said, positioning myself beside him on the bed. 'I've suddenly become very busy.'

'It's that brute of a man of yours, isn't it?' Ryan said. 'He has forbidden you to see me. I could tell from the way he looked at me that he disapproved. I'm so sensitive that way.'

'Well, he doesn't approve,' I said, 'but no man is ever going to tell me how to select my friends.'

'How bold of you, Molly, especially when that policeman is so forceful, so domineering.'

'Can you see me being dominated?' I chuckled.

'So did you come here for something special or just because you were pining for me as much as I was pining for you?'

'Actually, Ryan, I came for juicy gossip,' I said.

His eyes lit up. 'Juicy gossip. How divine. Now if that lazy-bones Jacques would only bring my breakfast we could both have coffee and my happiness would be complete.'

'My big news,' I said, 'is that I have taken a job in the theater. I'm to appear in Blanche Lovejoy's new play.'

'At the Casino? My darling girl, how did you manage that?'

'Let's just say I have a little secret assignment from Miss Lovejoy.'

'Anything to do with the ghost?'

'You've heard then?'

'My dear, the whole theater world is abuzz. Everyone is so thrilled that Blanche is finally being haunted.'

'Is she much disliked then?'

'Not disliked, but she has been known to play the grande dame a little too often, and she never forgives those who have insulted her.'

'So she does have enemies?'

'My darling, we all have enemies. Anyone who is successful has enemies.'

'Who would want Blanche's latest venture to fail?'

Ryan frowned, staring out of the window at two pigeons walking up and down the wide sill. 'I couldn't tell you that,' he said. 'It's her show, after all. One gathers she put up most of the money herself. Well, she'd have to, wouldn't she? She's getting a little long in the tooth to be the leading lady, especially since *Florodora* made sixteen-year-olds the standard fare. So it's not as if she pipped another actress at the post for the part.'

'A rival theater owner, maybe? Someone who doesn't want the Casino to be successful?'

'But it already is successful. If someone had wanted to bring about its downfall they'd have done it years ago. Now it's one of the best houses in the city.'

'What do you know about Robert Barker?'

'Dear little Bobby? Madly in love with Blanche, of course.'

'Is he?'

'Has been for years. Why else would he keep directing her plays and taking all that abuse from her. He keeps asking her to marry him and she keeps refusing. Not rich enough, for one thing. And not forceful enough. Blanche craves to be dominated.'

'Might he want to get back at her for all that abuse and rejection?'

'Only if he'd abandoned his quest, because she'd never have anything to do with him again if she found out he'd been doing the dirty on her.' Ryan's eyes opened wider. 'I see what you are getting at. You are hinting that it's not a ghost but a mere mortal who is making nasty things happen to dear Blanche?'

'That's exactly what I'm hinting. But I was there yesterday when the wind machine suddenly went off, all by itself. The whole cast was onstage. The stage crew was working together to finish a prop. The only people who weren't present were Mr Barker, who came through from the front house, and the choreographer, Desmond Haynes.'

126

'Dear Desmond,' Ryan's eyes became dreamy. 'How is he these days?'

'A friend of yours?'

'Former friend. Will you tell him that Ryan still misses him?'

So much for any thoughts of unrequited love for Blanche. So why had he been watching in the shadows that first time I was in Blanche's dressing room and then melting away before he thought I had seen him? 'You can't think of any reason why he'd want the play to fail, can you?'

'Dear Desmond? He is a perfectionist. If he felt that the play didn't meet his standards? But no, he'd have made sure it did meet his standards. Another forceful man, I have to tell you.'

'And he has no special relationship with Blanche? Former attachment? Former confrontation?'

'Relationship? Oh no. Desmond only likes beautiful people, like *moi*. And confrontation? I don't remember one, although he has his pride and Blanche did once do an impression of him at a party, I remember. She was brilliantly good, I have to admit, and Dessy was furious. But that was long, long ago. One doesn't carry a grudge over such small things. If one did, I'd have challenged half of New York to a duel by now.' Again the wistful look. 'I've never challenged anyone to a duel. Wouldn't it be divine? Think of the velvet britches and the white handkerchiefs and pistols at dawn and the mist swirling around. Of course, I absolutely can't stand the sight of blood, so probably not.'

I patted the covers to interrupt this fantasy. 'So to get back to the Casino, Ryan. There's no way into a theater besides the stage door if all the front entrances are locked, is there?'

'There is sometimes a cargo door when they need to bring in large pieces of scenery, but that's always kept locked, too. The only way in would be past the stage door keeper.'

'So it has to be an inside job. Maybe a member of the cast could somehow have . . .'

'Tell me who is in the cast,' he said. I reeled off those names I could remember and Ryan pronounced each of them blameless, except for Hiram Hunnycutt, who played the American millionaire. He was known to have tantrums about things like his billing on the marquee. Was it possible that he wasn't happy with the size of his part? And the maid, Collette, had also complained that she didn't have many lines. But in each case a small part in what Ryan described as one of the best theaters in New York was surely better than being out of work. Nobody working in what was destined to be a hit show would want to sabotage it.

Ryan's breakfast arrived and I accepted a cup of coffee. Ryan was ready to divulge more gossip and dying to tell me about the new play he was writing – about a freedom fighter bandit in South America. He had been in correspondence with the real bandit and couldn't wait to go to Bolivia to meet him in person. 'He sounds divine,' he said. 'So utterly rugged, and if one can go by the photographs, not a bad fashion sense, either.'

I had to laugh. 'Ryan, you are too much,' I said. 'Can you see yourself in Bolivia? I bet they don't have running water or proper sanitation, especially not where bandits live.'

'Oh I'm sure he's a remarkably civilized bandit,' he said. 'South American bandits are so romantic, compared to the lowdown animal behavior of New York criminals. You've heard about these brutal Sicilians, I take it? Utterly ruthless.' A wistful look came into his eyes as if he were almost hoping to be kidnapped.

I got up from my comfortable seat. 'Much as I would love to stay and chat, I have a lot to do before a dress rehearsal tonight.'

'So you really are going to be in the play? What is your part
– do tell?'

'I can't. You'll have to come to opening night and see for
yourself.'

'I'll never get tickets for opening night. Everyone will want
to be there.'

'Blanche is that popular, is she?'

'No, darling, to see if the ghost appears, of course.' He
laughed gaily and went back to attacking a boiled egg.

Sixteen

I left Ryan filled with the warm glow that always lingered after being in his presence and caught the Broadway trolley north to Oona Sheehan's rooms at the Hoffman House. It must have been my lucky day. Miss Sheehan was also in residence and prepared to see me. I was whisked up in the elevator, without bumping into the Divine Sarah this time.

Oona was bustling around, getting ready for her own theatrical performance, shouting instructions to the new French maid as that maid showed me into the drawing room. 'And, Yvette, my fur muff. I can't risk getting my hands cold. And the new jar of cold cream. You might as well bring that as well.' She broke off with a beaming smile. 'Molly. How lovely. Blanche tells me you have taken the case and words cannot express her gratitude. Have you been there yet? Have you seen the ghost?'

'I haven't seen a manifestation, but I've seen an example of its work,' I said, and told her about the wind machine. She was clearly delighted. 'How terribly chilling. So the place really is haunted. Poor Blanche. She would pick that particular theater for her big comeback. Now I bet she wishes she'd aimed lower and gone for the Fifth Avenue Theater instead. Not as glamorous but surely safer.'

Yvette appeared with the muff and the cold cream. 'Anything else, madame?'

'I'm afraid I can't offer you coffee, Molly. I have a matinee today, so I'm all a-dither. Was there something you wanted particularly?'

'Actually I wanted your impression of the cast and crew that Blanche has employed. I'm wondering whether any one of them might be trying to sabotage the play.'

'By pretending to be a ghost, you mean?'

'Exactly. I'm not sure I believe in ghosts, so I have to look at ordinary mortals as the first suspects.'

'Now, let's see. Who is in the show with her? Aubrey, of course, but he's a dear boy. Wouldn't hurt a fly. And Hiram. He's not the easiest man in the world but far too much of a sissy to do anything violent.'

'And Mr Barker?'

'Bobby? Adores Blanche, my dear. Positively adores her. Slavelike devotion. He would throw himself in front of any ghost to save her.'

'And Desmond Haynes?'

She paused. 'I do believe he and Blanche had a thing going once, but it was just a brief affair. You know how it is in the theater – grand passions that quickly burn out. I don't know on what terms they parted or how he feels about her now. But he hasn't had a big show to choreograph in some time so this is a great opportunity for him.'

She glanced down at the jar she was holding. 'I said cold cream, Yvette, not vanishing cream.' Yvette almost snatched the jar away and ran off into the bedroom. 'Oh, the girl is impossible. Just won't learn proper English,' Oona said in the same loud voice.

'And, Oona, one more thing,' I said. Actually it was two more things. 'About stage makeup. I have to buy some before tonight. Is there a particular shop where everyone buys their greasepaint sticks?'

'Darling, I have masses of the stuff. What do you need? Have Yvette show you my makeup box and help yourself.'

'But won't you be taking it to the theater?'

'I'm already well stocked in my dressing room. These are just emergency supplies.'

'Well, if you don't mind,' I said, but she was already calling, 'Yvette. *Venez ici.* Show mademoiselle to the box where I keep my makeup. There, my sweet. Yvette will take care of you.'

She was already turning away.

'And about the check you were going to send me,' I began, but she dismissed it with a graceful wave of the hand. 'Not now, darling. All a-dither. Must fly.' She half-kissed me on the cheek and was gone, leaving a trail of expensive perfume lingering in the air.

Yvette took me through to a dressing room and let me rummage through a drawer full of various types of makeup. Tempted as I was to help myself liberally, I just took the two sticks that Elise had suggested for me, plus the slim red one for my lips. I stopped at a drugstore on the way home to buy face powder, cold cream, and a roll of cotton wool. I didn't bother about my eyes. They'd be hidden behind glasses anyway.

While I was in the drugstore I also bought a bottle of Dr Claybourne's Strengthening Tonic, recommended to restore health to the frailest of invalids. I had never tried it myself, never having been what you might call frail, but judging by the testimonials on the bottle, it ought to do some good. I wanted to make time to take it to my girl in the hospital before I had to be at the theater. And somehow I had to squeeze in a visit to Miss Van Woekem first.

It was now lunchtime and I clearly couldn't spare the time to go home to eat, so I had to lay out all of five cents for a bowl of clam chowder and a roll at a stand-up counter. The clam chowder was a new experience for me, there being no clams in my part of Ireland, or if there were, we didn't eat them. But it was certainly sustaining enough to hold me until I had time for a proper meal.

Thus fortified, I set off for Miss Van Woekem's. The venerable old lady lived at one of the most elegant addresses in the city – Gramercy Park. This delightful square reminded me of Dublin and the grand Georgian squares I had seen there, but as most of my memories of that city were painful, I chose not to dwell on the comparison. The garden in the middle of the square still glistened with untrampled snow, probably because a high railing surrounded it and only residents possessed a key to the gate. It presented a pretty Christmas card scene as I approached along Twenty-first Street, with the brownstone and red brick buildings glowing and windows twinkling in the slanted sunlight. I went up the steps of Miss Van Woekem's house on the south side of the square and rang the doorbell.

The maid who had always been so disapproving of me in the past ushered me in with an almost pleasant 'The mistress will be glad to see you. She's in a proper state.'

This didn't sound like the lady I knew – from the old school and raised to show no emotion whatsoever. I stepped into the drawing room, which faced the park and was usually bright with sunlight. Today the drapes were drawn and I could scarcely make out the figure who sat, still and straight, in the high-backed chair with a rug over her knees. Her eyes were closed and she looked like an old stone statue.

'Miss Murphy to see you, ma'am,' the maid announced and the eyes shot open, instantly alert.

'Miss Murphy, how good of you to come so quickly. I can't tell you how much I appreciate it. Do take a seat and, Matilda, bring us coffee if you please. Or would you prefer tea, Miss Murphy?'

'Coffee would be fine, thank you,' I said. 'I came as soon as I could. I know you're not the kind of person to exaggerate or make a fuss, so I presumed it was truly urgent.'

'It is. Of the uttermost urgency,' she said.

'Are you not well? I see you have the drapes closed.'

'The bright light hurts my eyes,' she said. 'Tell me, are you engaged to be married to that rascal Daniel Sullivan yet?'

Since she was Arabella Norton's godmother, I wondered whether Arabella had suddenly decided that she wanted him back. 'How can we make any plans when Daniel is still under suspicion?' I asked. 'Some charges against him have been dropped, but the police commissioner is not willing to reinstate him with a clean slate.'

'Most annoying for you,' she said. 'So what is Captain Sullivan doing with himself?'

'Mostly bothering me,' I said and got a dry laugh from her. 'Actually, I've put him to work for me. It's not good to have too much time to sit around brooding.'

'I couldn't agree more,' she said. 'That is just what I have been doing and it is bringing me down to depths of depression I should not have thought possible.' It was so unlike her to admit to any weakness that I looked at her with concern.

'But I'm sure you didn't invite me here to discuss my private life,' I said.

'You're right. I don't think much of Sullivan myself, but I expect you'll bring him into line and handle him well enough. I asked about Daniel Sullivan because I rather hoped he might be able to assist us in a delicate matter.'

'Assist us?'

'You and I, Miss Murphy. I wish to engage your services professionally.'

'Oh dear, I'm afraid I'm too busy to take on another case at the moment,' I said. 'I take it the matter has to be addressed right away?'

'Immediately. And if you can't handle it yourself then maybe Sullivan can.'

'What kind of case is it?' I asked.

She leaned toward me, her old beaky face alive with emotion in a way I had never seen it before. 'My nephew is in grave trouble, Miss Murphy. I want you to clear his name.'

'Your nephew? What has he done?'

'You've read the papers, presumably,' she said. 'Nasty goings-on in Connecticut.'

'I'm afraid I haven't read about it,' I said. 'I don't take a daily newspaper.'

'You must be the only person in New York City not to have done so,' she said angrily. 'My friends and neighbors certainly have delighted in gossip about it – given my nephew's family connections, of course.'

'Then you'd better enlighten me,' I said.

'From what I understand there have been a series of violent and horrible robberies up and down the eastern seaboard recently. A bank robbed in Bridgeport, a company pay wagon intercepted in Greenwich, and most recently a botched bank robbery in New Haven, during which a bank employee was shot and killed, followed that same night by a robbery at the Silverton mansion, on the road between New Haven and Bridgeport. Again a servant shot and killed in a most callous manner.'

'I had heard about this,' I said, recalling the constable in Central Park, 'but surely the police don't think—?'

'That's just the problem. They do think,' she said. 'My nephew, John Jacob Halsted, is currently a student at Yale University, which, as you may know, is in the town of New

Haven. I won't say he is the ideal young man. His parents lavished too much money on him and have not brought him up as strictly as I would have liked. He is my youngest sister's only child, born to her late in life, which always results in spoiling the child in my observation. I would describe him as a dilettante, a lightweight – weak, but not essentially bad.'

'So why do the police think that he is involved in these crimes? Do they have any evidence?'

She sighed. 'Unfortunately, they have strong evidence. His parents bought him a rather stylish new automobile. Quite unsuitable and far too extravagant. This vehicle was found, crashed into a tree, in the Bronx, just off the main road between New York and Connecticut, on the morning after these robberies took place. My nephew is, apparently, a friend of Harry Silverton, the son of the family that was robbed that night, and his car was spotted driving away from the Silverton mansion just before midnight. It wasn't until dawn next day that the family discovered so many valuable items missing and their butler lying on the floor in a pool of blood, shot through the heart.'

'But all that doesn't prove that your nephew committed these crimes.'

'Ah,' she said. 'There's the rub. Under the seat in the car the police found a silver mustard dish, identified as one taken from the house. There was no sign of John Jacob, or the rest of the loot.'

'So they assume he has run off with it?'

'They have been looking for him for four days now, without success. His picture is plastered across the front pages of all the newspapers in the area. It is possible, of course, that he was injured in the crash. There was blood found at the scene. Maybe some kindly soul has taken him in, not realizing he is a wanted man. Maybe he wandered into the marshes and died. It is a desolate area, I understand, and it was a bitterly cold night.' She sighed again. 'Why he was driving toward New York I have no idea. Unless he was paying a surprise visit to his parents, who live just off Fifth Avenue, near the park.'

She broke off as the maid appeared with a coffee tray.

'You may open the drapes a little, Matilda,' she said. 'I don't want you spilling coffee on the rug.'

Matilda obeyed without a word and we sat in silence as cups were poured for us. I was unprepared for how haggard the old woman looked. I could see that her eyes were red and I suspected she might have been crying. Of course I pretended not to notice and sipped my coffee until the maid departed again. As soon as she had gone, Miss Van Woekem put down her coffee cup and glared at me. 'It is driving me mad, Miss Murphy. I need to know the truth. I am old, my dear. I may not live much longer but I can't die with this scandal and shame hanging over my head. I want my mind to be at peace with this matter. While I could believe that my nephew could have been sucked into a harebrained get-rich-quick scheme, I cannot believe that he would ever be involved in common robbery or violence. He is just not the type for it. Always a gentle boy at heart.'

'You say he is weak. What if he was led into it by a more forceful character?'

'We are an old and proud New York family, Miss Murphy. One of the four hundred, here since the time this city was called New Amsterdam. I believe in the end his family background and his upbringing would not allow him to let us down in this way.'

She was looking at me with imploring eyes. 'Will you not help me? I have come to admire your resourcefulness and your pluck. If anyone can come to the truth, it is you, my dear.'

'You flatter me,' I said. 'Most of the cases I've solved have been more through luck than skill.'

'Then it is that luck that I need,' she said. 'The luck of the Irish – that's what they say, don't they?'

I chose my words carefully. 'Miss Van Woekem, I would love to help you, but a case that would take me out of the city and as far as New Haven? That would involve time that I just don't have. I'm committed to being at the theater every evening for the foreseeable future, and I have other commitments as well.'

'Captain Sullivan then? Can you not persuade him to work for me? I am not a poor woman, Miss Murphy. I will make it worth your while. Find my nephew, clear his name, and you can set yourselves up in style when you marry.' She leaned forward again. 'You do still want to marry the captain, don't you?'

'I'm not completely sure yet whether I want to marry at all,' I said. 'To tell you the truth, I don't like the thought of being under the thumb of some man for the rest of my life. It seems to me that women are expected to surrender all freedom and individuality when they become wives.'

'Well said, Miss Murphy.' She clapped her hands and actually looked pleased. 'I knew you were a woman after my own heart. I had offers of my own, you know. I was no beauty but not plain, either, and I came with a good-sized fortune. But all of those suitors wanted to place me in a gilded cage. They wanted to protect me and advise me as if they were to be my father and not my husband. I never found a man who would take me on as his equal so I never married.'

'Sometimes I yearn for security,' I confessed. 'I have no money of my own and it's not easy living from hand to mouth most of the time. And I suppose I do love Daniel, but he has distinctly old-fashioned ideas about marriage. He'd never let me have a career if I married him and I'm not at all sure I want to stay at home and die of boredom.'

'Then it's fortunate you don't have to rush into it,' she said, eyeing me so intensely that I wondered if she had any inkling of what I had gone through a few months earlier. 'Maybe if you and the good captain work together on proving my nephew's innocence, he'll see what a waste it would be to lock you in your little gilded cage.' She reached out and grabbed my hand with her long bony fingers. 'You will approach him for me, won't you? You'll bring him to see me? You won't desert me in my hour of need?'

It was like being held in the bony grasp of a skeleton.

Seventeen

I stood in Gramercy Park with John Jacob Halsted's photograph in my hands, along with fifty dollars that Miss Van Woekem had pressed upon me to cover my expenses, taking deep breaths and trying to calm my racing thoughts. Why had I promised her that we would help her when I already had too much on my plate? I couldn't possibly jaunt up to Connecticut and back and neither could Daniel if he was supposed to be shadowing Mr Roth. I supposed I could conclude my investigation of the latter and report to the Mendelbaums that their future son-in-law was all that he claimed to be. But what if I had overlooked or failed to uncover some flaw? I didn't like to do shoddy work and I certainly didn't want to saddle the Mendelbaums' daughter with a less than perfect husband.

Maybe Daniel would have looked into his business and financial dealings today and I could report on those with confidence, I decided. Maybe he would even be home by now and I could brief him on Miss Van Woekem's problem. Since I was already in the area and Daniel's apartment was only just across town on Twenty-third, I caught the cross-town stage in his direction. It was still horse-drawn and painfully slow, but at least it saved my feet, on which I'd be standing later for much of a dress rehearsal.

To my annoyance Daniel wasn't home. I left him a long note, detailing everything Miss Van Woekem had told me and suggesting that he call on her in the morning to offer his services. So now it looked as if I'd just have time to squeeze in a visit to my silent girl in the hospital before I reported for duty at the theater.

My feet were beginning to drag as I walked along the side of Central Park to the hospital. The snow in this area had not been completely cleared away and it was hard going slithering over the icy surface. My feet dragged even more as I made my way up the steps to the hospital ward where she lay. I was hoping against hope for some kind of improvement, and also hoping to find Dr Birnbaum with her. I came into the ward and found a young fresh-faced nurse in the process of stripping the girl's bed.

'What happened to the young woman who was in this bed?' I asked, my heart beating faster. 'The one who couldn't talk.'

'I couldn't say, miss,' the nurse said, not looking up from her task. 'I was just told to strip this bed and that's what I'm doing.'

'Gone,' said a voice from across the ward, and I looked up to see an old woman staring at me. 'They came and took her.'

'Who did? Her family?'

'Men,' the old woman said darkly. 'Men in uniforms. Carted her off, they did. That's what they do when you can't pay. Cart you off.'

'I'm sure she was just being transferred to another hospital,' the nurse said quickly. 'We don't just abandon people in the snow, you know. This is the twentieth century. I could find out for you—'

'How long ago was this?' I asked the old woman, hearing my voice echo down the length of the ward, louder than I expected.

'Not long.'

I didn't wait to hear any more. I ran, my feet clattering down those tiled hallways. Down the steps at breakneck pace. I heard nurses yelling at me, but I didn't stop. Out at the front entrance I paused and looked around. Nothing. Life on the street proceeding in its usual tranquil manner. I rushed inside again and grabbed a surprised nurse. 'Is there another entrance – where the ambulances come?'

'Next to the casualty room, at the back.'

I broke into a mad run again. The hospital was a maze of hallways and I began to feel as if I were in one of those nightmares when you try to escape and can't. Then I saw it. A stretcher being carried down the hall in front of me.

'Stop!' I shouted. 'Wait.'

I put in a final sprint to catch up with it and found that I was staring down at a man with one eye closed, bleeding profusely from a head wound. He was moaning piteously and staff were already rushing to his aid.

'I'm sorry,' I muttered. 'I'm looking for someone else. A girl. Have you seen a girl being brought this way?'

They ignored me. I squeezed past them, out through the double doors and into the street. It was a narrow back alley, not at all fancy like the streets in this neighborhood. A windowless wagon, rather like those the police used, was drawn up outside. An empty wheelchair was standing beside it. A man was just about to climb into the driver's seat.

'Wait!' I shouted. 'Did you just pick up a young woman?'

'That's right.'

'And where are you taking her?'

'Ward's Island, miss.'

'Ward's Island?'

'To the hospital there where they can take care of her properly.'

'Holy Mother of God. That's – that's a lunatic asylum, isn't it?'

'That's right, miss.'

'Thank God I got here in time,' I said, the words spilling out between my gasps for breath. 'I'm her sister. We've just discovered where she was and I've come to take her home.'

The man looked worried. 'I don't know about that, miss. I've got my orders here.'

'They were only sending her to Ward's Island because they couldn't locate her family,' I said. 'And now I'm here. I've come to take her home.'

'I'm not sure, miss.' The man scratched his head and glanced up at his pal, already sitting at the front of the wagon, holding the horse's reins.

'You have to let me take her,' I said. 'She belongs at home, with us. She's not insane, you know. She's just lost the power of speech. With our loving care, I know it will come back.'

He was staring at me, his head cocked to one side. 'I've got my orders here,' he repeated.

'Let me see her,' I said. 'I know she'll recognize me.'

'Very well, I suppose.' He went around to the back of the wagon and opened the door. The girl was strapped to a gurney, trussed up like a chicken, staring out with terrified eyes. I climbed up and stood over her.

'It's her,' I said with what I hoped was conviction. 'It's our dear Mary, who we thought was dead.' I put my hand on her arm. 'It's all right, my love. I've come to take you home.' Without asking I started to untie the bonds that held her. As soon as she could sit up she clung to me, making little animal noises – the first sounds I had heard her make.

'Hey, stop that,' the man called, clambering up beside me. 'You've no right . . .' He yanked at my arm.

'You see. She knows me,' I said. 'Now please, let me take her home. If it was your sister, you wouldn't want her taken away to a place like Ward's Island, would you? Not when she could be safely home with her family.'

He finally agreed. 'I suppose not, miss.'

I opened my purse and took out my notebook, tearing out a page. 'Look, I'll write you a note, saying that her family arrived in the nick of time to collect her. That's all they cared about in there, you know. The hospital didn't want to be stuck with a destitute girl.'

I started to scribble. It wasn't easy with the girl clinging to my arm. When I had finished writing I reached into my purse. I just happened to have a dollar bill in it. I handed it to him with the note. 'And this is to thank you for your trouble,' I said.

He glanced at the dollar then up at me. I could see the wheels turning inside his head. Would he get into trouble if it got out that he was accepting a bribe?

While he was thinking, I undid the last of the straps that held her legs. She tried to stand but she was too weak. Besides, she was only wearing a flannel nightgown and she was barefoot. I took the blanket from the gurney and wrapped it around her shoulders.

'Can you lift her down for me? I'll borrow the wheelchair until I can find a cab.'

He did so and I pushed her off at a great rate, before he could change his mind. Then I flagged down a passing cab and had the cabbie lift her inside. She clutched at my hand as the cab took off. It was the second time in one day that someone had squeezed my hand almost hard enough to break it.

'What have I done now?' I said out loud.

The cabbie was a good sort and helped me carry the girl to my house. I opened the front door and got her inside, placing her in my one armchair. Then, of course, I had no idea what to do next. I was due at the theater any minute and I couldn't risk leaving her alone. She was staring at me with frightened eyes.

'You'll be just fine now,' I said, stroking her hair. 'You're safe with me. I'll make us a nice cup of tea.'

As soon as I put the kettle on the stove, I ran across the street and hammered on Sid and Gus's door, praying that they would be home. They were.

'Molly, my sweet. We're just in the middle of our Japanese lesson,' Gus said. 'I can now say "Do you like chrysanthemums" in Japanese. Most useful when we go there, don't you think?'

'I'm sorry to interrupt, but I desperately need your help,' I said. I tried to explain what I had done but the words just spilled out in a jumble.

'Hold on a moment.' Sid raised her hand. 'Calm down, Molly. We can't make head or tail of what you are saying. Are you trying to tell us that you kidnapped someone?'

'A girl,' I said. 'The girl I found in the snow. She still can't speak and they were going to send her to the lunatic asylum. So what else could I do? I pretended to be her sister and whisked her here. But now I'm due at the theater in a few minutes and I simply can't leave her alone, so I wondered if you'd keep an eye on her until I get back.'

Sid looked at Gus and gave a dramatic sigh. 'Life is never dull when you are around, is it, Molly, my sweet?'

'I'm so sorry. I know I acted rashly, but I couldn't let that poor girl go to Ward's Island, could I? I've heard what those places are like.'

'No, I suppose you did the only thing you could,' Sid said. 'But what now, Molly? What if she never recovers? What if she turns out to be a violent lunatic? What if you never trace her family?'

'Dr Birnbaum will work with her. He's promised to do so. I know he'll restore her speech and her sanity. I just know it,' I said, trying not to let my own doubts show. 'And with loving care and good food, she'll be as right as rain.'

'I hope so,' Sid said. 'Well, you know you can count on us. It will be a challenge to help to break through her silence, won't it, Gus? And you know how we love challenges.'

She gave me an encouraging smile. Somewhere in the distance I heard a clock striking the hour of four.

'The only thing is that right now I'm in a terrible rush,' I said. 'I'm due onstage at the theater soon.'

'Onstage? At the theater?' Now they really looked interested.

'It's too complicated to explain now. Another assignment. Come over and let me introduce you to the girl, if you don't mind. I don't know her name but I'm calling her Mary, because it's hard not calling her anything.'

I brought Sid and Gus into my living room. The girl started with fear when she saw them, but she didn't attempt to move, staring at them wide-eyed as they came toward her. They crouched beside her, stroking her hands and talking gently until I saw the fear leave her face. I made a pot of tea and handed her a cup. She looked puzzled, but then took a tentative sip. Soon she was drinking with gusto.

'I'll be back soon,' I said, in the hope that she could understand me. 'Until then you're in good hands with these ladies.'

Then I rushed out, already late for my costume fitting at the theater.

As I alighted from the trolley on Broadway, the newsboys were hawking the evening edition of the newspaper. 'Read all about it,' a scrawny little chap was shrieking in his high-pitched voice. 'Phantom haunts theater. Blanche Lovejoy's life threatened by theater ghost.'

'Jesus, Mary, and Joseph,' I muttered. It seemed as if Lily had been wined and dined sufficiently to spill the beans last night. I didn't fancy facing Miss Lovejoy.

Eighteen

I could hear Miss Lovejoy's strident voice booming through the vast expanse of backstage as I came in through the stage door and signed the book. She had definitely seen the evening papers by the sound of it.

'Trouble tonight, Henry,' I muttered.

He nodded. 'She came in with a face fit to curdle cream. If she finds out who let the cat out of the bag then one understudy better be ready to go on tonight. It couldn't have come at a worst time, with opening night only two days away.'

As I went up the stairs to report to Miss Lovejoy, I encountered her storming down the hallway.

'When I find out, I'll kill 'em,' she was screaming. She broke off when she saw me. 'Oh, it's you at last, is it? About time you showed up. You've seen, I suppose? All over the town. Couldn't be worse.' She wagged a threatening finger in my face. 'Who told the newspapers? I want you to find out which of them it was. I'm paying you to be my detective. You damned well better find out for me.'

'It may not have been anyone in the cast,' I said. 'At least not deliberately. There have been reporters hanging around the stage door every night. Perhaps they managed to overhear conversations. The girls were pretty upset when they came out of the theater last night.'

'I suppose so,' she said grudgingly. 'But it's your fault. I thought you'd have found out something by now. I'm paying you to find out whether it really is a ghost that's haunting me.'

'I'm not a miracle worker,' I said. 'I kept my eyes and ears open last night. I ran to investigate as soon as that wind started and nobody was there.'

'So it is a ghost. It has to be a ghost,' she said, giving the most dramatic shuddering sob. 'I knew it. The theater is cursed. My play is cursed. I'm ruined, ruined.' She started to walk down the hallway at a great pace. I had to break into a trot to keep up with her. 'I should have hired a spiritualist to begin with. Someone who knows how to communicate with spirits. A spiritualist could find out why the ghost hates me so, what I have done that it wants to bring about my ultimate destruction.' Her voice was loud enough to be heard in the back row of the upper balcony. 'We should find out who has died recently and died bearing a grudge against me.'

I tapped her on the shoulder as we came to the staircase. 'So does that mean you no longer require my services?'

'What?' She turned back to me as if she was surprised to find me there.

'You say you're going to hire a spiritualist to contact the ghost. So you no longer need me?'

'I suppose I still want you onstage, close to me,' she said. 'I need someone to protect me.'

'I can't protect you from a ghost,' I said. 'And I don't actually believe in ghosts myself. I'd like enough time to prove that your accidents are not caused by a spirit but by a real human who carries a grudge against you.'

'If only that were true.' She clasped her bosom. 'But who could that be? Everyone adores me.'

I didn't mention that half her chorus was not too fond of her, for a start.

'So you want me to go up to Madame Eva for my costume fitting, I take it?'

'Of course. Dress rehearsal at seven, as scheduled. The show must go on.' This was said loudly as several cast members were coming up the stairs. Then in a lower voice she said to me, 'But first run down to the stage door and see if a package was delivered to Henry for me.'

I went back down and the package was there. As I carried it up to Blanche's dressing room, I heard the chink of bottles inside. Blanche was obviously going to bolster her confidence with her calming mixture and with bourbon.

Madame Eva must have been a miracle worker. She had a costume more or less finished. It was a black-and-white gingham skirt, a white blouse, and a big black bow to be tied at my neck. I put it on while she clucked and fussed around me, pinning furiously, poking at my lack of a corset and muttering, 'Such a large waist. Well, there's nothing I can do about that.'

Finally, she helped me out of the skirt. 'Come back in one hour. It will be ready,' she said. 'And here are your wig and spectacles. Don't lose them.'

I left the wardrobe room and stood alone in the narrow hallway. I had an hour before I could pick up my costume, so I figured I should put that hour to good use. I combed every inch of the backstage area, trying to find places where someone could hide. I even hoisted my skirts and climbed a ladder up into the flies – that area high above the stage where backdrops and scene changes can be raised or lowered. I didn't fancy walking out across the narrow, precarious walkways, but I saw that there were plenty of opportunities for someone with a good head for heights to stand directly above the actors. I should bear that in mind.

I made my way to the dressing room feeling somewhat daunted. It was so dark and gloomy back there, so many corners bathed in shadow, so many nooks and crannies for someone to hide, waiting to commit mischief. Now if I could just find out who might want to do so . . .

I jumped a mile as a hand clasped onto my shoulder. I spun around to see Desmond Haynes standing right behind me, glaring at me with those dark, intense eyes.

'And just what do you think you are doing?' he asked.

'Me? I'm just having a look around,' I said.

'Having a look around, are you?' He snorted. 'You want to be careful, little girl. Theaters are not safe places. I don't know why Blanche was persuaded to hire you. It's not like her to go soft. But take this as a gentle warning. Do your job and stay out of trouble.'

'Maybe I should say the same to you, Mr Haynes,' I said. I stared him straight in the eye.

For a moment we stood there, his fingers digging into my shoulder. Then he released me. 'You should learn to be polite to me if you ever want to work again,' he said icily. 'Old friendships only stretch so far in this business.'

I came away shaken. Desmond Haynes was definitely upset by my presence. Was I finally on the right track?

An hour later I was in the dressing room with the rest of the girls, putting on my makeup.

'So you managed to buy your own greasepaint,' Elise said.

'No, I didn't have to. Luckily Oona had some to spare.'

A wistful look came over Elise's face. 'So it's true what they're saying, that you're Oona Sheehan's cousin?'

'Of course,' I said. 'How else do you think I'd have been given a little part in the play?'

'It must be nice.' She sighed. 'The rest of us have to fight for any part that's going, and sometimes do things we'd rather not, just to be hired.'

I finished my toilette and put on the black wig and then the spectacles. It was amazing how different they made me look. With the pigtails and the girlish costume, I didn't look much older than twelve.

At that moment the call boy announced overture and beginners. I made my way down to the stage with the rest of the girls. There was more tension in the air than the night before and whispered speculation about what might happen. The first act started and I noticed that the girls were decidedly alert, glancing around nervously as they sang and danced. But the whole act passed without incident. I was still busy making sure I stood on my exact mark each time and made my entrances and exits at the right moment. As the second act started, everyone was more relaxed. The chorus ran off stage at the end of the bathing scene and rushed up the steps to change into the ball costumes for the finale. I didn't have to change for the ball, so I stood behind the scenery in the wings, watching and waiting.

It was the big love scene between Miss Lovejoy's character and Arthur, the penniless painter. Just the two of them alone on-stage, singing one of the more memorable songs called 'Just Two People.' The scene was an arbor overlooking the ocean, with a small table covered in a red-and-white-checked cloth, on which were set a jug of lemonade and glasses. Miss Lovejoy was standing on one side of the table with Arthur across from her when suddenly the most amazing thing happened. The jug of lemonade leaped up in the air, came flying toward Miss Lovejoy and hurled lemonade all over her.

Miss Lovejoy screamed. Everyone came running, trying to calm her and wipe away the liquid from her face and the front of her dress.

'Now you have to believe it!' she was screaming. 'I told you it was a ghost but nobody believed me.'

Robert Barker came flying onto the stage, out of breath. 'Blanche, my love. Are you all right?'

'You saw it, didn't you, Bobby?' she shrieked. 'Everybody saw it. I'm not imagining things. Something hurled that jug of lemonade at me. Well, that's it. I'm not opening the show on Tuesday. I'm going to go home to Connecticut and forget about the whole damned thing.'

She rushed off the stage with Robert hot on her heels. At the edge of the stage he turned back to the rest of us, who were standing white-faced and open-mouthed. 'Don't worry,' he said. 'It's all going to be okay, I promise. I'll talk to her. The show will open as planned.'

As the other actors stood around in tight knots, whispering about what they had just seen, I went over to the table and examined it carefully. I picked up the jug, which had broken from the fall. There was nothing unusual about it. I looked carefully for a string or thread that could have jerked it off the table, but there was none. I searched the backstage area but there was nowhere close enough for anyone to have stood and made that jug move.

I was afraid I was beginning to agree with Blanche. Maybe it was time to call in a spiritualist.

Nineteen

By the time I got home, Sid and Gus had put my mystery girl to bed in what had been the O'Conner children's bedroom.

'We brought over some beef stew that we'd had last night,' Sid said. 'She seemed to enjoy it. Tucked right in.'

'Did she seem to understand you?' I asked.

'She understood that she was being fed good food,' Gus said, 'but as to whether she understood what we were saying to her, I couldn't say. We tried hard enough. We tried every language we could think of. I even tried my Japanese phrases although one can see that she is not from the Orient. We told her our names. Sid sang to her.'

'But she didn't say anything?'

'Not a word.'

I shook my head as I looked down at her. 'I hope we can find a way to get through to her. I'll visit Dr Birnbaum in the morning. If anyone can break through this veil of silence, he can.'

'How do we know she is not mute, or witless?' Sid asked.

'Dr Birnbaum says that she has the ability to speak but he believes that some great trauma has robbed her of her speech. He has seen similar cases in the hospital in Vienna where he worked with Dr Freud.'

'Dr Sigmund Freud?' Sid asked. 'I've been reading about

him. He is doing fascinating work on dreams and the subconscious mind. He claims we can suppress our innermost desires and fears but they are revealed in our dreams. Gus and I were going to keep dream diaries, weren't we, dearest?'

'We were, but we never got around to it. We always have too many projects,' Gus said. 'There are so many fascinating things to do in life that there simply isn't time for all of them.'

We tiptoed downstairs again.

'I'll look for books on the study of the mind tomorrow,' Sid said. 'Maybe we can help free the poor girl from her current prison. If only we could get her to jot down her dreams.'

'And sign language. We can teach her to communicate through signs,' Gus added excitedly. 'I'm sure there are books on communicating with the deaf and dumb.'

'But she hears, dearest.'

'But she doesn't speak, does she?'

As I bade goodnight to them I couldn't help thinking that I had never encountered such lively minds. Those males who think that we women are incapable of more than sewing and gossip should be forced to spend a day in the company of Sid and Gus.

In the middle of the night I was awoken by a horrible noise. I leaped out of bed and ran across the landing to the spare bedroom. The girl was apparently still fast asleep but was giving the most piteous moans.

I perched on the bed beside her. 'What is it, my dear?' I asked gently. 'Tell me what is frightening you.'

At this she began to thrash about wildly as if trying to ward off some evil. I had been raised in the Catholic church but had never given much credence to either God or the Devil. I couldn't believe that babies who died unbaptized would never go to heaven, or that people like myself, who slipped from the straight and narrow once in a while, would be condemned to hell. But as I watched her, I found myself wondering if she might, indeed, be possessed by the devil and that the person I should send for in the morning should be a priest rather than Dr Birnbaum.

I stroked her hair and spoke soothingly to her. 'It's all right, my love. You are safe now. Nothing can harm you here. The doors are locked. I'll protect you.'

Gradually the thrashing and moaning stopped and she drifted back into peaceful sleep. Which was more than could be said for me. I was already wound as tight as a watch spring from the jug-of-lemonade incident I had witnessed and I was just beginning to realize what a foolish, impetuous thing I had done by bringing the girl home here. If she was subject to such torments, then surely she couldn't be left alone, and I couldn't impose on Sid and Gus to watch her every time I had to go out. With no chance of going to sleep, I got up and wrote a list of things I should be doing next.

1. Dr Birnbaum. He may know a clinic that would admit her.
2. Mrs Goodwin. She might have discovered the girl's identity by now.
3. Daniel. He will have to bear the brunt of Miss Van Woekem's case.
4. Mr Roth. Try to conclude as soon as possible to give me more time for the happenings at the theater.

At least I wasn't going to be bored in the next days.

I must have drifted off to sleep in the early hours because I was woken by the sound of church bells. It took me a moment to realize that it must be Sunday. I got up and peeked into my girl's bedroom. She was lying there looking so still and peaceful that for a moment I feared she might be dead. But then I saw her bodice rise and fall in a gentle breath. My heart went out to her. Somehow she had become trapped in a nightmare world and I had to find a way to help her escape.

I dressed, made a pot of tea, and then took her up a breakfast tray with a boiled egg and the thin strips of bread and butter we used to call soldiers when I was a child. She woke, sat up, and ate like an obedient child. I talked to her all the time she was eating. 'Today Dr Birnbaum will be coming to help you. He is a nice doctor and he will try to get to the bottom of what is distressing you.'

If she understood, she gave no indication of it but dipped the bread into the egg yolk and took the strips mechanically to her mouth. After I had my own breakfast, I wrote a note to Dr Birnbaum, explaining the circumstances, and found an urchin by the Jefferson Market building to deliver it for a nickel. Fortunately, I didn't have long to wait for my reply. Dr Birnbaum arrived in person, looking even more dapper than usual with a gold stick pin in his neckerchief.

'My dear Miss Murphy.' He clicked his heels and jerked a little bow. 'I came immediately when I received your message. You say you have brought the girl to this very house?'

'I had to,' I said. 'They were about to send her to the insane asylum on Ward's Island and I couldn't let that happen.'

'But this is most irregular,' he said. 'This could be construed as kidnapping, you know.'

'I had no choice, Doctor. You don't believe she is insane, do you?'

'I believe she is out of her senses at this present moment, which may be the same thing. But I strongly hope that she may have a chance of recovering those senses, given the right treatment.'

157

'Which she wouldn't get at an insane asylum. They'd lock her up with mad people and she would be lost for ever.'

He nodded gravely. 'I fear that may be true. But what do you plan to do with her? You can't keep her for ever.'

'Did you place the advertisement in the newspapers as you said you would?'

'I did. Immediately after we parted company.'

'Then we may get a response as soon as tomorrow. Surely she has someone who is worried about her disappearance and will want her home again.'

'Let us hope so.'

'And in the meantime, I was hoping that you would be able to work with her until progress is made. You said that you are an expert in such conditions.'

'Hardly an expert. Nobody, not even Dr Freud, counts as an expert when dealing with the complexity of the mind. We are constantly making new discoveries, each more perplexing than the one before. I may well be going against the ethics of my profession by treating this girl in a place where she has no right to be.' He paused, stroking his beard; then before I could say anything he continued, 'But I must admit that our little friend challenges me. I shall write to Dr Freud for his opinion, and until her family is located I shall do what I can.'

'Can you see her today?' I asked. 'She is awake and has just had a good breakfast.'

'I was on my way to church,' he said. 'But I'm sure I can find a later mass, if I put my mind to it.'

'You're a Catholic? You go to mass?' I was amazed.

'What is so strange about that, Miss Murphy? Are you not one yourself?'

'I was raised in that religion. I no longer practice it. But I should have thought that a man of science, like yourself, would have little use for any kind of religion.'

'On the contrary. In my profession I am constantly reminded of the frailty of life and the power of prayer. And the existence of miracles.'

'So tell me, Doctor,' I said hesitantly, 'is it possible that she is possessed by the Devil? Last night she moaned piteously in her sleep and thrashed about as if in the clutches of something truly terrible.'

He looked at me kindly. 'I should say that the likelihood is that she has been in the clutches of something truly terrible. Some kind of assault.'

'But we were told that she was not badly hurt physically and hadn't been assaulted.'

'Let us still put the Devil as a less likely cause of her condition. If she will allow me to hypnotize her, then I may be able to persuade her to reveal her secret.' He placed his cane and his hat on the chair, then removed his overcoat. 'Very well, lead me to her.'

The girl reacted with fear as I ushered Dr Birnbaum into the room.

'It's all right, Mary,' I said. 'This man is a doctor. He's come to help you.'

'You've discovered her name?'

'I'm afraid not. I call her Mary because I have to call her something.'

He nodded, then pulled up a chair beside the bed. 'Mary, you and I are going to have a little chat.'

'I'll leave you to it,' I said, but the girl reached over and grabbed my hand, holding me as if she were lost in an ocean and I was her lifeline.

'All right. I'll stay. Nothing bad is going to happen to you,' I said. I sat at the bottom of the bed where she could see me. I glanced up at the doctor. 'It's so hard when we don't know if she can understand us.'

'Mary,' Dr Birnbaum said quietly. 'Blink your eyes if you hear me and understand me.'

The eyes sort of twitched, but you couldn't call it a proper blink.

'I take that as a confirmation,' Dr Birnbaum said. 'But you observed that she was trying not to blink. It may be that her conscious mind is attempting to block all communication with other people. If only I can succeed in hypnotizing her, I am sure some of these layers of resistance will fall away.' He reached into his pocket and took out his watch, which he then dangled in front of Mary's face. 'It's a pretty thing, isn't it, my dear?' he said. 'And listen. It has a charming tone to it.' He pressed a knob on the side and the watch immediately struck ten with a sweet, bell-like sound. Mary almost smiled.

'Now, young lady. I want you to keep your eyes on my pretty watch. Keep looking at it as it goes back and forth, back and forth.' He started to swing the watch gently in front of her face, all the while talking in a soft, monotonous voice. 'Your eyes are getting heavy. You are falling asleep.'

I don't know how well it was working on Mary, but I found myself drifting off. I shook myself awake with a jerk. Mary appeared to be lying there peacefully with her eyes closed.

'Can you tell us your real name?' he asked.

Silence. Her lips tried to mumble something but no sound came out.

'And where do you come from? Tell me about your home. Is your mother there? Your father?'

It seemed a spasm of pain crossed her face.

'Does she understand you, do you think?' I whispered.

Birnbaum held up a warning finger to me.

'Your parents are no longer with us, I suspect. So who looks after you now? With whom do you live? I want you to picture yourself at home, my dear. See your room. Your bed. Now the kitchen. Food on the table. Good food.' Dr Birnbaum talked on. She lay there, not resisting but not answering, either. It was impossible to tell whether she understood him or not but definitely the tone of his voice was getting to her. 'That night, my little one. Something happened to you that night. Where are you? Take yourself back. You go out in your pretty dress and shoes. Were you wearing a cape? It was cold. You are expecting a nice evening, a party, a theater – but something happens. Something goes wrong. Somebody comes.'

I saw her suddenly go rigid. Then her hands came up in front of her, jerking like puppet arms. She was fighting to push somebody or something away. Those horrible animal noises came out of her mouth.

'Who is it?' Dr Birnbaum demanded. 'Who do you see? What are they doing to you?'

Then through her torment I thought I heard a word. It was part of a tiny childish cry, a small whimpered word amid the moans, but I could have sworn she said 'Annie.'

'Annie?' I asked, forgetting that it was Dr Birnbaum who had her under his spell. 'Is that your name? Annie?'

The thrashing became so intense and the moans so piteous that Dr Birnbaum put his hand firmly on her shoulder. 'When I count to three and snap my fingers you will wake up. One. Two. Three.'

He snapped his fingers. The moans stopped as if they had been switched off and she opened her eyes, looking confused.

'Annie?' Dr Birnbaum asked gently. 'Is that your name? Annie?'

But her face registered no recognition.

'That is enough for the first time, I think,' he said.

'So she understood you?'

'That I can't tell yet,' Dr Birnbaum said. 'But the tone of my voice certainly opened her subconscious mind and unlocked the terrible event for a moment. As you saw, what happened to her is too terrible for her to confront, even in her memories. I cannot think what it could be. We must approach it cautiously or it may drive her over the edge for ever.'

He took out a little notebook. 'I will write a prescription for a sedative. I think sleep may just be the best medicine for her at the moment.'

I went to tuck in the sheets and blankets that she had kicked off and recoiled when I saw her feet. The nurses had obviously bandaged them, but she had partially kicked off the bandages. Her poor toes were bruised and bloody. She must have suffered frostbite, walking in those delicate shoes through the snow. I wondered how far she had walked. She had come from the north. How far north, I wondered. From the swank area near the park or beyond, in the not-so-respectable area of Harlem? It was possible that she had been brought to the park in a vehicle of some kind and then left there to die. If she had gone there on her own two feet, why? And where was she heading when she collapsed?

I put the bandages back in place and tucked the blankets around her feet again. Maybe the next day's post would bring us some clues.

Twenty

As we were coming downstairs, there was a loud knock at my front door, then I heard it opening and Daniel's voice calling from the hallway, 'Molly? Where are you?'

'Upstairs,' I shouted back. 'I'll be down right away.'

I hadn't thought about how strange it must look to see me coming downstairs with Dr Birnbaum at my heels, but I read it instantly in Daniel's surprised face.

'Hello, Daniel,' I said brightly. 'Dr Birnbaum has been visiting my patient upstairs.'

'Your patient?'

'The girl from the snowdrift. I brought her here in the hopes that Dr Birnbaum can restore her speech and her sanity.'

'You brought her here?' Daniel's impressive eyebrows rose. 'As if you don't have enough on your plate right now without looking after invalids.'

'I realize that,' I said, 'but I had little alternative. I had to stop them from carting her off to the lunatic asylum.'

Daniel shook his head. 'Molly, sometimes I despair of you. The word *sensible* just isn't part of your vocabulary. What were you thinking? We know nothing about this girl and you are certainly not in any way equipped to take care of someone who may very well prove to be insane.'

'With all respect, Captain Sullivan, I don't believe so,' Dr Birnbaum said. 'I have just tried hypnosis on the young woman and I think I can verify that she led a normal life until some recent and grave trauma, the shock of which was so terrible that she has retreated from the present, blocked all memories, and is protecting herself by existing in a safe cocoon of not knowing. With patient and gentle care I think we may well be able to bring her back.'

'And in the meantime who is to pay for her food and her care?'

'I shall not charge for my services,' Dr Birnbaum said frostily.

'And I don't mind feeding her.'

'But who looks after her when you are rushing around doing the thousand and one other tasks to which you have committed yourself?' Daniel demanded.

'That is a wee bit of a problem,' I agreed, 'but let us hope it won't be for long. Dr Birnbaum has placed advertisements in the newspapers. We are hopeful that someone will be looking for her and glad to have her safely home.'

'And if not?'

'We'll cross that bridge when we come to it,' I said firmly. 'I have taken on this responsibility, Daniel, not you. It's up to me to handle it.'

I saw him frown, but he said nothing.

'And I should bid you farewell, Miss Murphy,' Dr Birnbaum said. 'If I hurry I will be in time for the next mass at St Joseph's and still be able to make a luncheon appointment with friends.' He gave his funny little bow.

'Thank you so much, Doctor. I know you're going to be able to help her.'

'We shall have to see,' he said cautiously. 'Until tomorrow, then.'

And he went.

Daniel was still frowning.

'Molly, what am I going to do with you?'

'Nobody is asking you to do anything with me,' I said, 'except cherish me, perhaps. Love me.'

'You know I do,' he said. 'But I can't help wanting to keep you from all these difficult situations you get yourself into. It's human nature, Molly. The man wants to protect the woman.'

'I don't need protecting, Daniel,' I said. 'At least not most of the time.' Then I grinned, the frown left his face, and he wrapped me in his arms.

'You really are the most infuriating woman, do you know that?'

'Possibly,' I said, 'but I'm glad you've come. You got my note about Miss Van Woekem?'

'I've already been to see that lady prior to coming to you,' Daniel said. 'I understand that you volunteered my services – as your employee, I gather.'

'I didn't put it like that,' I said, 'and anyway it was Miss Van Woekem who suggested that you might have time and expert knowledge to help her.'

'As it was she left me little chance to refuse,' he said. 'I thought that today, being Sunday, we might take a trip to New Haven together. It is a day on which one usually finds people at home.'

'I would love to,' I said, 'but—'

'But now you have a young woman upstairs who needs constant care. If you must have her here, Molly, then you'd better hire a nurse.'

'I suppose so,' I said, 'but I can't locate a good nurse on a Sunday, can I?'

'Your friends across the street, maybe?'

'And I can't keep asking them to do me favors. They lead very social lives.'

He sighed. 'I would have preferred not to go to New Haven alone. And I had hoped that, being Sunday, it would be the one night when you would not have commitments at that blasted theater.'

'Your language in my presence is becoming remarkably coarse,' I said primly. 'You sound like Blanche Lovejoy.'

'She swears, does she?' He was looking amused now.

'Like a trooper.'

'And have you come face-to-face with the ghost yet? I saw the headlines in the newspapers. The press is lapping it up, making it sound as if the whole theater is under a curse.'

'It's not funny, Daniel. As a matter of fact I did witness the ghost yesterday. A jug of lemonade leaped off the table, all over Miss Lovejoy, and I'm dashed if I can explain how it was done.'

'Nobody within reach to accidentally nudge the jug?'

'Only two actors on the stage and neither of them touching the table.'

'A piece of black twine, maybe? A quick jerk?'

'I examined the jug and the table for something like that. There was nothing.'

'I don't believe in ghosts, spirits, phantoms, or anything of that nature,' Daniel said. 'Keep looking. There will be a logical explanation.'

'In the meantime Miss Lovejoy left in hysterics and has threatened to close the show before it opens on Tuesday. She's furious with me because I haven't managed to apprehend the ghost yet.'

'Then you sound as if you need a day out. Could the girl be left, if you put out food for her?'

'I'd rather not,' I said. 'I'm not sure how steady she is on her feet. What if she wandered off again, or fell down the stairs?'

'Blast it,' Daniel said, slapping a fist into his palm. 'Isn't there anybody you could call upon?'

'Do you think your landlady would keep an eye on her?'

'I suppose she might,' Daniel agreed.

'We could take her in a cab, I suppose,' I said, 'but I hate to disturb her again when she is finally lying peacefully. I have to go to the dispensary and have a prescription filled for a sedative for her. Dr Birnbaum thinks that sleep is the best medicine at the moment.'

'That's it. Then she'll sleep all day,' Daniel said.

'Daniel, I can't leave her, even if she's asleep,' I said.

'Then how do you plan to go to the theater every night?'

'As you say, I'll have to find somebody. Maybe the woman who comes in to do Sid and Gus's ironing may know of someone. I'll ask them.'

As if on cue there was a light tap at the front door. My face lit up. 'That will be them now.' I ran to open it, but no Sid and Gus stood there, instead an austere figure in navy blue.

'Mrs Goodwin,' I exclaimed. 'How good of you to call. Come in, please.' I ushered her inside. 'Look who is here, Daniel. You know Mrs Goodwin, don't you?'

'Captain Sullivan,' she said evenly.

'Mrs Goodwin. How are you?'

I noticed the difference in the responses instantly. Daniel's was hearty, cordial, hers was restrained. Perhaps she still was not completely convinced that Daniel had had no part in the death of her husband at the hands of a gang. Or perhaps she was merely being deferential to a superior officer.

'I am well, thank you, Captain Sullivan,' she said. 'A little tired after several shifts on night duty.'

'I know how that can be,' Daniel said. 'In truth I long to be back with such inconveniences, rather than idling my hours away.'

'Has your situation not resolved itself yet?'

'And won't be as long as John Partridge is police commissioner. I'm afraid that men like him do not want to lose face by admitting that they made a mistake. At the moment I am still on suspension, pending an inquiry which will probably never happen.'

'That is too bad,' she said. 'Your fellow officers often speak of you and wish you were back among them.'

'Fortunately, Partridge may only be commissioner a few more weeks,' Daniel said, 'and one hopes his replacement will look upon my case more favorably.'

'Would you both like some tea?' I asked. 'I haven't yet acquired the skill to make coffee.'

'Tea would be most welcome, thank you.' Mrs Goodwin smiled at me. 'I've come straight from night duty, but I thought you'd probably want to know the results of my investigation for you.'

'Investigation?' Daniel looked at me inquiringly.

'To see if any missing girls matched the description of our patient.'

'Oh, of course. Good idea,' he said. 'And have you come up with anything?'

'I don't believe so. Not based on the description that Molly gave me.' She took out a notebook and started reading off names.

'Frieda Hupfer. German. Ran off with unsuitable young man. Believed heading for New York. Described as blond, five foot one, well padded.'

'That's not our girl,' I said. 'She is sleeping upstairs. Come and see for yourself.'

'You have her here now?'

'Molly agreed to look after her for a few days, since she could no longer stay in hospital,' Daniel said quickly before I could reply.

'That was most generous of you,' Mrs Goodwin said.

'I felt responsible for her, since I was the one who discovered her,' I said.

We tiptoed up and looked at the sleeping girl. As we came down again Mrs Goodwin shook her head. 'Then I'd say that none of the young women on this list is she.'

'We've placed an advertisement in the newspapers.' I poured boiling water into the teapot and set out cups and saucers. 'And tomorrow we can revise it with a name. She has lost the power of speech but in her moaning we are fairly sure that she said the name 'Annie.''

Mrs Goodwin scanned her list again. 'I have no lost girl called Annie on this list,' she said, 'but as I explained before, New York is a magnet. Girls from all over the country run away to the big city. This Annie could have started out in South Carolina or even California.'

'It seems rather hopeless to me,' Daniel said.

'I disagree,' I said. 'Think of how she was dressed. She was dressed for an evening out. Silk dress, dainty shoes. That is not the mark of a runaway, nor a destitute girl. And she must have started out with some kind of outer garment, given the cold. She couldn't have come too far wearing those shoes or they would have been completely ruined. As I see it, she was expecting a pleasant evening, something terrible happened, and she ran away. I still think that someone in New York is looking for her. I'm confident we'll locate her loved ones.'

'I'll naturally keep my ear to the ground for any more reports of missing persons,' Mrs Goodwin said, tucking her notebook back into her cape pocket. 'You've undertaken quite a task here, I should think, Molly.'

I placed cups of tea in front of them. 'I'm going to have to hire a nurse,' I said. 'I don't want to leave her alone and I can't be in the house all day. I don't suppose you know where I might find a suitable woman?'

'We could always ask my neighbor, Mrs Tucker,' she said. 'You met her when I was in that accident. She's an awfully fussy woman. She'll drive you crazy, but at least she is responsible and she likes to be useful.'

'I remember her,' I said. 'I'd be most grateful.'

'If she accepts, it will only take you a couple of days before you'll stop thanking me.' She chuckled. 'But at least she's honest. And she will take care of the poor girl. As soon as I finish my tea, we could go and ask her.'

Twenty-one

I left Daniel minding the sleeping girl and went with Mrs Goodwin to see her next-door neighbor. That good woman not only agreed to come back with me right away but insisted on bringing a pot of her freshly made soup with her as well. So I was able to go to the dispensary to have the prescription filled, then go with Daniel to New Haven.

I hadn't asked Mrs Tucker how much she would charge for acting as nursemaid. I tried not to think about it, reasoning that I had an advance from Miss Van Woekem and I was going to make quite good money from the three cases I was currently handling. Daniel was obviously thinking along the same lines because, as the train came out into bright winter sunshine after leaving the Grand Central station, he said, 'At least you'll be making enough to pay that woman's wages. We'd better hurry up and close your case with Mr Roth. I think we can safely say he is reliable and responsible, don't you?'

'What about his financial reputation? Did you have a chance to check on that yesterday?'

'It was Saturday and the banks closed at two, so I didn't manage to accomplish everything I set out to do, but all indications were that he was a decent young fellow.'

'I'm so glad,' I said.

Daniel glanced across at me with a smile on his face. 'Why should it matter to you if he is responsible or not?'

'I like to conclude my cases in a positive manner,' I said.

Daniel was still smiling. 'Molly, you want to put the world to rights, that's your problem. If you were with the police, like me, you'd learn that most of the time we don't have it in our power to fix things. The world is a sad and broken place.'

'Not for me,' I said. 'I'm going to continue believing that I can help, here and there.'

He patted my hand. 'Molly, the eternal optimist.'

We were rattling across the railway bridge that separates Manhattan Island from the area to the north known as the Bronx. There were signs of new housing developments springing up but the railway line soon veered off to the right and crossed a desolate stretch of marshland at the edge of Long Island Sound. Black channels wound between snow-covered flat stretches of marshland, with dried rushes sticking up along the banks and the occasional sorry-looking tree, bent by the prevailing wind. It presented a bleak, wild scene so close to the city. It made me shiver, just looking at it, and I found myself wondering if John Jacob Halsted had crashed his car anywhere near here and had wandered off to perish in this bleak expanse.

'I don't see the road,' I said. 'Does it also cross the marshes like this?'

'It goes farther inland to cross into Manhattan,' Daniel said, 'but it will join the train tracks later on and more or less skirt the coastline all the way across Connecticut.'

'I was wondering where Miss Van Woekem's nephew ran his motor car into a tree,' I said. 'If he hasn't turned up yet, it's possible he was dazed and wandered off into an inhospitable area like this one.'

'I'm sure the police would have noticed if any tracks led

away from the vehicle,' Daniel said, 'but that is certainly something we should investigate further. I'll see if I can persuade one of my acquaintances to lend us an automobile for a day. That way we could retrace the route he took.'

'It does seem strange, doesn't it? A student at Yale, from a rich family, one understands. Why would he want to steal, and especially why would he want to steal from a friend?'

'Sometimes privileged young men like that do things as a lark, or because they have drunk too much or experimented with some kind of drug.'

'But not shoot one of the servants in the process,' I said. 'That sounds more like a hardened criminal. And you don't really think he could be mixed up in the other robberies that have taken place along this route, do you? Breaking into a bank, robbing a pay wagon?'

'I don't know what to think,' Daniel said. 'I don't know the boy myself. But I do know that even the best families can produce a wrong 'un from time to time. Maybe he is weak and easily misled. Maybe he has run up terrible debts and was desperate to find a way to repay them.'

'I find it very perplexing,' I said. 'Especially as Miss Van Woekem described him as a gentle boy. Natures do not change however desperate one is. I do not think a gentle person could kill with so little thought.'

Daniel nodded. 'I tend to agree with you. Maybe he was not alone. He could have worked with a more violent partner. We'll just have to see what facts come to light today.'

We left the marshes behind and moved into more civilized countryside. Here the land was cultivated, tamed into fields with trees and hedges between them. Cows and horses stood in the snow around bales of hay. Smoke curled from the chimneys of solid farm houses. On our right we caught glimpses of the water. We passed icy ponds with skaters testing their luck.

Buggies were leaving white-spired churches. It was the land of Currier and Ives and I gazed at it with satisfaction. I had rarely been out of New York and I enjoyed these occasional forays into a world that I knew so little about.

The train stopped in one old brick town after another: Greenwich, Bridgeport, and at last we came into New Haven. My first impression, as we came out of the train station onto Union Street, was of a well-laid-out town of fine brick buildings, built around squares. On a Sunday it had a deserted feel to it, with closed shops and empty streets. One got the impression that the whole town was taking a snooze after a big Sunday lunch. There was little evidence of snow here and we walked with ease through the town, following the directions we had been given to Yale University.

Yale's ornate tower was unmistakable and we headed straight toward it. The university almost took my breath away, seeing it for the first time across a green park. The only equally impressive sight of my comparatively sheltered life had been my first views of Dublin and Trinity College. But these buildings, in their red hues of brick, were warmer and for some reason this made them seem older and more distinguished. Again the campus had a deserted feel to it, apart from the occasional student hurrying off with books tucked under one arm. We stopped a passing student and asked where John Jacob Halsted roomed. He looked at us with distaste, thinking us to be reporters or morbidly curious, no doubt.

'We're here on behalf of his family,' I added quickly and he directed us to a dormitory building. The porter at the door was equally hesitant to let us in to talk to the young men in residence, but relented when Daniel informed him that he was a police officer from New York City.

'Such a tragedy.' The old man shook his head. 'We were all stunned here, you know. I'd never have thought it of him.'

'So you wouldn't have classed him as a wild young man, who might do something impetuous and stupid like that?'

The porter's face became guarded. 'Impetuous and stupid, maybe. I remember once he accepted a bet to walk along the parapet of the library roof. He made it too and almost got himself expelled afterward. But that's the sort of thing one expects from students. It's just high spirits, isn't it? I've seen him come home the worse for wear, of course. And he has been caught trying to sneak in after curfew. But robbing and killing? That I can't see.'

'We are of the same opinion,' I said. 'May we have a chance to chat with some of his friends, do you think?'

The porter looked at me as if I were a talking parrot who had suddenly started spouting Shakespeare. 'This is a gentleman's hall of residence,' he said. 'Young women are not allowed upstairs.'

'I run the detective agency that is looking into Mr Halsted's disappearance for his family,' I couldn't resist saying.

'Detective agency. Fancy that.' The old man scratched his head. 'I suppose I can't stop the police from asking questions, but I'd have to get permission for a detective agency.' His face conveyed the unsaid 'especially one run by a woman.'

'Then I'll ask the questions,' Daniel said quickly, sensing that my Irish was in the process of being roused. 'It will save you from getting permission. Correct?'

'Right, sir. Much obliged to you.' His face registered relief. He pointed up a narrow staircase. 'Now if you go up to the third floor, turn left, you'll find the young gentleman's room is the last one on the left. The rooms on either side of his are occupied by his closest friends. From what I gather, they are as baffled as I am about this whole nasty business, but maybe one of them can tell you something that will help you with your inquiries. Although the New Haven police have certainly grilled us all enough already.'

'I don't intend to do any grilling,' Daniel said. 'Come, Molly.'

Now I was definitely annoyed. 'May I remind you that this is my inquiry and that you are aiding me?' I muttered as we mounted the creaky wooden stairs.

'You saw how it is.' Daniel turned to answer me. 'A lot of men don't respond well to questions from a woman. We're more likely to learn something if they think they are talking to someone official.'

'Then next time don't say "Come, Molly' as if I were your dog.'

'I apologize, Miss Murphy. Would you be good enough to accompany me up the stairs?' Daniel grinned as he glanced back at me. He thought the whole thing was amusing. I was beginning to think there was no getting through to men.

Twenty-two

There was a distinctive smell to the building – old wood, furniture polish, and a hint of pipe tobacco. It was an old sort of smell, of a building that has existed for a hundred years or more. The upstairs hallway was narrow, wood-paneled, and dark. We made our way along it to the far end.

'Let's see if Halsted's room is unlocked, first,' I suggested. 'He may have left a letter or note that could be a valuable clue.'

Good idea.' Daniel tried the door. It opened and we went inside. 'Although I'm sure the local police will have been through his room thoroughly by now.'

'That doesn't necessarily mean they haven't overlooked something.' I started going through the papers on his desk. He was remarkably tidy for a young man, or perhaps the police had tidied his papers after they had examined them. There were class notes on philosophy and religion. A couple of scribbled observations led me to believe that Mr Halsted wasn't entirely shallow and, like a lot of boys his age, was starting to think about the meaning of life. I found myself hoping that he was alive and safe somewhere and that there was a perfectly good explanation for the crashed motor car that didn't involve him in robbery and murder.

The top drawer of his desk showed his other side, the side that Miss Van Woekem disapproved of: programs from local horse races, theater tickets by the dozen. Judging by these, Mr Halsted didn't spend many evenings studying. Daniel had been going through various boxes. 'He seems to have more than his share of debts,' he commented, 'but that was to be expected from what Miss Van Woekem said. Tailor. Three new shirts. Wine merchant – he owes the wine merchant fifty dollars! And look at this – eighty dollars owed to a jeweler. It doesn't say what for.' He closed the box again. 'The police will take this as confirmation that he needed money badly and would go to any lengths to get some.'

'We don't know that he couldn't pay his bills,' I said. 'Maybe these were just the outstanding ones to be paid at the end of the month. He may have been given a generous allowance by his parents that allowed this sort of lifestyle.'

'That's true,' Daniel agreed. 'I should pay a call to his folks when we get back to New York – with your permission of course, ma'am.'

'Permission given.' We exchanged smiles.

Daniel went across to the wardrobe and opened it. 'He certainly has enough clothes,' he said. 'However, I don't see any evening wear. For someone who went out in the evening as often as he did, that's odd.'

'He may have been wearing it when he disappeared.'

'Of course. But that would imply that he didn't plan to go out with criminal pursuits on his mind, wouldn't it? A man in formal evening attire would certainly be noticed if he had to flee through the streets.'

I started going through his jacket pockets and unearthed a small diary. Most of the entries were prosaic in nature: 'Philos. essay due.' 'Tutorial with Hammersham 10 a.m.' 'Lunch with Brodart.' It was rather strange to read entries for this week, appointments that he hadn't been able to keep. I checked the night that he disappeared. 'A and J? Ask S?'

'I wonder who or what A and J are?' I said. 'S could be Silverton. Didn't Miss Van Woekem say that he was friends with Harry Silverton, the son of the family where the robbery took place?'

Daniel nodded. 'And his car was seen driving away from the Silverton mansion at midnight at great speed. We should go and interview the Silverton family when we are finished here. I'll just go through the rest of his clothing drawers and it wouldn't hurt to check under his bed and his waste basket.'

'You want me to get down on my hands and knees?'

'You are younger and more agile than I.'

'And I am hampered by the restrictions of skirts and petticoats we women have to wear,' I said. 'Have you ever considered how hard it is to do what men take for granted while wearing long tight skirts? You should try leaping off a moving trolley or climbing a wall.'

'Most women don't want to do such things.'

'But I do. I'm going to have to start wearing bloomers on a regular basis.'

Daniel raised his eyebrows. 'All right. I'll look under the bed. I bet you're really afraid of finding spiders.'

'On the contrary. I grew up in a thatched cottage. Spiders were a normal occurrence.'

I pulled open the top drawer of his chest. A leather box contained gold cufflinks, collar studs, a ring with a square black stone. Next to it was a silver-backed brush set. Mr Halsted was certainly used to the good things of life. His handkerchiefs were monogrammed, his undergarments neatly folded. Either he was naturally neat or a college servant looked after him. But the chest of drawers revealed no other telling secrets. Daniel discovered nothing but dust under the bed. The waste basket was empty. We came out of the room and stood in the dark hallway.

'Now let's tackle the friends,' Daniel said. He took hold of my arm as I started for the nearest door. 'It may be wiser if I make the first contact,' he whispered. 'Young men could be alarmed by finding a pretty young woman standing outside their door. They might immediately leap to the wrong kind of conclusion.'

'Very well,' I said. 'I have no objection to your asking the questions. You have more experience at it than I anyway. I could learn a thing or two maybe.'

Daniel glanced at me as if he was trying to tell whether I was being sarcastic, then nodded and rapped on the door. It was opened by a ginger-haired young man whose bleary-eyed condition suggested that he hadn't been awake long.

'I don't know you,' he said accusingly. 'You've got the wrong room.'

'We understand that you are one of John Jacob Halsted's friends,' Daniel said with the sort of authority in his voice that only the police have.

The boy's expression changed to wary. 'One of his many friends.' He attempted to sound airy. 'JJ was everyone's friend. Generous to a fault.'

'You say was,' Daniel picked up on this as I had done. 'Do you believe him to be dead?'

'Either dead or whooping it up in South America,' the boy said flippantly, but then he added more seriously, 'I sure hope the silly coot is okay.'

'Do you mind if we come in and ask you some questions?' Daniel asked.

'Are you the police? I was already grilled by the police.'

'We're from New York,' Daniel said, carefully avoiding an

outright lie. 'We're acting on behalf of Mr Halsted's family, who are naturally worried about him.'

'Oh, I see.' His gaze lingered on me. 'You know JJ then?'

'I'm a good friend of his aunt,' I answered. 'She naturally wants to find out what has happened to him. All we have to go on are ridiculous rumors.'

'I suppose you can come in,' the boy said. 'Room's in a bit of a state, y'know. Rather a rowdy time last night and only got home at four in the morning. Had to climb in along the tiles.' He opened the door wide and ushered us into an unbelievably untidy room. My gaze went from the unmade bed to the items of clothing that littered the floor to the unwashed glasses on the table.

'Sorry,' he said again.

'What's your name?' Daniel asked. 'Mine is Sullivan and this is Miss Murphy.'

'It's Ronnie,' the boy said. 'Ronald Farmington the Fourth if you want the full thing. Of the Boston Farmingtons.'

'Of course.' Daniel smiled. 'And you're one of John Jacob's best friends, is that right?'

'Yes. Bertie, JJ, and I. We're thick as thieves. We hit it off instantly when we met as freshmen.'

'Is Bertie the one who has the room across the hall?'

'That's right.'

'Is he likely to be at home?'

'I should say so. He has a paper due tomorrow and he was up almost as late as me last night, so he'll probably be working away like a madman.'

'I'll go and bring him in then,' Daniel said. 'That way we won't have to ask the same questions twice.'

Poor Ronnie was very ill at ease as he cleared the debris of several weeks from an armchair and offered me a place to sit. He was just about finished when Daniel returned with Bertie, who was large and chubby with a round, good-natured face.

'Rum do about Halsted,' he said. 'I'm glad somebody's finally doing something about finding him.'

'So tell us everything you know about the night he disappeared,' Daniel said.

Bertie screwed up his face, thinking. 'It was a weeknight,' he said, 'but JJ poked his head in the door and said he was going to the theater. He said a new show was opening, a musical review.'

'He was keen on the theater, I take it,' Daniel said.

'Oh rather. Keen on any sort of nightlife – shows and vaudeville and cabarets. He liked pretty girls in skimpy costumes. They were definitely his favorite.'

'Do you remember which theater he was going to?'

Bertie shook his head. 'Can't say that I asked. It was such a regular occurrence that it never occurred to me to find out. Did he tell you, Farmington?'

'All I remember saying is that he'd get himself kicked out if he was caught climbing in late again this semester, and he said, "Don't be such an old fuddy-duddy.' He said what did he have friends for if it wasn't to sneak down and unlock the door for him from time to time.'

'So you agreed to do that?'

'Yes, of course. We'd never leave another fellow in the lurch, even though we gave him a ticking off about skipping out when he had a paper to write.'

'He gave us this angelic smile and said that he suspected his little excursion was really going to be worth it,' Bertie added.

'Meaning he was meeting someone there, do you think?' I asked. 'A girl?'

They looked at me as if they were surprised I was joining in the conversation.

'Could be,' Ronnie said. 'He was always falling in and out of love with some girl or another.'

'But he didn't tell you anything about the one he was going to meet?'

'No, I was rather busy, late on my own paper, you know. And my father had given me a devil of a talking to about my grades, so I was more concerned with my own problems.'

'Are there many theaters in town?' Daniel asked.

'Only three or four, counting the vaudeville place.'

'So someone might have remembered seeing him that night, if he was a regular.'

'They might,' Ronnie agreed.

'And I presume he didn't come home after the theater?'

Bertie shook his head. 'We waited up to let him in. He'd throw a pebble up at Ronnie's window and then one of us would creep down and open a downstairs window in the common room for him to climb through.'

'But two o'clock came and he still hadn't shown up,' Ronnie added, 'and we got fed up. We had early classes the next morning so we said "to hell with him" and went to bed. And next morning we found his bed hadn't been slept in. And Bertie said to me, "You don't suppose he went home with some floosie, do you?" We heard nothing more until the police came.'

'What was your reaction when the police told you what he was supposed to have done?' Daniel asked.

'Utter disbelief,' Bertie said. 'We told them that JJ would never have broken in and robbed a house, especially not a friend's house. He might have had his faults but he was loyal to a T. And as for shooting someone, JJ didn't even own a gun. I know because he made a joke about it once. He liked a girl but she was going with another fellow and JJ said, "I suppose I could challenge him to a duel, but I don't own a pistol, so that wouldn't be much use. And I don't suppose I could shoot straight even if I had one."'

'And why would JJ bother to steal things from someone's house?' Ronnie went on. 'Silver and jewelry and the like? He only had to ask his parents for money and he usually got it. They were potty about him and he was so good at getting around them.'

'So he hadn't run up any big debts that he couldn't tell them about?'

I saw the boys give each other a hurried glance.

'He did like to gamble,' Bertie said cautiously. 'Played cards for pretty high stakes, but if he owed money, I mean a serious amount of money, he never let on to us about it.'

'I gather the house he is said to have robbed belonged to a friend of his. A Harry Silverton?' I asked. 'Did you know him, too?'

'Only slightly. He was a senior when we came in as freshmen. He and JJ became pals because they played polo together. Both were potty about horses.'

'Did Halsted tell you that he was planning on visiting Harry Silverton that night?'

The boys shook their heads. 'Never mentioned him,' Bertie said. 'As I told you, we were both rather busy that evening and annoyed that JJ was going out when he should have been studying. Ronnie told him so. He said, "There are only so many classes you can flunk before they sling you out of here, you know."'

'And JJ only laughed and said we were turning into stuffy, middle-aged bores.'

'So did John Jacob spend a lot of time with this Silverton?' Daniel asked. 'Did they regularly spend evenings out together?'

'No, not evenings,' Bertie said. 'They went to the races

together on occasion, I know that, but Silverton wasn't one of his close pals. More like an admired older brother.'

'So if he admired Silverton, that would make it even less likely that he'd want to steal things from his home,' I said.

'I told you, JJ would never steal from a friend,' Bertie said firmly. 'If he was going to steal, he'd do it in a big way and rob a bank. Always one for flair, was our JJ.'

'You keep speaking of him in the past tense,' Daniel said. 'So in your heart you must believe that he's dead.'

'If he were alive, I think he'd have done the honorable thing and turned himself in by now,' Ronnie said slowly. 'He wouldn't have wanted his folks to worry.'

'Tell us about his automobile,' I said. 'Because that is the only piece of evidence that ties him to the crime. It was seen driving away fast from the Silverton mansion and one of the stolen items was found under the seat after it had crashed into a tree. Was it possible that he let someone else drive his motor car?'

'Drive Myrtle?' The two boys exchanged a glance and then chuckled. 'He didn't let anyone else drive her. Myrtle was his pride and joy. If he had five minutes to spare he was polishing the damned thing.'

'He drove fast?'

'Oh, yes. He liked to drive fast,' Ronnie said. '"Let's see if she'll do thirty-five," he'd say. Scared the pants off us sometimes. The number of narrow squeaks we had on country roads, coming around a corner and meeting a horse and cart.'

'So you weren't completely surprised to find that he'd crashed the auto into a tree?' Daniel asked.

'He shouldn't have been driving at all that night,' Bertie said. 'The roads were devilish icy. I told him he was crazy but he burbled on about Myrtle being sure-footed. He talked about her as if she was alive, you know.'

'So what do you think has happened to him?' I asked.

Bertie glanced at Ronnie again. 'I think he crashed the auto, wandered off to get help, got lost, and perished in the snow,' he said. 'That's the only thing that I can believe.'

Twenty-three

'So what did we learn from that?' Daniel said as we came out of the building and started to walk back toward the center of town. 'Not much, did we?'

'Only confirmation of what we had suspected,' I said. 'He wouldn't have robbed a friend's house. He wouldn't have shot anybody. He probably didn't need money.'

'We now know he was planning to go to a theater,' Daniel said. 'Too bad it's Sunday. They'll all be closed. We'll have to come back again when they are operating.'

I frowned as we crossed the green. 'If he was planning to take a girl to the theater, then why did he go to the Silvertons' house? You don't usually take a young lady to meet your pals. And what was he doing out of town with her late at night?'

'She may not have been entirely respectable,' Daniel said. 'Not all young men have honorable intentions, you know.'

'But if he didn't have honorable intentions, he wouldn't have been interested in driving out into the countryside, would he? I'm sure the girl must have had a room in town.'

'You're not supposed to know about such things,' Daniel said.

'Me? I've met my fair share of prostitutes, you know. Shared a jail cell with them once.'

Daniel just shook his head.

'Anyway, it doesn't add up if he met the girl. On the other hand, if he was hoping to meet a girl and she jilted him or never turned up, he might have decided to drive out to visit a pal, just so that he didn't have to go home early and lose face with his friends.'

'Possible.' Daniel nodded. 'Either way, the next step is to get ourselves out to the Silverton place and find out what really happened that night. I'd also like to hear the New Haven police's side of the story, but I don't know if I should speak to them, given my current circumstances.'

'I can speak to them,' I said.

Daniel snorted. 'I hardly think they will divulge the key elements of their investigation to a private investigator.'

'Did you never think that I might wheedle it out of them with my feminine charms?'

'I think that highly unlikely. We're trained to resist feminine charms.'

'You fell for mine,' I said with a satisfied little smile. 'At the very moment when you were supposed to be prosecuting me.'

'Be that as it may, I think it may be better if I have a quiet word with one of my fellow officers in New York. He'll be able to find out all the details of the case for me.'

'So how are we going to get out to the Silverton place?' I asked. 'I understood it was on the road between New Haven and Bridgeport.'

'Go back to the station and see if there is a cab willing to take us that far.'

'I'm starving,' I said. 'Don't police officers ever eat?'

'Not when we're on a case,' Daniel said. 'But in deference to the weaker sex . . .'

'Fine. If you can hold out, so can I. I don't see anywhere open in any case.'

'Maybe the Silvertons will invite us to tea,' Daniel said. 'And it may not be such a grand idea to go out there today. I don't like the look of those clouds.'

While we had been inside the dormitory building, a great bank of clouds had been building to the east. They looked as if they were heavy with the promise of more snow. I was tempted to agree that we should head back to New York, but a small voice inside my head whispered that I'd have no time to come up here again and I didn't want to leave my investigation in Daniel's hands. 'Oh, I think we'll be fine,' I said. 'As long as we find ourselves a covered cab. I remember getting drenched by a downpour in Ireland. I don't wish to repeat that.'

There were several cabs lined up outside the station, the horses with their faces stuck in a nosebag and the cabbies sitting under a shelter out of the cold wind. One of them rose to his feet reluctantly as he saw us.

'You need a cab, sir?'

'We need to go out to the Silverton mansion,' Daniel said. 'It's out toward Bridgeport, I gather. Do you know of it?'

'I know more or less where it is, yes,' the man said. He was thin and pinched and his cheeks were bright red with the cold. 'Quite a ways out. I don't know if I want to put my horse through that, in this cold wind.'

'Fine. If your horse isn't up to it,' I said, 'maybe you can direct us to a livery stable where we can rent a buggy of our own.'

'I didn't say he wasn't up to it,' the cabby said hastily. 'He's a good enough horse, but it's a long ride. Won't be cheap.'

'It doesn't look as if you have much demand for your services apart from us,' I said. 'Name your price and we'll decide if it's fair.'

The old man glanced shiftily from me to Daniel. 'I'll do it for two dollars, sir,' he said.

'Two dollars—,' I began but Daniel put a hand on my arm. 'Fine. We accept. Now let's get going before that snow starts to come down.'

The cabby helped me up and draped a rug over my knees. Daniel climbed in beside me. 'You drive a hard bargain,' he said.

'I'm glad you're finally realizing that I'm no blushing violet,' I said. 'I'm a businesswoman, on my own in a big city. I've had to learn to survive.'

The horse set off at a good pace, the sound of the hoofbeats echoing through empty streets. The squares at the center of town gave way to narrow streets of row houses, poor working-class neighborhoods where stiff laundry hung out on washing lines and hardy children played in the dirty remains of snow. Then gradually the town came to an end. We crossed a frozen river by a bridge. Some boys had made a slide on the ice and were taking turns at it. There was now snow on the road and the paved surface had given way to rutted track so that we bumped along, the icy puddles crunching under our wheels. If the road to New York is like this all the way, I thought, what on earth had made John Jacob Halsted drive his precious motor car as far as the Bronx? And he certainly wouldn't have done so with a girl in the seat beside him. She'd have been shaken up like a sack of potatoes.

About a mile or so out of town, the cabby stopped to ask directions at a tavern.

'It's just around the next bend,' he said with relief showing on his face. We passed a row of stately trees – elms, I believe, although it was hard to tell from bare wintry branches – and then came to a fine brick gateway. The wrought-iron gates were closed. Through them we could see a semicircular driveway in front of an impressive gray stone house, rising three stories high with a turret in one corner. The cabby stopped his horse on the street outside.

'Here it is. Silverton mansion,' he said. 'You want to go in there?'

'Of course. That's why we came,' Daniel said shortly.

'They expecting you?'

'No, but we're friends of the family,' Daniel answered.

'I hope so. I hear they don't take kindly to curiosity seekers, not after what happened. You did hear what happened, didn't you? How the young fellow robbed them of all their silver and jewelry and shot the butler who had been with them for twenty years or more?'

'Yes, we heard,' I said.

Daniel started to climb down and then offered me a hand.

'You want me to wait?' the cabby asked.

I could tell that Daniel was getting quite annoyed with him. 'We certainly don't want to walk back into town,' he snapped.

'I don't expect we'll be more than half an hour,' I said. 'Why don't you go back and get yourself a hot drink at the tavern, then meet us outside here.'

'All right, ma'am,' he said, touching his cap to me. 'I'll do just that.'

We left him turning the horse in a driveway across the street and I stepped through the gate as Daniel held it open for me.

'There's no lack of money here, is there?' I muttered as I took in the size of the edifice and the land surrounding it. 'What do you know about the Silvertons? How did they make their money?'

'Armaments,' Daniel said. 'Supplied both sides in the Civil War and the US Army ever since.'

We hadn't reached the house when the front door opened and a young man came out, pointing a shotgun at us.

'If you're more damned reporters, you'd better make yourselves scarce before I shoot,' he shouted.

'Are you Harry Silverton?' Daniel called back to him.

'Would you please lower that thing? We've been sent by John Jacob Halsted's family.'

'You don't think any connection to that rat would be welcome at our house, do you?' Harry said, but he did lower the gun.

'We are just trying to unearth the truth,' I said, stepping in front of Daniel in the belief that I'd appear less threatening. 'This is Captain Sullivan of the New York police and I am Miss Murphy. Mr Halsted's family is naturally worried sick about what might have happened to him. There has been no sign of him since his motor car was found almost a week ago.'

'Isn't it obvious what happened to him? He's made off with the loot. Probably on a ship to South America by now.'

'Might we come in for a few minutes and hear your side of this story?' I asked. 'All we have heard so far is bits and pieces and most of that is rumor and hearsay.'

'I suppose so.' Harry Silverton ushered us into a wide marble hallway, decorated with Roman statues and potted palms. 'You'd better come into the morning room. Mama is in the drawing room and I don't want to make her more upset than she already is.'

He opened a door to his left and we found ourselves in a corner room that was part of that turret. It was octagonal with windows looking out over the garden and was decorated with wicker furniture and Chinese wallpaper. In the summer, with the sun streaming in, I suspected it would be delightful, but not today. There was no fire in the grate and the room was cold. Silverton indicated a wicker armchair for me to be seated.

'We'll only take a few minutes of your time,' Daniel said, refusing the offer to sit himself. 'How well did you know Mr Halsted?'

'I considered we were good pals,' Harry Silverton said in a clenched voice. 'I met him in my final year at Yale. He joined our polo club. Damned fine horseman. I brought him home to meals. We stayed in touch after I graduated and went to work in the family firm. We went out riding together and to the occasional horse race.'

He paused, scowling out of the window at the snowy scene beyond.

'We would just like to hear exactly what happened that night,' I said. 'We've interviewed John Jacob's friends, and according to them, he was bound for the theater. Could you tell us whether he changed his mind?'

'No, he went to the theater all right. He telephoned me about ten thirty, I suppose it was, or maybe a little closer to eleven. How would I like to make up a party and go out for a late supper with him, he asked. At first I refused. It was a beastly cold night and I was tired. I'd been at the factory all day, working on a rush order that had to go out. I told him it was dashed late for supper and on a weeknight, too. But JJ wouldn't take no for an answer. He said I'd regret it if I didn't come with him and he'd already booked at table at Angelico's and I'd be in for a pleasant surprise.'

'Did he say what that surprise was?'

'I rather took it that he had a young lady set up for me. He said we'd be a jolly party. He even offered to drive out in his new automobile and pick me up. So I relented and went upstairs to change into my black tie and tails.'

Harry Silverton perched on the chair opposite me and talked on, looking down at his hands. 'I finished changing and he didn't show up so I was feeling seriously miffed, I can tell you. Then I heard the sound of an automobile engine revving up outside. I went to my bedroom window. It was dark out there but I recognized JJ's vehicle – well, that wasn't hard considering he'd splashed out on a spanking new job called a Cadillac, and had it painted bright red. And the strange thing was that it

193

was driving out of our gates and took off like a bat out of hell, heading away from town toward Bridgeport.

'Well, I damned him soundly to hell for putting me through all that trouble and then not even bothering to wait for me. I got undressed and went to bed. The next thing I knew it was morning and someone was screaming. I rushed downstairs to find one of our maids in hysterics. She had gotten up to light the fires and had discovered our butler, Cranson, sprawled on the floor in the servants' quarters, outside the butler's pantry. Naturally we thought he'd had a heart attack or a stroke. But when we turned him over we saw a dashed great pool of blood under him. And then we realized that he had been shot.'

He looked up at me and I nodded sympathetically. 'It must have been a horrible shock for you.'

'It was, I can tell you. Poor old chap. Never done anybody harm in his entire life and some cad goes and shoots him.'

'But you didn't hear a shot?' Daniel asked.

'The servants are below stairs and the butler's pantry is right at the back of the house, away from any rooms that we are currently using. I suppose one might have heard a pop and thought of an auto backfiring, but as it was, I heard nothing. I could have been in the shower, getting ready to go out.'

'Or it could have been after you'd fallen asleep.'

'That could have been possible,' Harry said slowly, 'except we now know what happened that night. When we checked the silver cabinet, the silver had all been taken. And my mother's jewels. The burglar had only taken the good stuff.'

'How come none of the servants heard anything?' I asked.

Harry shook his head. 'They had all gone to bed long before and their bedrooms are all at the top of the house. Cranson used to sit in his pantry and have a late glass of whiskey before he locked up. He must have surprised the burglar and paid for it with his life.'

'So you believe that this burglar was JJ Halsted?' I asked.

'I have no other choice,' he replied in a clipped voice. 'His vehicle was seen driving away at a great rate and later when it was discovered wrecked on the road to New York City, one of our pieces of silver was found under the seat.'

'Did anyone else see the motor car leaving your house or parked in your driveway?'

'No, just me. We're a lot of country bumpkins when it comes to bedtime. Father is always up at crack of dawn to be at the factory early and so we are in the habit of retiring before ten. The servants earlier than that since they are expected to be up before us.'

'And you believe that your friend, Mr Halsted, could really have shot your butler?' Daniel asked.

'Again, I don't know what else to believe.' Harry's voice rose in tension. 'I can only put two and two together. Halsted's auto is seen driving away. It contains an item stolen from our house and our butler is lying dead.'

'But if he intended to rob you, why telephone you to announce his arrival?' I asked. 'Wouldn't that put the household on the alert for him when surely he needed stealth to accomplish his theft?'

Harry frowned, considering this. 'I can only think that when he got here something gave him the idea. Perhaps he found the front door unlocked and let himself in. Perhaps an object caught his eye. A piece of silver maybe. He was short of cash. He thought why not? And then he decided to go the whole hog and raid our silver collection. He knew it to be a valuable one because my father had shown it to him.'

'Was it likely that Mr Halsted would be short of money?' Daniel asked. 'I understood that his family was most indulgent to him. I also understood that he did not possess any kind of firearm.'

Harry shook his head violently. 'I don't know. I just don't

know. I've been going out of my mind trying to make sense of the whole thing. Halsted was a good friend and I would have said a trusted friend. It simply wasn't like him to behave in this despicable way. But then maybe he had taken something that altered his personality.'

'Taken something?' Daniel asked quickly. 'Drugs, you mean? Halsted took drugs?'

'Not on a regular basis. Good God no. But he did like to experiment and try new things. I know he had tried cocaine and opium before now, because he told me. If there was some drug that can completely alter the personality, then maybe that is the answer.'

'I know of no such drug,' Daniel said. 'I know of drugs that will give a person courage and maybe cause the lines between right and wrong to blur, but nothing that will change the true nature – in spite of what that writer Robert Stevenson would have us believe with his Jekyll and Hyde.'

'Then I don't know what else to say,' Harry said. 'We understand from the police that this has not been the only robbery around here. Just that very day an attempt had been made to rob a bank in New Haven and it has been suggested that the same person carried out all of these foul acts because a bank employee was shot and the bullet was identical.'

'And do you think that could have been your friend?'

Harry shrugged. 'He loved excitement. You heard about the time he won a bet to walk across the library roof? He took great risks when he was riding and he drove and rode like the Devil. So who is to say that he didn't feed his craving with daring acts of robbery?'

'But violence? His aunt describes him as a gentle boy.'

Harry thought for a minute, then nodded. 'I should not have believed it possible that he is a cold-blooded killer. But there seems no other logical explanation.'

'We hope to get to the truth, Mr Silverton,' Daniel said. He put a hand on my shoulder.

'Mr Silverton,' I said. 'You said it was a dark night. Could you swear that the vehicle you saw driving away that night belonged to Mr Halsted?'

'I didn't see the driver but the automobile certainly looked exactly like the one Halsted had proudly shown me only a week or so earlier. And it's not even in general production yet. I'd swear to that in court. And they found our silver mustard pot under the seat, remember. How the devil did that get there if he wasn't to blame?'

We stared at each other for a while, then I sighed. 'We are going to get to the bottom of this, I promise you. We're going to find JJ Halsted and learn the truth.'

'Then I wish you luck,' he said. 'Nothing would please me more than to find my friend not guilty of this awful crime, but I fear I am already convinced there is no other explanation.'

He led us toward the front door and watched as we went down the front steps. The cabby was waiting for us out in the street and it had started to snow.

Twenty-four

The snow held off until we had reached the station, but as the train pulled out on its journey back to New York it started to fall in earnest, the white flakes swirling around the train windows.

'I hope we're not trapped in a blizzard,' I said, peering out into the grayness.

'We should be back before enough snow can pile up to stop trains from running,' Daniel said shortly.

He had hardly said a word all the way back from the Silverton house. I had decided he must be considering various possibilities in the case but now I looked up at him with concern.

'Daniel, is something upsetting you?' I asked. 'Something I've said or done?'

He sighed then blurted out, 'Molly, you must stop introducing me as Captain Sullivan. It's not right and it's deceptive.'

'But you are Captain Sullivan.'

'Not at the moment.'

'You know it's only a matter of time before you are reinstated. You've done nothing wrong, for heaven's sake.'

'I set up an illegal prize fight.'

'That half the police force attended.'

'Nevertheless, if anyone wanted to find an excuse to get rid of me, it was still illegal.'

'Why would anyone want to get rid of you? Your colleagues all think highly of you. It will all be sorted out soon.'

'I hope so,' he said. 'And until I am reinstated, I am not Captain Sullivan.'

'Very well.' I frowned. 'You're very touchy tonight.'

'I suppose I am. It has to do with the frustration I'm feeling. Being part of this case is only reminding me what I've been missing out on all this time. Cases I could have helped solve. And all the current trouble with the gangs. I'm one of the few cops who could do something about that. I think we may be in for a gang war, from what I hear. I know there was a big Italian gang funeral only the other day in the city. Black-plumed horses, bands, and the show. Makes me wonder who dared to bump off a gang member. And I can do nothing.' He slammed his fists together.

'You can help solve this particular case,' I said. 'I'd certainly value your skills because I'm stumped.'

He nodded. 'It's one devil of a puzzle, isn't it? I can't believe that Halsted committed those crimes, but then I know that not many people own a brand-new automobile like that, especially not in a small town like New Haven. And if he's really in the clear, then where the devil is he?'

'I wish I knew,' I said.

'I'll try and get my hands on an automobile,' he said. 'I hope I still have a few remaining well-connected friends. We should see for ourselves where the vehicle went off the road and see if anyone encountered Halsted after the crash. Although I'm sure the police will already have carried out a thorough investigation.'

'Which police department would that be?' I asked.

'Depends exactly where it happened. If it was in the Bronx then it's officially part of New York City jurisdiction. If it was farther out from the city then it would be the local police of whatever town was closest, and the investigation is not likely to have been as thorough. I'll ask a few questions. Someone in the department will know.' He turned to me. 'Are you free to come with me some day this week?'

'Tomorrow would be best because the show opens on Tuesday. After that I don't know how much time I'll have to spend at the theater. And we must finish up our investigation on Mr Roth, and I'd like to be around when Dr Birnbaum treats the poor mute girl.'

'You've taken on too much again, haven't you?'

I smiled. 'Better than sitting at home twiddling my thumbs. At least if I'm going to be able to pay the bills.'

'It's not right,' Daniel said. 'I should be providing for you. I want to, Molly. I'm waiting for the day when—'

I put my hand up to touch his cheek. 'Until that day it's you we've got to worry about. I want you back on the job, Daniel. I want you to feel happy again. I want my old Daniel back – cocky, arrogant, and fun.'

'Oh, Molly, I know what I want.' He looked at me and suddenly we were in each other's arms and he was kissing me passionately. It was lucky we had the compartment to ourselves. Who knows where that particular exercise might have led if a rap on the compartment door hadn't made us break apart guiltily. 'I need to see your tickets, sir,' said the ticket collector, looking distinctly embarrassed. 'I'm sorry to be disturbing you and the young lady.'

Daniel smiled. 'Sorry. We got a little carried away.'

'I quite understand, sir.' The ticket collector grinned knowingly. 'I was young myself once. Now I'm the father of seven. Make the most of it while you can, sir.'

With that he shut the door again. We sat with Daniel's arm around me all the way back into New York. When I got back home to Patchin Place I found Mrs Tucker sitting on Mary's bed with the girl asleep in her arms like a small child. She put her fingers to her lips as I poked my head around the door.

'She looks so peaceful,' I whispered.

'Now she does,' Mrs Tucker exclaimed. 'You should have seen her earlier.'

'What happened?'

'I was downstairs, doing some knitting, and suddenly I hears this unearthly noise,' she said in a low voice, smoothing the girl's hair as she spoke. 'I rushed upstairs and the poor thing is out of bed, rushing from room to room with this look of pure terror on her face, shrieking like a banshee.'

'Oh, no. What did you do?'

'It took me a while to quiet her down. I held her tightly in my arms, just like I'd hold my own children when they woke up with nightmares and suddenly she starts to sob. She cried and she cried and I kept telling her it was all right now. Then I gave her some of my soup, mixed her a dose of the sedative, and she went straight back to sleep.' She shook her head. 'Poor little thing. She was scared out of her wits.'

'That's exactly right,' I said. 'She has been scared out of her wits. We have an alienist coming to see her.'

'An alienist? What in tarnation is that?'

'He's a doctor of the mind,' I said.

'Never heard of such a thing. How can you treat the mind?'

'It's the latest thing. He tries to get through to the subconscious – that's the thoughts and fears we don't even know about.'

'Sounds fishy to me,' she said. 'I'll wager my good broth and loving care will work better than his mumbo jumbo.'

'Maybe both together will do the trick,' I said. 'And if we

find her family then that would be the best thing of all. She needs to be safely home again.'

'As long as it wasn't her family that brought on this terror in the first place,' she said knowingly.

'Oh, surely not,' I began but she shook her head. 'Have you not heard of fathers doing unmentionable things to their daughters?'

'Holy Mother of God,' I said, my hand coming up to involuntarily cross myself. This was something that hadn't crossed my mind before. I suppose I've always been naïve. Then I remembered. 'But the doctors say she hadn't been assaulted in that way.'

'Well, that's one blessing, isn't it?' Mrs Tucker said gently. 'Whatever happened to her, it was something terrible, I could tell that. I bet the crying did her a power of good. It was as if a damn had burst. I'll wager she'll be much better in the morning. Back to her old self, maybe.'

But the next morning there was still no indication that her speech or memory was returning. She greeted Dr Birnbaum with an apprehensive stare as he came into the room, glancing at me to make sure I was going to stay close by.

'Hello, my dear. And how are we today?' he asked merrily. Then he turned to me. 'I've some letters for you to read, Miss Murphy. Our first replies.'

'Does any of them look promising?'

'I doubt it,' he said, 'but one never knows. Take a look for yourself.' He handed them to me, 'Oh, and I've revised the advertisements, adding the phrase "May be called Annie." We'll see if that produces better results.'

I had been watching the girl. At the mention of the word *Annie* she became suddenly alert and her eyes opened wide with fear.

'It's all right, my sweet.' I went to her and patted her shoulder.

'Nothing bad is going to happen to you again. You are safe here among people who care about you. You do understand me, don't you?'

I thought I saw the slightest of nods, but I couldn't be sure. I opened the letters and read them out loud, one by one, hoping that I'd see some sign of recognition in an address or a signature. To be sure none of the missing girls matched the description of our young lady, but it was worth a try. Some of the letters were quite piteous and I realized just how many runaway girls there could be in the world.

After I'd finished the letters, Dr Birnbaum tried hypnotism on her again but once more she became horribly agitated when he said the word 'Annie,' and he had to stop. If she understood more than the word 'Annie,' she didn't let on. She was living in her own private hell and she wasn't going to let anyone else in.

'It may take time,' Birnbaum admitted, 'although in some of these cases it only takes one thing to trigger a response and return speech and memory to them. She may wake one day as if from a dream. If she does suddenly come to her senses, I want to be called immediately. It could be a very dangerous moment for her. Realizing the implications of the trauma she went through could be too much for her conscious mind and could result in permanent madness or suicide or even violence to those around her.'

I nodded, remembering my friends' concern that I might have taken on something too difficult and dangerous. 'I have now engaged a nurse to be with her when I cannot,' I said.

'That's a wise precaution.'

We all looked up at the sound of a horn tooting outside. I went to the window and there was Daniel, at the wheel of an automobile. I ran down to the front door.

'Are you ready for a ride?' he shouted over the noise of the engine.

'But what about all that snow yesterday?'

'It hardly snowed at all around the city,' he said jauntily as he jumped out of the automobile. 'And I'm sure they'll have taken the trouble to put down salt and gravel on the main roads out of town. So I think we'll be all right. I doubt if we'll make it all the way to New Haven, though. Have to leave that for another day.'

'I'll have to see if Mrs Tucker can look after our patient. I did warn her I might have to go out today.'

'She's going to prove satisfactory as a nurse, is she?' Daniel asked.

'Absolutely. She's treating our patient like one of her own children.'

'Well, that's one thing off your mind then,' Daniel said. 'I'll go and fetch her while you get ready, shall I? I bet she'll enjoy being seen driving away in an automobile!'

I helped him reverse the auto out of our alleyway and then off he went, his wheels spinning up slush from the gutters. I put on warm clothes, as my experience of automobiles led me to believe that they were not highly successful at keeping out the cold and damp. I was just tucking my hair under my hat when Daniel returned with Mrs Tucker.

'How is the lamb today?' she asked eagerly. 'I couldn't sleep all last night, worrying about the poor little thing. If I find the one who did this to her, he's going to wish he'd never been born.' And she waved her knitting needles in a threatening manner.

'I think we hit pay dirt on our choice of nursemaid,' Daniel said as we drove away. 'She's one of those women who relishes taking care of others.'

I laughed. 'When Mrs Goodwin was confined to bed after her accident, Mrs Tucker took it upon herself to look after her. She drove Mrs Goodwin mad. It was a real clash of wills.'

'So a sedated girl would be more to her liking,' Daniel said. 'Either way, it means I have you to myself again. We have the use of a stylish automobile and our time is our own.'

Twenty-five

I had to admit that it was a thrill to be seen driving up Fifth Avenue in a dashing motor car, with a handsome man beside me. The elegant neighborhood of the East Seventies soon faded, however, and the city became a collection of humble row houses mixed with ramshackle huts as we reached the northern tip of Manhattan Island. We crossed the icy bridge over the Harlem River with great caution and then had to proceed at a snail's pace because the main road wasn't as well maintained as Daniel had hoped. We passed signs of habitation, but it seemed that the towns were to the north of us. And we soon found ourselves in snowy countryside.

'Do you know where we are going?' I asked.

'We're going to a police station,' Daniel said. 'Just off the road here. It was apparently the first local station to respond to the accident,' he said. 'I'm hoping they can show us the accident scene and maybe answer some questions.'

We found the police station in a little main street next to H. Bingler, dry goods, and R. Murray, greengrocer. It was lucky that Daniel was known to the sergeant on duty. He sent a constable with us who was only too eager to come for a ride in the rumble seat of our automobile and show us the accident site himself.

'It gave Ernie and me an awful scare, I can tell you,' he said, leaning between us from the back seat of the auto. 'There was this horse less carriage, crashed into a tree, oil spilled out onto the snow, and not a soul in sight.

'"Where can they have gone?" Ernie says. "Someone must have been hurt, the way this thing's smashed up." '

'When was this?'

'It was the Wednesday morning. Later we found out that the vehicle must have collided with the tree the night before. But you'll see how it ran off the road at a bend, so it wasn't noticed until a farmer came by at daybreak.'

We rejoined the main road and soon the constable told us to stop in a wooded area where the road took a sudden swing to the right. 'It was smashed into that oak there,' he said, climbing out of the seat. 'See where it hit the tree?'

I could see a big gash in the trunk. I could also pick out dark patches in the snow. More snow had fallen the night before so it was hard to know if they were oil or blood.

'So the auto itself was pretty badly damaged?' Daniel asked.

'It sure was, sir. The whole front was smashed in. The steering-wheel column had been pushed clear out. I tell you, whoever was in there couldn't have walked away, that's my opinion.'

'And yet they did,' I said. 'Were there any trails leading off through the snow?'

The constable looked sheepish. 'Well, to start with we had no idea that this automobile was connected with a crime, so we looked all around to see if any wounded travelers had staggered away from the wreck and then collapsed. So a fair number of the tracks would be ours. But we saw no clear set of tracks leading away, I can tell you that. One strange thing. It did look as if a second vehicle had pulled up beside it at some time, then driven away again. It must have been another automobile because there were no signs of horses' hooves. I think that must have been a good Samaritan just checking to see if anyone was hurt. He found nobody and drove off.'

He looked at us for affirmation.

'Where is the wrecked automobile now?' Daniel asked.

'We had it towed to the yard behind the police station. We thought that whoever owned it might want to salvage any parts that he could. But nobody showed up, and then we found out that it matched the description of the automobile that drove away from the Silverton place. When we gave it a thorough search, the sarge came up with the silver pot. "It's part of the loot, boy,' he said to me, and it was.'

'So was the auto ever checked for evidence?' Daniel asked.

'Evidence?' the constable looked confused.

'You know – scraps of clothing, hairs, that sort of thing.'

'I don't think it ever was, sir. It was in pretty bad shape. Ernie says to me that it's nothing but a heap of junk and we should help ourselves to the wheels, 'cos they were still good.'

'You didn't, I hope?'

'Oh no, sir. By then word had come in that this particular automobile was wanted in a robbery.'

'Then I'd like to take a look at it,' Daniel said. 'You can learn a lot with a magnifying glass and close observation, you know.'

'Really?' The young man looked impressed. 'I know that Mr Sherlock Holmes was supposed to be able to pick up a cigarette end and tell you what kind of person smoked it, but I didn't think that kind of thing was done in real life.'

'They are using fingerprints these days,' Daniel said. 'Did you know that every fingerprint is different and they can be identified on most smooth surfaces?'

'No kidding, sir. Well, I guess I'd have to ask sarge if it's okay for you to take a look. I'd sure like to see you find them fingerprints.'

'I don't have a kit to do it with me,' Daniel said. 'But I could come back with one. But it's possible that clothing got torn in such a bad crash or even bits of skin and tissue were left behind.'

'Golly, sir,' the constable looked pale. 'You surely wouldn't want the young lady to see that?'

'The young lady has seen worse,' Daniel said. 'She's a bona fide detective, my boy.'

'No kiddin', sir?'

He looked at me as if I were an exhibit in Mr Barnum's circus.

I felt that I should warrant the label so I left the motor car and walked around to examine the accident scene for myself. The ground was truly trampled, and to make things worse, a horse and cart had been used to tow away the wreck. A light coating of new snow had fallen, blurring the outlines of foot-prints, so that it would now be impossible for anyone to pick up a trail in the pristine woodland beyond.

My eye was caught by a scar on a nearby tree. A horizontal line cut neatly along the bark, about chest level. I followed the line and saw some kind of blemish on a tree beyond. I held my skirts free of the snow and waded across to see.

'Daniel, come here,' I called, my excitement mounting. I pointed at the trunk. 'There is something stuck in the wood.'

Daniel produced a penknife and extracted it. 'Good eyes, Molly. It's a bullet.'

'And there is the path that it took grazing the outside of that tree trunk,' I said.

Daniel frowned as he looked. 'Someone was shooting into the direction we have just come. A falling out among thieves, maybe. One of them tried to run off?'

'He obviously succeeded, since no body was found,' I said. 'And remember what the constable said about the tracks of a second vehicle. Did another motor car catch up with this one and stop to offer help? Then why shoot?'

Daniel shook his head. 'Interesting question. Was it just coincidence that a second vehicle showed up? Had it come to help them? Or come to take the loot from them?'

'You're saying them, but we only believe that John Jacob Halsted was in the car, don't we?'

'He could have been working with a partner.'

'Who then tried to double-cross him and run off with the loot, knowing he was injured.'

'And Halsted shot at him to stop him from getting away,' Daniel finished with satisfaction.

'In which case, where is Halsted?'

'It could be that the partner was the one doing the shooting and that he managed to kill Halsted and bury the body somewhere close by.'

'Don't, it's too horrible.' I shuddered. I looked up at the constable who was watching us with interest. 'Were any dogs used in the search?'

'Wasn't no need. You'd have seen the tracks, plain as day, if they'd gone off through the woods.'

'We were just speculating that there could have been a falling out among thieves here. We've just found a bullet imbedded in that tree. So it's not beyond possibility that a body could be buried nearby.'

'I don't think so, sir. It had snowed, remember. The snow would be all disturbed, wouldn't it?'

'No harm in searching again, though,' Daniel said. 'Does anyone nearby keep hounds?'

'Yes, sir. Farmer over Hatcher's Corner way keeps a pair of coon hounds.'

'Did you ask at all the farms around this site, to see if the victims of the crash came to seek shelter anywhere?'

'Oh yes, miss. We asked, all right. And then when we knew it was a wanted man, we checked out barns and hen houses and everything. Didn't find nothing though.'

'My money would be on the second automobile,' Daniel said. 'It could even have been an arranged meeting, although I'm sure the crash wasn't intentional.'

'So you are suggesting that someone met Halsted and whisked him and the loot away?'

'Exactly.'

'Then who was doing the shooting?'

'Ah. That we don't know.'

It was cold and bleak standing there. I shivered. 'I think we've seen enough. I'm freezing,' I said.

Daniel helped me in and the constable climbed into the backseat again. 'Where to now, sir?'

'I think I'd like to examine the wreck,' he said, 'and then, if your sergeant wouldn't mind, I'd like to come back with an item of the missing man's clothing and go over the area thoroughly with dogs.'

'You won't find him, sir. He's long gone,' the constable said. 'We'd have heard by now if he was still hiding out around here.'

'Aren't there marshes nearby?'

'Well, yes, there is marshland along the side of the sound, about half a mile from here, it would be. But those marshes are awful bleak and exposed. Not easy for a man to find a place to hide in the wintertime. Not much fun in the summer, either.'

Daniel started the motor and reversed carefully. The road was icy and we had no wish to repeat the disaster. Soon, with the sergeant's blessing, the constable was opening up a yard in an alleyway and we saw the motor car for ourselves. It was a sorry sight, half hidden under a new dusting of snow. I felt sick and turned away. From the blackened state of the twisted metal, it looked like there had been a fire at some point. The red upholstery in the front seat was scorched and ripped. The backseat was intact, however, and Daniel examined it closely.

'Here's a small prize,' he said. And he held up a long blonde hair. 'Maybe Halsted wasn't alone that night.'

'We know he was hoping to meet a young lady,' I agreed, 'but why would her hair have been in the backseat?'

Daniel looked at me, went to say something, then thought better of it. 'Of course we have no reason to suppose that the hair was from that night. I'm sure that he frequently transported young women, given what we know of his way of life, but it might be worth checking whether a young blonde woman has disappeared from New Haven or the surrounding area.'

'It's too bad my speechless girl has chestnut hair,' I said.

Daniel shook his head. 'I think we should rejoice that she is dark, because otherwise it would mean that the great trauma that robbed her of her senses was suffered at the hands of Halsted, and I would hate to have to break that news to his aunt.'

Nothing else was forthcoming from the automobile. We spoke with the sergeant, then drove to farms in the area, but none of the farm folk had any information for us. If John Jacob Halsted had managed to walk away from the damaged automobile, he had not sought sanctuary anywhere nearby. At least, he had not come knocking on any door and no trace of him had been found in barns or outbuildings. I now truly began to believe that he was a scoundrel after all, and that he had managed to get away safely with the loot.

'The next step should be to approach this from the items that were stolen,' Daniel said on the way home. 'We'll get a good description of them and they'll have to show up somewhere. I'll make some inquiries. I have some connections with fences in the area. They'll let me know if any of the objects have shown up.'

'Poor Miss Van Woekem,' I said. 'I rather think that we'll have no good news for her, however hard we try.'

'You can't pass judgment until you know all the facts,' Daniel said.

'Now who is being the optimist?' I asked.

Twenty-six

On Tuesday morning I woke up with a knot in my stomach, as if something big was about to happen. Then I remembered – opening night at the theater. Although I had an almost invisible part in the play, tonight I'd be doing it before several hundred people. And tonight the ghost would have a full house to perform to. I had to admit that I felt angry and frustrated with myself. I'd been there, onstage, observing for two nights and had discovered nothing. If somebody was playing a cruel prank against Miss Lovejoy, then I had no idea who. I had reason to suspect Desmond Haynes, but he was certainly nowhere near that jumping jug, and I hadn't seen him anywhere near the wind machine, either. And Blanche had threatened not to open as planned. Why would Desmond want his show to fail? Why would anyone in that theater want the show to close? And yet there was only one way into the theater and that was past Henry.

I had a distinct feeling that Miss Lovejoy would be dispensing with my services very rapidly if I didn't make some progress. I just prayed that nothing would happen to mar tonight's opening.

In the meantime I had plenty to keep me occupied. I fixed breakfast for Annie, then stayed with her while Dr Birnbaum saw her. Although I didn't think we made any progress in the latest session the doctor seemed pleased. 'I sense a break-through may be coming soon,' he said. 'She is beginning to trust us, and complete trust is needed for hypnotism to work favorably.'

'I hope so,' I said. 'I'm disappointed that none of the letters we've received so far could be from her family. But maybe now that you've included the mention of the name Annie, it may trigger a response.'

As I showed the doctor to the front door, I found myself considering the alternatives I had so blithely put aside until now. If no family appeared, if sanity and speech and memory were not restored, what then? I knew I could never turn her out into the streets. But how could I saddle myself with the care of an invalid forever? Then my normal cheerful optimism took over and I decided I'd cross that bridge when I came to it. At this moment I had more urgent things to worry about, like walking across a stage in front of an audience without falling on my face.

I'd heard about stage fright before, but I never thought it would apply to me. In fact my mother was always scolding me for being too much of a show-off, ever since I got out of the pew in church and danced to the organ music (it was one of the livelier hymns). I was only three at the time but you'd have thought I'd brought the devil himself into the holy place, the spanking I got!

Since coming to America I'd been called upon to act various roles in undercover situations and managed to pull them all off successfully. So why should this latest role be any different? Why should I feel as if my insides were tying themselves into knots? I suppose it had to be because the potential for making a fool of myself was so great.

I was getting ready to leave for the theater when there was a tap on my front door. I hoped it was Daniel. I needed reassurance at this moment, and a good old touch of reality. Instead it was Sid and Gus who stood there.

'Well, here she is. The amazing disappearing woman,' Sid exclaimed as they came into the house.

'What do you mean?' I asked.

'My dear Molly, we've seen neither hide nor hair of you for several days now. We tried your door yesterday and on Sunday and each time it was opened by such a fierce harridan that we were forced to retreat.'

'She's the nursemaid I've hired to look after the girl while I'm away.'

'That's what we gathered. So your sleeping beauty still has not awoken from her enchanted slumber?'

'She's awake some of the time, although the doctor has administered sedatives to her. But she has neither spoken nor recognized that she understands us up to now.'

'And nobody has stepped forward to claim her?'

'Nobody, as yet.'

'Molly, what on earth will you do if she doesn't get better soon?' Sid asked, but Gus cut in gently, 'I expect it will sort itself out. It usually does with Molly. She lives a charmed life.'

'We came to offer you a treat and a respite,' Sid said. 'We have obtained tickets to tonight's opening of Blanche Lovejoy's new play – it's called *Ooh La La*. It's supposed to be very French and very naughty. What's more, there is a good chance that the theater ghost may put in an appearance. Do you want to come with us?'

I tried to stop myself from smiling. 'I'm sorry,' I said, 'but I have another commitment tonight. I've heard all about it, of course. And the theater ghost.'

'You're not spending the evening with Dreary Daniel, are you?' Sid said. 'That man has become excessively boring these days. Not a glimmer of a sense of humor at all.'

'I guarantee that I am not spending the evening with Daniel,' I said. 'Although I don't think you'd be too merry and gay if you had been wrongly dismissed from your job.'

'True enough,' Sid admitted. 'So you're sure we can't tempt you to join us at the theater?'

'I have an assignment for a case I'm working on,' I said.

'Not going out dressed as a street urchin again, please,' Sid said. 'Even Nelly Bly gave up on that as being too uncomfortable even for her.'

'No, this time I'm disguised as a schoolgirl,' I said with a smile.

'A schoolgirl – do tell!'

'I'd love to, but I can't. Later all will be revealed, I promise.'

'I suppose that will have to do then,' Gus said with a sigh. 'You are working too hard these days, Molly Murphy. You never seem to have time for fun.'

'I have to eat and pay the bills, Gus. I've no convenient aunts dying and leaving me a small fortune like you.'

'That's true enough,' Gus said. 'A steady income certainly does make life sweeter.'

'We must be off then, my sweet,' Sid said. 'Gus is determined to find a new feather for her headpiece. Scarlet, no less. I told her she'll look like a fallen woman but she insists.'

She gave me a knowing smile and took Gus's arm to lead her out. I couldn't help smiling as I closed the door behind them. Won't they be surprised tonight!

When I arrived at the theater there was already a crowd milling around on the street and the back alley was positively seething with newspaper reporters. 'Are you one of the actresses?' they asked me. 'Have you seen the ghost personally? Do you think it's going to put in an appearance tonight?'

I shoved my way through and signed in with Henry.

'It's a mad house out there,' I said. 'All those reporters grabbing at me.'

'You wait until afterward.' Henry nodded knowingly. 'You won't be able to push your way through the crush. Reporters and stage-door Johnnies and God knows what. If you want a word of advice, see if you can slip out through front of house. Unless you want to be whisked away to dine at Delmonico's, that is.'

He gave me a wicked little wink.

'There's a big crowd out front as well,' I said.

'They'd be fighting to get the last tickets,' Henry said. 'Let's hope Miss Lovejoy doesn't lose her nerve at the last minute and refuse to go on. There would be a riot.'

'Do you think she might?'

'She was as jittery as a kitten when she arrived a few minutes ago,' Henry said. 'I know it's first night and everyone suffers from first night nerves but not Blanche. She's usually the trooper, steady as a rock.'

'I'd better go and get ready,' I said.

I went on down the passage, but instead of going up the stairs to the dressing room I decided to check out the stage area for myself. That way at least I could see that no obvious traps had been set. I worked my way around the various flats and pieces of scenery. I opened drawers and trunks to make sure they contained nothing suspicious. I was just sticking my head down the mock well when I was grabbed from behind. I was so startled I almost toppled in head first, but strong arms yanked me out.

'And what do you think you're doing, young lady?' It was Wally, the stage manager, and he didn't look happy. Before I could answer he started to drag me away. 'Just wait until Miss Lovejoy hears about this! Ghost, my foot. I've never believed in a ghost.'

'I assure you I'm not the ghost,' I said. 'In fact I'm—' I hesitated, wondering how much I was allowed to tell him. He didn't give me a chance to speak but went on, 'I've had my eye on you ever since you showed up out of the blue like that. You're a plant, aren't you? You've been sent to make sure that Miss Lovejoy's show is a failure.'

'That's rubbish,' I said.

'Then why did I catch you snooping around where you had no place to be?'

'If you want to know, I was doing a bit of snooping because I also don't believe in the ghost and I wanted to check that there were no hidden wires or booby traps that were going to spoil tonight's show.'

He looked at me as if he were deciding whether to believe me or not. 'And why should you be so interested?'

Again, I hesitated to say that Miss Lovejoy had hired me just for that purpose. After all, Wally could be the ghost himself. He had full access to the backstage area and the knowledge to rig up spectacular effects.

'Why wouldn't I be interested?' I said. 'It's my first big break on Broadway and I don't want the show to close before it opens. And my father was a detective, you know, so I've picked up a few skills.'

'And what have you found then?'

'Nothing. Everything seems completely above board. I examined the jug and the table the other night, after the lemonade spilled all over Miss Lovejoy, and I found nothing then. If someone is doing this, they are darned clever.'

'I know I'd like to get my hands on them,' Wally said with a growl. 'Miss Lovejoy is a lovely lady. Generous to her friends. She don't deserve to be shook up like this.'

'We'll get to the bottom of it,' I said. 'I can keep my eye on the actors, and you can keep your eye on your stagehands.

If we see any of them acting suspiciously, then we'll follow them.'

'Right,' he said, still deciding whether I was trustworthy or not. 'You'd better get up there and into costume or there will be trouble,' he added.

I nodded and hurried up the stairs. I found the dressing room already a hive of activity.

'Well, look who has deigned to show up,' Lily said sarcastically. 'Think we're the big star already, do we? Practicing the grand entrance?'

'Not at all,' I said. 'I got tied up trying to get through the crowds down there.'

'I hope you didn't talk to the press,' one of the other girls said. 'Miss Lovejoy would kill you if you blabbed.'

'It's seems that somebody already did,' I said. 'The papers are full of every detail.'

I thought the room went suddenly quiet. Lily went back to putting moleskin between her toes, others turned to the mirror and started applying makeup. I made my way down to Elise at the far end. She was tying her ballet slipper.

'I hope this holds out,' she said. 'These shoes have seen better days and I've sewn this ribbon on so many times that the satin is starting to fray. And look at the toes. It's darning on top of darning. I think I'm going to have to spend most of my first paycheck on a new pair.'

'The company doesn't pay for your shoes?'

'Oh no. Costumes, yes, but shoes are a personal item, like makeup. We have to get them custom made for us. If you have a ballet shoe that doesn't fit properly, then your feet will wind up maimed for life.'

She went back to tucking in the ribbon ends. I started undressing, but a strange thought was forming in my head. I pictured my silent girl's feet. What if those blistered and raw toes were not a result of frostbite? What if she was a dancer and they were dancer's feet, made more irritated by her walk through the snow? She certainly had the lithe body for it and the delicate face and hands. Tomorrow I could borrow Sid and Gus's phonograph and play some popular dance tunes for her, to see if they produced a reaction.

I finished my makeup just in time before the call boy came around with the first warning. My heart was thudding as I followed the rest of the girls down to the stage to wait in the wings. Beyond the lowered curtain I could hear the murmur of a large crowd and the sounds of the orchestra tuning up. I could feel the excitement and tension in the air as stagehands glided past us, making last-minute adjustments to potted plants and spotlights. 'Break a leg,' the girls whispered to each other. I thought it was a rather odd thing to say, but I whispered it back to them.

Then there was a burst of applause.

'Conductor has come out,' Elise mouthed to me.

Then the orchestra struck up the lively first notes of the overture and we were instructed to go onstage. I found my hands were so cold and shaky that I could hardly hold the book. I took up my place on my mark and waited, giving a silent prayer of thanks that I didn't have to say a word. I knew that if I opened my mouth no sound would come out. The overture came to an end and the curtain started to rise. A great roar of applause came from the audience as they saw the girls in their tennis outfits. I could see the front rows, full of faces, and among them I picked out a scarlet feather and below it Gus's startled face. I studied my book and tried not to smile.

The girls launched into the opening number. The young men arrived in their automobile, getting another huge round of applause, and then Miss Lovejoy made her entrance. I had seen her onstage enough times now to know that she had a powerful

221

voice and a great presence. But tonight I could see why she was a star. There was something about her that would not let me take my eyes off her. When she spoke her voice was more powerful than ever. Her first funny line got a huge laugh and I sensed the girls around me relaxing. For the first time I fully realized that it was Blanche's show. The rest of us were only window dressing.

Twenty-seven

We got through the first act with no incidents. I remembered where I was supposed to be and got a good laugh when I was left onstage after the other girls ran off and had to be summoned by Miss Lovejoy. In the dressing room during the interval, the mood had changed. We arrived to find the whole place full of flowers. Some had cards on them, several of them for Lily. Others were addressed more vaguely. 'To the pretty little brunette at the end of the line.'

'That's you, Jewel,' someone said and handed out the bouquet. The girl blushed. 'I wonder who it is,' she said with a giggle.

'Hey, Lily, you could quit being in show business and open a flower shop with this lot,' someone yelled.

'One of them's not from that English duke, is it, Lily?' one of the girls asked.

'Not that I can see,' Lily said.

'Do you think he'll show up again?' someone else asked wistfully.

'If he does, then he's mine, so hands off,' Lily said. 'I always did fancy myself as a duchess.'

'You? A duchess, that will be the day!'

'You don't know how to drink tea with your pinky up!'

Lily looked haughty. 'Those *Florodora* sextet girls all married well, didn't they?'

'Yes, well, they were the stars. We're only chorus,' someone reminded her.

'But take a look at our leading ladies and gentlemen,' Lily said triumphantly. 'All over the hill, long in the tooth, and nothing special to look at. We're the ones they'll be waiting for tonight. You'll see. They've already seen our ankles in the tennis scene. You wait until they see us in our bathing suits!'

There was a great burst of laughter at this.

'I wish the censor hadn't cut that cancan number,' Lily went on. 'Then we could show them our bottoms, too.'

'Lily, you are the living end,' someone exclaimed.

'Oh, don't you go acting the prude with me, Connie Sharp. I know what you do in your spare time, and it ain't embroidering pillows, neither.'

Elise caught my eye and shook her head. 'Don't let them upset you, Molly. Most of us are good girls, just wanting to earn a living, same as anyone else. And if we happen to strike pay dirt and catch the eye of a rich young man after the show, then who is to blame us if we do what we can to make sure we hang on to him?'

'I'm not blaming anyone,' I said. 'But it seems to me as if Lily is courting trouble.'

'She is, Molly. She knows she's a looker and has got what they call sex appeal, pardon my language. One day she'll go too far.'

'So you all hope to meet a duke standing at the stage door, do you?' I asked as I reapplied makeup to my lips.

'Doesn't everyone? Of course not all the stage-door Johnnies can be trusted, you know. Some of them want too much in payment for a nice dinner, and some of them – well, they're just twisted, if you know what I mean. They don't just want normal things. I worked with a girl last year who went off with a young man she met at the stage door. He looked harmless enough but her body was found floating in the Hudson with signs of horrible torture all over it. They never did find the guy responsible, or if they did, his family was powerful enough that they paid off the investigation. So stick with me after the show and I'll let you know if I see a wrong 'un.'

'Thank you,' I said.

I had no time to hear more as we were summoned down to the stage for the second act. The girls ran down ahead of me eagerly, already thinking ahead to exciting post-theater parties and glamorous dinners. The orchestra started playing and the curtain went up. We were on. As predicted, the bathing scene was a great success. There was a gasp of horror (or was it delight?) from the audience when the girls appeared in their bathing suits with their legs exposed from the knee downward. If only they'd seen me swimming in the ocean at home, I thought. Then they'd really have had something to be shocked about!

I sensed the audience too had settled down in the second act. The laughter no longer had that tense, nervous quality to it. They applauded often and loudly, clearly enjoying the show. We reached the ballroom scene and I heaved a sigh of relief. The wind machine had been removed from the stage area. The wings were empty. In ten minutes it would be over. The band struck up the waltz number and the partners whirled around. 'The waltz, the waltz, most romantic of dances, the mood that entrances, just as if we were in Vienna,' they sang.

Then Arthur, the male star, led Miss Lovejoy out onto the floor. The couples moved to the side as they began to waltz – first, fast to the tempo and then slower and slower, until they were rooted to the spot, staring into each other's eyes. I was watching them so intently that I only caught the movement out

225

of the corner of my eye. Then someone shouted, 'Look out!' Someone else screamed as a pillar toppled across the stage. Miss Lovejoy leaped aside at the last second and the pillar crashed onto the stage, exactly where she had been standing.

The audience was in an uproar. Flashbulbs went off from reporters' cameras. Some people were still screaming, already fighting their way to the exits. I slipped off stage and rushed around the backstage area, keeping one eye on the pass door, through to the front of house, and the other on the stairs that led up from the stage. All I saw were stagehands and prop boys, standing wide-eyed.

'Did you see anyone back here?' I demanded. 'Was there anyone here who shouldn't have been? Anyone out of position?'

'No, miss,' they answered. 'There was nobody here at all but us.'

'And you could see each other? You'd have noticed if one of you slipped away to give that pillar a good push?'

'Oh yes, miss. We're not allowed to loiter in the wings unless we've got a job to do and then we have to stand in a particular spot, so that we're not in the way of the actors' entrances and exits.'

Over the tumult I heard Blanche's powerful voice. 'Ladies and gentlemen, please take your seats again. I'm sorry for the interruption, but we won't let it spoil our evening. We are professional performers. We won't let a little accident prevent our grand finale, will we? The show must go on.'

There was huge applause at this.

'Maestro?' Blanche indicated the conductor who lifted his baton, glancing around shakily. 'From the last reprise if you don't mind.'

The band struck up again and Blanche began to waltz with Arthur as if nothing had happened, leaving everyone onstage staring at her in open-mouthed admiration. I was staring at her, too, because something was wrong. I had watched her through the rehearsals and something struck me as different. Then I realized what it was. When I watched her before, I could see her absolutely in profile. Now I could also see the back of her head. Someone had moved her mark.

As soon as the curtain came down and we lined up for our curtain calls, I went over to examine. I could see where the first chalk mark had been erased and the new one put in. For the first time I knew what I had suspected all along: this was no ghost. Somebody had a personal vendetta against Blanche Lovejoy!

Up in the dressing room there was chaos. Some of the girls were in tears, almost hysterical.

'She was almost killed,' Connie was wailing. 'And it almost hit me, too. It slammed down right beside me. If I'd been off my mark, I'd have been a goner as well.'

'Don't be so dramatic, Connie,' Lily said. 'It missed you by a mile. And it probably wouldn't have given you any more than a nasty concussion either. It's only a stage prop, not real marble, you know.' She took the pins out of her hair and let it fall over her shoulders. 'I don't know about you, but I'm in serious need of champagne. Some guy outside better have a jeroboam with him, and it better be chilled and waiting in an ice bucket.'

I took off my makeup and changed out of my costume while beside me Elise was doctoring her feet. 'Have you worked with Miss Lovejoy before, Elise?' I asked her.

'Yes, once, three or four years ago. Miss Lovejoy hasn't had a show for the last few years. The public seems to want sweet young things these days, ever since *Florodora*.'

'But you've been working in the theater here?'

'Oh yes, I've been in quite a few shows now.'

'So can you think of anyone who hates Miss Lovejoy?'

'Hates her?'

227

'Yes, hates her enough to kill her or at least to frighten her?'

Elise looked shocked. 'Molly, you don't think . . .'

'That the pillar wasn't either an accident or a ghost? Yes, I do.'

'Oh my goodness. But it couldn't be one of us. The whole cast was onstage for the ballroom scene. And the stage manager would have spotted anyone who wasn't supposed to be backstage. And besides, Henry would never have let them in. He's really strict, especially now with all the young men at the stage door trying to sneak up to the dressing rooms.'

I sighed. 'I know. It does seem impossible, but I've witnessed three of these incidents myself now, and nobody has seen anything suspicious, or anybody where they shouldn't have been.'

'Then maybe it is the phantom after all,' Elise said. 'I did feel cold again tonight, didn't you?'

'That's because you were in a ball gown that was very décolleté,' I said. 'And I don't believe in ghosts.'

The dressing room was beginning to thin out, girls hurrying down to latch onto the best catches among guys waiting outside the stage door.

'Come on, Molly,' Elise called. 'You don't want to be the last.'

I gathered my own belongings and followed the throng down into the street. To tell the truth, I was anxious to witness the scene for myself. I also thought it might be rather nice to be enticed away with the promise of champagne drunk from a slipper, although I couldn't think that any young man would have noticed me with my severe spectacles and thick braids.

I could hear the uproar going on beyond the stage door and Henry's raised voice. 'Just wait patiently, gentlemen. They'll be out any second now. And no, you're not going up to meet them. I don't care who you are. If you were President Roosevelt himself I'd still keep you waiting down here.'

We came out to popping flashbulbs, eager reporters, and a whole army of young men dressed in white tie and tails, watching for us expectantly. Suddenly it was as if I was having a vision. I pictured John Jacob Halsted going off to the theater and then calling his friend to tell him that he'd arranged supper and a pleasant surprise. JJ Halsted was a stage-door Johnnie!

I had barely had this thought when Elise tugged at my arm. 'Watch out for that one over there,' she whispered. 'He likes to play rough.'

I followed where she was pointing and almost couldn't believe my eyes. The young man in immaculate evening dress was none other than my Mr Roth!

Twenty-eight

I barely had time to register this when I was set upon by my friends.

'Molly, you scoundrel. How could you keep it from us that you were in the play?' Sid shouted over the tumult. She pretended to shake me.

'We nearly died of shock,' Gus added. 'It was all I could do to stop Sid from shouting out your name. You were awfully good.'

'I didn't have to do anything,' I said. 'Just stand there.'

'But you stood there so well.'

'And guess who we found in the audience?' Sid said excitedly, then stepped aside to reveal Ryan O'Hare.

'Molly, my dearest, what can I say?' He stepped forward to kiss my cheek. 'If only I'd known that a great thespian lurked beneath that delicate little bosom, I'd have hired you for one of my plays long before now.'

'You and your blarney, Ryan.' I laughed as we moved out of the crush of the crowd.

Flashbulbs were still going off and the smell of sulphur hung heavy in the air while smoke curled around us. I heard one of the girls – Connie, I believe – saying loudly, 'And it almost struck me. I was lucky to get away with my life.'

'So I take it you haven't managed to unmask the ghost yet,' Ryan said. 'I must admit that ghostly toppling of the pillar was rather spectacular.'

'Is that why you were there?' Sid asked. 'You were hired to find the ghost?'

'Exactly.'

'And do you believe there really is one?' Gus asked. 'Have you seen it? Sid and I were dearly hoping to. We've always wanted to see a ghost for ourselves, haven't we, Sid?'

'Absolutely. I must admit it was rather exciting – the pillar crashing down in full view of everyone, just missing Miss Love-joy! We were agog, weren't we, Gus?'

'My dears, I was positively terrified,' Ryan said. 'Unlike the rest of you I can't abide ghosts. I grew up in a haunted castle and I hardly slept a wink until I was sent to boarding school. I'd stare at the wall all night to make sure it wasn't coming through into my room.'

'Well, you don't have to worry, because I don't think this is a ghost,' I said. 'I believe that someone is out to get Blanche Lovejoy.'

'Who do you think it is?' Sid whispered as she drew me out into the crowded street beyond the alley.

'I have no idea.' I glanced around to see if anyone could over-hear us. 'Each time it has happened, nobody has been spotted nearby. We've been able to account for the movements of prac-tically everyone, except for the producer and the choreographer, but they wouldn't be backstage during production. And if they were, they'd have been noticed. I've now witnessed three of these strange tricks and it's still a complete mystery to me.'

Out of the corner of my eye I noticed Lily getting into a hansom cab with a young man. Then I noticed that the young man was Mr Roth. I hoped she knew what she was doing. I'd have to ask her all about it tomorrow.

'Come on, Molly, we're taking you for a late supper at the Fifth Avenue Hotel.' Sid took my arm. 'We're meeting our friend Elizabeth, who is really you-know-who. She was in the audience tonight. I know she's dying to speak to you again, and to hear what's happening with the girl in the snowdrift.'

We climbed into a cab and off we went.

It was a merry evening and I came home after midnight to find Mrs Tucker sound asleep in my armchair. My girl was sleeping equally peacefully upstairs. I didn't have the heart to send my nursemaid home in the middle of the night so I brought down blankets to cover her, then went to bed. I woke in the morning to the smell of fresh coffee. Mrs Tucker was up and bustling around my kitchen.

'Comfortable chair you've got there,' she said, not looking up from making toast. 'I slept like a baby. How's she doing today?'

'I haven't looked in on her yet. I came down to see who was making coffee.'

'I've got the tray ready to take up to her,' Mrs Tucker said.

I opened the bedroom door for her then hung back as she went inside. The girl sat up as Mrs Tucker came in, and then, to my astonishment, she smiled. As Mrs Tucker had predicted, good old-fashioned loving care was breaking through before science could.

'We'll have you up and around and talking away nineteen to the dozen, won't we, my pet?' Mrs Tucker asked as she sat on the bed beside her.

She had just finished eating and Mrs Tucker was carrying down the tray where there was a knock at the front door. It was Daniel. He came in, waving a newspaper. Giant headlines proclaimed GHOST STRIKES THEATER STAR WHILE HUNDREDS WATCH IN HORROR.

'I've been reading about the near disaster at the theater last night so I came round to see that you are all right.'

'I'm fine, thank you. Come on in and have some coffee,' I said.

'Wonderful. Thank you.' He removed his hat and placed it on the hall table. 'I must say I'm relieved to find you unscathed. What a strange business. Presumably you didn't catch the perpetrator?'

'I rushed backstage as soon as it happened. The stage hands were standing there and they saw nobody.'

'Could it have been one of them?' he asked.

'I don't see how. They were all standing together. Anyone who pushed a pillar would have been noticed.'

'Unless they were all in it together,' he suggested.

'Why would they want to do it? What motive could they have?'

'Someone was paying them well enough to risk it? Someone wanted your leading lady out of the way – someone who was not connected to the theater, maybe, and wanted to make it seem as if it was a theater vendetta.'

'That's not a bad thought,' I agreed.

'I was a detective once, you know,' Daniel said.

'I'll go to see Blanche today and find out if anyone outside of the theater might carry a grudge against her.'

'I thought I might go back to New Haven and talk to the theater people there,' Daniel said. 'I believe I've covered all bases with your Jewish bachelor.'

'We've both covered all bases,' I said, 'and another thing I have to do today is to inform the family that hired me that they do not want Mr Roth marrying their daughter.'

'Why would you say that? What possible reason can you have? The man is a paragon. Do you think she would die of boredom?'

'He's a paragon who hangs around theater stage doors with a reputation of "playing rough," as one girl put it. I saw him outside the Casino last night.'

'Good God,' Daniel said. 'I'd never have thought it of him. Are you sure it was he?'

'Oh yes, and he went off in a cab with the chorus girl who is most generous with her favors.'

'Well I never.' Daniel shook his head. 'So you've concluded one case, at least. Now you just need to find a theater ghost and the whereabouts of JJ Halsted.'

'How are we ever going to do that, Daniel? Presumably the police across the country have been alerted to be on the look-out for him.'

Daniel thought for a minute. 'Well, if I were running the case, I'd work outwards from the car. We've tried local farm-houses and we're pretty sure he didn't hide out there. So where is the nearest station? Did anyone see him getting on a train in the morning? And if he had the loot with him, how did he carry it? Silver isn't particularly light.'

'Right.' I nodded appreciatively.

'And probably carriers have a regular route up and down that stretch of road. I'd ask if Halsted could have hitched a ride with any stage going into the city. And then it might be worth checking the steamship companies and finding out if anyone matching Halsted's description booked passage to somewhere like South America.'

'This is all presupposing that he's guilty,' I said.

'Then give me another explanation.'

'I can't.'

'Then we have to assume that something drove him to act in a way that was completely uncharacteristic for him – debts or drugs. And assuming he's guilty, the next step is to see if he has fled the country.'

'You're hired for the job, Daniel,' I started to say when there was another loud knock at my front door. This time it was Dr Birnbaum, who came in waving a letter.

'We've had our first reply to my second advertisement,' he said. 'It looks promising, I think.'

He handed me the letter.

I started to read.

Dear Sirs:

We saw your advertisement regarding a young woman called Annie who might be missing from home. One of our dancers, Annie Parker, failed to turn up at the theater last week and we have had no communication with her since. Her fellow dancers suspect she may have run off with a young man.

H. Goldman
Goldman's Theater
New Haven, CT

'New Haven, Daniel,' I shouted in glee. 'She's the girl who ran off with Halsted! I told you I suspected it, didn't I?'

'Let's go upstairs and see if we can jog her memory,' Daniel said, already heading for the staircase.

Birnbaum held up a warning hand. 'This must be done cautiously and correctly. Do you realize that your bursting in and confronting her with her past might push her over the edge into permanent insanity?'

'Very well, Doctor,' Daniel said, turning back to me. 'We'll let you handle it.'

Dr Birnbaum nodded gravely. 'I should like to work more with her today, but I regret that I am expected at a hospital. I just stopped by to give you the news.'

'Thank you for coming, Doctor,' I said.

He gave a curt little bow in reply. 'Before we take that next step it might be wise to know that we indeed have the girl from New Haven here, and it is not just a coincidence that the girl's name is Annie. I suggest you ask the theater owner for a picture of his missing Annie before we attempt any communication with our young woman.'

'Good idea,' I said. 'I'll write him a note.'

'And I must take my leave.' Dr Birnbaum headed for the front door.

'I was planning to go up to New Haven myself today,' Daniel said. 'I'll take the letter, if I may, and talk with the theater manager. Do you have time to come with me, Molly?'

I was going through a whole range of emotions. Relief that we might have found out who our Annie really was mingled with less noble feelings of indignation that Daniel seemed to be taking over my case, and suggesting I come along as his assistant.

'I'm not sure,' I said. 'Let me see. I have to be at the theater by five. I wanted a chance to speak with Blanche Lovejoy before that, and I suppose I should visit the Mendelbaums to let them know what I've discovered.'

'The Mendelbaums can wait,' Daniel said airily. 'This is the crucial moment in this case. You said you wanted to learn pointers from me about how a detective handles things and one of the rules is to always follow up on the vital clues yourself. I don't mind going to New Haven alone, but . . .'

He left the rest of the sentence hanging. I was now absurdly out of sorts. In fact I almost considered saying that I had changed my mind and nobody was going to New Haven. It was only the knowledge that Annie was lying upstairs that brought me back to reality and logic. Nothing mattered except getting that girl safely back to where she belonged.

'You're right,' I said. 'The Mendelbaums can wait. It's not as if the wedding is to take place tomorrow. But I do want to speak with Blanche so I have to be at the theater early. After what happened last night I want to double-check everything before the curtain goes up. And maybe persuade the stage manager to station men at all viewpoints backstage. We've got to stop this nonsense.'

'And if it turns out to be a ghost?' Daniel grinned.

'Then I'll call in the exorcist from the church, and leave them to it,' I said.

'You'd give up the chance to be a star?' Daniel was still teasing and, I suspect, a trifle annoyed that I was currently doing something so frowned upon by polite society.

'If you knew how terrifying it is to go onstage in front of hundreds of people,' I said. 'All right, Daniel. I suppose I can fit all this into one day if we leave right away. Can you stay on, dear Mrs Tucker?'

'I suppose I could,' she said grudgingly. 'You certainly can't leave that precious lamb alone.'

'Then run upstairs and get your hat and coat, Molly. We've a train to catch,' Daniel said.

Twenty-nine

You seem out of sorts today,' Daniel commented as the train pulled out of Grand Central. 'I'd have thought you'd be excited. Case with Mr Roth concluded and now we're about to ascertain the true identity of our mystery girl.'

'I suppose I'm tired,' I said. 'It's no picnic being up until all hours at the theater and then trying to lead a normal life.' I couldn't tell him the real reason for my displeasure was that he was acting like a typical male – trying to give the orders in what was my case and my detective agency. I know it sounds petty but I couldn't help feeling that if I didn't draw the line now, it would never be drawn.

'That's quite understandable,' he said. 'And of course that near accident at the theater last night must have played on your nerves.'

'You wouldn't have said to a male detective that something dramatic must have played on his nerves. You'd never have told a superior officer to go upstairs and put on his hat and coat.'

Daniel looked at me and laughed. 'You're being silly.'

'No, I'm struggling with the fact that you don't take me or my detective agency seriously. It's my case and you're helping me, and yet you're the one who asks the questions and acts as if you are in charge.'

'Only because most men wouldn't feel comfortable answering questions from a woman.'

'And you told me to go and put on my hat and coat, as if I was five years old.'

'Because we're in a hurry. If I'd been at police headquarters I'd have said the same to a fellow officer, only not in such polite phraseology. And if you want me to forget that you are a woman, stop being so damned sensitive.'

'Hmmph.' I turned away and glared out of the window. The sight of my reflection, a picture of righteous indignation, made me smile. 'You're right,' I said. 'It's just because it's you, Daniel, and because I'm thinking things through for the long term. I want to make sure I'm seen as an equal partner. I don't want to be trodden on.'

'Oh, I don't think anybody would manage to tread on you,' Daniel said. 'At least not without getting their ankles bitten.' He stood up. 'Let's see if there is a dining car on the train and we can have a cup of coffee and a bite to eat. I left without breakfast and I suspect you did, too.'

Thus fortified, we arrived in better humor in New Haven. It was a gray, cold, blustery day and I held my scarf around my face as we battled the wind up Crown Street to the theater. The box office was open and we were taken through to the office of the theater manager, a Mr Tweedie.

'So you've managed to find our Annie, have you?' he asked. 'That is good news. She was our star dancer, you know. We miss her sorely. There – that's a picture of her on that playbill.'

He pointed at the wall and a big poster affixed to it.

Come in to the Garden, Maude was apparently the name of the show. There were various photos of pretty girls with parasols and, in the center, a group photograph of several girls peeping around giant fans.

'There. In the center photograph,' he said. 'The one in the middle.'

He was pointing to a pretty fair girl with wide eyes like a china doll and hair in golden ringlets.

'The one in the middle?' I said as disappointment washed over me. 'That's not her.'

'Oh dear. What a pity,' Mr Tweedie said. 'I was so hopeful when I read your letter. We'd dearly like her back, you know. She was the most talented dancer we've had in years and quite a looker, too. The young men used to positively fight over her. That's why we suspected that she ran off with one of them. These girls do it all the time, you know. Think they are being promised home, respectability, security, when in fact the young man has no such intentions. All he wants is a good time. When he's done with them, they often wind up in the gutter. In fact there was another girl who—'

I turned away from the poster. 'I'm sorry to have wasted your time, Mr Tweedie,' I said, cutting off his rambles. I was so disappointed that I was ready to leave, but fortunately, Daniel asked, 'Tell me, Mr Tweedie, is a man named John Jacob Halsted known to you?'

'Halsted? Why, of course we've all heard of him. That's the young fellow from Yale who robbed the bank and then shot the Silvertons' butler in cold blood, isn't it?'

'Did you know him before that? Did he come to your theater?'

'I understand from the girls that he was one of the young men who hung around the stage door,' the manager said. 'But the young gentlemen from Yale do so in droves, every night. I can't say I would recognize his face if I saw it.'

'He drove a smart red motor car,' I said. 'The latest model.'

Tweedie nodded. 'Yes, I did see a vehicle like that in the alleyway behind the theater from time to time.'

'On the day that Annie disappeared?' I asked.

He shook his head. 'I can't remember,' he said.

We came away subdued and silent.

'I was so excited. I was sure our girl was Annie,' I said at last. 'It would have been so wonderful.'

'Not for Annie,' Daniel said. 'Because something terrible would have happened to her between leaving the theater and being found in Central Park.'

I nodded.

'Do you think it's possible that Annie and Halsted might have cooked this up together and that they are now somewhere sufficiently far away, enjoying the spoils?'

Daniel frowned. 'I suppose it's possible,' he said. 'In any case, I'm afraid you're right again and we're back to square one with the girl. I think you may have saddled yourself with an enormous burden here, Molly. I told you at the time that I thought you were being unwise.'

'Dr Birnbaum and Mrs Tucker will cure her between them, I know they will,' I said. 'She smiled at Mrs Tucker today. That's a huge breakthrough, isn't it?'

'It doesn't sound like it to me, but if you think so . . .'

'I do.' I glanced up at him. 'It means she's coming to trust us and regard us as her friends. I bet one day she'll suddenly start talking again.'

'And like most women, she probably won't shut up,' Daniel said, then dodged as I went to hit him with my handbag.

The return journey seemed to take forever. The weather deteriorated and the heavens opened, peppering the carriage windows with cold rain.

'I was thinking that I should leave the train at the station closest to the automobile wreck,' Daniel said. 'I can question them as to whether Halsted was seen there. And then I should check with the steamship companies to see if anyone matching Halsted's description bought tickets for two to South America.'

'Why South America particularly?' I asked.

'Because it's where people go if they are running from the law. There are certain countries where foreigners are welcome and no questions are asked.'

'I see.' I stared out at the bleak, desolate landscape and said a silent prayer that Halsted and Annie were indeed enjoying their ill-gotten gains in South America and not lying somewhere in those marshes.

Daniel got off the train, leaving me to cross the bridge into Manhattan alone. I arrived home to be met at the front door by an excited Mrs Tucker.

'Good news, Miss Murphy!'

'She's speaking again?'

'No, but you've had a letter. Her family has been found.'

'Oh, that's wonderful news,' I said. 'Where's the letter?'

'On the kitchen table. That German doctor brought it round. It must have come in the second delivery.'

I was already rushing ahead of her down the hall to the kitchen. It was on cheap lined paper, the kind that comes out of a child's school copy book.

Dear Sir or Madam:

My heart was full of joy when a friend show me your notice in the newspaper. You see, I believe from your description this girl is my betrothed, Anya Bartok. She was expected to arrive from Hungary on a steamship last week. I went to meet the ship but I never found her. She is a simple girl. She comes from my small village and speaks no English.

If you would be kind enough to meet me tomorrow morning at eleven, under the clock at Grand Central Terminus, you can conduct me to her and I will be able to take her home.

Mr Laslo Baka

'That's it,' I said excitedly. 'Why she couldn't understand us! She only speaks Hungarian. Nobody spoke Hungarian to her! I'm so happy, Mrs Tucker. She's going to be going to people who can take care of her.'

'Hmmph,' Mrs Tucker said. 'I'd like to get a good look at him myself, before I let her go with him. Why didn't she meet him at the boat? That's what I'd like to know. And what if he was the one she ran away from?'

I hadn't considered this.

'We'll take a good look at him tomorrow,' I said. 'We won't let her go if we don't like the look of him.'

Thirty

I could hardly get through the rest of the day, I was so excited. Whatever terrible thing had happened to her, our girl Annie now had a good chance of recovery among those who loved her.

I went off to the theater earlier than usual, determined to get somewhere at last with this baffling case I was pursuing. There was a crowd around the theater, even at that time in the afternoon. A big sign across the glass doors read sold out and men were waving tickets. 'Five dollars,' one was shouting. 'Five dollars for a front row seat. See the ghost up close.' People started fighting to get their money out and pay him. It seemed that a lot of people were dying to see our elusive phantom.

'People are fighting for tickets out there, Henry,' I said as I arrived, rather battered and windswept at the stage door, having run the gauntlet of reporters as well as ticket hunters.

'Oh yes. Everyone wants to see the ghost for themselves,' he said. 'You wouldn't believe the trouble I've had fending off newspaper reporters all day.'

'Henry,' I said, 'you see everyone who goes in and out. Has anyone suspicious or unsavory showed up, wanting to talk to one of the stagehands, maybe?'

Henry frowned. 'I'd have sent him packing if he did. They

can leave messages with me, but I'm not going to leave my post to fetch anyone from the stage.'

'I see.' This wasn't going to get me anywhere. I left him and made my way upstairs. I found Martha alone in Blanche's dressing room.

'The mistress hasn't arrived yet,' she said, scowling at me in her normal unfriendly fashion. 'Gone to her doctor to get more tonic for her nerves, poor thing.'

'As a matter of fact, it's you I wanted to talk to,' I said, 'because I'm sure you know Miss Lovejoy better than anybody. I want to know whether she might have any enemies outside of the theater.'

'What do you mean by that?' Martha asked sharply.

'I mean that the falling pillar almost killed her yesterday. I was wondering if somebody could have paid off a stagehand to give it a push at the right moment, somebody who had a reason for wanting Blanche out of the way.'

Martha's old face stared at me, puzzled. 'Who would ever want to do that? Everyone loves her. She's the most beloved actress in New York. Always has been.'

'Another actress maybe? One who is jealous of her? Or a jilted lover?'

'The only jilted lover is that Barker fellow, and he never gives up. She won't have him, you know. She's holding out for something better.'

I came out of the dressing room with all kinds of crazy thoughts in my head. What if Robert Barker's devotion had turned to hate? He was a small man and small men often have an exaggerated sense of pride. He was also the director, with the power to hire or fire anyone in the theater. He could have enlisted the help of anyone to do his dirty work. Maybe he had bribed a couple of stagehands to be in it together, each the alibi for the other. But how would I ever prove it?

I walked slowly along the passageway, wondering if I would dare to confront him. He might have been a small man, but he was probably stronger than me and not hampered by tight and impractical women's clothing. No, I'd have to be more subtle than that.

And then there was Desmond Haynes, whom I hadn't seen at all yesterday. Was it just that the choreographer's work was done as soon as the show opened, or was he lying low so that he could be the ghost and create an accident? Again, I had no good reason for his wanting to kill or harm Miss Lovejoy, just tidbits of hearsay and gossip. I wished I knew more about the theater, which taverns theater folk gathered in, for example. I'd have to go back to Ryan and see if I could enlist him as my spy in places where gossip might be overheard.

I came around the corner and bumped into Miss Lovejoy herself.

'Molly, what are you doing here so early?' she asked.

'In case you've forgotten, you hired me to get to the bottom of the ghost story,' I said. 'I thought I'd take a peek around backstage for myself before the show opens today, just to make sure there are no contraptions rigged up to harm you.'

'Contraptions?' She shook her head. 'You mean deliberately rigged to fall on me?'

'It's possible,' I said.

She was still shaking her head in bewilderment. 'I can't believe that anyone would want to harm me. Who would want to do that? Everyone here is so grateful that I've given them a chance to be in one of my hit shows.'

'What about your friend Mr Barker? Is it possible that he has grown tired of waiting for you?'

'Bobby?' She gave a merry peel of laughter. 'Bobby will be faithful to me until his death, I assure you. And as for rigging up contraptions – he is the most meek and mild little fellow. He once turned a horrible shade of green when he found a mouse caught in a trap.'

'And Desmond Haynes?'

'Dear Desmond? Well, between the two of us, my dear, his interest doesn't lie in girls. We had a brief relationship once but it led nowhere. I could see at the time that his thoughts were straying in other directions. And he is the consummate professional. He would never do anything to damage the success of his show. He's with the girls now at the rehearsal studio, you know. Putting them through their paces once more before they take to the stage tonight. He'll work himself into an early grave, will our Desmond.'

'Then somebody else?' I said. 'Can you think of anybody who might have joined this company harboring a secret desire to get revenge on you?'

She laughed again. 'If it was a secret desire, how would I know about it? But the answer is that nobody in the cast knows me well enough to want revenge. Our paths have only crossed when we have been part of the same company, and frankly, I was always the star – set quite apart from the rest of them.'

She patted my shoulder as if I were a slow child. 'I'm sure you mean well and you're trying really hard, but I think you're wasting your time, and mine. You haven't been able to find out the truth or to protect me so far, so I'm afraid I have to conclude that you don't possess the skills to solve something as bizarre as this. So maybe we should call our relationship quits. I'll pay you for the time you've put in and that will be that.'

'Miss Lovejoy,' I said, angrily now, 'last night you were almost killed on the stage. If you had been standing another foot to the left, that pillar would have crashed onto your head. Now, I don't believe it was a ghost that gave that pillar a shove. I believe it was someone backstage. Maybe more than one person in a conspiracy, and I would like to get to the bottom of it. It appeared to me that your mark onstage had been deliberately moved, although I can't prove this. I ask you to give me another week at least. Either that or call in the police right away and have guards stationed around the stage area.'

She considered this, frowning. 'It would make everyone so nervous, having great burly men stationed everywhere.'

'And it doesn't make them nervous having pillars fall and nearly kill people?'

She sighed. 'Maybe you are right. I wish I knew what was best. I tried to keep this away from the newspapers, but now look what's happened – everyone witnessed that pillar falling last night, so now the whole country knows about it. I don't want to be defeated but I don't want to live in constant fear, either. I am at my wit's end, Molly. My wit's end.'

She put her hand up to her head in a wonderfully dramatic gesture.

'Give me a few more days, Miss Lovejoy,' I said. 'Then I really think that you should call in the police.'

'Very well,' she said. 'I am in your hands, Molly.'

I left her and conducted a quick tour backstage. No wires attached to pillars, nothing suspicious or dangerous to be seen. I went back to my dressing room and got ready for the evening's performance. The curtain went up. The house was packed. One could sense the electricity in the air. Was the ghost going to make an appearance? I could feel them all holding their breath, prepared to be scared and delighted at the same time. But for once the ghost was well behaved, and we went through the whole performance with no incidents at all.

'Maybe the ghost has realized he can't make Miss Lovejoy quit,' one of the girls was saying as I came back into the dressing room after the curtain calls.

'She's a tough lady all right,' someone else agreed. 'Look

how she stood there calmly last night and said the show must go on. I got chills up and down my spine.'

'It didn't hurt our attendance, did it?' another girl chimed in. 'Miss L. was terrified it would keep the people away if the news got out, but look at tonight's crowd. They couldn't wait to see the ghost for themselves.'

'Yes, well, I have some ideas on that score,' Lily said, then went on calmly untying her ballet slippers.

'Meaning what?'

'Oh, nothing.' She flung a ballet shoe into her box.

'How was your beau last night?' I asked.

She looked at me as if I were a worm that dared to address her. 'It's none of your business,' she said. 'But let's just say that he wasn't my cup of tea, and when it came down to it, he was downright stingy with the money he put out.' She turned to Connie. 'And he had some funny ideas,' she muttered, thinking I wouldn't overhear. 'Lucky for me I got a whiff of what he wanted to do before we left the restaurant. So I played the distressed virgin. Great tears trickling down my cheeks. Imploring the saints. That always works. He took me home.'

'What did he want to do?' Connie asked.

Lily whispered something into her ear. Connie went bright red. 'He never did?' she demanded. 'The louse.'

I came out of the theater into the throng in the alleyway. Mr Roth was there again. I wondered if, in the interests of good investigation, I should go with him myself tonight, but I reasoned that I didn't have Lily's skills in making a getaway at the right moment.

Thirty-one

I opened my eyes to the smell of freshly brewing coffee again, lay contentedly for a moment, then wondered why I had such butterflies in my stomach. I had already made it through my first two nights onstage. It wasn't Christmas. But something big was about to happen. Then I remembered and sat upright. This morning I was to meet Annie's betrothed, and by tonight she could be safely among those who could take care of her.

I came down to a breakfast laid on the kitchen table, and a tray ready for our girl upstairs. It struck me that having Mrs Tucker to stay overnight again had not been such a bad idea.

'Well, here we are then,' she said. 'Maybe the last meal I shall make for the poor, dear soul.'

'I am very grateful, Mrs Tucker,' I said. 'I believe you've made all the difference to her.'

'I've done my best,' she said, looking pleased. 'I think I was born to be a nurse, you know. If I hadn't married Mr Tucker, I'd have maybe gone into nursing. And how was I to know that the louse would go and die at forty, when it was too late for me to take up a useful profession?'

She picked up the tray. 'I'll just take this up to her. The doctor should be here soon. Between you and me I don't think he's doing a darned thing to help the young thing. Just makes her cry most days and then tells us he's making progress.'

Up the stairs she went like a ship in full sail. I sat down and helped myself to the oatmeal and toast she had prepared. I had just finished when Dr Birnbaum arrived.

'A momentous day, wouldn't you say, Miss Murphy? I just wish I could be here to see the young lady handed into the care of her loved ones.'

'You can't stay?'

'Unfortunately, I am to address the New York medical society at a luncheon today. I have to be there by eleven thirty and I must go over my speech before that. It is a very important occasion for me. There are many doctors who still resist the thought that the mind is something that can be treated by scientific methods, that dreams are mirrors into the world of the subconscious.'

'Then I wish you luck,' I said, 'although I also wish you could be here to help me decide.'

'Decide what?'

'Whether to let the girl go with this Laslo person.'

'My dear, if he brings proof that he is her family, then you have no choice but to release her to him. It's not up to you to judge.'

'I suppose not.' I sighed. 'I've come to feel so responsible for her.'

'I'm sure it will all turn out magnificently. Maybe one sight of the young man who is her betrothed and her memory will return instantly. I've seen that happen before, you know – patients coming out of comas at the sound of a beloved voice.'

'At least being Hungarian explains one thing – why she doesn't understand us. Hungarian is a strange and difficult language, not related to any other. She must have thought we were beings from another world, jabbering at her. No wonder she was so afraid and unwilling to trust us.'

I nodded. 'That certainly does explain things.'

'And now I must hurry up and see my patient. Would you please leave the gentleman my card and tell him that I will be happy to continue working with the girl if they wish, at her new address.'

'You're very kind.'

'On the contrary. She presents me with my biggest challenge to date. I would love to return home to Dr Freud with such a case documented.'

He went up the stairs. I heard him greet Mrs Tucker and then say something to the girl that I didn't understand. After a few minutes he came downstairs again. 'I tried addressing her in Hungarian,' he said. 'I know a few phrases. But it seemed to make her more distressed, so I stopped.'

I closed the door behind him, still wondering. If the sound of Hungarian being spoken made her more distressed, how could I be doing the right thing in handing her over to this young man? A suspicion came into my head. What if she had arrived, an innocent virgin from Hungary, pledged to a man she hardly knew, and what if he had tried to have his way with her as soon as he got her home? Might she not have fled into the snow, hoping to find a friend? I was going to give Mr Laslo Baka a good grilling before he took Annie away.

I dressed with care and then took the El to Grand Central, giving myself plenty of time to reach the meeting place first. I stationed myself under the clock, as instructed, and waited. It was smoky and noisy in there with the sound of puffing loco-motives competing with the shouts of porters and the hubbub of the crowd. I waited. The clock struck eleven. Nobody came. An absurd hope rose inside me that he had changed his mind and I wouldn't have to give up Annie to him. Of course, like many of my notions, it bordered on the ridiculous. I had neither the time nor the means to care for her in the long run, but I realized I'd harbored this stupid secret fantasy that one day she'd open her eyes and say, 'I am restored to my former self, thanks to you, Molly Murphy.'

I hadn't taken into account that her former self might have been deranged.

As the big hand on the clock jumped on to ten after eleven and I had decided to leave, I saw two men hurrying toward me. One was tall, lanky, and dark-haired, with a sad face and drooping mustache, and the other short, stocky, clean-shaven, and distinguished-looking, with an impressive head of iron-gray hair worn beneath a dark homburg. They both wore dark overcoats of what seemed to be good quality, and the older one carried an ebony cane with a silver tip.

'Miss Murphy?' It was the older one who spoke. He held out his hand. 'May I present my nephew Laslo Baka. Unfortunately, he speaks only little English. He came from Hungary two years ago.'

He nudged the younger one, who held out his hand. 'Happy to meet you, Mees Murphy,' he said.

'And I you,' I replied.

'We are so grateful you rescue our beautiful girl for us,' the older one went on. 'We think she is lost forever.'

'We don't yet know that it is your girl,' I said.

'Of course. But we are hopeful. You find this girl lost the day after she should have arrived from Germany on the ship.'

'How was it that you failed to meet her at the ship?' I asked.

The old man muttered something to the younger one, who muttered a reply.

'He say he was a little late. They were digging up the streets around the docks. The cab take longer than it should. He gets out and starts to run. It is farther than he thinks and when he gets there – the gangways are already down and people are going ashore. My nephew asks for her. He goes on board and asks for her. They think she already went ashore.'

The young man muttered something else, waving his arms as he spoke. 'He is frantic. He is desperate. He search the whole of New York for her.'

'What do you think happened?' I asked.

'What I think,' the old man said grandly, 'is that sometimes no good rats wait for these ships. They pounce on girls alone. They lure them away and want to force them into prostitution.' He looked at me with a penetrating gaze. 'What was the girl wearing when you found her?'

'She was dressed as if for a party or the theater. A white silk evening dress. Little evening slippers.'

'No coat? No shawl?'

'No. Nothing.'

'You see, I am right! These rats, they dress her, tell her is for party, and then she find what is for. She escape. She run.'

It did seem possible.

'So now we take cab. We go to her, *si*?'

'Do you have a photograph of the girl you are looking for?' I asked.

'Unfortunately, no. This girl is from primitive village, far from city. No photographer. But I bring you letters.' He opened his overcoat and produced some papers from an inside pocket. He bowed as he handed them to me. 'One from her father. One from priest to say on which ship she comes.'

I stared at the letters. They looked as if birds had been hopping over the paper, creating a series of wild scratches that hardly resembled words. Finally, I did manage to pick out the word Budapest and then Bremen on one of them. The older man looked over my shoulder and jabbed at the letter with his forefinger. 'This say Anya is so happy that she will meet Laslo again. She looks forward to her new life in America.'

'We don't yet know that it is the same girl,' I said.

'We will know her when we see her. We go?'

He took my arm and firmly escorted me from the station and out to the hansom cabs.

'It's quite a way to my house,' I said. 'Are you sure you don't want to take the El?'

'No, today is important day,' the uncle said. 'Today we take cab.'

He hailed a hansom and helped me in with great courtesy. The nephew scrambled in behind him.

'So where do you live?' I asked.

'Brooklyn. We live Brooklyn. Nice house. Backyard. Good place for girl.'

'Is her name really Annie?'

'Anya,' he says. 'Sometime we call her Anni. Is affectionate little name, no?'

The cab ride seemed to go on forever. I kept telling myself that these were good people. They were well dressed. They had enough money to take care of her. She would be fine. From time to time I glanced at the younger one. He had a beaky nose and dark, sad eyes. But he seemed mild enough. He had taken off his gloves and I noticed that his hands were not those of a laborer.

'What kind of work does your nephew do?' I asked.

'He work for me,' the old man replied. 'I own a business.'

'What kind of business?'

He looked at me scornfully for a moment. 'Trade. Buying and selling.' Then he laughed and patted my hand. 'You a young lady. What you know about business?'

'I run one,' I said. 'I own my own detective agency.'

I thought he looked startled for a moment, then he chuckled again. 'You – a detective? What you look for, lost pussycats?'

'Actually my agency is quite successful,' I replied haughtily. 'I located you, didn't I?'

'Anya will not have to work.' He dismissed me with a wave of his kid-gloved hand. 'My family will keep her safe and well fed. You can be assured of that.'

Another long silence.

'So tell me again, how you find her?' he asked. 'Was it just chance?'

'Pure chance. I was walking through Central Park, with my gentleman friend, and we stumbled upon the body. I thought she was dead. She wore no cloak. Only dainty evening slippers. But we managed to revive her and brought her to the nearest hospital. Then the hospital didn't want to take care of her any longer, so I had her brought to my place.'

'Central Park?' he said. 'This is far from ship. How does she get to Central Park, I ask myself. She can tell you nothing of this?'

'She doesn't speak,' I said. 'She appears not to understand.'

'Ah. She will understand Hungarian and tell us what happened to her. You are kind young lady. We thank you.' He nodded to me graciously.

We pulled up at last at the entrance to Patchin Place.

'Nice house. Small,' the uncle said.

He picked his way in his polished patent shoes through the remaining slush to my front door. I let them in. They stood in my hallway, looking around.

'You say she remembers nothing?'

'Nothing. The doctor who is treating her says she has experienced a very traumatic event.' I saw this might be beyond the scope of his English. 'Something very bad happened to her.'

'Exactly what I tell you. Some rat try to make her do bad things.'

'She's up here, in the bedroom. Do you think she will know you?'

'Me she will not know. I came to America when she is little girl. My nephew, she will know him, I am sure. He left our village five years ago to work in Vienna. He work there until I tell him to come to New York. When he want wife, I say take nice girl from our village and the girl's father arrange with me. But she should remember his face, I hope. He has not changed much in five years.'

I led them up the stairs.

'Tell me,' I said. 'Was Anya a dancer?'

'Dancer? No. Her parents have bakery. Make bread. Good girl.'

I opened her door and went in. Mrs Tucker was sitting beside her.

'Dr Birnbaum has kept her mildly sedated,' I said. 'He gave her something to make her sleep a lot.'

They came to stand beside me. I heard the intake of breath.

'It is her. Thank God,' the old man said and crossed himself. The nephew did likewise.

'You're sure?'

'I would know her anywhere. She look just like her mother. When I was a young man her mother and I were sweethearts.'

I touched her hand. 'Anni? Something wonderful has happened. Here is Laslo, come to take you home. You remember Laslo?'

Her eyes opened and focused on the young man bending over her. 'Anni?' he said, then rattled off a string of Hungarian at her. She stared at him blankly.

He took her hand. She shrank away from him, looking scared, and grabbed at Mrs Tucker for support.

'She may not remember anything at all,' I said. 'In which case she won't remember you or where she is or why she's here.'

'Tragic,' the old man said. 'So sad. What she needs is to be among her own people. I am sure she will soon recover, God willing.'

Laslo had knelt beside her, stroking her hair and murmuring strange-sounding endearments. He sounded genuinely concerned and my heart warmed a little to him. Annie, however, glanced up at me with a worried look on her face and tried to push his hand away.

'It is so sad. She does not remember him.' The uncle wiped his eyes. 'Come, Nephew. We will take her home. My wife makes the good noodles, the goulash. Look how thin she is! Soon we will make her fat and healthy again, you see.'

Laslo took the blanket from her bed and wrapped it around her, then he gathered her up into his arms. She made a pathetic little whimpering noise. Mrs Tucker leaped forward. 'Hey, you make sure she's kept warm enough. And you treat her properly now.'

'Of course,' the uncle said.

Laslo started to carry her downstairs. She lay in his arms unresisting, which seemed to me a good sign. I caught up with the uncle.

'Can I have your address, please? I know that Dr Birnbaum wants to go on treating her, if that's all right with you.'

'We don't need strange doctor. We have Hungarian doctor.'

'But he is an alienist – a doctor of the mind. He was beginning to have success in getting through to her with hypnosis. He reckons he can find out what happened to her that night and why she is so afraid. You can work with him and translate for her.'

The old man shook his head firmly. 'This I do not like. We do not believe in such things. She will come back to us with

258

love and with good food. You see. She just needs to be with her own people. Then all will be well.'

'I'd like your address anyway,' I said. 'Just in case.'

'Of course. It is twenty-nine Brook Street. Brooklyn. You are welcome to come and visit her when she recovers more.'

'Thank you.' I stood in the doorway as they made their way toward the waiting hansom. 'Take good care of her, won't you,' I called after them.

'Of course. Goodbye.'

The cab started up and disappeared from view.

Thirty-two

Mrs Tucker and I looked at each other in silence.

'You shouldn't have let her go,' she said.

'What choice did I have? They are her family – or she is about to be part of their family.'

'Then why wasn't she wearing a ring, if she was promised to him?'

'Maybe they don't in their society. Maybe he was going to give her the ring when they met here in America, or maybe it was stolen from her in Central Park. Who knows, maybe she was robbed of all her possessions.'

Mrs Tucker shook her head again. 'I didn't like the look of them, myself.'

'They looked prosperous enough,' I said. 'And they are taking on a tough assignment, restoring her to health, so they must care about her.'

'I'm glad you got their address. If I were you, I'd go and check on her for myself. Just in case.'

'I will,' I said. 'And I expect that Dr Birnbaum will want to as well, even if they don't wish him to continue with his treatments.'

I felt bleak and empty as I went upstairs. Mrs T. was already bustling around the room, stripping the bed and folding the sheets for the laundry.

'They walked off with your blanket as well,' she said accusingly. 'The darned cheek of it.'

'They're welcome to the blanket,' I said, 'as long as it keeps
her warm.'

Then I started to cry. I don't know why I felt so strongly
about her, but ever since I stumbled over her in Central Park I
felt as if she were calling to me to protect her. And I had just
let her go.

Still, I now had one less item on my plate, one less thing to
worry about, which was good. This could be a day for sewing
up loose ends, to use yet another house hold metaphor. I would
go to see the Mendelbaums with my report. I just wished I
could tie up my theater case as well. It irked me that I was no
closer to unmasking the ghost. And now Blanche had virtu-
ally decided that I was useless and was going to terminate my
contract at the end of the week. My only chance of getting
anywhere was to enlist Ryan O'Hare as my spy. He heard all
the theater gossip. Surely someone must have dropped a hint if
they knew anything at all.

Mrs Tucker had finished tidying up. 'Well that's that then, I
suppose,' she said, looking sadly at me. 'You'll not be needing
me anymore.'

'I suppose not, Mrs Tucker. And I'm most grateful to you.
You did a wonderful job looking after her. Let me give you
what I owe you.'

I went to the drawer in the kitchen cabinet and took out the
money. I gave her more than we had agreed on.

'That's very generous of you, miss,' she said. 'I'll make you
a nice macaroni pudding for your lunch, before I go, shall I?'

'No, thank you. I'm not hungry.'

'It's all for the best,' she said as she collected her hat and
shawl.

'I hope so,' I whispered as I stood alone in my dark hallway.

Then I saw my gloomy face in the mirror. No use in standing around moping. At least I had one case I could conclude successfully. I spruced myself up, put on my long woolen cape, and headed uptown to the apartment of the Mendelbaums on the Upper West Side.

I was greeted by a prim maid and shown into the front hall while she went to announce my arrival. I could tell instantly that my timing had been bad. I could hear the chink of dishes and the sound of luncheon conversation coming from a door on my right. After a short wait Mrs Mendelbaum appeared, wiping her hands on her napkin.

'Miss Murphy,' she said, looking a little flustered. 'How nice of you to call. Unfortunately, I am currently entertaining guests to luncheon.' She shot a worried glance toward the dining room.

'I'm sorry, I hadn't realized the time,' I said. 'I should call back later, when your guests have gone.'

'That might be better,' she said, 'Unless you would care to join us? We're already halfway through the main course, though.'

'No, thank you. I don't think that would be appropriate, or fair to your guests,' I said. 'Should I return in an hour or so?'

'Very good,' she said. 'That would be an excellent idea.'

She looked much relieved as she headed back into the dining room and I made for the front door. I spent an hour kicking my heels in a ladies' tea room on Amsterdam Avenue, where I suspected the cheese sandwich had been on display in the window for several days, then returned to the Mendelbaums' apartment building.

'Mrs Mendelbaum is expecting me,' I said to the maid this time. 'She asked me to return in an hour and I have done so.'

'Very good, miss. Come this way then.' She took me down

the hall to the doorway past the dining room and ushered me inside. 'Miss Murphy has returned as requested, madam.'

I stepped into a warm sitting room and was surprised to find that Mrs Mendelbaum was not alone. She jumped to her feet as I came in.

'Oh, Miss Murphy. So soon? I'm sorry but my luncheon guests haven't all departed yet.'

I wasn't going to disappear again. It was a long trip for me to the Upper West Side.

A young woman who had been sitting on a sofa also got to her feet. 'We were just leaving, weren't we, Leon?'

I looked at the young man whose hand she was tugging to pull him up from the sofa. It was Mr Roth.

'There's no rush, Lanie,' he said. 'Let us digest our luncheon, for goodness sake.'

Mrs Mendelbaum's eyes darted from Mr Roth to me. 'Miss Murphy, may I present my daughter Lanie and her betrothed, Mr Leon Roth.'

'How do you do,' I said and politely shook hands.

'I suggest you two go on your walk, if you're going,' Mrs Mendelbaum said. 'You know how early it gets dark at this time of year.'

'Yes, I am determined to walk to the park and back,' Lanie said. 'Come, Leon.'

He got up, unwillingly, and followed her from the room.

Mrs Mendelbaum's gaze turned to an elderly woman. 'And you, Mama. Isn't it time for you nap?'

'I can tell when I'm not wanted,' the old woman said, rising from her chair with difficulty and shuffling out of the door.

Mrs Mendelbaum and I stood facing each other in awkward silence.

'Please take a seat, Miss Murphy,' she said at last. 'It was good of you to come.'

'Rather awkward under the circumstances,' I said. 'I see you have already made up your minds about the suitability of Mr Roth as a husband for your daughter. You didn't need my help after all.'

'It was our daughter who rushed things along, Miss Murphy. She took one look at the young man and fell hopelessly in love. She is an impulsive girl, and she has her father wrapped around her little finger. He doesn't deny her anything she wants.'

'I wish you could have waited until I submitted my report,' I said, 'because I believe I have uncovered some not-so-savory details about Mr Roth.'

'Oh dear. How vexing.' She glanced at the door as her daughter's high-pitched laugh echoed down the hallway, followed by the slamming of the front door.

'They've gone,' she said with a sigh of relief. 'Now please feel free to speak. You do not think it wise that Lanie should proceed with this engagement?'

'I don't, Mrs Mendelbaum.' I leaned closer to her. 'I followed Mr Roth for several days and I am disappointed to report that his moral character is not all that it should be.'

'Mercy me,' she said. 'What can you mean?'

'I mean that he hangs around stage doors and picks up chorus girls.'

She put her hand to her impressive bosom and started to chuckle. 'Is that all? Surely every young man in New York has had a yen for chorus girls at some time or other. It's a natural part of growing up, Miss Murphy.'

'But I heard rumors that he does not treat them well. That he is – well, rather rough with them. That he makes strange demands of them.'

'What kind of demands?'

Since I hadn't been privy to that conversation I couldn't

supply her with details. 'Just that they were afraid to go with him. That should be enough to warn you, shouldn't it?'

Instead of agreeing with me, she shook her head, still smiling. 'This is of no importance for Lanie's future, Miss Murphy. After they are married there will be no more evenings at the theater. No more chorus girls. The boy will learn to settle down and be a good husband and doting father. We shall make sure of that. I was more concerned about his financial status.'

'His financial affairs seem above reproach,' I said. 'He is thought of highly among his colleagues and at his bank, one gathers.'

'Then that is all that matters. Young men are expected to sow their wild oats, Miss Murphy. You're no more than a slip of a girl yourself. You have probably led a sheltered life and never encountered such things, but young men with a good income make a practice of wining and dining chorus girls. They may get drunk and act foolishly from time to time. But it all stops when they marry.'

'But are you not concerned that he may treat your daughter roughly? He may make strange demands of her?'

'My daughter is used to getting her own way, Miss Murphy,' she said firmly. 'I don't think she'll have any problem keeping Leon Roth in order, and if she does, then Mr Mendelbaum will soon straighten him out. Everyone listens to Mr Mendelbaum, if they know what's good for them.'

She stood up again. 'I'm so glad you came and I thank you for the information. I owe you a fee, don't I? Let me find my checkbook.'

She went to a lady's writing desk, beautifully carved in mahogany, and opened the roll top. Then she scrawled something on a check and handed it to me. 'I think we agreed on one hundred, didn't we?'

'I hardly like to take it if I did you no service,' I said.

'Take it. Of course you should take it. You put in the time and effort, didn't you? You supplied us with the facts. Now it is up to us to decide whether we should act on those facts. And knowing my daughter and how headstrong she is, I'd say there is little likelihood that she will let Leon Roth out of her clutches again. And I suspect they will be blissfully happy.'

She waved the check back and forth to let the ink dry and then put it firmly into my hands.

I left the house with a bad taste in my mouth. Should I have been more forceful in my condemnation of Leon Roth? Was Lanie Mendelbaum destined for a hard time ahead? Then I told myself that it was none of my business. I had been hired for a job. I had done the job. What they did with the information I supplied was their business. As my friends had told me, I got too emotionally involved with my cases. I should learn to keep all emotion out of my work.

Thirty-three

After I left the Mendelbaums', I paid a satisfying visit to my bank, then I checked a nearby clock and decided I might just have time to find Ryan at home before I had to report to the theater. I went all the way back to Washington Square and to the Hotel Lafayette, only to find that Ryan wasn't there. This was turning into a most vexing day. I was just leaving the hotel again when who should be coming along the sidewalk but Dr Birnbaum, who also resided at the Lafayette.

'Ah, Miss Murphy,' he said, raising his hat to me and clicking his heels at the same time, which was no mean feat. 'I have just been to call on you. I was most anxious to hear how things went this morning.'

'Our girl has been taken away by her relatives,' I said.

'Well, that is good news, isn't it? So all was well? They recognized her immediately?'

'They did.'

'And it was too much to expect that she recognized them?'

'She certainly didn't seem to. If anything she looked worried when they spoke to her.'

He nodded. 'Only natural. Her brain was trying to put the pieces of the jigsaw puzzle back together. Something inside her was saying that she should know these people, but she

267

probably associates them with home and knows that they are in the wrong place. She didn't even react to their speaking Hungarian to her?'

'She didn't answer them, or even look as if she understood.'

'It will take time. We just have to be patient. At least with loving care she may make dramatic improvements. You told them that I would like to continue treating the patient?'

'I did, but they insisted that they would rather have their own doctor. They seemed suspicious of alienists.'

'Only too frequent a reaction, I fear. But you took their address, did you?'

'I did. And I remember it. It is twenty-nine Brook Street, Brooklyn.'

'Excellent.' He produced a little notebook, took a pencil from the side of it, and jotted down the address. 'I think I will call on them anyway and again offer my services. I can say modestly that I have a better chance of restoring her to health than any other doctor in New York, except for Meyer, maybe.'

'I'd be glad if you did call on her,' I said. 'I'd like to know she was safely settled and being looked after well.'

'I will report back to you then,' he said. 'But I shouldn't keep you out here in the cold. Were you looking for me at the hotel?'

'No, for Ryan, actually. But he's not home.'

'When is he ever home? He flits around like a dragonfly, that one. So may I offer you some tea before you go on your way?'

'It's kind of you, but I have to make my way back to the theater,' I said.

'Ah yes, the famous play. Were there any ghostly manifestations last night?'

'No, the play went smoothly.'

'Fascinating.' The doctor stroked his light blond beard. 'What is your own deduction, Miss Murphy? Have you personally seen this spirit?'

'I have seen its acts,' I said. 'I have seen a jug of lemonade throw itself over Miss Lovejoy. I have seen a pillar topple and nearly hit her. But I can't believe it is the work of a ghost. I'm sure it's a vindictive person, but I can account for everybody's movements and I have no idea how these tricks were done.'

'If it were an illusionist show, like that rascal Houdini's, then you'd have your answer. Those fellows can make things appear and disappear before your very eyes. Most unnerving.'

'Unfortunately, this is a simple musical comedy. No illusionists as far as I know.'

I left him and went on my way to the theater, deep in thought. This was a suggestion that might be worth pursuing. Somehow I should be able to check whether anyone in the cast had worked as an illusionist or with an illusionist at any time. At least this gave me something positive to do and I walked up Broadway from the trolley with a more sprightly step.

There was another large crowd milling around the front entrance. I even overheard a bookmaker taking odds on whether the ghost would appear tonight. I pushed through to the stage door and was on my way up to the dressing room when Robert Barker called to me.

'You, girl.'

I stopped and looked back at him.

'Miss Lovejoy wants you onstage.'

'Onstage? Now?'

I could feel my cheeks flaming. Had I got something wrong? Was the performance on Fridays at an earlier time and nobody had told me?

'Yes, now,' he snapped. 'Hurry up. She needs you there.'

I ran back down the stairs, past the prop room, and negotiated the backstage area. Through the side curtains I could see that the stage lights were full on. I stepped out into their glare, shielding my eyes. I saw that Blanche was standing alone at the front of the stage. The curtain was up and she was addressing invisible people in the audience.

'Here she is now,' I heard a male voice say.

Blanche turned around, saw me, and held out her hand in a welcoming gesture.

'Oh, Miss Murphy. I'm so glad you've come. Do join me. I decided the time for secrecy was passed, so I called a meeting of the gentlemen of the press.'

I took her hand and she pulled me beside her.

'As I was saying, gentlemen, it was perhaps naïve and foolish of me to think that I could ever keep this strange phenomenon a secret from the world at large. You see I feared, again wrongly, it seems, that word of a phantom haunting this theater would drive away our potential audience and spell ruin for our show. But you heard about it anyway. You always manage to, don't you? You are so clever that way. So I called this conference today to bring things into the open and let the world know what we've been going through these past weeks.'

Her voice cracked at the end of the sentence.

'So there really is a ghost, is there, Miss Lovejoy?' a voice shouted from the blackness.

Blanche glanced around her, as if fearful that the ghost might overhear.

'I can come up with no other explanation,' she said. 'Strange things have been happening since we started rehearsing here. A jug of liquid hurled over me. The wind machine suddenly came on at full strength in the middle of a scene. A strange face at a window when I looked out.'

'You don't suspect that someone is playing tricks on you? Someone wants you to lose your nerve and close down the play?'

'That did cross my mind,' she said. 'That is why I hired this young woman. Gentlemen, may I present to you Miss Molly

Murphy? Miss Murphy runs a private detective agency. I had friends who spoke highly of her skills. So I hired her to do some snooping around and to find out who might be behind these strange events. She has now been with me for two weeks, taking part in every performance, and I regret to say that she is as perplexed as the rest of us.'

'So you don't think these acts were carried out by a normal human hand, Miss Murphy?'

'I wouldn't say that,' I said. It felt strange to be speaking out to invisible people lurking in the blackness. 'But as yet I haven't found anybody who would have had the opportunity to be in the right place to carry them out.'

'She was on the spot instantly when they happened,' Blanche said, before I had finished. 'She rushed off to search, and nobody was there each time. How do you explain that? Believe me, gentlemen, I wish I could explain it. I wish it could all be linked to a jealous actress who wished me harm. But I know Miss Murphy has done all she can and she still can't give me a plausible answer. Which leads me to only one conclusion: this theater is haunted.'

'Is the ghost likely to make an appearance any time now, do you think?' one of the men asked, with a chuckle.

'It is no laughing matter, let me assure you of that,' Blanche said, glancing over her shoulder. 'Were you here when the pillar toppled over? It is a huge piece of scenery, almost too heavy for one person to move alone, and yet it toppled during the middle of a scene and just missed me. Had I been a few inches to my right, I should not be here talking to you now, gentlemen.'

'So what do you plan to do now, Miss Lovejoy?'

Blanche paused. 'I am at a loss for what to do. I can't continue to endanger the lives of my cast, can I? I have tried a private detective and she has failed to come up with any plausible answer. My next step should be, I suppose, to call in the police, to call in bodyguards, and station them around the back-stage area. But how will we manage to put on a lighthearted comedy with so much gloom around us? And if it is indeed a specter that is causing all this mischief, what good will they do? I don't want to shut down the play, gentlemen, but I may have no option.'

'Oh no. Surely not,' were muttered comments from the dark-ened auditorium.

'How can we continue to act when we live constantly in fear?' she asked. 'When our nerves are on edge and we fear an attack at any moment?'

'But the public loves the show,' someone said. 'You saw them outside, clamoring for tickets. I understand that it's sold out for weeks.'

'I'm well aware of that,' Blanche said. 'And you know how I hate to disappoint my public. I have been a trooper all my life. I have always believed that the show must go on, but at what cost, gentlemen? At what cost? So I am taking one last desper-ate step to find out what malevolent being haunts this theater and why it wants our destruction. I have been in touch with the famous spiritualists, the Sorensen Sisters. They have gra-ciously agreed to come and hold a séance in this theater, to see if they can make contact with the spirit and maybe persuade it to leave us in peace.'

There was a rumble of excitement from the audience but Miss Lovejoy held up her hand. 'You will have to excuse us now, gentlemen. I have to dress for curtain-up in forty-five minutes. The show must go on. Thank you so much for coming. God bless you all.'

She blew them a kiss. The curtain came down and she turned to make a grand exit, leaving me standing there.

I hurried after Miss Lovejoy and caught up with her as she mounted the stairs.

'You can't call in the Sorensen Sisters, Miss Lovejoy,' I said. 'I know. I investigated them last year. I am sure they are frauds. They can't contact spirits any more than you or I can.'

I faltered at the end of this sentence as just a small doubt crept into my voice. During their so-called séances they had shown me something that later proved to be true. Could that just have been coincidence? They had certainly fled quickly enough when I threatened to expose them.

'But they are wonderful, Miss Murphy. Everybody says so. I have friends who swear by them. And you have not managed to prove or disprove our ghost, have you?'

'No, but I am still convinced that you are dealing with a malicious person, not a spirit.'

'Then tell me how these things were done. You saw that wind machine. The whole cast was onstage. Nobody could have sneaked past the backstage crew without being spotted. And what about that jug? You saw it. It flew into the air by itself.'

'But it's always you it is aimed at, Miss Lovejoy. Why should a spirit take such a dislike to you? Much more likely to be a disgruntled person, someone who feels that you tricked them or let them down at one time.'

She shook her head violently. 'I can think of nobody in my cast to whom I could have possibly behaved badly.' Then she patted my hand. 'I know you've done your best, Molly dear. You've tried hard. But this is something outside your sphere. I had hoped with all my heart that you would find a human culprit and we could all breathe easier. But you haven't, have you? I am terminating your services as of now.'

'Now?' I asked. 'As of this minute? You don't even want me in the show tonight?'

'Frankly, I don't see any point in it,' she said. 'Why don't you go home and have a free evening for a change? And spare a thought for us here, never knowing when that thing will strike again.'

I took a deep breath. 'If you no longer need my services, Miss Lovejoy, then I require my fee.'

'Send me the bill, my dear girl. I'll be delighted to pay whatever you ask.'

She waved me away as if I were a bird that had flown too near her.

Thirty-four

I stomped out of the theater in a black mood. I wondered whether I should say goodbye to my fellow young ladies in the chorus, but I didn't want to go up there and admit I was being given the boot. I'm not one that takes failure gracefully. I was really angry as I passed Henry and stepped out into the night. I couldn't tell if I was more angry at Miss Lovejoy or at myself. I had been given an opportunity and I had failed.

I started to walk blindly down Broadway, pushing my way through the crowd. Newsboys were shouting out the latest headlines. Something to do with the ghost and the theater, from what I could hear. By tomorrow they would include the news about the spiritualists. Fine, I thought. Let her pay good money to hire those old quacks. A lot of good they'd do her.

Then I stopped dead in my tracks. Something wasn't right here. The way I had been brought onstage at the perfect moment. The grand announcement to the press. It had all been staged for the maximum effect. Blanche hadn't needed me there to make that announcement, in fact she had already told me that my services would no longer be needed. Then it dawned on me: Blanche was putting on another play. She had cast me in the role of ineffective detective, as often happens in these little melodramas. She hadn't expected me to come up with anything because there was nothing to uncover.

I stood there, unmoving, while the crowd surged around me. Then I made my way out of the main stream of people and found a little café, where I sat with a cup of strong coffee, trying to put my thoughts in order. I was tempted to walk to Daniel's place and talk the thing through with him. But after all my talk of being an independent woman and able to handle my own business life – very well, thank you – I could hardly go running to him when a perplexing problem turned up.

I sipped the coffee and tried to make sense of what had just happened. I thought through each of the incidents onstage – the face at the window that nobody else but Blanche saw, the wind machine, the jug of liquid flying all over her, and then the pillar falling, missing her by inches. Was it possible that Blanche had somehow orchestrated these things herself? It was, after all, her play. Maybe she and Bobby Barker had thought this up between them – even rigged it up between them. But why? The jug of lemonade was just annoying, but the pillar could have cost her her life.

Unless – unless she knew it would miss her because she had carefully moved her own mark a foot to the left. She was a veteran actress. She knew that timing was everything. She had timed the events to perfection.

The words *veteran actress* played over and over in my brain. I toyed with my spoon and gazed at the crowds surging past the window. Everyone had commented that Blanche was getting long in the tooth, too old really to play the ingenue, especially at a time when the *Florodora* girls had set the standard of beauty at a sweet sixteen.

So Blanche wanted to make a big comeback on Broadway. She had the play. It was good. She would shine in it, but . . . But she had to get people into the theater. And what better way than a mystery? Poor brave Blanche. The show must go on. What a trooper, continuing with a play even when her own life was in danger. And even a real detective couldn't find any human explanation for the shocking events that had happened.

I saw it all now. When I had been brought in Blanche had seemed desperate to keep any news of the phantom out of the press, knowing full well that one of her cast would be bound to spill the beans, thus creating that delightful atmosphere of secrecy. She had built the tension perfectly and had achieved the desired result. The show was sold out for weeks. And I had played my part and was no longer needed.

I was really angry now. I suppose I was still too much the naïve little country bumpkin, but I had been used too many times recently. I wondered if Oona Sheehan was in on Blanche's little scheme from the beginning and had calmly enlisted me for a second time to be made a fool of. I was about to go and confront her here and now, and let her know exactly what I thought of her. Oh, and to collect the money she still owed me.

Then I decided no, I'd go and confront Blanche instead and let her know exactly what I had discovered. I wasn't such a bad detective after all, was I? I was sure that she had hired me because she knew I would fail, but I hadn't failed. I'd come up with the truth, all on my own. And I'd make sure Blanche paid me well for my services, or I'd let the word out about what she was doing.

That stopped me in my tracks, of course. Threatening her like that was pretty close to blackmail and I wasn't about to sink to that level. This would need more thought. I wasn't sure how to handle this situation. Part of me thought that the sensible solution should be to take my fee, walk away, and say nothing. After all, what harm had she really done, apart from ruining a costume or two? Except for that one costume that caught fire and could have resulted in harm to a chorus girl, the accidents had all been aimed at herself and heaven knows that people have done even more outlandish things to try to gain the public's attention. Mr Houdini had supposedly had himself locked into a box and been dropped over a bridge in London to gain notoriety. Probably all was fair on the stage as well as in love and war.

But I did not like being duped in this way. I did see that if I confronted Miss Lovejoy, she could play the wronged innocent and demand proof of how I came up with these slanderous sayings, and of course I could give her none. I hadn't managed to discover how any of the accidents had been caused.

It was then that a devious idea came into my mind. Blanche might well have something spectacular planned for tonight and not want my observant eyes around at the time. Well, I would show her. I'd slip back into the theater – after all, only Blanche knew that I'd been dismissed – and take up a good position where I could observe without being observed. I marched right back to the stage door and went back inside.

Henry looked perplexed. 'Didn't you already sign in once tonight?'

'I had to slip out to buy some more face cream,' I said, smiling sweetly, and then hurried past him. I made as if to climb the stairs, but instead I went into the backstage area. All was quiet and dark there. The set was ready for curtain-up and the stagehands were probably taking a well-deserved smoke outside. I looked around to see where I might hide and not be noticed. Then the idea came to me that I could climb up one of those ladders into the flies. I could then perch on one of the crosswalks and have a perfect view of the stage. If anything happened tonight, I'd let Miss Lovejoy know that I was prepared to talk to the press should she try any more of her tricks.

I looked around once more and then found a ladder and

began to climb. It is not easy to climb ladders in tight skirts and pointed shoes, trust me. I took it slowly and carefully and came out to a little platform, high above the stage. I don't usually have a fear of heights but I have to confess that it did look an awfully long way down. I stood on the platform, holding onto the ladder that disappeared into darkness as it continued up to an even higher level. At eye level with me a walkway spanned the stage and behind it various backdrops hung, waiting to be lowered into place. It was a remarkably small space I was standing on and I didn't want to let go of the ladder.

I had no idea what time it was and how long I would have to wait up here before curtain-up. It also occurred to me that I would be well and truly stuck after the performance started. Too bad for me if I needed a visit to the unmentionable. I wondered if I dared hitch my skirts up and sit, with my legs dangling over the edge. I was just considering how I might accomplish this when I felt the ladder vibrating in my hands. Someone was climbing up toward me. I was well and truly trapped, unless I dared to brave the walkway across to the other side. It was only about a foot wide, with thin railings on either side, and looked about as appealing as walking a tightrope.

It would surely only be one of the stagehands, I told myself, as I peered down to make out the top of a head coming toward me. He'd get a fright when he saw me, but I'd explain how I'd been instructed to keep a secret watch on Miss Lovejoy from up here and all would be well. I stood back against the wall and waited. A face appeared as a white blob in the blackness. I gasped as Desmond Haynes hauled himself up beside me with one fluid movement.

'So?' he said. 'May one ask what you are doing up here? Taking up an aerial act, are we?'

'May one ask what *you* are doing up here?' I answered,

sounding braver than I felt. He was a slim and elegant young man but he stood a good deal taller than me.

'As for that, I often study my choreography from above,' he said. 'The patterns emerge, you know.'

'May I point out that nobody is onstage yet.'

'How true,' he said. 'So would you care to answer my question, or should I summon the police right away and have you arrested as an intruder?'

'Have me arrested? I like that,' I retorted.

'Blanche told me she had fired you. So I ask you once again, what do you think you are doing up here?'

I tried to come up with a clever answer but my brain wouldn't work in the rarified atmosphere of this great height. All I could think about was holding onto that rail for dear life in case he tried to push me down.

'Whatever it was,' I said, 'I now have the answer to my problem. It was you all along, wasn't it? I saw how alarmed you were when I joined the company.'

'Oh, you're right,' he said. 'I have been keeping an eye on you, and I can't tell you how relieved I am that you won't be allowed into this theater again.'

'I bet,' I said.

'I told Blanche from the beginning she was a fool to hire you. Anyone could tell instantly that you'd never been an actress, never even been onstage. So now that I've got you here, I'm going to find out the truth. Who sent you? Who is behind this?'

'Behind what?' I stared at him defiantly, eye to eye.

'Do you want me to spell it out?'

'Finding out the truth about you, Mr Haynes? Is that what you mean? Finding out that you were the one behind all those so-called accidents?'

I knew I was taking a huge risk. I kept telling myself to shut up but somehow I couldn't. It's always been a failing of mine.

I saw his eyes narrow. He was frowning at me. 'Nice try,' he said, 'but you won't get away with it.'

'What do you plan to do? Try and hurl me to the stage? Oh, believe me, I'm no delicate little flower. I can deliver a nasty kick when I have to. And I've got a good set of lungs on me. One scream from me and everyone will come running.'

He was still frowning.

'How can you live with yourself, that's what I'd like to know,' I went on, having now got my steam up. 'Miss Lovejoy thinks you are her friend. She hired you. She gave you a job.'

'I am her friend.'

'Then why try to wreck her play?'

'Wait a minute,' he said. 'Are you trying to say that you were not planted here to cause the accidents?'

'What? I was brought here to keep an eye on Miss Lovejoy,' I said. 'Strictly undercover, of course. I'm a private detective.'

'Good God,' he said. 'And all along I thought you were the one up to no good.'

'And I thought you were the one acting suspiciously.'

'It seems I might have been under a misapprehension. I was so worried about these damned accidents. I thought somebody wanted to close our show before it started.'

'But they've had the opposite effect, haven't they?' I asked. 'Your show is a huge hit. It will run for months. People will come just to see if the ghost makes an appearance.'

'You're right,' he said. 'So do you think there is a ghost? I can't really believe that, but I've no other explanation. God knows I was watching from the stalls each time and saw nothing.'

'And I was positioned onstage, in the glare of the lights, where it was impossible to see what was going on backstage.'

He nodded. 'Whose idea was that?'

'Blanche's. She wanted me near her. For protection.' I

wondered about saying more. Should I hint that I suspected Blanche herself had orchestrated the whole thing? He was, after all, her friend. 'Leave me up here this evening,' I said. 'And don't mention this to a soul. By the end of the night I may have seen something that can provide proof, one way or another.'

'All right,' he said. 'One way or another, I'd certainly like to know.'

Thirty-five

Almost as soon as Desmond Haynes had climbed down, things started to happen. There were stirrings below, then the sound of electric switches being thrown, and the stage was bathed in light. Out beyond the curtain I heard the scrape of chairs and the orchestra tuning up. The whisper of voices floated up to me from backstage. Louder sounds, muffled by the curtain, came from front of house, hinting that the theater seats were filling up.

Then I saw the chorus girls lining up below me, ready for their first entrance. A round of applause sounded as the conductor came out. The tap of a stick and the overture started. The curtain went up. More applause. The girls ran onstage. More applause. The first song. The arrival of the motor car with the young men, and then I held my breath. Blanche Lovejoy made her first entrance. She was sparkling tonight. The audience roared at her jokes, clapped wildly at her songs. And nothing went wrong.

The first act finished and the lights were dimmed. I was becoming stiff and tired up here, but obviously I couldn't get down for another hour. Were there to be no more ghostly appearances, I wondered, now that Miss Lovejoy had won over her audience and assured a sold-out house?

The second act got started. We came to a scene when the girls are onstage alone. It was a naughty song about how they would like to dance the cancan at the Moulin Rouge. At the end of it, the girls line up to do a high-kicking number in their underwear. Very risqué. I was enjoying the absolute symmetry of their line when suddenly something went flying down onto the stage. It struck the girl on the end of the line on the head, knocking her to the stage with a sickening thud. The girl beside her was pulled down to her knees. There were screams from the girls onstage as well as from the audience. The orchestra faltered as male actors rushed onto the stage. They lifted the thing off the girl and turned her over. It was Lily.

'Is there a doctor in the house? Somebody call a doctor!' someone was yelling.

I had just started to climb down when I thought I saw a flash of movement, high on the wall on the other side of the stage. Did I dare to try and cross the catwalk? I didn't have the nerve, and besides, I didn't want to confront any kind of adversary at this height. I climbed down as quickly as I could. As my foot hit the bottom step I was grabbed.

'Got ya. This is the one who done it,' one of the stagehands shouted. 'I caught her coming down.'

'Don't be silly,' I said. 'I was up there spying for Miss Love-joy. Besides, what ever it was that dropped, fell from the other side of the stage. Now let go of me and let's see if we can catch the person that did it. Come on. Follow me.'

He did, unwillingly. We rushed around the back of the set.

'Did anybody climb down from any of the ladders over here?' I demanded of the stagehands who were standing look-ing shocked.

'Nobody.'

'Then I suggest some of you go up there and look for the one who did this. He or she will still be hiding up there.'

Again they did as I said, looking at each other uncertainly.

I turned to see the scene onstage. The curtain had been brought down. There was a buzz of anxiety from the audience. A group of people were kneeling or standing around Lily. I could now see that the object that had fallen was a sandbag, one of those used to secure the backdrops when they are hauled up into the flies.

'She's dead,' I heard somebody say. 'It must have broken her neck.'

Then I saw Blanche Lovejoy. She was standing there with a look of utter horror on her face. She had turned so pale that her face was almost green. I had seen her when the lemonade had been thrown over her, when the pillar had fallen, and she had looked shaken each time. Now I realized that she had been acting before. That had been stage fear. This was the real thing. Blanche Lovejoy was terrified.

All around me I could hear whispers about the ghost, quiet sobbing. I stepped out onto the stage. 'Somebody call the police,' I said.

'The police? No, not the police,' Blanche said quickly. 'This was either the work of the ghost or a horrible accident. Somebody left a sandbag balanced in the wrong place or a rope broke. And it couldn't have been aimed at me this time. I wasn't even onstage in that scene.' She sounded hysterical.

'Someone's been killed. The police need to investigate,' I said. 'If you don't call them, I'll do so myself.'

'What are you doing here, anyway? I fired you,' she said.

'Keeping an eye on you, Miss Lovejoy. Making sure you stayed safe.'

'And I did, didn't I?' She put a hand to her mouth. 'It was poor dear little Lily . . .'

I left the stage, trying to make sense of what had just happened. Lily, the one who couldn't always be trusted to keep her mouth shut, who had made some interesting hints that she knew something . . . I started to climb the stairs from backstage to the dressing rooms. It had just occurred to me that maybe there was a walkway around the wall that led straight to the upper level without crossing the backstage area at all. It had also occurred to me that certain people were in the theater but not onstage when the accidents happened. People I had overlooked because they were so unlikely.

I ran along the narrow hallway and pushed open the door of the wardrobe room. Madame Eva looked up in surprise, pins sticking from her mouth.

'Whatever is it, my dear?' she asked.

'One of the chorus girls has been killed,' I said. 'A sandbag fell on her. You didn't see anyone in the hallways up here, did you?'

'My dear, I have been trying to fix the costume that had lemonade thrown all over it,' she said. 'I haven't had time to wander around. Poor Miss Lovejoy, she will be desolate.'

I closed the door and ran down the hall to Blanche's dressing room. Martha looked up as I came in without knocking.

'What do you think you're doing?' she demanded. 'You don't just barge in here.'

She was dressed all in black, her little bird eyes darting as I came toward her.

'You planned this whole thing between you, you and Blanche, didn't you? A great way to bring in the customers – let them think the place was haunted. And why not bring in a simple girl detective so that you can show the world that even a professional couldn't solve your little mystery.'

'I don't know what you're rambling about, girl,' she muttered. 'Go on, get out of here. I've got work to do, ironing Miss Lovejoy's dress.'

I noticed how easily she moved across the room. She was

old, but she was still sprightly. And she was small. Had she somehow managed to hide herself in that table, maybe rigged with a little trapdoor, to knock over the jug at the right moment?

And then, of course, the bigger question – was she strong enough to have positioned a sandbag to fall on a chorus girl who couldn't keep her mouth shut? Ridiculous, I thought. How could an old woman like her climb up and down ladders, let alone drag sandbags?

'Go on. Beat it. Clear off, I say.' She came at me with the iron in her hand. 'Your services are no longer wanted here.'

'I'm sure they are not,' I said, backing away slightly because I could feel the heat from the iron. 'The last thing you and Miss Lovejoy want is a detective who has uncovered the truth.'

That may have been a stupid thing to say, but I was banking on the fact that I could fend off an old woman if necessary. Fortunately I didn't have to put this theory to the test. The door burst open and Blanche came in.

'Martha. She's dead. A sandbag fell on her and she's dead. How could that have happened?'

There was a horrible silence during which the women stared at each other. Martha's face was defiant.

'You didn't?' Blanche said in a trembling voice. 'You couldn't have done.'

She didn't notice me as the open door now hid me from her.

'You silly girl,' Martha said sharply, 'did you want to risk the truth coming out? Do you want to be the laughingstock of New York City? Blanche Lovejoy had to fake her own ghost to bring in the customers because she was too old and fat to be a leading lady any longer?'

'Stop it!' Blanche shouted. 'This has gone too far. And now they'll close us down anyway.'

'Of course they won't if you keep your mouth shut,' Martha said. 'I rescued you from the gutter, girl. Don't you ever forget that. You and that baby of yours. You'd never be where you are today if it wasn't for me. You owe me a great debt.'

'I know that. And we'll be all right, won't we. We'll just keep quiet and say nothing. There's no way anyone can ever prove this was anything but an accident. Nobody else suspects.'

'She does,' Martha said, pointing at me.

Blanche spun around. 'You!'

'Yes, Miss Lovejoy. I'm not quite as simple as I look,' I said. 'I'm sure you hired me because you thought I'd never come to the truth, but I did.'

'We'll have to get rid of her somehow,' Martha said, pushing between me and Blanche, the iron still in her hand. 'Lock the door, Blanche. Your headache powders. They should knock her out and then we can dump her somewhere.'

'No!' Blanche shrieked. 'Don't be silly. This has gone too far already. There is to be no more killing, Martha. A little hocus-pocus to bring in the crowds is one thing, but killing people?'

'That Lily would have gone on blackmailing you, and you'd never have known when she'd forget to keep her mouth shut. And this one – this one is dangerous.'

She waved the iron at me again in a threatening manner.

'Do you promise not to go to the police if I let you go?' Blanche asked in a trembling voice.

'I don't need to go to the police,' I said. 'They'll be here by now. The truth will come out whether you want it to or not. Your friend Desmond Haynes – he already suspects. We spoke before the show tonight. And if Lily figured it out, you can bet she shared her suspicions with some of her friends. She was never one to keep her mouth shut.'

'But Lily – they'll never be able to prove it wasn't an accident, will they? You can't prove it wasn't an accident?'

'I don't know. It depends if there were any witnesses,' I said.

'I recommend that you tell the truth, Miss Lovejoy. Otherwise you'll never be able to live with yourself.'

'We've got to get rid of her, Blanchie,' Martha insisted, shaking Blanche's sleeve. 'If not, we're ruined.'

'We're ruined anyway, Martha,' Blanche said. 'You don't think they'll keep the theater open after this, do you?'

'But I did it all for you, Blanche. I've done everything for you.' Her old voice cracked. 'I've worshipped you. I've given up my whole life for you.' She started to cry.

'Don't cry, my sweet. We'll make it all right.' Blanche took Martha into her arms and they clung together, swaying piteously in their joint misery. I took the opportunity to slip out of the room.

Thirty-six

Once outside in the dark hallway, I wasn't sure what to do next. I could hear sounds coming up from down below. Loud voices, the tramp of feet. It sounded as if the police were already in the building. Was it up to me to tell what I knew? Suddenly I just wanted to get away, back to my own world. I never wanted to see the theater or Blanche Lovejoy again.

I ran down the stairs and out the stage door. The news of the latest accident had already reached the press. The alleyway was packed with reporters and the curious. I was grabbed and manhandled as I stepped through the door.

'They say a girl was killed. Was it the ghost again? Did you see the ghost? How did she die?' The questions were shouted in my ears as arms grabbed me.

Then another arm was placed firmly around my shoulder. 'Come on, Molly, we're getting out of here,' said a calm voice in my ear, and Daniel was leading me firmly through the crowd and away. I had never been more glad to see him.

'Are you all right?' he asked as soon as we were safely away from the mob.

'Yes, I'm fine. How did you know?' I asked.

'I thought I might see the play for myself tonight,' he said.

'I wanted to witness your acting prowess. Imagine how disappointed I was when you didn't appear onstage.'

'Miss Lovejoy fired me.'

'Not for your lack of acting ability, I assume.'

'No, because I had already played my part and she no longer needed me.'

'Your part?'

'Innocent girl detective who has been unable to prove or disprove the existence of the ghost.'

'But you stuck around anyway?'

'Yes, and I'm glad I did.'

'You saw who killed that girl?'

I hesitated. No, I hadn't actually seen anything more than a hint of a movement. 'Not actually saw, but I think I know.'

'And it wasn't a ghost?'

'No, it wasn't a ghost.'

'The police are already there. Do you think you should go back and . . .?'

'No,' I interrupted. 'I don't want to go near that place again. I've had enough, Daniel. Take me home. If the police don't get a confession, then I'll step forward. Right now I want to be as far away as possible.'

'You think you're in danger, yourself?'

'Possibly,' I said. I turned and looked up at him. 'Daniel, I'm so glad you're here.'

'And I'm so glad you're here, trust me,' he said. 'When you didn't appear onstage and then the word went around that somebody was dead, I was all set to burst in through that stage door and rescue you.'

'The dashing hero as always,' I said, putting my hand up to his cheek. He took my hand and kissed the palm. 'Your hands are cold,' he said. 'Where are your gloves?'

'Oh dear. Lost somewhere in that theater, I suspect. I'm not going back for them.'

'Do you want me to take you home?' Daniel asked. 'Have you eaten this evening?'

'Not really. A cup of coffee, I believe.'

'Then shall we go and have a meal somewhere?'

I almost opened my mouth to say, 'you don't have any money at the moment, Daniel.' I swallowed back the words just in time. 'I suppose we do have reason to celebrate,' I said. 'I've just concluded two cases.'

'Two?'

'I gave my report to the Mendelbaums this afternoon, and I have deposited the check.'

'And they are happy that their daughter is marrying a boring and respectable young man?'

'They are happy that she's marrying a dubious rogue,' I said. 'And a stage-door Johnnie with strange ideas about—' I couldn't say the word *sex* in front of Daniel, even though we had shared more than words on the subject.

'I suspect many rich young men go through that phase in their lives,' Daniel said.

'I hope you didn't.'

'I was never rich enough nor at leisure. Do you fancy Muschenheim's Arena? It's fairly close by.'

'A little pricey for us, isn't it? I may never get the money out of Blanche Lovejoy.'

'Write up your bill and I'll collect it for you. And also what Oona Sheehan owes you. I guarantee they'll pay up.'

Of course they would, I reasoned. Knowing what I knew, they'd have no choice. And Daniel was an intimidating presence.

'I am your employee, after all,' Daniel said. 'I have to earn my crust somehow.'

'Not employee, affiliate,' I said.

'How about partner?'

'You want to go into partnership with me?'

'That's right. Say to hell with the police department. Why should I wait around, holding my breath, for them to admit they made a mistake and wrongly accused me?'

'But your job, Daniel. Your status. You were one of their best officers. It would be quite a come-down to work the small-time cases that I get.'

'Do I get the feeling that you don't want to work with me?'

'On the contrary. Nothing would please me more. But we have your career to think of. And our future. You're an important man, Daniel. You have a fine future ahead of you.'

'Not anymore,' he said bitterly.

'Of course you do. It will all come right again, you'll see,' I said. 'Come on then, we'll have a slap-up meal and drown our sorrows in a bottle of wine.'

I slipped my arm through his and we marched down Broadway to the restaurant on Thirty-first.

'This is more like it,' Daniel said, taking a sip of claret as the waiter put a large steak in front of him. 'I've been living on edge for too long now, and so have you. You're looking quite pale and drawn. You need some good red meat.'

I nodded. 'It hasn't been easy and today has been a strange, strange day.' Then I told him about the Hungarians and about Annie going with them.

'But that's good news, surely,' Daniel said. 'I'm relieved to hear that you no longer have to take responsibility for her. She's gone where her own people can take care of her.'

'I hope so,' I said. 'I kept asking myself whether I was doing the right thing in letting her go.'

'Why? Was there something wrong with these men?'

'I don't know. They seemed respectable enough. They seemed very concerned about her.'

'Well, there you are then. The girl should never have been your responsibility. Let her go and stop worrying. So the only case we still have on the books is Miss Van Woekem's nephew, and I doubt that we'll ever get to the bottom of that one.'

'Did you have a chance to visit the steamship companies?'

'I did,' he said. 'None of the shipping lines remembers selling a ticket to someone who resembled John Jacob Halsted.'

'And trains?'

'I showed his picture around at the train station that was closest to the wrecked car. Nobody remembered seeing him there, either. Nor at any of the businesses along the little main street there. The man has completely vanished, Molly. I think we have to assume that he is lying dead somewhere in a snowdrift. I don't know how we'll tell the old woman. It will break her heart.'

'What else could we possibly do?'

'I have no idea. But right now what we are going to do is enjoy this meal before it gets cold.' He attacked his steak with relish. I followed suit.

'I'd better take you home,' Daniel said as we came out into the chilly night air. 'That wine was certainly heady.'

'I'm just fine,' I said, although I could feel the effects of the wine all through my body.

Daniel looked at me and smiled. 'I don't want you falling over on the ice.' He hailed a cab and helped me inside. In the dark confined space I was very conscious of his closeness and it seemed very natural for his arm to come around me and for my head to rest on his shoulder. 'Now this is more like it,' he said. 'It seems we've been at odds recently. I've had the feeling that you've been keeping me at arm's length.'

'With good reason,' I said. 'I know what happens if I let you get any closer than that.'

He laughed and squeezed me tighter.

We proceeded slowly down lower Fifth Avenue to the Washington Square arch and then stopped at the entrance to Patchin Place. Daniel jumped down to help me out. His hand was warm and firm in mine. 'Here, take my arm,' he said. 'It's still icy in the alleyway.'

We reached my front door without incident. Conflicting thoughts were racing inside my head. He was going to ask to come inside. I knew that I should turn him away but I didn't want to. I also knew what was likely to happen if I let him in. I fumbled for my key, conscious of how close he was standing beside me.

Suddenly the door opposite was thrown open and Sid and Gus came rushing out.

'Molly, it is you!' Sid shouted. 'Gus said she was sure she spotted you coming down the alley. I'm so glad we've caught you.' She noticed Daniel at this juncture. 'Oh, and good evening to you, too, Captain Sullivan.'

Daniel nodded politely.

'Molly, please tell us that you don't have to be at that horrible theater tomorrow night, because we have something wonderful planned.'

'I don't,' I said. 'My assignment at the theater is over.'

'Hooray for that,' Gus said. 'We were quite out of sorts because we hadn't seen you for absolutely ages, weren't we, Sid?'

'She was,' Sid said. 'Positively pining. Wouldn't eat her food. I've had to tempt her with foie gras and truffles.'

'You two!' I laughed.

'Can you come in for a while?' Sid asked. 'We have to tell you our plans for our wonderful costume party tomorrow night. We're all going to come as our favorite literary character and we're going to cook meals that feature in several well-known novels. There will be prizes and Ryan is bringing some of his theater friends—' Again, she glanced at Daniel, who was scowling now. 'You are invited, too, of course, Captain Sullivan.'

'Not exactly my cup of tea, thank you,' Daniel said. He tapped my arm. 'I think I had better be making my way home, Molly. It's getting late.'

'Oh, all right, Daniel.' I held his sleeve. 'Look, won't you reconsider and come to the costume party with me tomorrow? We've had so little fun recently. We didn't even manage to go skating in Central Park.'

'I – I'm afraid I have to go home this weekend, Molly,' he said. 'My father's health is not improving and I can tell that my mother is worried about him.'

'You're just saying that because you don't want to come to a party with my friends, aren't you?'

'Not at all,' he said. 'I'm concerned about my father, Molly. I have to go home.'

'Very well. Then you'd better go home, hadn't you?' I said coldly. 'Give my regards to your parents. Or haven't you told them about me yet?'

'I've hinted,' he said, glancing across at Sid and Gus still standing there at their front door. 'But now is not exactly the time to spring something on them.'

'Of course not. Well, in that case, thank you for bringing me home, Captain Sullivan.'

He looked at me, went to say something else, then his gaze turned to Sid and Gus. 'I bid you goodnight, ladies. Goodnight, Molly,' he said and walked away without any kind of farewell kiss.

'I fear your brave captain doesn't enjoy our company the way you do,' Gus said.

'Too bad for him,' I replied. 'He doesn't know what he's missing.'

Thirty-seven

The party on Saturday night was noisy, crazy, and a lot of fun. Ryan came as the Scarlet Pimpernel and Elizabeth, aka Nelly Bly, appeared as Huck Finn. She commented that she might as well use her hard-won expertise in passing as a small, ragged boy. I was Jane Eyre, not because she was my favorite literary character – although I did like the way she threw a book at her cousin – but because I owned the plain sort of clothes a governess would wear.

'What a pity Captain Sullivan isn't here,' Gus said. 'He'd have made a lovely Mr Rochester.'

'What a pity indeed,' I thought, still annoyed that Daniel ran a mile from having anything to do with my friends. He had probably had no intention of going home this weekend until he wanted an excuse to get out of the party. Did he really believe that our future together would only include friends of his choosing? I pushed the uneasy thoughts aside and enjoyed myself thoroughly. It had been a long time since I had enjoyed an evening so much.

It was strange to have a whole Sunday to myself. It was even stranger to wake up on Monday morning with nothing really to do. Even the house was in good order, thanks to Mrs Tucker, who had done more than her share of dusting and polishing while she had been with me. I had been complaining about having too much work to do, but now I drifted around the house, bored and annoyed. I thought of paying a visit to Daniel to see how his father was faring, but then decided against it.

Then it came to me that I should let Mrs Goodwin know the outcome of the story with the mute girl, after she had taken such an interest and worked on my behalf. I didn't expect to find her at home on a working day, but I wrote her a note and asked her to stop by at her earliest convenience so that I could tell her the latest in this saga. I had scarcely made it back home myself when she showed up on my doorstep.

'I was thinking of you today, as it happened,' she said as I invited her inside and seated her in my best armchair. 'I've just come from the morgue, where I was taking a look at a young woman called Annie.'

My heart leaped alarmingly. 'Annie? It wasn't my girl, was it? You remember how she looked – elfin face, lots of chestnut hair?'

Mrs Goodwin looked surprised. 'She is no longer with you then?'

'No, some Hungarian men came for her.' I related the entire story.

'And you were not happy to let her go?'

'Of course not,' I said. 'At least, I suppose I am happy for her that she's among her own people. It's just that I expected her wits would have returned and she would have recognized them when they spoke to her. But she didn't.'

'It doesn't always work that quickly in such cases,' Mrs Goodwin said. 'If the brain has suffered considerable trauma it needs time to heal.'

'And now you've got me worried that she might have met a bad end.'

Mrs Goodwin smiled. 'You can rest easy. This girl was quite different. Pretty, pale, blonde little thing from what we can tell – she had been in the river for a while.'

'The river?'

'East River. She was pulled out close to Ward's Island. Who knows where she went in. She could have floated with the current from farther north.'

'I see,' I said. 'How did you know her name was Annie? Did a family member come forward to identify her?'

'No, it was easier than that. Her undergarments had her name inked on them. Annie P.'

I started. 'Annie P? That couldn't be Parker, could it?'

She nodded. 'Possibly, why? Do you know an Annie Parker?'

'A girl named Annie Parker, who meets your description, went missing from a theater in New Haven, Connecticut, just before I found the girl in the snowdrift,' I said.

'Is that right?'

'And she may be connected to a case I'm working on – trying to find a young man called John Jacob Halsted who robbed a mansion just outside New Haven.'

'Halsted?' she reacted sharply. 'Half the police force is looking for him. Why are you involved?'

'Working on behalf of his family. They want to know the truth about him and where he is.'

'So do we all,' she said.

'Well, one thing I've found out is that he frequented the theater in New Haven and that he was planning to take a young lady out for a late supper – possibly Annie Parker. We did wonder whether they might have run off together to South America, but that doesn't seem to be the case. She could have been in his motor car with him when it crashed. She could have been dazed and wandered off and fallen into the marshes nearby.'

'Hardly,' Mrs Goodwin said shortly. 'She had a bullet hole in the middle of her back.'

'She was shot?'

'She was shot. So if your Mr Halsted was with her, I'd say that things now look even worse for him.'

'Oh dear,' I said. 'It all seems so unlikely from everything we've heard about him. He certainly liked a good time and he liked spending money, but he had plenty of it and his friends describe him as someone easygoing who didn't even own a gun. I can't see a person like that being involved in these horrible crimes they are ascribing to him – robbing banks, shooting people willy-nilly . . .'

'As to that,' Mrs Goodwin said, 'it would now appear that Mr Halsted is probably not responsible for at least some of the crimes in that area. I gather they have arrested a man in connection with the pay-wagon robbery in Greenwich.'

'They have?'

'Yes, lucky coincidence, actually. The New York police have had their eye on an Italian gang who have been causing us grief. They call themselves the Cosa Nostra and come from Sicily, so I understand. Anyway, we conducted a raid on their houses and one man we rounded up matched the description of the bandit who had robbed the payroll wagon. Now we think that they have found these outlying small towns to be easy pickings without the police supervision of the city.'

'So John Jacob is no longer wanted for these crimes?'

'He's still wanted for the robbery and murder at the Silverton mansion,' she said. 'The evidence against him there is overwhelming.'

'Yes, I suppose that is pretty damning,' I said. 'I'd certainly like to know if Annie Parker was involved with him and if it is her body that is now lying in the morgue.'

'I can take you back there to see for yourself,' she said,

'although I warn you, she's not a pretty sight. When a body has been in a river for a few days, the fish have had a good nibble at it.'

I shuddered. 'I think I'll do without the morgue visit then,' I said. 'It certainly sounds very like her. But I'm thinking that perhaps I should go up to New Haven and talk to the other girls in the chorus up there. Annie may have confided her plans for that night to one of them.'

'Now that you tell me this, I've thought of something else that could be done. I'll see if the bullet was extracted from her, and then maybe we can find out if it matched the bullet that shot the servant at that mansion.'

'Good idea,' I said, getting quite excited now. 'Will you come with me up to New Haven?'

She shook her head with a smile. 'Oh no, my dear. I've just had ten hours on the beat. All I'm going to do now is fall asleep. But you go. You can handle it well enough on your own. I've great faith in you.'

'All right,' I said. 'I'll go then. I believe that most theaters are dark on Monday nights, but I'm sure I'll be able to locate where the girls are lodging.' I picked up my cape from where I had tossed it across a kitchen chair. 'Can I make you something first?' I asked. 'A cup of tea? A sandwich?'

She smiled again. 'Oh no, thank you, my dear. You go about your tasks and I'll be off to bed then. How did my nosy neighbor work out as a nursemaid?'

'Wonderfully,' I said. 'She couldn't have been better. My girl adored her and had actually come to trust her. I think if we'd had another week or two, we'd have restored her to her old self.'

'Amazing.' Mrs Goodwin nodded. 'It just shows that she's the type who needs to be kept busy then, doesn't it? Next time she shows up on my doorstep, I'll find a task for her to do.'

301

She got up and adjusted her bonnet. 'Good luck in your hunting then, Miss Molly. Let me know what you find.'

We left the house together, she for her bed and I toward Grand Central Terminus. I stared impatiently out of the window as the train crawled through Manhattan and then crossed the bridge to the Bronx. It was a gray December day with mist hovering over the low-lying ground. I watched keenly as the marshes appeared in the distance to our right. The first of the marshy area must have been a good half-mile from the place where the motor car hit a tree. If Annie had been in the car, how had her body wound up in the marshes? Had the car been ambushed, knowing that it contained the loot from a burglary? In which case, had John Jacob also been shot and his body dumped into the nearest creek?

I shuddered and pulled my cloak around me, even though it was warm in the compartment. It is always tragic when a young life meets a violent end. John Jacob had seemed a likable young man and Annie Parker was a vibrant beauty. And yet someone had robbed and murdered at the Silverton mansion and all the evidence pointed so firmly to John Jacob Halsted. I just hoped I'd be closer to the truth by the end of this day.

We passed through Greenwich and then Bridgeport and finally came to New Haven. It was bitterly cold and the sidewalks were icy as I made my way toward the theater. I hoped I might find the manager in his office again, but the building was closed up and there was no sign of life. I walked around the back and discovered an alleyway with what was presumably a stage door. No luck there, either. I was just walking away when I heard a sound above my head. I looked up to see a woman taking in her laundry, farther down the alley. The garments were stiff with frost and crackled as she pulled them from the line. I called out to her and asked if she knew where the chorus girls from the theater lodged.

'Are you thinking of joining them?' she asked. 'It's an awful hard life, so they say.'

'It's my little cousin I've come to visit,' I said. I've found that the mention of family members always reassures people.

She nodded and gave me directions with a clothespin still stuck in the side of her mouth. I came out of the alley and turned right at the Bank of Connecticut on the corner. The lodging house was on a dingy side street with scruffy children playing kick the can in spite of the cold. Their breath hung in the air like smoke. They stopped playing to look at me curiously as I went up the steps and knocked on the front door.

A slovenly middle-aged woman opened the door and stood staring at me with her hands on her hips.

'Well?' she demanded.

'Is this where the girls from the theater lodge?' she asked.

'Some of them, yes.'

'Did Annie Parker stay here?'

'Her? Don't talk to me about her. She skipped off owing me a month's rent, she did. If you're a relative, I expect to be paid.'

'I'm not a relative,' I said. 'I'm a private detective and we're investigating Miss Parker's disappearance.'

'Go on with you!' She shook her head in half disbelief. 'What's she supposed to have done?'

'Could I come in?' I said. 'It's freezing out here. I'd like to talk to some of her friends if they're at home.'

'Where else would they be on a nasty cold day like this?' she said. 'When these girls have a day off, they sleep. Come on then. Wipe your feet.'

I thought this last command was a little excessive, given the state of the floor, but I followed her into a shabby sitting room. There was the barest hint of a fire burning in the grate and two girls were sitting in armchairs with blankets around their shoulders. They looked up as I came in.

'This young lady wants to know about Annie,' she said. 'She's a detective.'

They shot me worried looks. 'A detective? So it's true then. She has done something bad?'

'I don't know yet,' I said. 'It's possible. It's also possible she might be dead, so anything you can tell me about her, and about that last night when she disappeared, would be most helpful. Do you happen to know if she went off to meet a young man that night?'

'She was a great one for the boys, Annie was,' the younger of the two girls said. She had a fresh-scrubbed face and looked not much older than fourteen. 'And they sure liked her. You should see the gifts she got – flowers, candies, even perfume.'

'Did she have a special boy?' I asked.

'There was some guy who came to the stage door. She liked him. She said he was a big spender and she always had a lot of fun with him, and if she played her cards right she'd be out of this crummy place and living in luxury.'

'Did she tell you his name?'

The two girls exchanged glances. 'We kind of thought it might be that Yale guy who robbed the mansion. Anyways, the police came and asked questions about him.'

'Do you happen to know if Annie had a date that night?'

'She did.' The older, sharper-looking one said, 'She had a dress with her, to change into after the show. She said she was going out for supper. We didn't think much of it. She was always going out with some guy after the show.' She lowered her voice. 'Mrs Stubbs locks the front door at midnight and Annie often doesn't show up until breakfast next day. You can guess what she's been doing.'

'So Annie definitely went on a date that night, but nobody saw her leave with a man?'

The younger one frowned. 'Well no. She went off with Jessie that night, didn't she?'

'Jessie?'

'The other girl that's gone missing. Jessie Edwards.'

I gasped. 'Another girl went missing that night too?'

'Oh yes. Annie took Jessie with her. I think they were going out to supper with a couple of guys. And they didn't show up for breakfast next morning. That must have been some supper, we said. We were kidding around, you know. Only when they didn't come back for the show that night, there was big trouble. We thought maybe they'd run off with the rich guys and they didn't need to be in no stinking chorus anymore.'

'Tell me about Jessie,' I said.

'Jessie? She was different from Annie,' the older girl said. 'I don't know why Annie liked her so much. She was fairly new. Came from somewhere out in the boonies – Massachusetts I think. And she was real shy. A good dancer, though. She'd studied classical ballet, she said. And she and Annie really hit it off. They became bosom buddies. Did everything together. So sometimes Annie would take her on dates with her and introduce her to guys. "She's never going to hitch a guy by herself,'Annie would say. Although she was pretty enough.'

'What did she look like?' I asked although I thought I already knew.

'Skinny, petite, dark hair . . .'

'Little elfin face, pointed chin?'

'That's right. Do you know her?'

'I think I do,' I said. 'And she and Annie went off together. Did anyone happen to see a swank red automobile that night?'

'I didn't, but Lizzie said she'd seen that auto again and I guess that was the one she meant.'

'So it was possible that Annie and Jessie went off in the

automobile. Could we ask the other girls to find out if anyone saw them leave?'

The older one shook her head. 'The police already asked everybody that. They showed us a picture of the automobile. Real nice it was. But you know those two rushed out that night. They were off and away before we'd finished taking our makeup off.'

'Did Jessie wear a white dress that night?'

The younger one screwed up her face, thinking. 'I believe she did. Yeah, because some wisecracker made a joke about looking like a virgin and that Annie had given up wearing white at her christening.'

'I presume the police have been through Annie's and Jessie's things? Have they contacted their families?'

'I don't think they had families to contact,' the older one said. 'I know that Annie ran away from home when she was a kid, and I believe that Jessie grew up in an orphanage.'

'Would you happen to have a picture of them that I could take with me?' I asked.

The younger one got to her feet. 'We've got some playbills out in the hall. That shows all of us.' She flopped out in her slippers and came back holding out the playbill we'd seen in the manager's office. I looked at it again, Annie, front and center, and now, as my eyes scanned the rest of it, my girl from the snowdrift smiling demurely from the back row.

Thirty-eight

I was so mad at myself that I could scream. If only I had studied that photograph carefully when I had seen it in the manager's office, instead of just looking at Annie, I'd have spotted Jessie then and I could have stopped those men from taking her away. An awful fear clutched at the pit of my stomach. Who were they? Why had they pretended to be her relatives? With a name like Jessie Edwards she certainly had no links to Hungary. And more to the point, what could I do now to get her back?

I visited the local New Haven police station and reported everything that I had found. They were polite enough but I got the feeling that they weren't taking me too seriously. 'Oh yes, miss?' one of them said, barely stifling the grin. 'You say she was found in a snowdrift and then kidnapped by Hungarians? Are you sure you haven't been reading too many novels?'

I came away angry and frustrated. I had learned nothing from them that I didn't already know and they were not the least bit interested in helping me. It was going to be up to me to rescue the girl myself. If she's still alive – the words flashed through my mind.

The train trip back to New York went on forever and I tried to formulate a plan. At least I had an address. I'd have to come up with a pretext for visiting Jessie – maybe a necklace that she left behind at my house. And what then? I could hardly drag her off by myself, could I? I decided to appeal to Mrs Goodwin for help. She'd know what to do. She may also have heard of a Hungarian gang that kidnapped girls. I felt sick inside. Mrs Tucker had suggested that maybe the girl ran away from white slavers. Had I delivered her right back into their hands?

I leaped off the train the moment it came into the platform in New York. I knew that Mrs Goodwin would be sleeping, but this was a matter of life and death. I just prayed that Daniel had come back and headed straight to his house on Twenty-third Street. The wind off the Hudson was bitter as I leaned into it, hurrying toward Ninth Avenue. His landlady met me in the front hall.

'Captain Sullivan hasn't returned yet, Miss Murphy,' she said.

'He's been away all weekend, has he?'

'That's right. Went off on Saturday morning to visit his folks. I'll tell him you stopped by when he returns, shall I?'

'Yes please. Ask him to come and see me the moment he gets back. It's urgent.'

'All right, my dear.' She ushered me back out into the street. I walked away feeling angry and disappointed. Just how long was he going to stay away this time? What if his family persuaded him to stay with them until Christmas?

I pushed such worries aside and decided that the only person I could turn to was Mrs Goodwin, sleep or no sleep.

I went home first to find the address to which the Hungarians had taken Jessie. I was in the process of opening my front door when the door across the alley opened.

'There you are at last, Molly,' Gus called to me. 'We've got Dr Birnbaum here, waiting for you to come home.'

'Dr Birnbaum?'

'Yes, in a very disturbed state. He has some bad news, I'm afraid.'

I hurried across to Gus and was shown into their drawing room, where Dr Birnbaum was sitting next to the fire. He leaped to his feet.

'Miss Murphy. At last. These two young ladies were so kind. They invited me to stay until you returned home. I came to find you with the most disturbing news.'

'About our girl?'

'Of course. I decided this morning that I would go to visit her, to make sure she had settled in well and to offer my services in person. Frankly, I didn't think that any doctor they could produce could have the skill with such a difficult case. Anyway, I went to Brooklyn and the address they gave you does not exist. There is no Brook Street.'

'No Brook Street,' I echoed. 'I suppose I'm not surprised. I have just made a discovery of my own. The girl was not Hungarian. She was a dancer from a theater in New Haven, Connecticut.'

'Then why did they claim her as their relative?' Gus asked.

'I wish I knew. I can only assume the worst – that they wanted her for some evil purpose.'

'I wish I had been there when they came to collect her,' Dr Birnbaum said. 'I have some fluency in Hungarian. I might have been able to reason with them.'

'We only have their word that they were Hungarian, don't we?' I said. 'I wish you'd been there, too. At least you could have told me whether they were genuine or not.'

'Did you hear them say anything in that language?' Birnbaum asked.

'Yes, but since I don't speak it, it meant nothing to me.'

'Nobody speaks it,' Birnbaum said. 'It is one of the strangest languages on Earth. It bears no similarity to any other spoken language.'

I stared at him, as an idea crossed my mind. 'Then that is why they claimed to be Hungarian,' I said. 'A language that nobody else speaks. They could claim that the girl didn't communicate with anyone because she couldn't understand them.'

'Did the language sound like this?' Birnbaum asked and rattled off what sounded like a string of gibberish.

'I don't think so,' I said. 'And one of them said *si*. Is that yes in Hungarian?'

'No, Spanish or Italian.'

Sid entered the room at that moment. 'Oh, Molly, I didn't hear you come in. What have I missed?' she asked.

'Molly has found out that the girl from the snowdrift was really a dancer from New Haven,' Gus said breathlessly, 'and she's been kidnapped by two men who said they were Hungarian but probably weren't. And they left a false address.'

'Goodness,' Sid said. 'So what do you propose to do now?'

'I wish I knew,' I said. 'It will be like trying to find a needle in a haystack. I fear the worst for that poor girl. I can only think of one reason that those men would want her.'

Gus frowned. 'In the state she was in? She is an invalid. She requires constant attention, Molly. Who would want to undertake such a challenge? There must have been a very strong reason for hauling her off with them.'

I nodded. 'I suppose you're right. I just hope she's still alive.'

'Why would anyone bother to kill her when she neither speaks nor recognizes anybody? One could say she was scarcely alive in her current state.'

'It could be a case of mistaken identity, I suppose,' Sid said. 'Perhaps she resembled strongly the real Hungarian girl they were looking for.'

'Then why give a false address?'

Sid couldn't answer that one.

'I am going to see my friend Mrs Goodwin,' I said. 'She

works for the New York police. She may know what to do, because I certainly don't.'

'We are going to have dinner with Elizabeth,' Gus said. 'We should ask her opinion. She had handled some tricky situations during her career.'

'By all means ask her,' I said wearily.

Gus came over to me and put her hand on my shoulder. 'You did everything you could and more, Molly. If you hadn't rescued her, she'd have been shut up in an institution by now.'

'Perhaps she would have been better off there.' I found that I was fighting back tears. I always find it hard to take when people are kind to me.

'And she never was your responsibility, you know,' Sid added. 'You did a kindly act, but she is not yours to worry about.'

'All the same, I feel responsible,' I said.

Dr Birnbaum gave an embarrassed sort of cough. 'I should be going,' he said. 'I am to meet some colleagues for dinner. Perhaps I shall refer the matter to them. We are a small fraternity. Surely one of us would hear if a fellow alienist was called out to treat a mute girl.'

It was about the best we could hope for. I collected the false address from my house and then set off straight for Mrs Goodwin. I rapped on her door until I heard slow feet coming down the stairs.

'Oh, it's you,' she said, still bleary-eyed.

'I'm so sorry to disturb you,' I said, 'but I couldn't think where else to turn.'

'It's a hazard of my profession,' she said. 'You'd better come in.'

I went through into her warm kitchen and poured out my story to her. She sat nodding gravely. 'So this girl may have been part of the robbery at the Silverton mansion,' she said.

'She may have been in the red automobile when it crashed.'

'In which case something awful happened to her. Maybe she escaped when Annie was shot.'

'Escaped from whom? That's the question,' Mrs Goodwin said.

'Is it possible that it was from those men who claimed to be her family? But why would they want to find her again?'

'Obviously to silence her because she might be able to identify them,' she said in her matter-of-fact way.

'Then we'd already be too late.'

'I fear that may be the case.'

'But where does John Jacob Halsted fit into all this?'

'Either he was part of the gang or rival thieves got wind of his big haul and set up an ambush.'

'In which case . . .' I began.

'He's probably also dead.'

'This is terrible,' I said, 'Is there nothing we can do?'

'You can give me a description of the two men who came to collect the girl. I can pass it around at police headquarters and see if it rings a bell with any of our officers. I take it you've told Captain Sullivan. He was always closely involved with the gangs.'

She saw me stiffen. 'I'm not saying he was working with the gangs,' she said. 'I think his innocence has been well proven in that matter, at least to me. But he has a better inside knowledge of the criminal classes in this city than any other officer I can think of.'

'I can tell you right now that he'll not be persuaded to work with anything to do with the police force,' I said. 'He's very bitter and angry. But he is helping me on the John Jacob Halsted case and it does seem that the two are linked somehow. Very well, I'll go and speak to him this evening.' I got up, then looked back at her and smiled. 'I'm sorry to have disturbed your rest. And I appreciate everything you're doing to help.'

'Glad to do it,' she said, 'although if we are dealing with the criminal classes, I wouldn't hold out too much hope that the girl is still alive.'

'No,' I agreed. 'But I have to keep on trying until I'm sure.'

Thirty-nine

I spent a miserable night, tossing and turning, consumed with guilt. I had had a chance to save Jessie and instead I had delivered her to men who could have no good reason for carting her away. And Daniel wasn't around just when I needed him. A fine sort of assistant he was turning out to be – running home to his parents when we were in the middle of a case. You can see my state of mind was not quite rational. When I get upset I've been known to blame everybody, including myself.

At first light the next morning I was up and pacing. How was I going to find those men again in the whole of New York City? They had given me a Brooklyn address – was at least the Brooklyn part of it genuine? And even if it was, what hope did I have of locating two men who would fit the description of half the immigrants in the city. Well, not half the immigrants – the older man especially had been well dressed, had well-manicured nails and a good-quality cloth for his overcoat, and carried an expensive-looking cane. And he ran his own business, although I remembered he had skirted the question about what kind of business that was.

I tried to make myself something to eat, but I couldn't swallow. In the end I decided to go across the street and see if Sid and Gus were awake. Not only were they awake but their house smelled of freshly brewed coffee and Sid had already been out to get French rolls from the bakery. Of course they invited me to join their breakfast.

'We've been up for hours,' Sid said. 'Gus is in a painting mood and went straight to her easel. I positively had to drag her away to eat breakfast. If I didn't take such good care of her, she'd starve.'

I had to smile at this because Augusta looked to be far from starving.

'Sid does exaggerate,' Gus said, returning my smile. 'You can tell which of us is the writer.'

'I'm sorry to interrupt your breakfast,' I said, 'but I had a horrible time sleeping last night.'

'Of course you did. You're worried about that girl,' Gus said. 'Have you passed along the details of those men to the police?'

'To my friend Mrs Goodwin,' I said. 'I know she'll do what she can, but how does one track down two immigrants in New York City?'

Nobody could answer this.

'Have a hot croissant and some coffee, you'll feel better,' Sid said, pushing a plate in front of me. I tried to eat, but I couldn't. *The New York Times* lay on the table beside me. While they ate I thumbed through the pages, glancing at the headlines. Then I paused, reading a small article on an inside page: 'Police raid Italian gang headquarters. Leading Sicilian crime figure taken into custody.' And underneath was an engraving of a man who looked very like the uncle who had come to visit me.

'That's him,' I shouted, almost making them spill their coffee. I tapped the paper with my finger. 'I'm almost sure that's him. The older one who came to pick up Jessie.'

Sid peered over my shoulder. '"Salvadore Alessi. Known

to his gang members as the Don. Ruled over a brutal gang in which disloyalty was rewarded with death. Thought to be responsible for variety of crimes in and around New York, including protection rackets, bank robberies, and contract murders."' She glanced up at me. 'This does not sound like a very nice man, Molly.'

'And he's got Jessie.'

'Given his reputation, one should conclude that Jessie is probably no longer alive,' Sid said gently. Gus gave a little gasp.

'I've got to know,' I said. 'At least the police can give me the address.'

'Molly, you are not going to the house of an Italian gang.'

'It's says this Don man, this gang leader, was taken into custody,' I replied. 'At least I can find out if the police found a girl in the house when they raided it.'

'I'd assume the gang had more than one house and a dozen places where they could have hidden her if they'd wanted to keep her alive,' Sid said. 'But why would they want to keep her alive?'

'Why would they want to kill her?'

'They suspect she knows something, perhaps,' Gus said. 'She saw something that night. They fear she could identify them if she regains her sanity.'

I got up. 'I have to go,' I said.

'Molly, you cannot go looking for a violent Italian gang.' Sid held my arm. 'For heaven's sake, be sensible. Go and tell Captain Sullivan if you must and then let him deal with them for you.'

'Daniel's still away,' I said, feeling close to tears. 'He went to his parents' house and hasn't yet returned. Mrs Goodwin will help me, if I can find her. She's probably still at work. She works a night shift. Thank you for the breakfast. Sorry, I'm not hungry.'

After this torrent of words I fled, dashed home to get my cloak, and then took the trolley straight to police headquarters on Mulberry Street. There I found the officers to be as unhelpful as I always remembered them.

'The matron, you mean?' one of them said. 'Have you looked in the shelter next to the Tombs? That's where you'd find her.'

I've never been known for my patience and calm nature. I was about to explode when I saw someone I recognized coming down the stairs. It was Detective McIver, who had previously been partnered with the infamous Quigley and worked under Daniel. I hadn't found him too helpful, either, but that was at a time when I was still suspicious of him.

I saw him start when he recognized me. 'Miss Murphy, is it not? Do you have news about Captain Sullivan?'

'No good news,' I said. 'The current commissioner won't reconsider his case so he waits in limbo until a new commissioner is appointed in January.'

'A nasty business,' he said. 'If you see him, please tell him that I look forward to his return.'

'I will. Thank you, Detective.'

'So what brings you here today?' he asked.

'I was looking for Mrs Goodwin,' I said. 'Would you happen to know where she might be found? I know that the police use her on special assignments and I need to talk to her urgently.'

Detective McIver shook his head. 'I've no idea. She comes and goes. I haven't seen her today anyway.'

'Then maybe you could help me,' I said. 'I understand there was a raid on an Italian gang last night.'

'You read about it in the paper this morning, I suppose.'

'I did. And I have a particular reason for wanting to know more details on that raid. Can you tell me which officers were involved?'

He looked at me and laughed gently. 'I don't think we're about to give out information like that, Miss Murphy. For one thing, these Sicilians have a nasty habit of getting even. I don't want one of our officers shot in the back. And why might you be interested?'

'I believe they kidnapped a friend of mine,' I said. 'A young girl. I need to know whether she was found at their house when the police raided.'

'I know of no young girls,' McIver said. 'Of course I wasn't on the site, but . . . Was the kidnapping reported to police?'

'No. I didn't realize who these people were until I saw the newspaper this morning.' And I spilled out the whole story – the girl in the snowdrift, the hospital, the Hungarians, the theater, New Haven . . . I think it must have come out as a garbled mess. Anyway, by the end of it McIver nodded patiently. 'If you give me a description of the young woman, I can ask questions for you.'

'Thank you. You're very kind.' I took out my notebook and wrote all the details I could think of.

'I'll do what I can,' he said. 'But you're not to think of going up to that neighborhood yourself. These are the most dangerous kind of thugs. And some of them have undoubtedly evaded our net and would be waiting for you.'

'Very well,' I said. 'I've put my address on the paper. You'll let me know if you have any news, won't you? And if you see Mrs Goodwin, would you tell her that I need to speak to her?'

I left then, having found out a vital clue. He had said 'up to that neighborhood.' That meant not in the Italian neighborhood around police headquarters that they were calling Little Italy. It meant another neighborhood in the city. Not Brooklyn or anywhere outside the city, because he'd have said, "over there." It shouldn't be that hard to discover where Italians might have settled in upper Manhattan.

I came out of police headquarters and immediately found an Italian café. They were most helpful. Apart from this area, the big concentration of Italians in the city was on the upper East Side, between 95th and 125th in an area they called Yorkville.

I didn't wait any longer. I made my way to the Second Avenue El station at City Hall and rode the train all the way up to 99th. Up here was a ramshackle area, still being built. Streets of tenements were interspersed with squatters' shacks, tacked together from any materials they could find, and between them were unbuilt lots and even small market gardens. To my right I had views down to a narrow stretch of water, with more land on the far bank. I didn't realize at the time that it was Ward's Island. To my left was open land and I realized with a thrill that it must be the northern end of Central Park.

Had Jessie been brought here once before and somehow escaped into the park? Was I finally on the right track? I wandered aimlessly northward until I heard Italian spoken. The streets leading off Second Avenue became full of life. Women carried on shrill conversations from upstairs windows as they aired out their bedding, or hauled in laundry. Children ran around, shouting to each other in high, melodious voices that mingled with the sounds of the pushcart men, calling out their wares. It was rather like the Lower East Side transplanted northward.

On the corner of 115th Street, a man was standing on a stool, trying to fix a broken window.

'Excuse me,' I called. 'But can you tell me if any Sicilians live on this street?'

'Sicilianos? Pah.' He spat onto the sidewalk. 'We don't need them no-good sons-of-bitches. They're not Italians. They're dogs. Cut their grandmother's throats for a dime, they would.'

I waited for this outburst to subside. 'So where might they be found?'

'I think you find them on One Hundred Twentieth, but I'd stay away if I was you. Nothing but trouble those Sicilianos.'

I ignored the second warning that day. What harm could come to me walking down a street in daylight, especially an Italian street, with so much life going on. I walked until I came to 120th Street. It seemed quieter here. Two old women dressed head to toe in black were walking together, heads down, carrying shopping baskets. A group of men stood on a stoop in animated conversation, expressing themselves with their hands as much as their mouths. From their raised voices, I expected them to break into a fight at any moment, but then one of them laughed, so I supposed the discussion had been good-natured after all.

I didn't feel like approaching them with my question – after all, they might have been involved with the Sicilian gang themselves. And the old women obviously didn't speak English. Then I saw a figure I could approach – a young Catholic priest, his long cassock swishing along the ground as he walked.

I crossed the road to speak to him.

'Sicilians? Yes, it's mainly Sicilians on this street,' he said, 'all the way down to the corner grocery. After that it's Milanese.'

'I read in the papers that there was a raid on a house around here last night,' I said.

He frowned. 'And what interest might you have in that? Just morbid curiosity? Not wise in neighborhoods like this.'

'I have a personal interest,' I said. 'I believe this gang kidnapped a friend of mine. I wanted to know whether a young girl was found in the house when the police raided it.'

He looked grave now. 'I survive well with these people

because I don't go sticking my nose into their business,' he said. 'This is a serious charge you're making.'

'I'm not making it up. It's true. They came to my house and took her away. They claimed they were her relatives. I've been so worried about her.'

'You should ask the police who conducted the raid what they found,' he said. Clearly he wasn't going to be of any help.

'Can you at least tell me which house it was?'

'I believe it was number twenty-nine. On the next street,' he said. 'There's nobody there now. The place is empty. They carted off the lot of them. But they'll be out right away. They're wily, these Sicilians. And they'd never get anybody to testify against them – nobody who wants to stay alive, that is.'

I thanked him and made my way to the next street. The whole street had an empty air to it after the noise and bustle of Second Avenue. Twenty-nine looked like any other house in the row – newish red brick with white trim around the windows. I stood gazing up at it, wondering what to do next. Then farther down the street I saw a door open and a woman came out to shake out a cloth. I ran over to her.

'That house.' I pointed. 'The police come last night?'

She frowned. I couldn't tell if she didn't understand me or didn't want to talk.

Then a male voice from inside yelled something and a big man in undershirt and braces stood beside her in the doorway.

'What you want?' he demanded.

'I'm asking about the house over there. The police came and took the men away.'

'*Stupido*,' he muttered. 'The *polizia* – they can't do nothing. What they think they can do, huh? These men are Cosa Nostra. The police – they no touch them.'

'We'll see,' I said. 'Did you see the raid yourselves? There was a young girl. Did the police find a young girl?'

The man directed rapid-fire questions at his wife. She responded and then put her hand to her forehead in an international symbol meaning crazy. I looked at the man, waiting for an explanation.

'She say young girl – they come and take her before. To the crazy house. The crazy wagon come.'

'The crazy house? You mean the insane asylum?' Hope surged through me. She wasn't dead. She was probably in the safest place in the country right now.

'*Si*. One, two days before.'

'Thank you.' I shook his hand, then his wife's.

I knew where at least one asylum was, and that was on Ward's Island. Now all I had to do was find out exactly where Ward's Island was and how to get to it. I made my way down to the dock on 125th where I knew that ferries docked.

'Ward's Island?'

The sailor I asked laughed. 'You're looking at it. If the water wasn't so cold, you could swim across. There's a little ferry, down a ways. Keep walking and you'll see the sign.'

I did as he suggested and found the ferry was no bigger than a large row boat. The old man who ferried me grinned as he handed me ashore. 'Make sure they don't lock you up and keep you here,' he said. 'It's a terrible place, right enough. You should hear the cries and the groans sometimes. You can hear them in Manhattan when the wind's in the right direction.'

I tried not to think about his warning as I marched up to the front entrance of a grim brick building. I couldn't help noticing the bars on the windows. Inside I was met by a nurse in a crisply starched uniform. 'Did you not read the sign?' She tapped at the wall. 'Visiting days are the first Saturday of every month, but only for those patients deemed suitable to receive visitors.'

'I've come to reclaim a young woman who was admitted

here by mistake,' I said. 'She would have been brought here within the last three or four days.'

'By mistake, you say?'

'Yes. She was being looked after by myself and treated by an eminent doctor of the mind. She should never have been brought here and I'm here to take her home.'

'I see.' She regarded me coldly. 'And the name?'

'I'm not sure under what name she would have been admitted. Probably Anya something.'

'You say you don't know the person's name?'

'I know her real name. It's Jessie Edwards. But I fear she was admitted under a false name or no name at all. Now, can you look in your records and see if a girl was brought here in the past few days?'

'I can do no such thing,' she said. 'Our records are confidential.'

'Even if a mistake has been made?'

She glanced down at a book on her desk. 'The only person admitted here recently who matches your description was admitted by her family. I take it you are not a family member?'

I was so tempted to lie and say that I was, but I decided this might complicate things even further. 'No, I'm not, and neither were they. They had kidnapped her.'

Her eyebrows shot up. 'You can prove this?'

'No, I'm afraid I can't.'

'Then what exactly is your interest in this case?'

'I'm a friend of the young woman. I was looking after her until she was kidnapped.'

She frowned at me as if trying to read my mind.

'What was the name of these people who committed a young woman against her will?'

'I don't know what name they would have used,' I said. 'They are really Sicilian gang members. They may have claimed to be Hungarian.'

'Really.' She shook her head in disbelief. 'And do you not think that our staff would be aware if a perfectly sane individual was brought here against her will? This is not the dark ages, you know.'

'Unfortunately she is not in her right mind at the moment,' I said. 'She has lost her memory and her power of speech.'

'Which would indicate that she actually belongs here, would you not say?'

'She needs treatment, but she was getting good care from me and from a doctor who is a friend of mine.'

She regarded me for a long while then she sniffed and said, 'Young woman, you are wasting my time. If you really believe an injustice has happened then come back to me with the authorities and with proof. Personally I think everything you've said is a load of baloney.'

'It's not. They really did kidnap her.'

'Someone whose name you don't know was brought here by relatives, who are not relatives but you don't know their names, either, and she really is in a current catatonic state. I don't think you're going to find anyone who takes you seriously, miss. I don't know what your game is, but I suggest you leave.'

'Let me talk to someone in charge,' I begged.

'Until you can show me that the people who signed her over to this institution were not her family members, I am not prepared to mention this to any of my superiors. Until then you have no right to be here. Good day to you.'

'If I could just see her,' I said. 'I know she'd want to see me. She'd want to know that something is being done on her behalf.'

'Good day to you, miss.' She deliberately turned her back on me.

'Now look here,' I said angrily. 'I'm not leaving until I see someone who will at least listen to me.'

The nurse rang a little bell on her desk. Two large men appeared. 'Have this young woman escorted out, please,' she said. 'She is trying to make trouble.'

Forty

I stood on the Manhattan shore and looked across at Ward's Island, overwhelmed with anger and frustration. To know that my girl was in that terrible place and that I had no way of rescuing her was driving me crazy. What could I do? If Daniel had returned he might know how to approach this. But then he might also tell me that it was none of my business. The girl had been destined for that very asylum when I kidnapped her myself. And who knows – in spite of the reputation and the moans and the groans, maybe she would receive some treatment there that could help her.

Of course that's when I thought of Dr Birnbaum. He was well known in his field. He could probably gain entrance to such an institution and he could see if Jessie was all right and being cared for. Feeling much better, I hurried to the nearest El station, and sat impatiently while the train crawled slowly southward through Manhattan until it reached Eighth Street. Soon I found myself at the Hotel Lafayette. I hardly expected Dr Birnbaum to be in his rooms in the middle of the day, but I could leave a note for him, and by the end of the day I'd have an ally who could save Jessie for me.

'Dr Birnbaum?' the man at the reception desk said. 'I'm afraid he's not here.'

'I realize that,' I said, trying to sound calm, 'but I wish to leave a note for him to be delivered the moment he returns. It's urgent.'

'If it's urgent, I'm afraid that's not going to do much good,' he said. 'The doctor was called out of town unexpectedly this morning.'

'How long will he be away?'

'I couldn't tell you but he did take quite an amount of baggage with him.'

'You don't happen to know where he went?'

'It is not my job to ask the guests where they are going, miss,' he said solemnly. 'It could have been back to Europe, I suppose. He did tell us to retain his room, so I expect he'll return in good time. If you care to write the note, I'll see that he gets it as soon as he returns.'

I wrote on hotel stationery, but my heart just wasn't in it. How could I possibly wait to see when Dr Birnbaum might return, knowing Jessie was in that place? Then I decided I wasn't going to wait. Mrs Goodwin would probably be home in bed by now and I was going to risk waking her.

I hurried to Tompkins Square, hammered on Mrs Goodwin's door, and was finally rewarded by slow footsteps coming toward me. It was clear she had been in a deep sleep.

'Oh, Molly, it's you,' she said. 'What drama do we have today?'

'A terrible one,' I said, and spilled out the whole story. 'We have to do something,' I concluded. 'They wouldn't listen to me. It will take an official visit from the police before we can get her out of there.'

'Very well.' She nodded. 'I'll see what I can do. Captain Paxton was the senior officer in the raid on the Sicilians, so he would have to be the one to take this up.'

She went upstairs to get dressed and I left her feeling more hopeful. It was now in the hands of the authorities. They would make that hatchet-faced nurse admit them and release Jessie back to me. I realized I might be taking on a long-term problem, that supporting another person would not be easy, but I'm always of the Mr Micawber school of thought that 'something will turn up.' So I walked home with a spring to my step, already planning how I might make Jessie's bedroom more cheerful, or perhaps give her mine so that she got the morning sun.

I waited impatiently all day. There was almost no food in the house, but I dared not leave to go shopping, in case I missed Mrs Goodwin. Evening came and still no Mrs Goodwin. Still no Daniel, either. I paced the house like a caged animal, up and down the narrow hallway, waiting for that knock on the front door. By eight o'clock I realized she wasn't going to come.

I told myself to calm down and stop fussing. Obviously Captain Paxton had more on his mind than the fate of one girl. I couldn't expect him to drop everything, to risk jeopardizing his case against the Sicilian gangsters just for me. That night I dreamed about Ward's Island, but it wasn't Jessie who was locked up there, it was me. It was a horrible nightmare with half-human creatures dancing around me, screaming and moaning and laughing. They prodded me with sticks and one of them said, 'This one's sane,' and another shouted, 'Not for long!' at which they all cackled with laughter and a voice in the background whispered, 'You'll never get out, you know.'

I woke screaming, then lay in the darkness with my heart pounding. I had to do something today. I couldn't wait any longer. As soon as it was light I made my way to police headquarters. As I walked up Mulberry Street I saw her walking ahead of me, in conversation with a male police officer. I didn't stop to think that perhaps I shouldn't approach her when she was on duty. I'm afraid I yelled out her name and broke into a run. She turned in surprise and waited for me.

'Molly, my dear, I can't talk now,' she said. 'We're on our way to interview a girl in a brothel. I get off duty at ten and I'll come straight to your house.'

So I had to wait yet again. At least she'll have good news when she comes, I kept telling myself. At last there was the knock on the door and I ushered her inside.

'Would you like a cup of tea?' I asked. 'Come and sit down.'

'I won't stay.' She remained standing just inside the door. 'I'm afraid I don't have very encouraging news for you, my dear. I told your story to Captain Paxton and he's not prepared to intervene.'

'What?' I shouted. 'He knows those gangsters have shoved an innocent girl into an insane asylum and he's not going to do anything?'

She put her hand on my shoulder. 'Molly, he considered it carefully, I assure you.'

'Oh, I bet he did!'

'But in the end his opinion was that the girl was currently out of her mind and thus belonged in an insane asylum, even though she was admitted there by dubious means.'

'Did you tell him I'd be prepared to take care of her?' I demanded.

'Molly, you have no claim on her. You're not a family member. You'll have to let matters be for now. I'm sure if she recovers her senses they'll release her.'

'No they won't.' I could feel tears stinging in my eyes.

'I don't know why you're taking this particular case so personally,' she said. 'You're a detective. You know the world is full of sadness and injustice and you have to remain detached from your work or go mad yourself.'

'But she's not my work. I found her,' I said. 'I believe I was meant to find her. Meant to save her. And save her I will, one way or another.'

After she had gone I sat at my kitchen table, staring out at the December grayness. The world outside matched my mood – swirling fog, bare branches from which moisture dripped. How could Daniel have deserted me when I needed him? If he'd been in charge of the case, and not that stupid Captain Paxton, then all would be well. At least he'd have been able to comfort and reassure me. I realized that sometimes I fought too hard to be a strong and independent woman. Maybe I had shut him out one time too often and he no longer thought that I needed or wanted him close to me. I was almost ready to rush up to Westchester, find him, and make him come back to New York with me. But my pride wouldn't let me do it.

I tried to tell myself that Jessie would be all right. This was, after all, the twentieth century. Great strides were being made in treating the insane. There were other doctors like my friend Dr Birnbaum who now specialized in the sick mind. Maybe she was in the right place. Maybe they'd cure her.

Then I decided I'd write a letter to the head of the asylum, asking to be notified as soon as he saw any improvement in her, letting him know that I was willing to take care of her myself. He'd be a reasonable man. I'd have her out in no time at all.

I wrote the letter, weighing every word I put down. At last I was satisfied and had completed a whole page with no blots, which in itself was a miracle for me. I found a stamp and set out to post it. But even as I dropped it into the mailbox, I found that I couldn't keep the old worries at bay. What about that dream I had had last night? Was it a warning that the asylum was a terrible place? After all, Nelly Bly had gained notoriety by having herself committed and thus exposing the horrors of such places.

I stopped in midstep on the sidewalk. I'd go and see Elizabeth and find out the truth. So I turned away from Patchin Place and made for the Fifth Avenue Hotel. Hot chestnut men and Christmas carolers reminded me of the approaching season. It certainly didn't feel like a time of goodwill to all men!

Elizabeth had obviously just risen and was still in her robe having breakfast in her suite, but she looked pleased to see me.

'Molly. You have news about your silent girl?'

'News, but not good. It seems she has been admitted to the insane asylum on Ward's Island.'

'Mercy me. That's not good news, as you say. Is there nothing you can do about it?'

'I've tried everything I can,' I said. 'I've just written to the doctor in charge. Everyone has told me that the girl belongs in there. So I came to you. I have to know – is it such a terrible place, do you think? Will she be treated and cured?'

I saw the answer from her face before she spoke. 'Molly, those places are one step away from hell,' she said. 'In spite of the article I wrote, and the public outcry at the conditions, I've come to believe that little has been done to improve things. We've no way of improving them, you see. We just don't know how to treat the insane. Most of the time we just don't bother.'

'Then I want you to help me,' I said. 'You managed to have yourself admitted to a similar institution once. I want your help in getting me admitted there.'

She shook her head firmly. 'You don't know what you're saying.'

'Of course I do. But it's the only way. Once I'm in there, I'm sure I can find Jessie and manage to convince a kind doctor or nurse that a terrible injustice has been done.'

'You may not find a kind doctor or nurse. Some of the people who work there are the worst sort of bullies – those who delight in inflicting suffering on those with no voice and no power.'

'At least let me try it,' I said. 'What have I got to lose? If a family member can commit a person, then surely you can claim to be my relative. You can have me admitted and then, a couple of days later, reveal who you are and why you admitted me. People will listen to you. I'll be whisked out again and I can bring Jessie with me.'

'Jessie?'

'That is the girl's real name. Jessie Edwards. She was a dancer in Connecticut.'

'Amazing. So not foreign after all?'

'No. It must be as Dr Birnbaum suggested – that a great and horrible event robbed her of her senses and her power of speech.'

Elizabeth shook her head again. 'Then what would happen to her if she was rescued from that place? The insane are not always easy to care for, you know.'

'I can help her, Elizabeth. My doctor friend is a renowned alienist and I have a devoted woman to be her nurse. The poor girl has suffered enough. I've got to do all I can.'

'Then why not let your doctor friend help her?'

'Unfortunately, he's been called away, and I've no idea where or for how long. Don't you see that a few days in a place like Ward's Island might push somebody into madness for ever?'

'Yes, I do see that,' she said.

'So won't you help me? You can summon the wagon to have me taken away. Tell them I'm having delusions or I'm violent or even that I'm like Jessie and I've lost my memory and can't speak.'

'Violent and delusional would be better,' Catherine said. 'If you'd just lost your memory, any loving family member would take care of you until you regained it. I'd have to show that it was beyond my power to care for you and that you were a danger to yourself and others.'

'But not too dangerous, or I might be locked away from other inmates.'

'Very well,' she said after a long pause. 'If you really want to go through with this, then I'll come with you to your home and contact the asylum from there. It will look less suspicious than from a hotel. And you'll need to pack a bag – only pack clothes you don't care about losing, as they'll probably be stolen from you if they are too fine.'

We took a cab back to Patchin Place. I went upstairs and threw my oldest night attire and undergarments into the bag. I wasn't going to risk taking a change of dress. I didn't own enough clothes to willingly sacrifice one outfit. I also packed my hair-brush and tooth powder, although whether I'd be allowed to use either was debatable. I unpinned my hair and made it stand out wildly, giving me a definitely mad appearance.

Then Elizabeth went to find a public telephone and I rehearsed my role. We had decided that I had become delusional. I was convinced that I was a foreign princess, being held captive by my sister Elizabeth, and that I kept trying to escape. That way I would not be deemed a danger to other inmates, but would be too much for my poor sister, given her own current health problems (we hadn't quite decided on these, but we'd just hint).

Elizabeth returned, looking grave. 'They will be here before the end of the day,' she said. 'And they will be bringing papers for me to sign, committing you to the care of the state.'

'I see.' I swallowed hard. It suddenly sounded very real and very final. 'And we'll give it two days, shall we?' I added. 'That should give me enough time to locate Jessie and make sure that she's all right. And who knows, I might even have a chance to speak to a person who would listen to the truth.'

'Who knows,' Elizabeth said.

I thought of going over to Sid and Gus to say goodbye, but I had a suspicion that they wouldn't let me go through with this.

I wasn't at all sure that I should go through with it myself. The sensible side of me kept saying that Doctor Birnbaum would be back in a few days and that he'd be able to rescue Jessie, but I couldn't shake off this terrible feeling of dread and need for haste. What if he had gone back to Europe and stayed there for months? Something inside me whispered that if I didn't get there soon, it would be too late. I wasn't sure why those ruthless men had committed Jessie to the institution – maybe they had been tipped off about the police raid and wanted her safely stashed away. But maybe they could equally have bribed a guard to bring about her demise in a way that didn't look suspicious.

Anyway, the wagon had been summoned. There was no going back now. And I had Nelly Bly working with me. She had done braver and more risky things than this and had survived. She'd make sure I stayed safe.

At four o'clock there was a hammering on the front door. I was just finishing a slice of bread and jam and a cup of tea. I leaped up, my heart hammering as loudly as those knocks. So this was it. Doom was knocking. I heard Elizabeth go to the door and heard her say, 'She's in here. She's quiet right now, and I think she'll go with you if you agree with what she asks you.'

Two men came into the kitchen. I looked up at them and recognized one of them from the time I stole Jessie. But I managed to keep my face in a worried stare and went on eating bread and jam as they handed Elizabeth papers to be signed.

'Molly dear,' Elizabeth said, as she handed the papers back to them, 'these nice men have come to take you on a little trip.'

'I'm not Molly. I keep telling you,' I said. 'I am Princess Alexandra.' I turned to the men. 'They took me from my castle in England, you know,' I said. 'Have you come to take me home and restore me to my royal seat?'

'Yes, that's right.' One of the men dug the other in the ribs.

'Say Your Royal Highness when you address me,' I said.

Another dig in the ribs. 'Oh, of course, your royal highness.' He smirked. 'Now, come along nice and easy. We've got to make our way to the boat that will take you back to your palace.'

'Make sure she doesn't escape during the trip,' Elizabeth whispered to them. 'She's become an expert at running away.'

'Then we'd better put on the jacket, Fred,' one man said to the other.

'Oh, I don't think that's necessary,' Elizabeth said quickly. 'If one of you sits beside her and you keep the doors shut.'

'Best to be safe,' the first man said. 'Fred here lost a patient a couple of weeks ago and he got in one hell of a row about it.' He produced a white canvas jacket and came toward me. I whimpered in alarm and backed away.

'It's your royal robes, your highness,' he said, and slipped my arms into it, lacing it up down the back. Then, to my horror, I found that there was no opening for my hands. The laces were pulled tight and suddenly my arms were wrapped around myself in a tight hug. I shot Elizabeth a frightened glance.

'You'll be all right, Molly dear,' she said. 'These men will take good care of you.' But I could see that she looked worried, too.

'Let me give you a kiss,' she said. As her face came close to mine she whispered, 'It will only be for two days, and I'll try and check on you all the time.'

The men put big hands on each of my shoulders and marched me out of my door and down the alley. Then they literally bundled me into the back of a wagon. I heard the doors close with grim finality, shutting out all light, as I sat on the hard bench. I was almost hurled to the floor as the wagon took off and had no way of steadying myself. I pressed myself into a corner and tried to stay upright. It wasn't easy and when I slipped down to my knees, I stayed there on the floor, rather than risk another fall.

After what seemed to be an eternity, the wagon came to a halt. I heard the sound of the door opening. 'Come on, get out,' one of the men shouted, no longer gentle and kind. He grabbed at my arm and yanked me down to the ground, where I fell to my knees again. This time he grabbed my hair and made me stand up.

'You're hurting me,' I protested.

'You'd better get used to it, sweetheart,' he said. 'Now march. The boat's at the end of the dock.'

This was no friendly little rowboat but bigger and enclosed. They half-carried, half-pushed me onto the deck and inside a nasty little cabin. Then they shut the doors again, leaving me in complete darkness as the boat chugged across the narrow stretch of water. I almost fell over as we bumped against another jetty. Then the door opened and this time there were warders in uniform, looking remarkably like prison guards.

'Come along then. Get moving,' one of them said. They grabbed me and marched me between them from the dock to that big front door. It opened. I was taken inside, and the door clanged shut behind me. I was an inmate in an insane asylum, whether I wanted it or not.

Forty-one

Without having time to catch my breath, I was hustled down a long tiled hallway and another heavy iron door was opened with a key. I was shoved through into a holding area. It was dank and cold and the only small window had bars on it. There was a bench along one wall but I paced rather than sat. Time went by. Outside the light was fading. I began to worry that I'd be held in a solitary cell like this and never have a chance to talk to Jessie.

Then I heard the tramp of approaching feet and then a hatchet-faced woman in a nurse's uniform and another man who looked like a prison guard came in.

'Name of Murphy,' the nurse said, looking up from a clipboard. 'Committed by sister. Delusional and tries to run away.'

I decided I had better keep playing my part.

'This isn't my royal palace,' I said in a haughty voice. 'Guards, I command you to take me to my palace immediately.'

The man glanced at the nurse and chuckled. 'Right away, your majesty. You'll find a couple of Napoleons and Queen Victoria waiting for you, if I'm not mistaken.'

The nurse, however, did not smile. 'Did she bring a bag?'

'Yeah. They have it.'

'I need my bag,' I said. 'It has my crown in it. Make sure it is brought to me. And please remove this ridiculous garment. It is most uncomfortable.'

'The garment stays on until you've been evaluated,' the nurse said. 'Is Dr Arnold still in the building?'

'No, he's gone,' the man said.

'Then take her to Female Four.'

'You should probably take the jacket off her if she's going in there,' the man said. 'She'll need her hands to defend herself.'

'The inmates are not violent in Female Four,' the nurse said.

'She'll still need her hands free,' the man said flatly.

'Very well,' the nurse said. 'Upon your head be it if she claws someone's eyes out during the night.'

He spun me around and untied my back. I sighed with relief as my arms dropped to my sides. He yanked my jacket off and I wiggled my fingers, enjoying the freedom of movement. 'Right, come on then.' He pushed me forward, out of the door through which they had just entered. Another long hallway stretched out ahead of me. On either side were doors with small barred windows. As I passed one of these, a creature flung itself at the bars, snarling. I saw frightening bloodshot eyes and matted hair before I was propelled onward.

My heart was now beating very fast. Why had I ever thought that this was a good idea? I didn't even really know for sure that Jessie was an inmate here – what if I was going through all this for nothing? Then I told myself that Nelly Bly had done it and survived and I was every bit as tough as she was. I held my head high like a princess and strutted ahead of my jailer.

At last he opened a door and pushed me inside. The first thing that hit me was the stench. The place smelled like a latrine, only worse. Was there no WC available?

'New one for you,' the guard barked. 'Another one thinks she's royalty.' He shoved me inside and slammed the door shut behind me. I heard a key turning in the lock. The room was dark. No lamps of any kind had been lit and the daylight, outside the two small windows, had almost faded. All I could make out were shapes, some sprawled on the floor, some huddled in corners. There were whimpers and then a burst of crazy laughter. I stood frozen in the doorway. A creature in a gray shift, with hair even wilder than my own, drifted over to me and touched my face. 'Are you my own precious child?' it asked in a cracked voice. 'My own precious child come back to me?'

'Leave her alone, Minnie,' a sharp voice said, and I saw a figure very different from the rest of them: a huge woman with a bosom like a vast shelf, several chins, and a spiteful piggy face. 'So you're another princess, are you? Well, let's get one thing straight in here, your highness. You do what I say, all the time. You disobey me and you'll be sorry – believe me, you'll be sorry. When I tell you something, you say "yes, ma'am." Got it?'

I turned puzzled eyes on her. 'Have I been abducted?' I asked. 'Is this the enemy's dungeon?'

The gargantuan woman laughed, a big chuckle that shook all the chins. 'Oh yes, my dear, this is the enemy all right. Now go and sit down and behave yourself. Don't talk to the other inmates unless they talk to you. You never know who's feeling cranky today and some of them can pack quite a punch. If you're lucky you'll get food soon. Better eat quickly.'

'Can you tell me where I sleep?' I asked. 'And what about my things? Where are my nightclothes?'

She laughed again. 'Oh, you're a rum one, you are. You're going to keep me amused for days. You'll be given your clothing in the morning at morning inspection.'

'But I must have my hairbrush,' I said. 'Where is my servant to brush my hair?'

She tugged at my hair. 'This don't look like it's seen a brush in a while. But it will get combed tomorrow morning, don't you worry.'

There was a stone bench that ran along the wall. I went and sat on it. My eyes were getting used to the gloom now. I saw there were about twenty women in the room, of all ages and shapes. Some were muttering to themselves. One was hugging herself and rocking back and forth. Yet another was sucking her thumb. Poor pathetic wretches, I thought, until I realized that I was now one of them.

How could I possibly find out about Jessie? I was supposed to be delusional, so how could I ask sane questions without arousing suspicion? Were there other wards for females more violent than this, or more disturbed? Maybe I'd find out how the place worked in the morning.

At that moment there was a clanging sound in the hallway. The inmates rushed to line up at the door. Our wardress opened the door. 'Make sure you stay in line and keep your hands to yourselves,' she barked. We marched down the hallway and into a large room. Long tables ran the length of the room, with benches on either side of them. Every one of these places was now being taken by women in identical grayish shifts. I followed the woman in front of me. At every place there was a bowl of what looked like a watery soup with bits of cabbage floating in it and a thick slice of bread. The women from my room scrambled to take their places and started wolfing the food into their mouths right away. I eased myself onto the bench and looked for a spoon but found none. The other women already had their bowls at their lips, draining the liquid, chomping away on any solid pieces they found. I put my bowl to my own lips. It was too hot to drink yet. Suddenly it was snatched away from me by a big flabby creature across the table.

'Hey,' I shouted, but it was too late. She had already tipped the contents down her throat.

'That's not nice, Irma,' my wardress said, then she and the servers burst out laughing. 'I told you to be quick, didn't I?' she said.

'May I get some more?' I asked.

'One bowl per inmate. That's the rules.' The servers were still laughing.

'That's not fair,' I retorted, forgetting that I was supposed to be confused and deluded.

'You'll learn soon enough,' someone said. 'Better hang on to your bread or that will be gone, too.'

I tried to eat it. It was stale, thick, and smeared with such disgusting butter that I could hardly swallow it down. I looked up and down the rows. There seemed to be about three hundred women in the room. Some were eating like animals, making strange noises, but some sat primly and ate daintily. It seemed that not all were as insane as the occupants of my room.

Almost immediately a whistle sounded. The women got to their feet and were led out of the dining room. I scanned the other lines of inmates, looking for Jessie, but couldn't see her. Then a scuffle broke out. One woman tried to run away. Immediately she was pounced upon by two nurses. Her arms were twisted up behind her back and she was forced to her knees.

'I'm not insane,' she shouted. 'I'm as sane as any of you. My family has locked me away, that's what they've done. Locked me away. Let me talk to a doctor. Please, let me talk to somebody.'

I felt quite sick as she was led away. My group was marched to a bathroom where we were instructed to wash our faces and hands and use the WCs. I was horrified to find that there were two rough towels for all of us, and that some of the women had nasty sores on their faces. I washed willingly enough in cold water and dried myself on my own sleeve. After that we were taken to a dormitory with a long row of iron beds in it. Another gray shift was laid out on each bed. We changed and lay down on the scratchy sheets. It was freezing cold. I lay shivering, curled into a ball. Dear God, what had I done?

I must have drifted off eventually because when I awoke, cold gray light was filtering in through those windows, both of which were open, letting in freezing air. A whistle had blown. Those inmates who didn't respond immediately were yanked out of bed by a leg or an arm and there was much cursing and growling. We were marched to the bathroom again, had cold water splashed over us, then changed into our day clothes. I was given a garment identical to the rest of them. We were made to sit on the edge of our beds while our wardress combed out hair. She was so brutal with the comb that tears spouted by themselves from my eyes. She then pulled back my hair into a braid. 'And don't take it out,' she said.

Then off to breakfast. It was a bowl of lumpy oatmeal, three dried prunes, and a cup of very weak tea. This time I held onto my oatmeal. My flabby friend reached across and grabbed the prunes. She was welcome to them. The tea was just like drinking warm and slightly soapy water. The oatmeal was equally unappetizing.

After breakfast we were lined up for our morning walk. Once around the island in that bitter wind. The gardens were nicely landscaped and must have looked attractive in summer, but in midwinter there were only sad dead lawns and bare trees. We passed other groups of women, going in a counterclockwise direction. At one end of the island newer buildings had been built; these had bigger windows and no bars. The sign over the door said, RESEARCH INSTITUTE.

I was so busy staring at this new building that I almost missed her. Jessie was passing me in another column of women. She was stumbling along as if in a bad dream, her eyes staring blankly ahead of her. As we drew level she looked up and for a moment I thought I saw recognition in her eyes.

'Jessie,' I said.

She turned back to look as we were marched away. Had she remembered me? I wondered. And would she be glad to see me? Maybe she blamed me for delivering her to her tormentors. Maybe she'd want nothing to do with me.

When we came inside with stinging cheeks and numb fingers, we were put to work at housekeeping tasks. Making beds, sweeping floors, washing floors. In the middle I was called over and taken to a small room where a young man sat at a table.

'I'm Dr Field,' he said. 'And what is your name?'

It suddenly occurred to me that maybe all those inmates who couldn't or wouldn't communicate were in one room. I stared at him blankly.

'You don't want to talk today?'

I kept on staring.

'You're not a princess today then? Who are you?'

I remained silent.

'Do you understand what I'm saying to you?'

No response.

'Interesting,' he said, scribbling something on a sheet of paper. 'Complete withdrawal. Shutting herself off from a situation she doesn't like. We'll try again another day. Nurse, take her to Dr Meyer's ward. He might be interested in her.'

I wasn't sure if this was a good thing or not. I allowed myself to be led away. Out of the main building, across a courtyard, and up some steps. Then into another dreary room, as cold and bleak as the first one. The sound of coughing greeted me.

'New?' a stone-faced nurse asked my escorts. 'Violent?'

'Wouldn't communicate this morning. Delusional yesterday.

The doctor thought Dr Meyer might want to take a look at her, when he gets back.'

'All right. Leave her here. Well, don't just stand there,' she said to me. 'Find a place and sit down.'

I wandered aimlessly around the room and found myself staring at Jessie. She was curled up in a corner, hugging her knees to her, her head buried in her hands. I sat beside her. She didn't stir. At last an orderly came to the door. 'Bring out Rodriguez. The doctors want to take a look at her,' he said.

As the nurse dragged a bewildered-looking woman up from the floor, I leaned closer to Jessie.

'Jessie?' I whispered. 'It's Molly. Remember me?'

I saw disbelieving eyes turning in my direction, a flash of recognition, then a warning sign in her eyes. I thought I saw her mouth 'don't know me,' before her head sank into her hands again.

I sat quietly beside her. Occasionally she glanced at me. I longed to talk to her and reassure her, but the stone-faced woman's eyes were constantly on us. After a long morning we were summoned to the dining room. Down the steps, across the courtyard, and into the dining hall. In the confusion I drew close behind her.

'I've come to save you,' I said in her ear. 'I'll get you out of here, I promise.'

I heard her intake of breath so I knew she had heard and understood me. Unfortunately, she was shunted away from me at table. Lunch was a piece of plain boiled fish and a potato. Again it was hard to swallow but at least nobody from this new room tried to grab my portion.

After lunch we were marched back. Some inmates dozed in the afternoon, curled up like animals on the benches or the floor. There was no form of entertainment provided for us, no reading material, no sewing. A person committed here really would go mad soon, I realized. I looked around the room, wondering how many women truly belonged in a place like this and how many were committed by families who wanted them out of the way. I saw how easily the staff had accepted the Sicilians' word that they were Jessie's relatives and how they had needed no proof that I was insane before I was carted away.

Jessie was either sleeping or pretending to. Suddenly the door was thrown open and two male orderlies came in. One was carrying a large can. 'Louse patrol,' one shouted. 'Line up. Come on. Move it.'

Our nurse went around prodding and pushing us into a line. I was a good way from Jessie. Each person had her scalp inspected. Those that failed were sent to the bathroom, where I suspect they would be doused with whatever was in the can. When the male orderly came to Jessie I watched in disbelief as his hands slid down from her head and one of them disappeared inside the front of her shift. She recoiled in horror and tried to pull his hand away. The orderly merely laughed and fondled her breasts more aggressively. He had a horrible piggy face and a mouth with missing teeth.

I forgot that I wasn't supposed to speak. I leaped out of that line and flung myself at the orderly.

'Leave her alone, you filthy lout,' I shouted. 'Take your hands off her right now.'

Instantly the orderly turned on me, knocking me across the room with a backhanded blow to my face. He and his fellow were on me right away, with the nurse also standing over me. As I struggled they brought both arms behind my back and one of them knelt on me. 'Get a jacket. This one's violent,' the nurse shouted.

'Let her go,' a voice screamed and Jessie was tugging at them, flailing away like a mad thing.

A whistle was blown. There was the sound of running feet. Someone dragged Jessie away. Someone else was kneeling beside me. I felt my sleeve pulled up and pain as something was jabbed into my arm. Everything started to blur. There was a roaring in my ears and I knew no more.

Forty-two

When I opened my eyes, I was lying staring at a strange ceiling. I tried to raise my head but I felt sick. Gradually I looked around and saw that I was in a small, windowless room. An electric lightbulb shone down from the ceiling. The metal door had a window in it at face height. The only furniture was the shelf on which I was lying. Apart from that there was only a bucket in the corner. I had been in a jail cell before now and it looked a lot like this.

I tried to sit up. The world swung around. How long had I been here and – more to the point – where was I? I realized that my rash intervention yesterday had ruined everything. Now instead of being in a room with Jessie and with a chance to speak to Dr Meyer, whoever he was, I was in some kind of solitary confinement for violent inmates. Fear began to overtake me. What if they professed no knowledge of me when Elizabeth came to collect me? Was it already my second day and time to be freed?

I staggered drunkenly over to the window and looked out onto an empty hallway. On the other side were similar rooms with windows in their doors, but no sound, no movement. I sat and waited. I couldn't tell if it was day or night. By the growlings of my stomach I thought that I had probably missed supper. What would happen to me now? I wondered. Would I ever have a chance to speak to a sympathetic person who would listen to my case? I realized that I was now probably classed as violent. Would that give them an excuse to keep me here?

I sat, sunk in deepest gloom, telling myself over and over what an idiot I was. Why did I think I could do these ridiculous things? Daniel had warned me several times that I was like a cat with nine lives and I was using them up all too quickly. Daniel – would he have returned yet? Did he wonder where I was? I missed him horribly. I'd have given anything to feel his strong arms around me. At that moment I didn't want to be strong and independent. I wanted to be protected and loved and cherished. I wanted to be out of this place right now. Had Elizabeth told Sid and Gus of our plan? Was she at this moment coming to rescue me? And then the nagging fear – would she find me, now that I had been placed among the violent?

Hours dragged by. At last the door was opened and a tray was pushed into the room, the door then closed hastily behind it. On the tray was a bowl of soup, a slice of gray meat, and a thick piece of bread. Not breakfast then. But was this lunch or dinner? And on what day? I dipped the bread in the soup and ate both that way but could not swallow the stringy meat.

At last I heard the sound of voices faintly outside in the hallway. I rushed to the window. A group of men, some wearing white coats, were moving down the hall. Two of them were deep in conversation. It took me a second to register that one of those men was Dr Birnbaum.

'Dr Birnbaum!' I shouted his name.

He didn't appear to have heard me. Maybe there was a racket coming from other rooms. I grabbed the tray that had not yet been picked up and hammered against the door with all my might. 'Dr Birnbaum. It's me, Molly. Molly Murphy. Help me.

Get me out of here,' I screamed. He didn't turn around as the group of men disappeared down the hallway and were gone.

I sank back onto the bench in deepest despair. No hope. Daniel, come and find me, I whispered. I must have dozed off because I woke with a start as the door opened. Two burly guards jerked me to my feet. 'Come on. Move.' They half-carried me out of the door and down the hallway. I began to feel hopeful again. Elizabeth had arrived and I was to be released. Everything was going to be all right.

We passed through a door into another world. This one smelled of disinfectant, like a hospital, but it was clean and bright and I was manhandled into what looked like a doctor's office. There was an examining couch and a table with medical instruments on it, including a long and wicked-looking syringe. My captors continued to hold my arms tightly, their big thumbs digging into my flesh. Through a half-open door I heard a man speaking: 'I know it sounds barbaric, but I have to tell you that it has produced some remarkable results. Injecting them with typhoid seems to work better than the other diseases. It produces the highest fever and a reasonable percentage survive. And of those who do, some seem to be permanently cured.'

'Interesting,' another man said. 'I should certainly like to witness this.'

The door was pushed open and a large florid man in a white coat came into the room. 'So this is the next candidate for our little experiment, it is?' he said jovially, and I realized what the syringe on the table was for.

I struggled to stand up. 'Wait. No. Listen to me. I am not insane. Ask Nelly Bly. She's coming to get me out today—'

Then I heard the words, '*Gott im Himmel*. Miss Murphy?'

The first doctor stepped aside and Dr Birnbaum was standing behind him, staring at me in disbelief.

'Miss Murphy. What are you doing here?' he demanded.

'I was trying to rescue Jessie,' I said, still gasping for air. 'They said you'd gone away. They wouldn't let me see her, so this was the only way.'

'My dear Fraulein.' Dr Birnbaum came over to me.

'Watch her, doctor. She's a lively one,' the orderly said.

'I believe I can handle her, thank you,' the doctor said. 'My dear colleague, this young lady is as sane as you or I. I can personally vouch for her.'

Hands released me. Soon I was sitting in Dr Meyer's office, explaining my presence. Even as I said the words I realized how ridiculous and impatient I had been. 'I didn't know how long you'd be away,' I concluded lamely.

'So you took matters into your own hands.'

'With the help of Nelly Bly.'

'Nelly Bly?'

'The famous reporter. She went undercover in an insane asylum once. She was my co-conspirator. She was supposed to come and release me by now, but everything went wrong. I found Jessie and one of the men started fondling her. I tried to pull him off her. They gave me some kind of injection and that's the last thing I remember.'

'So our girl is here?' He looked pleased. 'How is her condition? Any improvement?'

'She can speak,' I said. 'And understand. I didn't have a chance to talk with her, of course, but she came to my defense so she might now be in a cell like the one I was in.'

'Which girl is this?' the other doctor asked.

Dr Birnbaum explained and someone was sent to fetch her.

'I can't tell you how glad I am to see you,' I said to Dr Birnbaum as the other doctor left the room. 'I thought you'd gone away, maybe back to Europe.'

'Europe? I told the hotel I had been called away for a few

days, that's all. Dr Meyer invited me to come and stay with him and witness his latest experiments.'

'You've been staying here all the time?' I looked at him and started to laugh.

Soon after that Jessie was brought to us in a pleasant sitting room. She came in looking terrified, and the look in her eyes when she recognized me and Dr Birnbaum was wonderful. I embraced her and she started to cry. We stood there clinging to each other and crying. I believe even Dr Birnbaum wiped away a tear.

'You're safe with us now,' I said. 'We're going to take you home.'

We were treated very differently on the return voyage to Manhattan and helped ashore into the arms of a very worried Elizabeth.

'Molly, I can't tell you how glad I am to see you,' she said. 'They told me you had been taken to the wing for violent patients and there was no way they were going to release you to me. I was just on my way back to round up some reporters and a police escort. I thought we might have to storm the place.'

'All is well,' I said. 'And this is Jessie.'

'The girl in the snowdrift?' Elizabeth beamed at her.

'I remember now,' Jessie said slowly to me. 'There was snow. Lots of snow. The whole world was white. You carried me out of the snow.'

'What else do you remember?' I asked.

'Not very much. Bad men. Horrible things, but all a blur, like a nightmare. I know that I was very afraid.'

'Those men are now locked up in jail,' I said.

'When did your power of speech return?' Dr Birnbaum asked.

'When I saw those men again, suddenly things started to come back to me. I knew they were bad and I was afraid of

351

them,' Jessie answered in no more than a whisper, like one who is surprised to discover she has a voice. 'But I knew I had to pretend to be witless if I wanted to stay alive. My plan was to get strong enough to run away. But then they lost patience and decided to send me to the asylum until my wits returned. Then I truly despaired, until this lady came for me.'

'Molly,' I said. 'My name is Molly.'

A cab took us back to my house. Dr Birnbaum sat and talked with Jessie while I made us all a good meal.

'What I don't understand,' I said, 'is why they wanted to keep you alive and wait for your memory to come back.'

She frowned for a moment and then she said slowly, 'Because I am the only one who knows where the loot is buried.'

By the next day we were able to piece it together. 'You left the theater with Annie and John Jacob Halsted to go out to a late dinner,' I prompted as Dr Birnbaum and Elizabeth sat beside us in my living room.

'Annie?' She closed her eyes and a great shudder went through her. 'They killed Annie,' she said at last.

'I know.'

'They would have killed me, too.'

'I'm sure they would. So what happened when you reached the Silverton mansion? Did Mr Halsted rob the place? Did Annie help him?'

Her pretty eyes opened wide. 'It wasn't JJ,' she said. 'We got there and JJ stopped the automobile to open the gates and suddenly this man jumped into the front seat and he held a gun up to Annie's head. He shouted at JJ to drive as fast as he could or he'd kill us. He had a great sack with him. JJ did what he said and drove away. When we came to a wooded area the man made us stop. He made us get out and clear away the snow and hide the sack with branches over it and then pile snow on top. And when we had finished, he turned to JJ and he said, "We don't need you anymore," and he shot him. Just like that.' Her voice trembled and tears started to run down her cheeks. 'Then he made Annie and me cover his body up with branches and snow until it was hidden. Then he made us get into the car again. He had that gun beside him in the front seat all the time.' She looked up at us hopelessly, tears trickling down her cheeks.

Elizabeth put a hand onto Jessie's arm. 'You don't have to go on right now. It's not wise to distress yourself so much after what you've been through.'

'No, I want to tell you,' Jessie said. 'When we came to a town he found a telephone at a tavern. He took us in with him and he had the gun pointed at Annie's side. He said if we made one sound, we'd both be shot. We knew he meant it. He made a telephone call to someone.'

'In what language?' I asked. 'Did he speak English?'

'His English was not too good,' she said. 'He was speaking Italian, I believe. Then he made us get back in the auto and he drove really fast toward New York. We came around an icy bend and he lost control. We skidded into this big tree. I was thrown out and I don't remember anymore.'

She paused. I handed her a glass of water and she took a sip. 'Now comes the hard part,' she said. 'When I came to, I was lying on the ground in the darkness. I crawled around and I found Annie. She was badly hurt and in a lot of pain. I saw that the man was still in the front seat of the car, but he looked as if he was dead. I wanted to go and get help, but Annie didn't want me to leave her, so I stayed with her. We were sure that help would come eventually.

'Then, after a long time, we heard a sound and a motor vehicle of some sort was coming toward us. I jumped up and waved my arms. It stopped. Three men got out. They saw our wreck and they started speaking fast in Italian. One asked me what happened and I told him. Then they talked fast again. They took the dead man and put him into the trunk of their auto. Then they saw Annie. She was lying there and couldn't move.

'I said, "Please help my friend. We must get her to a hospital." And do you know what they did? One of them took out a gun and fired it at her. Bang. She was dead. I tried to run away. They fired after me and I thought they'd kill me, too, but they ran after me and grabbed me and shoved me into the automobile. They put Annie's body in the seat as well, beside me. When we came to a creek, they stopped and threw her body into the water. Then they drove on.' She looked up with despair written on her face. I took her hand. 'That's when it all becomes hazy,' she said. 'I know we crossed a bridge and I knew I had to escape. I remember jumping out and then I just ran and ran. That's all I know.'

After I had settled Jessie, I sent a note to Mrs Goodwin and asked Mrs Tucker to resume her role as nurse. After all I had been through, I didn't feel up to facing Miss Van Woekem with the news just yet. Mrs Tucker arrived and proposed that Jessie go back to her house to recuperate. 'I've all my own cooking utensils there,' she said, 'and this young one needs good, nourishing food.' I thought that was a splendid idea, just in case any of those gang members ever came looking for her at my place.

'I don't know where I'll go after that,' Jessie said. 'I don't think I can go back to New Haven. I couldn't bear it.'

'Let's not worry about the future,' Mrs Tucker said. 'All we have to do right now is fatten you up.'

'Not fatten me up or I'll never be able to dance again.' Jessie actually smiled.

'If you want to dance again,' I said, 'I know the very person.

Blanche Lovejoy owes me a favor.' As I said this I realized that Blanche's maid had killed somebody. Now that I was home again, I should find out if she had confessed to the police. She ought not to be allowed to get away with murder.

The afternoon post arrived as I was getting Jessie ready to leave with Mrs Tucker. One of the letters was from Blanche Lovejoy, the other from Daniel. At last he bothers to write, I thought angrily, and read the other one first. It contained a check and a note thanking me for my services. And at the bottom an extra sentence in small letters. 'Martha took her own life last night.'

So Martha had made the final sacrifice for the woman she loved so much.

I glanced at Daniel's letter and almost decided not to read it. But curiosity got the better of me. I never could resist an unopened letter.

My dear Molly,

Please forgive my long silence. My decision to go home last weekend was a good one. I arrived to find my father's condition had deteriorated. He continued to grow steadily worse and finally slipped away from us last night. He went peacefully. I was beside him when he died, for which I am truly thankful. The funeral has been arranged for Saturday.

Now I have a request of you. I know how busy you are, but I would like you to come for the funeral. It is my regret that I never introduced you to my father. I would like you at my side for the funeral.

Please let me know which train you intend to take and I will meet you at the station.

My love forever,
Daniel

I sat and stared at that letter for a long time while conflicting emotions went through me. The first, of course, was guilt. I had taken Daniel's desire to see his parents as an excuse to miss a party, when all the time he had known how serious his father's condition had been. And now he needed me beside him. If I went I would be cementing my position as his intended. I would, in effect, be saying yes to marriage.

Then suddenly I realized that I was only thinking of myself. Daniel was grieving. I remembered the hollow feeling I experienced when my brother was killed and the terrible realization that I would never see him, or my other brothers, again. The least I could do was go to Daniel's side. And I realized that I wanted to be with him. I wanted to share his grief and joy, just as I wanted him to share mine. As to what that might mean for our future, we'd just have to let things take their course.

I went back to Jessie and Mrs Tucker. 'You're sure Jessie will be all right with you?' I asked. 'Because I have been called away for a while.'

'Don't worry about it,' Mrs Tucker said. 'Jessie and I will do just fine, won't we, my pet?'

At least one thing had ended satisfactorily, I thought, as I watched them go.

Postscript

New Year's Day, 1903

JJ Halsted's body was located in a remote woodland. The stolen items from the Silverton mansion were found buried nearby, a few pieces of silver and some jewels. Three lives, almost four, had been squandered for such useless trifles. But at least Miss Van Woekem could now have the consolation of knowing that her nephew died with no stain to the family honor.

Later I introduced Jessie to Blanche. I saw Blanche's eyes flash with interest when she heard that Jessie was an orphan from Massachusetts. It was too much to hope that I had produced her long-lost daughter, although stranger things had happened, but I could see that Blanche wanted to believe this and thus took Jessie under her wing. So something else ended happily.

And Daniel and I – well, we have been spending Christmas with his family in Westchester. His mother has taken to me quite well, almost leaning on me as a daughter in her time of grief. And I, deprived of a mother at the age of fourteen, have been enjoying the closeness and warmth of family life. With the New Year has come new hope. A new police commissioner will be sworn in this week and we are hoping that he will take speedy action to reinstate Daniel as a captain of police. After that, who knows. I have to think that our story will also end happily one day.